THE ENCHANTED

www.rbooks.co.uk

THE
ENCHANTED

Charlotte Bingham

BANTAM PRESS

LONDON · TORONTO · SYDNEY · AUCKLAND · JOHANNESBURG

TRANSWORLD PUBLISHERS
61–63 Uxbridge Road, London W5 5SA
A Random House Group Company
www.rbooks.co.uk

First published in Great Britain
in 2008 by Bantam Press
an imprint of Transworld Publishers

A CIP catalogue record for this book
is available from the British Library.

ISBN 9780593055946

Addresses for Random House Group Ltd companies outside the UK
can be found at: www.randomhouse.co.uk
The Random House Group Ltd Reg. No. 954009

The Random House Group Ltd supports The Forest Stewardship
Council (FSC), the leading international forest-certification organization.
All our titles that are printed on Greenpeace-approved FSC-certified paper
carry the FSC logo. Our paper procurement policy can be found at
www.rbooks.co.uk/environment

Typeset in 11/14½pt New Baskerville by
Kestrel Data, Exeter, Devon.
Printed and bound in Great Britain by
Clays Ltd, St Ives plc.

2 4 6 8 10 9 7 5 3 1

For perhaps the only actor, playwright,
singer and painter ever to train
a winner under Rules.

IRELAND IN THE LATE 1970s

Prologue

They come upon her one blustery spring morning with an April tide running up the white sand shore. She is just standing there, looking out to sea, still as a statue in a square. She could indeed have been a monument for all they know as they slide carefully down the end of the cliff path to get a closer look at her. There are three of them, father, son and daughter, the children full grown into late teenage, the wind from the sea blowing their long dark hair back from their heads as quietly they approach her, afraid of scaring her, wondering when she will sense them and if when she does she will make a sudden dash for continued freedom.

Yet even as they approach she stands quite still. She must hear them, know they are there, but not a move does she make. She just stands there still, looking far out to the sea. And now they are near they see she is pregnant and greatly so. At first glance it would seem she is about to give birth there and then, which might explain her stillness, so they take even more care lest they should frighten her into delivery. She is astonishingly lovely. Wild certainly, so it would seem, for what else could explain her presence here on this lonely stretch with no one in sight of her and no visible means of reaching the beach unless from round the corner of the cliffs through the seas? Yet she is more beautiful than any wild one they have ever seen before. In fact she looks every inch an aristocrat with her fine head, her perfect limbs and her noble bearing.

They are only a matter of feet away from her now, and at last she turns and looks at them and when she does they can see the past in her large wise eyes. From dark brown orbs there shines a sense of times before, times that seem to stretch back to when everyone was wild and untamed and the gods ruled the land from strange and wondrous kingdoms. They put out hands, not to catch or touch but to make peace, and it seems she has no fear of them for she just keeps looking at them, her eyes unmoving from theirs. The father watches, then says he thinks she wants to be taken and sure enough, when the girl with the long dark hair stretches closer to her, with a last look at the sea she turns herself round and begins to walk towards them.

Yet they know better than to touch her, so they wait to see if they can discover what she wants. The girl turns away as if to walk back down the beach and when she does so she finds she is being followed. They all walk away now with nothing said, no questions asked and no promises made. The wind off the sea is dying down and the tide has turned and is running out fast so that by the time they reach the head they may walk round it safely without need to climb any path. Soon they are approaching home with her walking easily behind them, her stomach swaying with every pace as if her advanced pregnancy is no burden to her whatsoever.

But what none of them saw, as far as is known, was the man on the beach now far below them, a young man with long wet blond hair and eyes the colour of sea coral. He stands where she had stood and quite as still as she had been, looking after her to where she has gone yet making no move to follow her. He stands in the very edge of the sea, as darkness falls and an April moon rises to shine on waters that stretch into the blue of the night, until there is nothing more to see or hear and finally then he moves, turning and walking back into the sea, away from the life of the land.

Chapter One

New Life

She lay in the deep, dry straw prepared for her delivery. Someone knelt by her head, gently pulling one of her ears; the other one stood by her tail, watching, waiting, smoking his pipe as he did so, well used to such times. Nothing was said. There was silence, broken only by her breathing, which had become deeper, more powerful and urgent, as the foal moved inside her, ready now to be born.

'I'd say we're under orders.'

'You'll be fine. I'm here. You'll be just fine,' the girl murmured.

The mare's head tilted back once as birth began in earnest, nostrils widening, eyes half closing. She gave a groan that caused her to shudder massively, while her flanks heaved with the effort.

''Tis all right, girl,' the man said, bending lower, his pipe still stuck in the corner of his mouth. 'Come on now – you'll be all right.'

'She's not comfortable, Da.'

'I'd say she is not as young as we would like her; 'tis more of an effort, so.'

'Whatever her age, she has the look of the eagle, and the mark of the prophet's thumb in her neck.'

'Whose horse is she, I wonder? A fine mare like this has to belong,' Padraig said, shaking his head.

'She's come out of the sea, so she has. She's a horse of Mananan. She's come from the kingdom under the seas.'

'Whether she has or hasn't, she has to belong to someone,' Padraig repeated. 'A thoroughbred mare like this is not a tinker's donkey. She probably escaped from one of the farms beyond and got herself cut off be the tide.'

He took off his hat to bang it against his leg, before replacing it.

'But don't I know every one of the horses in these parts? She has to have come from much further abroad.'

Kathleen interrupted him. 'This is not going to be easy, Da. Look, the poor mare is never going to do it on her own.'

'There's never any need for the vet, Kathleen. You know that.'

Kathleen shook her head. They were poor, it was true, but not so poor that she could bear to let the mare die, when it was evident the foal was stuck.

'I'll go call Mr Sweeney, Da. He's only ten minutes away. I'll pay for him myself, so I will.'

'If he's home. And if he's sober, which I doubt, and never mind the payment; didn't he take a mountain of hay from me last year and divil a penny from him.'

'I'll go call him anyway.'

For once the vet was at home. He muttered thickly that he'd be there as soon as he could, and when Kathleen returned to the stable she found things were no better, and said so.

'And no worse, either, girl,' Padraig protested, as he struggled to find the foal. 'The foal's just not presenting itself – not the right way. I'm trying to turn it now.'

The mare seemed to be giving up the struggle. Kathleen could see it in her eye and in the damp dark sweat that had broken out over her skin. She arched her neck, trying to look round at her flanks, but overtaken by another contraction she threw her great head back into the straw and kicked out in a sudden spasm.

'Careful, Kathleen. You don't want to have her catch you. Where's Mr Sweeney got to anyhow?' her father grumbled. 'I'm doing me best here, but it seems a fore leg is stuck. And for the life of me . . .'

Padraig had both hands in the mare now, but all he could get hold of were the unborn foal's hindquarters. If they couldn't turn the foal they knew they were lost.

The vet arrived a quarter of an hour on in slippered feet, the bottoms of his flannel pyjamas showing under the legs of his trousers and the end of a Sweet Afton stuck to his top teeth. He lurched over to Padraig and all but fell to the floor as he bent down to start his examination.

'We need more light here,' he said.

'More light?' Padraig growled. 'The mare's throwing a foal, not a moth, man.'

'More light and some whisky,' Sweeney repeated. 'We're on for a long haul. And some rope, child!' He called to Kathleen as she rose to go. 'We'll have to pull this fella out.'

Padraig saw it was wrong. He knew the rope was on wrong. He couldn't really see how Sweeney had it attached but he just knew the drunken oaf had it wrong.

'Get away, man,' he said angrily, pushing the vet aside.

'No, Da, let me. I've the smaller hands and arms – let me do that.'

'Where is it now, Kathleen?' Padraig asked her as she took his place, and Sweeney collapsed against the wall of the stable, drinking whisky from a half-bottle clothed in brown paper.

'It seems to be round the neck,' Kathleen muttered, feeling the warmth of the foal, feeling it was still alive, still moving.

'God help us all,' Padraig sighed. 'Take it off there, Kathleen – if you can – and you take yourself home, Sweeney. Sure you're a disgrace to your profession.'

But the vet wasn't going anywhere until the bottle was done. He just eyed his neighbour and drank some more while Kathleen slowly unwound the lethal noose and as her father instructed tied it firmly round the foal's chest.

'If we can ease him round now, child,' Padraig told her. 'If you can turn him now at all – then we can help him out.'

Kathleen prayed as she started to turn the unborn foal. The mare opened her eyes and turned slowly to look, sensing help, even perhaps sensing salvation.

'I think I have it done, Pa,' Kathleen said, the sweat running down into her eyes. 'The head's presenting itself now.'

'Good girl yourself,' Padraig told her. 'Now all we must do is gently ease him out – gently so – and pray to God the mare gives us a bit of help.'

Padraig took hold of the rope while Kathleen tried to guide the path of the foal. She could see the head now through the sac, bent down to the animal's chest, and as she saw it beginning to be born the mother took the very deepest breath Kathleen thought she had ever heard an animal take, and groaned mightily. As she did so, her foal was eased out into the world by loving hands, until it lay by its mother, still wrapped in its caul.

'Is it alive, Da? Please God let it be alive.'

'It's alive all right, Kathleen girl,' her father replied, taking a large handful of clean fresh straw and beginning to clean the newborn. 'By some wondrous great miracle 'tis well alive – and there you are, 'tis a colt, too. A fine chestnut.'

Kathleen gazed at the foal, all leg and little else, soaking wet and covered in its birth, the faintest signs of breath barely discernible.

'You sure he's all right, Pa? You sure he's alive?'

'He's alive, Kathleen – don't fret. How's the mare now? Is the mare all right?'

Kathleen went to her head, kneeling down to stroke her head, her ears. 'She's exhausted, Da. She's barely breathing . . .'

'But she is breathing, girl?'

Kathleen bent closer to watch and listen. She counted the breaths and the intervals between them.

'About ten seconds apart. They're deep – and getting deeper. But she's breathing real slow.'

'And wouldn't you, after what she's been through?' Padraig finished cleaning the foal and stood up. 'The mare'll need stitches, Sweeney, though she's not too bad considering. Get up, man,' he said, for the vet was now sitting in the straw. 'Get up and finish the job we have just done for you. For all our sakes, get on with the stitching.'

He went to the corner of the stable and retrieved the vet's bag, while Sweeney shook his head as if trying to get some sense into it. Kathleen stood watching mare and foal.

'How we got him out, girl.' Padraig sighed, shook his head and turned his pipe back the right way round to try to relight it.

'It was a miracle,' Kathleen said quietly. 'We must thank St Francis.'

'Isn't he the man?' her father replied. 'Isn't he just the man?'

As Sweeney set about his work, another miracle happened,

a miracle that they both watched, struck silent as always by the marvel, as a creature not yet twenty minutes old somehow and against all odds struggled up from its bed – half up one moment, down the next, on three legs a second later, then down on its knees again – standing all at once and sensationally up on all four and staying up, balancing on a quartet of long, slender limbs that looked as though if someone suddenly opened the door the draught would snap them.

'Would you ever?' Kathleen laughed. 'Will you look at that?'

'He's not over large, even for his age.'

'He's beautiful,' Kathleen said defensively, moving a step closer and holding out her hand for the foal to sniff. 'He's enchanting.'

'Show me a foal that's not beautiful.'

They went outside to take the air, and stare at the stars, to catch their breath, and ever afterwards Kathleen would wake in the night and blame herself for that, for in that time Sweeney, the drunken son of a drunken father, did his worst, and they lost the mare. But for a few minutes – oh, dear God, but for a few minutes – they could surely have saved her.

There was no time for tears, as there never is on a farm; no time even to curse Sweeney. They must do what they could. Padraig ran to the telephone as Kathleen tried to give comfort to the foal who stood looking down at his fallen mother with uncertainty already in his milky eyes, unsteady still on his lanky legs while Kathleen with one arm around him put her free hand to his mouth in the hope that he would suckle it until her father returned and she could boil and cool him some milk. But as soon as he was called her brother arrived, and was at once dispatched to prepare the feed.

By a miracle, and on only his fourth call to neighbouring farms, Padraig located a mare who had lost a foal not half an hour before. He was offered the stricken mother at once as a foster, and knowing the urgency the neighbours had her loaded in their horsebox and delivered to the farm just as Kathleen was trying to interest the foal in a bottle of warm cow's milk.

'Here, girl,' the groom who'd brought the mare across said to her, handing her a tin. 'Himself said you'd be in need of this, in case you've none yourselves. 'Tis colostrum. He always keeps some frozen for just these times.'

The groom had brought another container as well, a much larger one, a packing case from which he produced the skin of the dead foal, helping them to drape their own live foal in it before leading the mare into the next-door stable. Hoping the disconsolate creature would accept the stranger as if it were her own, Kathleen passed a head slip over the nose of her foal and led it to where the foster mare stood waiting, ears back and tail swishing.

'Wait now,' the groom advised Kathleen, putting one arm out in front of her to prevent her progress. 'She's a kick in her, this one.'

He had hardly spoken before the mare lashed out, a blow which might well have caught the foal and finished it had Kathleen not been stopped in her tracks. Once the mare had calmed down, Kathleen slowly led her foal to the mare's head so he could be seen. The mare looked down on the strange sight, the uncertain newborn swaddled in the skin of her own dead foal, and slowly flared her nostrils at him. For a while she did nothing more than regard the interloper, making no move to familiarise herself with him, her nostrils still wide, one eye fixed on the creature standing unsteadily by her side. Then at last, as Kathleen was beginning to despair, the mare slowly lowered her nose until it rested on the foal, and left it there. The foal staggered at first under the sudden weight;

then, as if sensing something, turned its head to look up at the creature standing over him. The eyes of the two animals caught and held and then the mare flared her nostrils even more and blew gently down at her foot.

'They're met,' the groom said quietly. 'He'll be on her in no time at all.'

So he was, too, helped by Kathleen who went round to the far side of the mare and slipped a hand under the animal's stomach, the same hand the foal had suckled earlier. A minute or so later a soft warm mouth found her fingers, and Kathleen slid her hand slowly back to the mare's teats. First time, the foal refused, insisting on fingers rather than teats, but the next time Kathleen kept her hand just out of reach until the youngster took hold of the mare and began to suckle.

'I'd still give him the colostrum,' the groom advised as he prepared to leave. 'For that's not his own mother's milk. And we all know the meaning of that, so we do.'

'If there's ever a thing we can do,' Padraig said, walking him through the dawn light to the horsebox.

'You can let us know when he's to win his first race,' the groom replied, stopping to light a smoke. 'Which he will. For I see he has the mark of the prophet.'

'He does.'

'So there you are.' The groom smiled. 'Be sure now to tell us.'

The foal belonged to Kathleen. Not that it was ever said. It was simply understood, so much so that from that moment on Padraig was always to refer to the foal in such a way, as in *you'd best go see what that foal of yours needs*, and later *that colt of yours is fooling about in the paddock again*, and even later, as he raced with his companions in the fields, *that horse of yours has come on a stride or two. Will you look at him go, daughter of the house?*

But though he flourished, and filled out well, and strengthened nicely, fed on the good grass that sprouted on top of the limestone, he never grew tall.

'He's not had his mother's milk, that's why,' Kathleen would state when she and her father leaned on the fence and watched the young stock graze. 'Though the mare, God rest her, his mother was a good size.'

'Size isn't all in a horse, Kathleen, until you come to sell it, and then isn't it everything?'

'He could run over timber, Da. If he has any toe, sure he might be a hurdler, who knows?'

'If there was only three more inches to him, girl,' Padraig replied, lighting his pipe, 'he could make us a million, but today all they want is a good big horse. They're not wanting anything but size now – what they all calls *a fine stamp of a horse*. As if any of them has the eye, as if any of them has anything but a chequebook. Chequebook breeding, I call it. You'll be lucky if you find an owner for him, and then only if you give him a case of whisky to go with the little horse.'

'Ah well, if he's too small to sell, then maybe we'll keep him so,' Kathleen said hopefully, hopping up and over the fence to take the colt his afternoon treat of a sliced carrot and calling back, 'You never know – he might win *us* something!'

When he was weaned and turned out, Kathleen fell into the habit of hiding herself unseen in the long grasses of the paddocks, two or three hundred yards away from where he was cropping grass with his companions. She would crawl on her hands and knees to her chosen hiding place, making sure her foal was downwind of her, then lie on her back, waiting. The first time he found her, it took him six minutes by Kathleen's watch. Ever after that, no matter what time of day she hid nor how carefully, he would come in search of her.

Rarely did it take him longer than a couple of minutes to find her; the average was a count of fifty.

Kathleen would lie, always in a different place, flat on her back with her eyes closed, waiting. At first she would hear the delicate pounding of his young hooves as he came to look for her. Not a sound would there be from her, until she opened her eyes and found herself being observed by two round brown orbs, after which he would nudge her, buckle his legs and lower himself to the ground to settle beside her. Finally when it was time for Kathleen to return to her work he would walk slowly beside her to the gate, where she would give one last pull at his ears or a ruffle on his neck before letting herself out. The moment she unlatched the gate he would dip his head, kick out his hind legs, turn on a sixpence and gallop off back to join his friends, and one in particular, a pretty little dark bay yearling filly out of a mare owned by the neighbouring farmer. Kathleen watched the friendship grow between the two young horses, hers becoming attached to the filly as if they were meant to be together, never leaving her side, running with her, and grazing by her side. And when one of them got down to doze in the grass, the other would always stand sentinel.

She never put a leading rope on the colt. Instead she would call him at first with a whistle, but soon all she needed to do was appear at the gate and he would come to her. Finally she would arrive at the gate only to find that he was already waiting, more often than not in the company of his girlfriend, whom Kathleen had christened Finoula.

Her brother usually broke the horses. Liam was good with them, but of late he had grown tall and gangly, and with his sudden growth had come a loss of balance. His hands had grown heavy, too; as a boy he'd had the touch of a girl, his father would tell him – *not farmer's hands, boy*, Padraig would say.

'You don't want farmer's hands. A horse is in its mouth. A horse is all its mouth. Would yous like a great bar of steel being banged on your teeth as if ye'd no feeling? Indeed you would not, so keep those hands light – like your sister there. She is holding ribbons, boy – ribbons of silk, not chains like ye're holding there! Lighten your hands and sit through the horse – don't sit on him like that! Sit through him, boy! And when you're thinkin' of stoppin' him, do just that! Think it – don't pull the bit through the back of his head! Sit down – sit back – change your weight now – and easy! Ease him back – *ease him! Sure he'll have no mouth on him be the time ye're done, boy!*'

Padraig Flanagan might not look much on the ground, a short round-shouldered man who limped from a boyhood riding accident, but up on a horse he was a changed man. Flanagan was a part of every horse he rode. He rode from the leg and the seat, and although he'd the Irish habit of a forward foot, once he had hitched his irons up to racing length and perched himself on the horse's withers he was nothing but balance. Then he would ride his work, all the weight transferred down to the middle of his gumbooted feet, the reins clutched double in a bunch behind the horse's neck, his eye firmly fixed through the animal's ears on a point in the middle distance.

'But I want to back him, Da,' Kathleen pleaded. 'Boyo will expect me. He won't want Liam. Boyo won't go for him. I know it. Don't go asking why – I know Boyo and please, please let me back him, Pa, please?'

The colt had always been known as Boyo, since to begin with Kathleen could think of no suitable or indeed possible stable name for him. *He'll come to his name, one day*, she'd reasoned. *If I can't think of a name now it's because I haven't the right one ready.*

Padraig knew as well as Kathleen did that she must be

the one to back him, but he also knew that when it came to horses nothing worthwhile ever came easy. He said he'd think about it. Said he would mull the matter over, give it every consideration.

'Very well,' he finally announced. 'Since you've done nothin' but keep at your poor father every day for the past two months about the business of backing your horse, I have finally made up me mind, so I have.'

Kathleen knew better than to prompt her father.

'Kathleen here is too light and too weak, I'd say, Da.'

'And I'd have to agree with you, boy,' Padraig replied with another nod. 'I'd have to agree with you there . . .'

'It's only common sense, Kathleen, seeing that you are a girl.'

'Am I now, Liam? I never noticed.'

'I'd have to agree with you, Liam,' their father continued, raising his voice, 'if you were right and if I thought you might fare better – but since you are not right and you would not do better I have to disagree with you.'

'Ah come on, Da – sure you're only teasing me?'

'I am not so,' Padraig replied. 'I am commissioning Kathleen here to put a saddle across this horse of hers and that is that.'

Padraig was all too aware that Kathleen had already been about the business. He had caught sight of her putting a roller on the colt's back, then following it by gently easing on a saddle; witnessed the horse eating his dinner with the saddle still on him, although as yet ungirthed; seen his daughter from a distance down the field walking the horse in a bridle, then with a saddle on, later with a sack of potatoes slung across the saddle; and finally watched from afar as she carefully tightened the girth under the saddle and let the irons swing loose against Boyo's side, although, to be sure, it was only the way they always did things with the young horses.

So when it came to it, it was as if the horse had always had a saddle on his back, for what with the weight of the potatoes, and much else, when she had finally slowly and carefully swung her right leg over the saddle, having stood in the left stirrup only while her father had taken a light hold on the animal's head, and sat herself down as lightly as she could, the horse only moved an ear. When she felt his calm she nodded at her father, and Padraig let go his hold and stood back, allowing him another chance to take flight, but still Boyo only stood, ears pricked, eyes bright.

'We're going to walk on now, sweetheart,' Kathleen told him quietly. 'I'm going to pick up the reins, I'm going to ease you forward – and we're going to walk on.'

She gave the horse only the lightest squeeze with her legs. The moment she asked him, he moved – not a sudden burst of activity, but a rhythmic, well-measured pace, easing into an elegant walk that took him in a generous left-handed circle round the small railed paddock. Later she stopped him, turned him, and had him walk round on the other rein. Finally she walked him in four diagonals and one straight line, before calling to her father to take hold of his head while she dismounted as gently and carefully as she had mounted.

'That'll do fine for today, young man,' she said, patting then kissing his neck. 'You did just grand.'

Handing her father the saddle he was waiting to take, Kathleen slipped the bridle off and left the paddock, the horse keeping pace with her. She walked to the main field fifty yards away, and opened the gate. Boyo followed her, but once in the field he didn't run off to join his companions. Instead he stood staring out to the distant hills and the sea beyond, with a look that reminded Kathleen of his mother, the day the three of them had found her on the beach. Then he got down and rolled slowly and pleasurably in the well of dry mud by the gate, got up again, shook himself off and chose as his grazing spot a place not five hundred yards but five feet away.

Kathleen leaned on the gate and watched him. She watched him until she heard her father calling.

Padraig was waiting in the yard, smoking his pipe as usual, and leaning up against a closed stable door.

'The day is not long ahead when we have to sell Boyo, you know that, Kathleen?'

'I know that, Da,' Kathleen replied, quickly picking up the yard broom and beginning to sweep. 'But not today.'

'We're not here to keep horses as pets.'

'Well, I never. You know, I never knew that.'

'It's as well to remember it, Kathleen. We can make no preferences, and we are poor people, as I have always told you.' Padraig took his pipe from his mouth and eyed the smouldering tobacco. 'Every horse we have is born to be sold.'

'There's the matter of his passport still,' Kathleen replied. 'You'd have to have that sorted out.'

'Don't I already have it that?' Padraig put his pipe back in his mouth and drew on it before continuing. 'Not that it need be a real concern of yours—'

'I'd have thought not knowing which stallion bred him and with no papers for the mare it'd be a real concern for us all.'

'Then for your edification I say our neighbour John Slattery has franked the necessary documentation that says the sire was his stallion,' Padraig said, carefully watching his daughter. 'King of the Sea was your horse's sire, and it shows the dam was Mananan's Girl—'

'The mare you had to buy back from the Heaslips?' Kathleen exclaimed. 'But she's as barren as a hill in Greenland!'

'All that's needed is a name on the passport,' her father replied. 'And your Uncle Noel in Ballydehob has verified the document.'

'You never had Uncle Noel do that, Da?' Kathleen asked, wide-eyed.

'I had so. Sure he's a veterinary himself, is he not?'

'He's a vet for small animals, Da!' Kathleen protested. 'He's a family pet man. The only horses he ever sees are on merry-go-rounds!'

'And that's for us to know, girl, and for nobody else,' Padraig replied firmly. 'It won't be the first time a man's had to go this route, don't you worry. The horse is a thoroughbred, there's no doubt of that, and since he's gelded now there'll be no career at stud to worry about. Sure the breeding's only words on a racecard. What matters is what the horse does, that's what matters.'

'But Da—'

'That's enough of your buts, my girl. We'll have no more on the matter, so be about your work. We have plenty enough on our hands.'

'We're short of chaff, Pa,' Kathleen muttered, eyeing her father as she swept round his feet, trying to get him to go. 'You'll need to cut some more.'

Her father remained where he was and put another match to his pipe of tobacco.

'Mick Finnegan has a horse he can't be backing,' he said, blowing the match out from the side of his mouth. 'His lad has a leg broken, and the horse is getting skittish. I said I'd send you along.'

'Is that right?' Kathleen wondered. 'And will he pay me?'

'I doubt it,' Padraig replied, taking a satisfied look at his now properly lit pipe. 'But sure you can always try axing him, but I doubt he has ever given a girl money, however good she may be.'

Kathleen said nothing more. Her father walked off and she watched him go, his pipe leaving a curl of blue smoke in the air. Sure it was a man's world. They had the paying of every-thing so they had the say of everything, it seemed, just as it didn't seem fair. She began sweeping the yard as clean as she could get it, wondering what was going to happen and how much longer she would have her horse to herself.

Still, she had time enough. Time enough to enjoy watching her youngster grow and, in bringing him on, time enough to relish their rides on the long empty beaches and their treks up into the hills beyond their small farm, time enough for them to grow so close they became all but inseparable, time enough to watch the friendship between the two young horses grow; and yet she knew somewhere the wheels were already in motion that would bring the strangers across the water in their search for good horses. And when that day finally came, as Kathleen knew that it surely would, then she would lose him, and she also knew that when she had lost him she would spend her spare time wondering where he had gone and what his poor fate might be.

ENGLAND IN THE EARLY 1980s

Chapter Two

Under Orders

'I didn't know you was interested in racing, Mrs D.,' Evie Tranter said, coming to a stop in front of the television and holding her feather duster in front of her as if it were a bunch of flowers. 'All the years I've been coming here, I'd never have put you down as being interested in horse racing.'

'It's just something to watch while I'm waiting, Evie,' Alice replied, taking another look at her watch. 'I know nothing about racing. I've never even been to a race meeting.'

'My Den's never off the track, if you ask me,' Evie continued, her eyes fixed on the screen, sitting herself down in the chair next to Alice. 'And if I was having a bet, he's the one.' She leaned forward to poke the screen with the end of her duster. 'W. Swinburn. My Den says he don't know how to lose.'

The telephone rang, giving Alice an excuse to break up what was obviously going to turn into what Evie liked to think of as one of their nice cosy moments. 'Excuse me, Evie. That might be Christian. To say why he's late.'

As it happened it wasn't her son. It was her solicitor, ringing to remind her that she really needed to return the documents she had been sent, so they could settle her late husband's estate.

'I promise I'll do them and return them straight away, Mr Pimlott,' Alice told him. 'It's just that I have to go to the country today, but I'll take them with me and drop them in at the post office.'

'While I have you on the telephone, Mrs Dixon . . .' The lawyer cleared his throat. 'If I could just run another couple of things past you? It won't take a minute.'

Alice did her best to concentrate on what she was being told but as always legalese bored and baffled her. Everyone knew that the way the law was written was purposely to cheat people of any understanding of what was being done to them. And as her solicitor rambled on Alice stared at the street scene outside, thinking of anything except what he was saying to her, her mind going blank as usual. She watched an overdressed woman walking past the old bookshop opposite with a poodle on a lead and thought that nowadays poodles seemed to have gone out of fashion, remembering the time when a smart woman was rarely seen without a poodle on a lead.

When she and Alexander had first moved into what was then only a two-bedroomed house, Kensington still had the feel of a village. Walking through Holland Street and the other back streets, they could have been in the country. In those days, friends who lived in Mayfair used to refer to *travelling out* to see them, very much in the way that Alice now thought of going to see her daughter and son-in-law in Richmond. Yet now Kensington had changed so much that even Evie was always giving it as her opinion that you couldn't tell the High Street from Oxford Street. This statement was usually followed by an *if-I-was-you* lecture about Alice's being better off moving out to a leafy suburb where she would be safer and healthier.

Of course Alice knew that Evie was right, that not only Kensington but the whole of London had changed, and of course it would be more sensible to move out, the most sensible move of all being to Richmond, so she could be near Georgina and the grandchildren. But try as she did to interest herself in this most sensible of ideas, Alice finally found against it. It was just too . . . well, *sensible*.

'Told you he'd win, Mrs D.,' Evie announced when Alice had put down the telephone. 'That W. Swinburn. Won by a street. Like I said, never rides a bad race.'

Alice inwardly sighed with relief that the race was now over and Evie could resume her household chores.

'You thought any more about moving, Mrs D.?' Evie enquired, flicking her duster along the line of Alice's favourite set of eighteenth-century prints, as always, and with unerring accuracy, managing to knock each one slightly crooked. 'You was saying about moving out near your son-in-law and daughter, which as you know I think would be no bad thing. It would be no skin off of my nose – I could still do the journey just as easily from Battersea to help you, and it would be so nice for you and Georgina. And those lovely grandchildren of yours.'

'Yes, I do see it would be nice for Georgina, Evie.' Alice looked out of the window again, but this time to see if there was any sign of her son. 'I'd obviously be much handier for babysitting and so on. I do see that. Limitless unpaid babysitting and school runs would be attractive, I can see.'

'Now then, Mrs D.,' Evie chided her. 'That doesn't sound at all like you.'

'That's probably because I'm not quite sure what me sounds like any more.'

'Come again?'

'It doesn't matter, Evie, really.'

Alice turned away. There were times when she thought, *There's lots of life in me still. I'm not going to just give in and become some sort of housekeeper and nanny* – but there were just as many times when she missed her husband Alexander so much, she no longer saw the point in anything. 'I'm just going to make sure I've left everything as I should,' she continued, heading out of the sitting room. 'It's something Mr Dixon always did whenever we went away, and I still can't get into the habit.'

Sammy, her devoted West Highland terrier, who had been sitting perched on the arm of her chair, jumped down and followed his mistress into the kitchen.

'Leftover life to kill,' Alice said to herself. 'Whatever that means, Sammy. But that's not what we want to do, is it? Spend the rest of our life killing time.'

In the weeks following Alexander's sudden death she had nearly been rushed into agreeing to go and live in the basement of Georgina and Joe's house in Richmond. Still stunned by her loss, she had thought it seemed only sensible to be near a married daughter, until her best friend Millie stepped in.

'Too soon to make up your mind about anything, duck, much too soon,' her oldest friend kept insisting.

Alice had to listen to Millie, if only because when Millie had lost her husband many years before, instead of wasting time on self-pity, she had ignored her family's protests and sold the rambling family home, moving to a cottage with a few acres where by sheer hard work, endeavour and determination she had made really quite a considerable success out of producing the kinds of jams and chutneys in which small local country delicatessens revelled – with the result that she was now not just self-supporting, but vaguely prosperous.

'Best of all, Allie, I don't have to rely on someone else. Number one rule of widowhood: whatever you do, don't get in tow with some man, just because you're feeling lonely. You should see the way some of the widows behave. Talk about ravers. I mean, you should see.'

Now, as Alice waited for Christian to give her a lift down to Millie's cottage where she had been invited to stay, she put her thoughts on hold. She would only think about the fun they were going to have.

The telephone rang again.

'I'll bet that's Georgina, Sammy,' she said to the little dog. 'I don't know what it is, but there's something about the way it rings when it's Georgina. It just sounds different.'

'Mum? Hi.'

'I thought it would be you, Georgie. How are you? How's tricks?'

'Why did you think it would be me? I didn't say I'd ring.'

'Sorry. What I meant was I thought it *might* be you.'

'Aren't *you* meant to be in the country?'

'If you thought I was in the country—'

'I just wanted to ask Chris something.' Georgina sighed. 'If he's arrived yet.'

'Do you know something I don't know?'

'How? I just thought I'd ring on the off chance.'

'Meaning you thought I'd still be here.'

'I wouldn't be ringing otherwise, would I?'

'Let's start again, shall we?' Alice said, bending down to stroke Sammy. 'How's tricks?'

'I do wish you wouldn't always say that, Mum. I mean, what does it mean?'

'It's old-fashioned for how's everything, really. How are Will and Finty?'

'Same as they were last night when you saw them. So Chris hasn't arrived yet, surprise surprise?'

'Punctuality is not your brother's strongest suit.'

'He *is* taking you all the way to the country, Mum. That is *seriously* good of him, you know.'

'I know, Georgie,' Alice replied, still stroking Sammy, if anything a little faster. 'And it's very kind of him.'

'I think you should give him something for the petrol. Seriously.'

'I have every intention of so doing, Georgina. I wouldn't dream of not—'

'There's no need to get in a fluff.'

'I am not in a fluff.'

'You called me *Georgina*. You *seriously* only ever call me *Georgina* when you're annoyed. I only rang to speak to Chris, you know.'

'I'll tell him to call you, shall I, when he gets here? Except hang on . . .' Alice said, listening. 'That might be him now.'

After she had let her son in, she left him talking to his sister on the telephone while she ran a last check on the flat and her luggage, telling Evie that she too had best be on her way since she had to put on the alarm.

Finally she found herself standing around waiting for Christian to finish his conversation with Georgina – which seemed to be a very earnest one, judging from all the *seriouslys* being bandied about – before they were able to make a move.

'Georgie wants a quick word before we go, Mum.' Christian waggled the telephone at his mother and handed over the receiver.

'Mum. Look. Can you babysit next Friday? Be good if you could.'

'No, I shall be away. I told you – I'm going away for the week.'

'Couldn't you come back a bit early, though? Like Friday? You know what the traffic's like at the weekend.'

'I'm going away until Wednesday week, actually.'

'O-*kay*,' Georgina continued slowly, obviously determined not to let this one go. 'You could come back up by train. Joe could meet you.'

'Georgina,' Alice said slowly. 'What's happened to your regular babysitters?'

'One of them's got a filthy cold and Joe's seriously off Tina. He thinks she nicks things, mostly his Scotch. Seriously – you could zap back up by train on Friday, no sweat. We've got tickets for this gig then there's a do afterwards—'

'Darling, I really can't,' Alice interrupted. 'I really can't trek all the way up from Dorset just to babysit.'

'Oh, thanks, Mum.'

'I just couldn't.'

'Thanks a bunch. It's not just pleasure, you know. It's business. Joe has to be there.'

'I'm sure you'll find *someone*, darling.'

'And *darling*'s as telling as *Georgina*, Mum. At least it is the way you say it.'

'I'll ring you from Millie's,' Alice finally said after a short pause, feeling herself weakening.

'Don't bother. I'm sure we'll manage. 'Bye!'

Georgina hung up, leaving Alice to stare blankly at the humming receiver.

'What did she want?'

'Wanted me to come back up to babysit on Friday.'

'Man – Georgie really is something else.'

Alice clipped Sammy's lead on his collar. 'Anyway. Sorry to keep you, Christian. We can go now.'

'Mum?' Chris said as he took the bags he had let his mother carry and put them in the back of his Golf GTI. 'I wonder. Can you bung me a ton? Just for my hols? I'll pay you back end of the month.'

'I lent you a hundred and fifty only last month, darling.'

'Yeah . . .' Chris said, getting in the car at the same time as his mother. 'But that was for the rent – I don't have any spending money. And I'm going to look a right dweeb with Dan and Matt if I can't ante up.'

'I don't know what you're all talking about half the time,' Alice grumbled, opening her handbag and sorting through the myriad contents up to and including two Bonios for Sammy. 'Most I can do is fifty – and I want it back at the end of the month.'

'Good as done, Ma.' Chris grinned, pocketing the loot. 'You are such a star.'

Jamming the car into first gear and keeping the brake on, Chris spun the wheels of the GTI then fast-started it into the outward-bound traffic, throwing Alice backwards in her seat before she even had time to do up her seat belt.

'Great wheels, eh?' He laughed. 'Blow your rocks off.'

Clutching the grab handle above her head and Sammy on her knee, Alice found herself wishing that she'd hired a car to take her to Dorset. Not only would it have been safer, but it would have been a lot cheaper.

Christian put a tape in the cassette player.

'Are we going to have this all the way to Dorset?' she wondered as they sat in a traffic jam at the top of the Earl's Court Road.

'Sorr-*ee*!' Christian stared out of the window as a pretty girl in a fashionable bright blue silk dress sashayed by on the opposite side of the road. 'Don't you like The Clash?'

'It is a little . . . how can I say . . . loud.'

'OK. Bit of the old Radio Middle-of-the-road? Yes?' Christian asked, switching to the radio.

'Anything would be better than the whoever they were.'

'The Clash, Mother,' Christian said in his talking-to-old-people voice. 'Just the best punk band of all time, that's all.'

'Oh, we're going to have to go back to the house,' Alice said suddenly. 'I left the television plugged in.'

'You what?' Her son stared at her incredulously.

'I know, I know,' Alice sighed. 'But your father always said you have to pull the plug out of the wall.'

'No way, Mother. Seriously.'

'I shan't enjoy a minute of my holiday otherwise.'

'Ma . . . ?'

'Please?'

With a histrionic groan, Christian turned off at the traffic lights on the Cromwell Road and drove his mother back to her house, where he ran in to pull the plug out for her.

'Oh God, Mother.' Returning, he peered through the passenger window and chucked the keys into her lap. 'It was *off.*' He climbed back into the car. 'For that, I choose where we have lunch.'

'The least I can do,' Alice muttered, doing up her safety belt. 'Sorry.'

'OK.' Christian nodded. 'Music of my choice as well. OK?'

'Whatever you say.'

An hour and a half later, as they were speeding their way west down the hill that leads back up to pass Stonehenge, they both saw that the traffic ahead was coming to a standstill fast.

'Now what?' Christian said, lowering his window to try to get a better view of what was causing the jam. 'There's some idiot jumping up and down in the middle of the road.'

'I do hope there hasn't been an accident,' Alice said, quickly taking the chance to turn the music down.

'I hardly think they've stopped to have a picnic, Ma,' Christian replied. 'This isn't going anywhere. I'm going to take a look-see.'

He hopped out of the car and disappeared, running along

the verge. He was back a couple of minutes later, looking grim.

'Just don't look when we get to go past. Some idiot's run over a horse.'

Sitting and sketching no more than a quarter of a mile away on a hillock to the north of the prehistoric stones Rory had no idea of the cause of the accident. It was true that at one point he had noticed a traffic jam forming, but since that stretch of the A303 was a notorious bottleneck for westbound traffic he had thought nothing of it. A little later he had become aware that there might have been an accident of sorts as he spotted the arrival of a police car, but again, given that it was a long straight road, he simply put it down to yet another lethally impatient driver. Soon it started to rain again, so he threw in the creative towel and went home.

He had hardly had time to park his old Land Rover and walk into the stable yard before he knew something was up, and not just from the look on the lads' faces. Normally the yard at Fulford Farm was a cheery place, underwriting the amiable nature of Rory's father, Anthony, who had been training race-horses in a charming and deceptively laid back way ever since he had left the army. The yard might not be smart – in fact first-time visitors were generally dismayed by the really rather down-at-heel appearance of an establishment where none of the stable doors matched or fitted, tiles were falling off roofs, and every drainpipe seemed to run at a different angle – but a closer inspection would reveal that the horses' beds were clean and deep and the jumbled boxes surprisingly draught-free and spacious, and the tack was spotless. There were no fashionable matching anoraks for the staff at Fulford, where the horses pulled out to work every morning this side of late, attired in a variety of rugs and sheets that looked as if they might just have been snatched from one of the dog beds lined up against the walls of the Guv's far from spotless office, but, more important than anything else, the horses were healthy, and well cared for. Not that this made much difference to the luck of the establishment, which could be described, at best, as being sporadic.

Anthony Rawlins had had his share of national hunt winners, or rather more correctly had once had his share of winners, but in the past half a dozen years his tally had fallen, and the yard still existed thanks mainly to the goodwill and affection of a small but loyal band of owners who would rather enjoy their racing than be part of one of the increasingly impersonal large training yards. Fun had always been Anthony Rawlins's target. He couldn't abide trainers who referred to racing as an *industry* and thought of their owners as *mushrooms* – fed on rubbish and kept in the dark.

The last season had been the worst ever at Fulford Farm, a horrendous six months during which he had lost three horses, one in a schooling accident and two of his most promising young chasers on the racecourse. It had taken more out of him than even he had realised, a fact which had never hit him harder than at this moment.

'It seems the saddle slipped,' Anthony told Rory when his son found him in his office. 'Something must have spooked the mare, because it was very out of character. She might even have been stung, who knows? Anyway, she dumped Teddy, jumped the wire and disappeared into the heart of the plains.'

'It wouldn't have helped if the saddle was still on her.'

'Wasn't on when the lorry hit her,' Anthony replied, lighting another cigarette from the end of his last one. 'Anything might have happened. But God knows how she got where she did. Someone said they saw a horse charging east along the road from the roundabout just past Stonehenge, but if she'd come down the road from Larkhill . . .'

'If she was on that road,' Rory agreed, as his father petered out, 'yes, why hadn't she headed for home? First thing the older horses do – bolt for home. I remember when I came off Ozzy at Larkhill, he headed straight back here.'

'We'll never know. That's horses. They have their ways.'

Moss Daisy, the mare who had just been killed on the road, happened to be the yard's favourite, not only because she had won two particularly competitive handicaps at their local racecourse, but also because of her character. With a saddle on her she had been a street fighter, but in her box and in the paddocks she had been a lop-eared dozy old softie, with an addiction to Extra Strong mints. Everyone loved her, and now she was gone and her lad was bereft.

'I've told Teddy it wasn't his fault,' Anthony said. 'These things happen. That's racing, as if he didn't know.'

'Did he check his girths before they galloped? I know it sounds like an obvious thing to ask, Dad—'

'He said he did and if he said he did, he probably did. But it happens. It happened to me once in a Members' Race up at Larkhill, just as I was coming to win it.'

'Sure, Dad. During a race it's understandable, but before a gallop?'

'It was an accident, Rory,' Anthony said, cutting his son short. 'And even if it wasn't, it's not going to bring the mare back.'

Of course his father was right. Even if the lad had been to blame, the how and why of the accident was only academic. They both knew there was a possibility that Teddy had failed to check the girths prior to doing some fast work, but then they both also knew that, if that were the case, the lad's guilt would be punishment enough.

'You're looking a bit tired, Dad,' Rory murmured over dinner that evening.

'Hardly surprising, old lad,' Anthony said, pouring the wine. 'All things considered.'

'You haven't had a break in ages.'

'That's because I don't like *breaks*, as you call them, chum. It was different when your mother was alive, but now, what's the point?'

'It would get you away from here, that's the point. You really should get away, just for a few days – fishing or something. You've got a good staff here. And I can keep an eye on things.'

His father regarded him over his wine glass, but said nothing, turning his attention to his food.

'Tell you what,' he admitted finally. 'I was actually thinking of going to Ireland.'

'Horses?'

'That time of year. If I do go, I don't suppose you'd feel like coming? We could put in a few days' fishing first, then amble along and look at some *harses*. Could be fun.'

'Yes, OK. I must admit I've always wanted to go.'

'And you've always refused.'

'Because there were always reasons.'

'One particularly good reason.'

'Don't go there.'

'Wasn't going to, old boy. Where angels fear to tread department. So you'll come, then?'

'Of course.'

'It'll be fun. We'll have some fun.'

Anthony went to bed that night feeling a little more cheerful than he had expected, the loss of Moss Daisy being slightly mitigated by the knowledge that he had persuaded his son to come with him to Ireland. Not that he was feeling particularly fatalistic; it was simply something he had been wanting them both to do – before it was too late.

'No need for all that kind of thinking. Mustn't look back,' he scolded himself as he sat on the edge of his half-made bed smoking the last cigarette of the day. 'It's just losing the mare, it's getting to you, making you soggy round the edges. Can't have that.'

It would do them both good, going away. They'd get in some fishing, on the Ban maybe, then take their time driving through Cork where he'd look up old horse friends and introduce them to his son and heir. If anyone needed a break it was surely Rory, after all he'd been through at the hands of his long-time girlfriend, the minx who'd spun him at the eleventh hour, just when they were all set and under orders to go up the aisle.

Anthony had liked Penny well enough, but he'd never trusted her, not for a moment. She was pretty and amusing and had *seemed* devoted to Rory, at least whenever the three of them were together, but there was something about her face in repose that struck a warning note.

'What do you really want out of life, old boy?' Anthony found himself asking Rory, out of the blue, as they were driving to the airport a few days later. 'I know we've talked about it before, but what do you *really* want?'

'You know what I really want, Dad.' Rory tried not to sound embarrassed, and failed.

'I don't have to leave the place to you, you know. I can just as easily sell up, let you have your bundle and go and live in a warm air bungalow somewhere. There's no obligation to you as far as Fulford Farm goes.'

'What else would I do? It's something you've brought me up to do, you and Ma, to take over.'

'Mmm. But. What about your painting? Your drawing?'

'There are an awful lot of people who are a great deal more talented than me.'

'There are even more people who can train better than me, but that didn't stop me.'

'We don't have to talk about this now, you know. It's time to have fun.'

'You bet,' Anthony agreed, as Rory headed the car on to the airport approach road. 'Let the *craic* commence.'

They stayed for five days in an old inn at Glenbeigh in County Kerry where they fished the local river by day and by night. Anthony caught over a dozen good trout and Rory caught his first salmon, a decent six-and-a-half-pound fish which tasted as well as it had fought.

The September weather was soft and full of sunlight, so golden in fact that the two men were loath to leave their small hotel with its semi-tropical garden and wonderful views over the sea and Rossbeigh Strand, and to compensate made a booking for a ten-day fishing holiday the following year. Then they packed their stuff into their hire car and set off for Cork. As they left the weather broke and the first rains of autumn blew in off the Atlantic.

The following morning they found themselves standing for what seemed like an eternity on the edge of an unkempt and rainswept field just outside the undistinguished town of Cronagh, some thirty miles on from Cork city.

'I'm just glad we had the *craic* up there in Kerry, Dad,' Rory said, zipping his old Barbour jacket up to his chin. 'This is not a place to spend quality time.'

'You'd be surprised, old chap,' Anthony returned cheerfully. 'It breaks out in the most surprising places over here.'

'What does exactly?'

'Life. Life Irish style.'

'Not here, surely? This isn't just a place that time forgot. This is a place it never visited. That town. How about that for dismal? It's got more bars than houses.'

'Wisht, as they say,' his father replied. 'Hold your hour. You haven't seen anything yet.'

At this point the long-awaited, bedraggled figure of Sean Phelan appeared out of the mists and rain, leading a miserable mud-covered horse for inspection.

'I think you showed me this poor chap last year, Sean,' Anthony told the dealer after a cursory inspection. 'Probably the year before as well.'

'I did not so!' Phelan protested as he tried to pull the recalcitrant horse out of the mud and up on to the patch of weed-covered concrete by the gate. 'Sure I never had this fellow last year, so I did not! If I'd had him I'd have sold him be now. You just take one look at him yourself and see the quality.'

'All I can see is skin and bone, Sean,' Anthony insisted. 'And the same two scars on its knees as it had last year.'

'Scars?' Sean yelped. 'What are you talking about, Mr Rawlins, sir, forgiving your presence? This horse is entirely unblemished!'

'I remember these scars, Sean. Two of them across both of his knees – where last year you yourself said he'd grazed himself getting out of the horsebox.'

'Where?' Phelan began another of his elaborate pantomimes, pushing his rain-drenched hat to the back of his head as he bent down to stare at the unfortunate animal's fore legs. 'Jeeze, would you look at that now – however did he come by those things? Sure he hadn't a mark on him this morning.'

'Is that so?' Anthony wondered mock-seriously. 'So how come I can see old stitch marks?'

'Stitch marks?' Phelan said. 'This is getting worse be the

minute. Someone's been at him, that's what they've been, at him, they have.'

The dealer made a mighty show of clucking his tongue and shaking his head in mock shock and dismay at the discovery of wounds inflicted on the miserable horse well over twelve months ago.

'If you've nothing else to show me, Sean . . .' Anthony said with a private wink to Rory, sinking his freezing hands into the deep pockets of his old raincoat.

'This is a grand animal, Mr Rawlins – you'd have to be as mad as a hawk to spin him, the way you are intent.'

'That is a poor old creature, Sean, fit only for one thing. And you're as big a rogue as ever you were.'

'I am not so!' Phelan protested, dropping the horse's leg, which he had been tenderly nursing, and slapping away the half-starved animal on its rump with his hat. 'The thing is you've not got the eye for him. Not for a good 'un, you just haven't the eye, Mr Rawlins, sir, saving your presence.'

'Ah well, Sean.' Anthony paused and mock-sighed. 'Let's just hope my misfortune is someone else's great luck.'

'Ach,' Sean growled. 'Away with ye! You'd have spun Arkle, so ye would!'

'OK, Dad,' Rory said once they were in the car and out of the dealer's earshot. 'What in God's name brings you to this godforsaken place anyway?'

'Believe it or not, my son,' his father replied, 'I got the Mighty Midge from old Sean Phelan.'

'You're putting me on!' Rory stared at his father in amazement. 'The Mighty Midge? Who won the Cathcart?'

'My one and only Cheltenham winner. He came out of the very same field as that poor old wreck. I always come back here, just in case, in spite of what they say, lightning does strike twice.'

'But it never has.'

'You know as well as I do, old boy. God knows how he bred it, and you know what sort of horse that was.'

'If only he hadn't broken down . . .'

'*If onlys* keep us all in the game. Racing's full of *if onlys*.'

'You said yourself he'd have been a Gold Cup horse.'

'Racing's also full of *might have beens*. Time for a jar,' Anthony decided. 'Don't know about you, but I am *cold*.'

Rory glanced at his father. It was unlike him to complain, and while it had certainly been wet it really wasn't cold.

'You OK, Pop?'

'I'm fine, old chap. Just wet through. It's all right for you young ones, you don't feel it like us old warriors. Now get us to a bar double quick.'

Rory drove them back into Cronagh, pulling up finally outside a bar grandiosely entitled in red and white neon *Finnegan's Exclusive American Cocktail Lounge*. Inside it was definitely not as advertised, being dimly lit, poorly furnished and fogged with a thick pall of cigarette and pipe smoke. It wasn't particularly busy, although, as Anthony said to his son while they waited to get served, given the number of bars in such a sparsely populated town it was a testimony to the natives' drinking abilities that so many pubs were able to trade at all.

'Soft auld day,' the man next to them at the bar said, with a sideways nod of his head.

'Dirty old day,' Anthony replied, knowing the score.

'Ah well,' his neighbour sighed, sucking at his pipe. 'There's a lot worse to come. How was your pal Sean?'

'Big a rogue as ever,' Anthony said, as if the man's question had been anticipated.

'Trying to sell you that dammety auld gelding again. As if you hadn't seen enough of it.'

Anthony smiled and took a sip of his Paddy Powers. 'Will you join us?' he asked.

'I'll have a John Jameson,' his neighbour said.

'A John Jameson for my friend here,' Anthony directed the tall poker-faced barman.

'Large, Donal,' his neighbour added.

'As if I would not,' the barman intoned, as if saying Mass.

'And from a fresh bottle, too.'

'I have no fresh bottles, Michael.'

'You have so. Under here.' Michael tapped the bar then nodded his head once to underline his point. 'I like my whisky without the water, Donal.'

'And don't I know?'

'So let's have it out of a fresh bottle then.'

'There are plenty of other bars, Michael Doherty.'

'And aren't they all run by your relatives? Now do the decent thing, Donal, and show our guest here your good manners.'

The squabble finally over, the four of them drank, the landlord pouring himself a generous ball of malt from the freshly opened bottle. He charged Anthony for it, but Anthony knew better than to protest, since he knew from experience that there were plenty of free ones in the offing now a new bottle had been broached.

Some time later he found himself being advised by Michael to go to see a very particular horse. Michael had laid his head on the bar with his face turned towards Anthony, and was doing his best to focus on his drinking partner.

'Padraig Flanagan has him,' he said in a stage whisper. 'But shh! No one's to know I'm telling you that.'

''Tis a fine horse Padraig has so!' a voice from somewhere down the bar assured Anthony. 'A man'd have no one at home not to go and see it now.'

'Don't you go sayin' I'm sending you,' Michael said from

his semi-recumbent position. 'He'll be thinkin' I'm after the finders.'

'That's finders as in keepers, right?' Anthony wondered with a frown, trying desperately not to let go.

'Finders as in fee, friend,' Michael replied, before rolling off his seat and sinking slowly to the floor.

By now Rory had the flavour too, and was sitting happily smiling at his reflection in the far from clean mirror over the bar. Anthony took him by the shoulder, but it seemed Rory wasn't that keen to move, turning round to his father and putting a finger to an area near his lips.

'Shh!' he advised. 'There are people sleeping here.'

'Come on, chum,' Anthony said, keeping hold of him with one hand and searching for his car keys in his pocket with the other. 'We're off to see a horse.'

'Ye'll not be driving yerselves, so you won't,' an enormous man in a large brown overcoat warned him, taking the keys from his hand. 'Ye're in no fit state to take ahold the wheel. I shall drive to Padraig's.'

'And you reckon you are?' Anthony asked him, trying to draw himself up to his full height but still finding himself a good foot shorter than the giant swaying over him. 'In a fit state to drive, that is?'

'I am not, for I have drink taken,' the giant replied. 'But there's no need for concern on my behalf, man. There'll be no problem if the Garda stop me.'

'I see,' Anthony said, scratching his head. 'And I wonder why would that be, chummy?'

'Because I have no driving licence,' the giant said. 'Now come along, man, and show me to your vehicular.'

Realising he himself was far too drunk to drive, let alone make any sense, Anthony followed the large man out of the bar, dragging Rory with him, and pointed out the red hire car parked immediately outside. His chauffeur nodded and got in the back seat.

'I thought you were going to drive.'

'I am so,' the man replied. 'Where's your problem?'

'I've always found it easier to do that from the front seat.' Anthony opened the driver's door with an exaggerated bow.

'I have not me spectacles, man. I have them lost,' the giant told him, shoehorning himself into the driver's seat with some difficulty, being far too tall for the economy-size vehicle, and trying without much success to get the key in the ignition. Anthony took the ring from him and, after encountering a similar problem, realised they were his house keys rather than the car keys. Finding the right ones in Rory's pocket, he managed to get the engine started, pushed his swaying son into the back, went round to the front passenger seat, slammed the door shut on his coat and nodded to the man hunched over the wheel.

'Full steam ahead, captain,' he said. 'Full steam ahead.'

'You shall have to direct me, man,' the giant said, unable to lift his head properly. 'You'll have to indicate the route for I find it hard to see the road in front.'

'You can actually drive, old man?'

'Indeed I can. I have been drivin' vehiculars since I was a gossoon.'

'Motor vehiculars?'

'All manner of vehiculars. Now then – how are we doing?'

'We are doing fine,' Anthony replied. 'Just fine. But that's probably because we're still stationary.'

The giant crashed the stick into third gear and the car lurched off very slowly.

'You're on the pavement, old chap,' Anthony said, having cleared a patch of condensation off his window. 'Apparently headed for a chemist's.'

He leaned over and corrected the steering in time to return the car to the mercifully empty road.

'That is a sensible thing you are doing here, man,' his driver told him. 'You make sure to do that now if I go a little off beam.'

'Perhaps it'd be better if I did the driving entirely,' Anthony suggested.

'You should have thought of that before you started the drinking,' the giant replied. 'But then you still may, of course, provided you are content to spend the rest of your day in gaol.'

'The rest of my *day*? For being drunk at the wheel?'

'The Garda Milligan has a scorched earth policy here, man. He comes down like a mallet on drink drivers.'

And so on they lurched in third gear at all of five miles an hour, with Anthony calling the directions from the passenger seat. By a small miracle and some fifty hair-raising minutes later, they arrived unscathed at a smallholding halfway up a hill, most of which was totally wreathed in mist and rain.

'Padraig Flanagan's as ever was,' the giant deduced once he had levered himself out of the car. 'Pray to God he is still alive.'

'Why? Is there a chance he might not be?' Anthony enquired.

'We none of us know when we may be called, do we? Or when we may be spared. Padraig!'

Reeling from the man's enormous bellow, Anthony shook his head and tried to get his bearings, then went round the back of the car to wake his son.

'Padraig! Padraig, 'tis I, Yamon! 'Tis I Yamon and a stranger come here to see The Horse!'

'How tall are you?' Anthony said, gazing at the figure before him. 'Just exactly how tall *are* you?'

'Shorter than the mother, but not the father. The mother is still our tallest.'

'That doesn't precisely answer my question. You must be over seven feet.'

'The mother can open an upstairs window with no use of a ladder. Padraig!'

The summons echoed round the misted landscape like a fairytale ogre's roar. Back the name came at Anthony – *Padraig! Padraig!* – whereupon at about the fourth or fifth echo the small round figure of Padraig appeared, limping his way across the yard and pulling his old battered hat down over his eyes against the rain, then turning his pipe upside down as an added safeguard.

'What is it possessin' you, Yamon? Ye'll wake the whole county!'

'I have a stranger here, Padraig! Come to see The Horse.'

'I'm standing right beside you, Yamon,' Padraig chided him. 'There's no more need to bellow. And how would he know about The Horse?'

'He had heard tell.'

'And I wonder what has he heard tell, Yamon?'

'That you have this horse, so you have. And that he's something special.'

'Which horse in this country isn't?' Anthony asked, with half an eye on Rory who was slowly pulling himself out of the car. 'Every horse I'm shown is something special.'

'It'll be no skin off my nose if you don't want him, sir,' Padraig said, eyeing him up from under his rain-sodden hat. 'I have several interested parties and the horse isn't even advertised.'

'Did you breed him yourself, Mr Flanagan?' Anthony enquired, looking round at the ramshackle yard.

'I did not, sir,' Padraig answered with perfect truth. 'Though indeed he was born here. The mare came to us in foal.'

'Ye'll not be wasting your time, friend,' Eammon, pronounced Yamon, loudly assured him. 'Padraig here always has fine stock.'

'I certainly don't mind looking, Mr Flanagan,' Anthony said, even though he was more than half convinced he was wasting his time. 'If you want to show him to me, no harm in looking.'

'We'll see,' Padraig grunted, now eyeing both Rory and Anthony. 'First I'd say you're both in need of a cup of tea.'

Nodding sideways towards a small cottage at the top of the yard, Padraig limped off, expecting them to follow, which they duly did, Yamon included. Padraig went straight to the kitchen at the back, calling ahead in Gaelic as he went. Anthony entered the room well ahead of Rory, who was still outside, taking a lot of deep breaths in an effort to clear his head. A girl with her back to Anthony, dressed in a heavy black Aran sweater and a dark green skirt under a white apron, was busy washing dishes in a bowl at the sink. Padraig said something to her in Gaelic that caused her to turn and stare at Anthony in silence. Then, wiping her hands on her apron, she took the garment off, threw it on the draining board, nodded to Anthony and ran out of the kitchen.

'Something I said?' Anthony enquired lightly, struck by the extraordinary beauty of the young woman.

'Don't mind her now,' Padraig said, taking his hat off and slapping it against his leg. 'My daughter Kathleen. She has her days. Don't mind her at all.'

When Rory appeared at the doorway, Padraig invited his guests to sit at the table and moments later had poured them cups of the strongest tea from a pot that was already standing hot on the hob. A tall gangly young man was the next to show, coming in from outside dressed in a short black oilskin and agricultural gumboots. Padraig addressed him also in Gaelic, whereupon the lad nodded and ambled back out into the rain, taking with him a bridle that was hanging on the back of the door.

'Mr Flanagan has a horse he thinks he might show us, Rory,' Anthony said.

'I keep feeling I'm dreaming,' Rory said slowly, blinking his eyes as if to try to focus on the proceedings. 'Am I?'

'Has the horse done anything, Mr Flanagan?' Anthony asked, guiding his son to a chair by the table. 'Has he raced at all?'

'Has he raced at all.' Yamon sighed, then repeated himself loudly. 'Has he raced at all indeed!'

Padraig eyed the big man and poured himself a cup of tea, stirring the sugar in with the stub of his pipe. 'He has so, sir,' he said to Anthony. 'We gave him a couple of runs tail end of the last season. He ran in a point, then in a hunters. At Tramore.'

'And?'

'I was happy enough,' Padraig said with a nod, returning to his tea.

'That doesn't tell me much, Mr Flanagan. How happy?'

'He'd have won his point be a mile,' Yamon said from where he was standing by the door as if keeping guard, his head bowed under the low ceiling, arms folded across his chest. 'He'd have won it be a mile if he hadn't been run out of it.'

'A touch of the might have beens?' Rory wondered, glancing at his father.

'The boys had a hot horse running,' Padraig said, now sucking at his pipe. 'So they ran our fella out at the last with their other runner.'

'Knocked him halfways to Skibbereen,' Yamon added. 'He'd have won be a mile.'

Anthony nodded, pushing his empty teacup away from him and lighting a cigarette. 'And the hunter chase?'

'Sure the lad fell off of him!' Yamon suddenly bellowed, as if still infuriated. 'The lad only went and fell off of him!'

'And I suppose he'd have won that too by a mile?'

'At the very least, man!' Yamon bellowed. 'At the very least!'

'He was twelve lengths clear at the last, sir,' Padraig said. 'And well on the bridle.'

'And?'

'The boy looked round to see where the others might be, the horse jinked, and the boy fell off.'

'Why run him in a hunter chase?' Rory asked, beginning to come to. 'If he hadn't yet won his point? Or even his points, as in more than one.'

'I was persuaded,' Padraig replied. 'That's for why.'

'Who persuaded you?' Anthony enquired.

'I did, sir,' Padraig said. 'He's an exceptional horse, d'you see, and there's a bit of money to a hunter chase while there's next to none for a point.'

'But if he had won, old chap,' Anthony continued, 'he'd have been out of novice class and straight into handicaps.'

'This horse is no novice, man!' Yamon thundered. 'This horse has been here before! This horse has nothing to learn, man!'

'Your man here means the horse would have had then to run straight in handicaps, Yamon,' Padraig said.

'This horse could run straight in a cup race, Padraig!' Yamon insisted. 'Ye could send this horse straight to Cheltenham and live in clover the rest of your days!'

'If we're going to have a look . . .' Anthony said, consulting his watch, mindful that he and Rory had a plane to catch later – a later which was fast becoming sooner.

'Sure you can have a look now all right,' Padraig agreed, opening the back door. 'The boy should have him fixed.'

They all went out into the yard, Anthony lending half an ear to Padraig's imaginative account of the horse's bloodline. It was still pouring with rain, but Liam had set up a course of makeshift jumps fashioned from barrels, boxes, planks and even broomsticks, and was leading a horse already saddled up from a stable.

'In the name of God,' Anthony said in some dismay. 'You're not going to put the horse over these?'

'Of course not,' Padraig replied. 'Sure we'll warm him up first, Liam?'

Liam took his instructions, nodding as he fastened on a riding helmet that was at least one size too small for his head. Then with a leg up from his father he began to trot the horse round the enclosure.

'There isn't a lot of him, is there?' Anthony observed when Padraig had come back to stand beside Rory.

'He only appears that way with the boy being tall,' Padraig returned.

'OK,' Anthony said. 'But you're not exactly tall and I was judging the animal more by you.'

'He must be under sixteen hands,' Rory added, peering through the rain.

'He just walks small,' Padraig assured them. 'He's a different size altogether when he's jumping.'

As Liam began to trot the horse, Kathleen emerged from the stables, a small oilskin-clad figure with her face half obscured by a large man's cap, and leaned with her back against the wall, watching the proceedings. She saw her brother was having trouble getting the horse to trot sweetly for him, but she ignored his call to her. She had little time for those who came to buy their horses, particularly the smart, moneyed ones from across the water.

'He's quite green, isn't he, old man?' Anthony said to Padraig. 'Doesn't seem to know how to use himself.'

'Use himself?' Yamon roared. 'Use himself indeed! Use himself?'

Padraig took his hat off and threw it to the ground, shouting something in Gaelic to his son, who shouted back to him in the same language.

'Subtitles?' Rory looked at his father.

'All I know is *caed mille failte*,' Anthony replied with an apologetic smile.

The more Padraig and his son shouted at each other, the more the horse began to misbehave. It was as if he deliberately wanted to put on a bad display.

'Put him over the jumps now, boy!' Padraig called. 'You have us all bored. Go on now! Have him jump something! Watch now,' Padraig advised his English visitors. 'Now you'll see some form.'

Liam got the horse half straight but it was immediately obvious that the animal was far from settled since he began to prance on the spot and buck when he saw the jumps in front of him.

'Go on, Liam boy!' Padraig shouted. 'Go on! Go on now!'

Liam tried to do as he was told, shortening the reins and kicking the horse on, but as soon as he did so the horse's head came up and he put in a monumental buck that all but had Liam on the ground.

'Really, old chap,' Anthony said politely. 'Thank you, but I think we've seen all we need to see.'

'You have not,' Padraig insisted. 'You'll not go till you've seen him jump!'

Grabbing a Long Tom that was propped up against the shed,

Padraig hurried over and cracked the whip sharply behind the horse to try to encourage him to get himself straight and go forward, but its only effect was to make the animal shoot ahead as fast as he could, the suddenness of his bolt causing the ill-prepared Liam to fall off sideways. He managed to keep hold of the reins, but far from stopping the horse he simply got dragged behind it as it charged around the yard, between them knocking over practically every barrel and plank set up for the horse to jump.

'Well, he can certainly bolt.' Anthony laughed. 'And if it was a bolter I was after, old chap, I would look no further.'

'Pull that horse up, boy!' Padraig shouted at Liam as he was swept past them yet again at full pelt. 'What in all the saints' names do you think you're doing?'

But all Liam could do now to save himself was to let go of the reins and slide across the yard to crash into a small shed, which at once began to shake as if on the verge of collapse. Seeing this, Padraig rushed over to the jerry-built structure and shoved a heavy prop against one wall to prevent yet another disaster while the horse went on galloping headlong round the yard.

'I also note he doesn't object to the hard going,' Anthony remarked wryly to his son as the sparks continued to fly. 'So that's something.'

'Someone should take a hold of him, Padraig,' Yamon advised loudly, 'or you'll be paying for a new set of shoes earlier than you wanted.'

But in spite of Padraig's madly flapping arms and shouts of *Will you not whoa there now!* the horse persisted in its wild journey until Kathleen could stand it no longer. Her ardent desire not to see her horse taken from the yard was at war with her wish that her pride and joy should not disgrace himself, and it was pride that finally won the day. Just as Anthony and

Rory were about to leave, she pushed herself quickly away from the wall against which she was still leaning and whistled sharply. Recognising the sound, the horse stopped at once, slithering on the wet concrete before turning back to the caller.

'Come here, will you, you crazy loon,' she said softly to the horse as she walked towards him with her hand held out. 'Come here before you do yourself a mischief. Come here and show them what you can do.'

Straightening his tack and calming him almost at once, Kathleen set him right, then, hopping on to one of the few still upright barrels, vaulted lightly and easily into the saddle. As soon as she was up the horse settled, pricked his ears, snorted and began to walk out like a dressage animal. Liam reset the jumps while Kathleen continued her display, now trotting the horse, now extending his trot, and finally cantering him in a perfect collection round the inside of the course.

'You're not really going to ask him to jump on this surface?' Anthony wondered. 'It's not only concrete, but wet concrete.'

'I wouldn't ask a thing of him, Mr Rawlins,' Padraig replied, 'if I knew he couldn't do it.'

'Most of those jumps are at least four foot, Dad, and a couple are even higher,' Rory muttered in amazement.

'Not our horse, old boy,' his father said. 'Ours not to reason why.'

'They're off their chumps,' Rory said, feeling his head beginning to throb. 'But the girl certainly can ride. Look at that seat.'

'I already have.'

They watched, both privately coming to the conclusion, without publicly remarking on it, that now the horse was standing up and moving properly he looked bigger and stronger than he had when he had ambled out of his box as if he was a donkey setting off for work in the peat bogs.

By no means a big horse, nevertheless he now looked nearer sixteen hands than fifteen, and considerably more athletic than before. He had the air of a street fighter, an animal that as soon as it was saddled up and faced with a challenge seemed to change its physical appearance, prepared to take on all comers, to see anyone off. Getting him ready to jump Kathleen gave him one stroke down the neck, rose up in her irons into the jumping position, then gathered him up.

'Go on, fella,' she whispered to him. 'Show them what you're made of.'

Now the horse moved forward with quite a different look in his eyes, tight held and bouncing into the first of the jumps. No one could quite believe what they then saw, not Yamon, not even Padraig, and certainly not the two visitors from England. From a standing start on lethally wet concrete the horse flew round the yard jumping everything in his way with plenty to spare, arching his back and tucking his fore legs well up as he rose. He didn't touch a plank or a broomstick. He simply skipped over the jumps in the style of a seasoned show jumper. Kathleen took him round twice before easing him up and bringing him to a standstill in front of the two Englishmen.

'Well done, Miss Flanagan,' Anthony called up to her. 'And you, little horse,' he added, patting the horse on his neck. 'Well done you as well. That was some display.'

Kathleen nodded her thanks, despite her feelings.

'Would you like to see him pop over a hedge in the field now?' Padraig enquired. 'The ground's a bit sloppy but he'd not mind that. He'll go on anything.'

'He's like a wave when he jumps, man!' Yamon assured them. 'Like a great big wave when he races, overlapping the fences and flowing like the sea itself!'

'I'll take your word for it,' Anthony said, inspecting the horse more closely now, lifting up and flexing each fore leg before running his fingers down the tendons, satisfying himself that the legs were cool as could be and the tendons clean and sharp. 'If you were going to sell him, Mr Flanagan . . . ?'

'I'd be axing you for twenty thousand of your English guineas, sir.'

'You can axe away, old chap, but I wouldn't go anywhere near that sort of figure.'

'If we were in the sales at Doncaster you would have to, sir.'

'But we're not, Mr Flanagan, and if you really are thinking you might sell him, I might offer you ten thousand English guineas.'

'And I'd take not a drop under nineteen firm,' came the reply. 'And I'll not haggle further.' Padraig spat on his hand in preparation of sealing the deal, watched now in horror by Kathleen who in the heat of the moment had quite forgotten what the purpose of this visit might be.

'And I'd not budge over ten and a half, Mr Flanagan.'

'Then we have no deal, sir. And you have missed out on the chance of owning something exceptional.'

'Da,' Kathleen chipped in, sliding down from the saddle and pulling the reins over the horse's head and under his chin.

'This is nothing to do with you, girl, this is men's business,' Padraig said without looking at her. 'Now do your horse good, and that's an end to it.'

Kathleen glanced round at their two visitors, but they were both taking one last look at the horse before he was returned to his box. She said something to her father in Gaelic, but was met with a dismissive wave of his hand.

'Eighteen nine and the horse is yours,' Padraig said.

'Sorry, Mr Flanagan.' Anthony sighed. 'It's a nice enough

animal, but not at that sort of money. Now my son and I have a plane to catch.'

'Eighteen five hundred,' Padraig offered. 'And that's it.'

'Thank you but no thank you. If the horse sticks, you can always give me a call in England.' Anthony gave Padraig his card, then shook his hand. 'He's a nice little horse and I'm sure he'll pick up a race somewhere.'

From the look on both Padraig's and Yamon's faces it was as if they had insulted Mother Ireland herself, while Kathleen, with a face like a thundercloud over Dingle Bay, took her precious charge back to his stable.

'Time to mosey along,' Rory muttered. 'If you fancy keeping your scalp.'

With one last nod Anthony and Rory hurried off to their car and made good their escape.

Exhausted by his recent experiences, Anthony settled down to sleep as Rory headed the car for Cork airport, and Rory had to defer the questions he had stored up to ask, every one of which concerned the little horse.

But they didn't get very far before the matter was once again brought to their attention. Just as they were clearing Cronagh town itself, a desperately battered old truck pulled out in front of them and came to a halt. Forced to stop, Rory saw Padraig Flanagan behind the wheel with the giant Yamon sitting beside him, head bent and knees up almost under his chin. Oblivious of the fact that he was causing a minor traffic jam, Padraig got out of the truck and came round to the passenger window of the hire car, on which he rapped his knuckles sharply in order to wake Anthony.

'Fifteen thousand five hundred,' he barked through the still closed window. 'Fifteen and a half thousand of your guineas and the horse is yours!'

Anthony frowned for a moment, then shook his head and instructed Rory to drive round the obstruction and be on his way. Padraig got back in the driving seat of the truck and followed them, sounding the horn constantly.

Forced to another stop ten miles on by a flock of sheep wandering across the road, in his driving mirror Rory saw Padraig hop out from the cab once again to appear at his father's window.

'Ah but you're a hard man, Mr Rawlins,' Padraig gasped. 'Fourteen thousand flat says the horse is yours.'

'I really don't have that sort of money to spare, old man,' Anthony said firmly. 'Drive on, Rory.'

With the road ahead now clear of sheep, Rory floored the accelerator, leaving Padraig throwing his battered old hat to the ground in despair. Half a mile on, they joined the main trunk road to Cork where driving as fast as he safely could Rory left the battered old farm truck miles behind them.

Reaching Cork airport in plenty of time, they returned their hire car then went to check in. There was a good hour still to spare before their flight, so they went to the café and had something to eat and a couple of cups of strong coffee. Settled at a table overlooking the runway neither of them was aware of the two figures stealing up on them quietly from behind.

'Eleven thousand five hundred, Mr Rawlins, sir,' said Padraig's voice softly in Anthony's ear. 'The very final offer.'

Anthony didn't even look round. He just eyed his son, winked, finished his coffee and yawned. 'Nine thousand seven hundred and fifty,' he said finally. 'English guineas.'

'Ten thousand five hundred.'

'Ten thousand flat,' Anthony replied. 'Not a penny more.'

'Done,' Padraig agreed, and spat on his hand. 'You're a hard man, but a decent one, and I have the papers here.'

Sitting himself down, he produced a bundle of papers

including a bill of sale from his top coat pocket, together with an old cracked biro which he handed to Anthony.

'You have yourself the best horse in Ireland.' He nodded. 'Good luck with him now. And may he bring you joy.'

Anthony leafed quickly through the papers then signed the bill of sale.

'Dad . . .' Rory said quietly.

'In a minute, old man,' Anthony muttered as he wrote a cheque. 'First things first.'

'Dad,' Rory persisted.

'Hush now,' Padraig cautioned. 'Your father's busy here.'

Anthony handed the cheque over, then gathered up the sheaf of papers.

'The passport, Dad?' Rory said quietly.

'Rory.' His father looked at him, clearing his throat. 'I do know what I'm doing.'

'The boy's right, Mr Rawlins,' Padraig said, putting a hand to his inside pocket and producing an equine passport. 'I nearly forgot it meself, so I did. There now.' He handed over the document. 'It's been a rare pleasure, and may your shadows never grow less.'

Then the Irishmen were gone, even more suddenly than they had arrived.

'I hadn't forgotten the passport,' Anthony grumbled, suddenly feeling very tired. 'And old Flanagan knew as well I did no passport, no deal. That's just the way it is.'

'But you hadn't – we hadn't checked it, Pop.'

'We heard how he was born back at the yard, and the horse is obviously thoroughbred.'

'I don't remember hearing the breeding.'

'You were probably still six sheets, old lad. By . . . who was it? And what was the mare again? Mananan's something or other. Mananan's Girl, that's it. By some stallion of his neighbour's

67

that I've never heard of – King of the Sea, that's the boy. By King of the Sea out of Mananan's Girl.'

'You won't be able to put that on the racecard,' Rory said, handing his father the open passport. 'You're going to have to put by King of the Sea out of mare unknown. The dam wasn't registered.'

Anthony frowned at him, then studied the passport.

'Well, that's not the end of the world. She'll be in the part-bred register, no doubt.'

'Whether she is or not, Pop, I'm thinking it doesn't exactly bolster the horse's value. If you're thinking of selling him on, or finding an owner.'

'He's a cheap horse, Rory. And even with an unregistered dam—'

'A useless unregistered dam,' Rory corrected him. 'And an equally useless sire, if you don't mind my saying.'

'We should still be able to sell him on, perhaps for as much as twenty. People are throwing money around these days. After all, he is Irish, and all they want at the moment in England are Irish horses.'

'Big, well-bred Irish horses with some form. And what do you mean by *we* should be able to sell him on?' Rory threw his father a droll look.

'Figure of speech, old boy, figure of speech,' Anthony said, swallowing hard as he felt a pain hit him mid-chest. 'And there's our flight called.'

Anthony suffered his first heart attack on the plane just as they were coming in to land. By the time they got him off the plane and into an ambulance he was suffering a second one. His life, hanging by a thread, was saved only by the speed and efficiency with which he was transferred to the nearest hospital, where he was placed in intensive care.

'Any idea of his chances?' Rory waylaid a doctor at the first available opportunity. 'He's always been a pretty tough character.'

'He'd need to be, Mr Rawlins.' The doctor looked past Rory to someone else coming towards him. 'That second attack was severe. Nine out of ten on the graph, I would say.'

Despite being warned that there was little chance of his father's recovering consciousness that night, Rory stayed at the hospital as long as he could, hoping in some helpless way that if he stayed around so would his father. Finally, in the very smallest of the small hours, he drove himself back to Fulford Farm, the emptiness of the roads giving him plenty of time to try to sort his thoughts out.

On the morning they had left for their trip to Ireland Rory had received a letter informing him that he had won a scholarship to study at the famous Savarese school of art in Florence. Of course he'd applied for it, although with no more than the faintest hope. At nearly twenty-eight years of age he knew it was high time he knuckled down, but he also knew he was getting far too long in the tooth to be a student. Naturally, being well aware that his father wanted him to take over at Fulford, he had said nothing to Anthony about Florence or the scholarship, not even when Anthony raised the subject on their drive to the airport. Now his father's sudden illness meant that Rory was faced with a very real dilemma. Basically, sell up Fulford, or take over.

If his mother Evelyn had not died in a terrible train crash only eight years before, everything would have been very different. They had been such a happy family. His father and mother had been devoted to each other, and because of Evelyn's seemingly everlasting patience and understanding as well as her innate good humour his father had managed his small yard with considerable success, even achieving a third in the Grand National.

But then Anthony's sweet-tempered wife had been killed because some idiot had made a terrible mistake with a set of points, and everything, right up until this present moment, had subsequently gone downhill, not fast, but bit by little bit, unwinding itself; Anthony losing his grip, Rory not on hand as much as he should have been, reluctant to muscle in on a grieving father. Wrong decisions had been made, the farm income had declined, staff had left unexpectedly and, on top of it all, compensation for victims in the rail accident had been interminably delayed because of the usual series of appeals, counter-appeals and counter-counter-appeals in the wake of the official report. Then when the money had finally been paid over, sums that were far too little in the opinion of most people, much of the received capital had to be utilised in helping make good damage already done to Fulford Farm, all of which had added up and brought them to this moment.

He unlocked his father's office door and went and sat behind his desk, in his chair. He had to get a grip. He had to get a grip and make decisions, in case his father never recovered.

First things first, he thought. First he would have to do something about the apparently useless horse his father had bought in Ireland. To buy an undersized and inexperienced horse with no notable breeding, regardless of how much had been drunk, seemed to Rory to be yet another example of the kinds of wrong decisions that had brought Fulford to its current state of near bankruptcy.

He stared round the room at the photos of the old glory days, of fine horses winning their races, of owners being presented with cups, of his mother and father and himself standing smiling beside horse after horse and owner after owner, remembering the good days, the happy ones, the times when the future had seemed safe and secure. Not like now. Now his father lay dangerously and possibly mortally ill, his mother had long been gone, and the yard was all but on its last legs, with yet another owner about to remove two decent horses and the only incomer being an undersized Irish squib. Something had to be done, but what that thing was for the life of him Rory could not imagine.

He could send the incoming animal straight to the sales, of course, but given the provenance of the creature he doubted whether they would get more than two thousand pounds for it. He sighed and scratched his head with a pencil in the faint hope of firing some sort of inspiration, but nothing was forthcoming. He was absolutely sure that his father had no old friend or owner on his books who was looking specifically for a small and underbred horse. Those in the know liked their steeplechasers to be big, athletic and strong enough to do the job, which this Irish horse was most certainly not, failing, it would seem, on all counts. What his father could have been thinking when he finally agreed to buy it was beyond Rory's comprehension – and, on top of everything, at this particular moment when thanks to the wretched government and the latest set of restrictions from Brussels, farming was in such difficulties that Fulford Farm could not support Fulford Racing Ltd, as it had so often done previously.

'If the old man gets better, the way things are we're going to have to shut up shop and buy him a nice little warm air bungalow,' Rory sighed to himself, watching the dawn break. 'Failing some sort of miracle.'

He stood up, and was about to turn off the office light when his eye was caught by a photograph of his mother. She was on her favourite hack, a part Welsh part thoroughbred bay gelding, the wholly delightful old Brown Jack. She was smiling happily into the camera, totally relaxed, as was her horse, the sunlight catching at the sheen of Brownie's coat and the polish on his mother's immaculate black riding boots. Behind them stretched the lush green of the summer paddocks and the light ochre of the cereal fields beyond, the whole a picture of elegant ease, a study of one of the most intrinsic elements of English country life, a beautiful woman on a fine horse in the fold of the countryside.

But there was something else about the picture, something that held Rory back. It was as if his mother was trying to talk to him, to send him a message.

'I must be tired,' he said to himself, as his dog Dunkum stretched himself out at his feet, ready to move back to the warmth of the kitchen. 'I must be imagining things. Photographs do not speak.'

Yet there was something most definitely in his head, and the more he listened the more he heard his mother's pretty voice. *Remember, Rory,* she was saying. *Just remember we never know where our good luck is coming from.*

What good luck? he wondered as he let Dunkum and himself out of the office just as the stable clock outside struck six, finding himself for once at odds with his mother. He did know one thing: any luck they might be getting would most certainly not be contained in the horse transporter that would shortly arrive at the stables from the Emerald Isle.

Chapter Three

Grenville

By now Grenville Fielding had resharpened every Venus HB pencil in the small silver container on his dark-green-leather-topped partner's desk, trimmed the dirty edges from his Staedtler Tradition eraser, carefully polished with a tissue the gold nib on his Parker 51 fountain pen – a present from his father on the occasion of his twenty-first birthday exactly twenty-five years ago – arranged his ivory ruler in a perfect parallel with the black leather correspondence folder that sat dead centre on the desktop, shot the cuffs of his freshly laundered and ironed dark blue and white striped shirt, and finally adjusted his Garrick Club tie before sitting back to review the day's play.

'Good,' he said to himself after a moment's reflection. 'Highly satisfactory, in fact. Could not have come at a better time.'

To celebrate the new business that had just come his way, he decided he would allow himself his first gin and tonic of the evening a quarter of an hour earlier than usual, assuring himself that if he drank it more slowly than was his habit, in the end it would come to much the same thing.

'It will come to very much the same thing, Grenville,' he said aloud as he rose to walk slowly to the skilfully distressed Georgian wardrobe that he used as a drinks cupboard. 'As long as we sip – and do not gulp.'

Carefully pouring a double London Gin from a silver-plated bar measure over two large cubes of iced Malvern water and adding precisely half a bottle of Slimline tonic to the Waterford tumbler, he dropped in a thin slice of freshly cut lime and then took the drink over to the window that looked out on to the iron-railed garden reserved solely for use of the residents of the square.

'Perfect,' he sighed, but then quickly stepped back as he caught sight of Lady Frimley walking a pair of small Tibetan dogs in the garden square below, and staring up at his window. When she raised one gloved hand in a vaguely royal gesture, it became really rather too obvious that she had seen him, which meant he was forced to wave back, rather less royally. He even managed a smile.

'She must walk those dogs of hers about twenty times a day,' he said out loud to himself, still smiling down at the woman far below him.

Like so many, Grenville had found out that there was only one drawback to living in a smart London square, and that was that the place was still filled with so many of the old guard that you were always dodging sherry parties, not to mention invitations to the theatre where one set of crumblies in the auditorium sat enthralled by a cast of another up on the stage, most of whom were seriously trying to remember where they were, or in what play.

But then living where he did also brought its advantages, since many of the old things around him had chosen him as their investment counsellor. Few invested very large sums, all of them having grown understandably ever more cautious with age, but none the less it all added up to something rather than nothing, and the more it added up the happier Grenville became. A few, such as Lady Frimley, had resisted the temptation to invest, but he had high hopes that she too would finally succumb to his lures, although, as he had come increasingly to realise, success was something of a double-edged sword. The greater his number of investors, the more invitations he received to attend very dull dinners, generally held in ancient restaurants and clubs with old-fashioned menus, peeling wallpaper, and inordinately tiresome company.

The previous year, Grenville had actually had to take the decision to try to find younger, rather than older, people on whose behalf he could invest. Recent good fortune had come from the word-of-mouth recommendation of one of his clients, the Honourable Pelham Augustus Dashwood, to someone he met in the Long Room at Lord's, a moderately charming but singularly undistinguished actor by the name of Jeremy Bell, who had recently amassed a small but satisfactory fortune by way of the deaths of two maiden aunts and a homosexual uncle who had owned a modest brewery. Bell was uncertain as to what precisely to do with his new-found wealth, but as is so often the way with actors, had been unable not to mention the windfalls several times *en passant* to Dashwood, who, by coincidence, had himself come into a certain amount of money as a result of the more than convenient theft of an antique Bugatti racing car he had inherited from his godfather. Dashwood had then kindly recommended Grenville and so Grenville had taken on fresh, rich blood without so much as the raising of a finger.

As it happened, Grenville was a very wise and happy choice, because he really did have the knack of making money in unexpected places. More than that, he had a brilliant sense of timing, of making an investment at just the right moment – and of course, from Grenville's point of view, managing someone else's money was a gift, particularly when it came with no strings attached, just orders to go full steam ahead. The job required a minimum of effort, and yielded a most satisfactory income. Dashwood's faith in Grenville was completely justified, and so he was soon followed by others of his kind, Old Etonians all – or, as they preferred to say, the alumni of *Slough Grammar*, this affectation generally followed by a loud bray of undeniably Etonian laughter. Most conveniently of all, Dashwood's friends still thought it vulgar to talk about their money, and so were more than happy to hand over substantial handfuls of their unearned to be invested by someone they understood from Dashwood was a Chap Like Them, something which, as it happened, Grenville certainly was not. Nevertheless, because Dashwood had made Grenville his investment manager, everyone now thought Grenville was of the same ilk as his sponsor. It was a case of class by association, really.

Now, for want of anything else to do, and because he was anxious to avoid being waved at again by Lady Frimley, Grenville went to the looking glass over his chimney piece and regarded himself carefully.

For someone in his mid-forties, he was good-looking in an unremarkable sort of way. Tall, slim, hair greying a little round the edges, what he liked to think of as honest eyes, hands perhaps slightly too heavy to be those of a patrician, but at least the signet ring was on the correct finger, the little finger of the left hand, and the Asprey's cufflinks in his striped Turnbull and Asser shirt were of a discreet medium size and fashioned from old gold, unlike the overlarge decorations sported by so many of his peers. Looking at his mirrored image he had no doubt in his mind why he passed so easily as a gentleman. He looked like a gentleman.

Yet he had a problem, which he was pondering once

again as he stood carefully sipping his gin and tonic, and this was the fact that in many ways he was now possibly a little too successful. He badly needed some sort of stimulus; he needed to feel energised again because, quite frankly, at the moment he felt nothing at all. That was the trouble with all this achievement. Being fairly wealthy and successful seemed to mean that he now felt less about everything, which was very disappointing. Grenville had always thought that the more you had the more you would feel; he had imagined success brought more colour to your life, yet this seemed not to be the case with him. It had merely brought a feeling of emptiness, as everything in which he invested went up and up, and his clients became so fat and content they ceased even to ask after their investments, and consequently about him. Instead he imagined them all sitting around congratulating themselves on their perspicacity and innate brilliant business sense, ignoring the fact that it was he who had precipitated their success.

'What one needs,' he said to himself, back to idly staring out of the window now that the coast was clear of Lady Frimley, 'what one needs is for something to happen which is out of the general run of things. One *really* needs a chum or two to come in with one on something stupendously trivial, perhaps. One needs a silly situation, instead of a pounds, shillings and pence one. One needs to do something totally frivolous instead of always doing the sensible thing. Ah, yes – yes, but what?'

The fact that he could find no answer to his own question made Grenville feel even more like an old bachelor who had been too busy making money to realise that life was passing him by, not to mention someone whom others had passed by as well. It made him feel unwanted, which in fact he now wondered whether he truly was. Except for the money he made for people, he was not actually needed by anyone, not as a person. If he dropped dead tomorrow the most that his acquaintances would say at his memorial service probably would be that he was *a good sort of chap, splendid with the old lucre, but lived just for his work really. Reason why he never married probably, and had so few close friends – too caught up in his work.*

The telephone rang and the sound brought him out of his long reverie. When he picked up the receiver he heard a voice which immediately brought even further dejection, at once making him feel like a lonely little boy all over again.

'Hello, Mummy,' he said, hoping he had contained his small sigh of anguish. 'How are we today?'

Chapter Four

The Singleton

Lynne carefully crossed her long and elegant legs, hooked a tress of blond hair back over one ear and smiled at her solicitor. He too smiled but with less brilliance, and Lynne was unsurprised to see that he had coloured a little, too. Mr Morgan was a short, curly-haired Welshman much prone to embarrassment. They were an odd duo, but however different their natures might be, between them they had at last got Gerry on the run, so much so that it had now become one of their running jokes, like something out of a British situation comedy: *I say – we've got old Gerry on the run, what?*

Certainly, whenever Lynne entered Mr Morgan's office she was always happy to share their jokes in order to take her mind off the stale and musty smell of the room, as well as off Miss Fanshawe, Mr Morgan's squat, bespectacled secretary who kept peering through the glass partition that divided her office from his. She actually watched them so closely, and with such regularity, that Lynne had come to the conclusion that the secretary thought that she might have some kind of designs on her boss, which added to her amusement.

On this particular visit Miss Fanshawe was at her spying

in spades, constantly up and down from her desk to pop into the office wearing her best *Does Mr Morgan need me?* expression. But as it happened Lynne was in far too good a mood to mind if Miss Fanshawe stuck her nose right against the glass partition and left it there. Today was a marvellous new day. Lynne stroked her pale grey cashmere shawl-collared cardigan, which exactly matched her new pale grey T-shirt, thinking that if she now played everything right today really could be the first day of the rest of her life.

She stretched out her legs once more, noticing happily that they shone with that well-known iridescence provided by only the most expensive hosiery, stockings that beautifully set off her pleated white linen skirt and white Victorian-style half-boots. She was just the right mix of expensive clothing and startling good looks, and the best thing of all was that once again she knew it. Small wonder then that Mr Morgan kept feeling his shirt collar as he doodled on the legal pad in front of him.

'But to come to the point, Mrs Fortune—'

'It would appear you've just broken yours,' Lynne said, smiling. The solicitor's eyes had caught her legs and the point of his pencil had snapped on the page.

He laughed awkwardly in acknowledgement and plucked a fresh pencil from the mug on his desk. 'Very good, Mrs Fortune – yes, very good indeed.'

'You know, now everything is being so nicely wrapped up, Mr Morgan,' Lynne said, 'I think I shall miss hearing all about you and Mrs Morgan hitchhiking around the States and visiting sites of special interest, I really will.'

'Oh, you're far too kind, Mrs Fortune.' Mr Morgan dabbed at his forehead with a handkerchief. 'But before we get distracted, I really must come to the point,' he repeated, doing his unsuccessful best to refit the left lens that had just fallen out of his glasses. 'I have to say you have been the very personification of patience, Mrs Fortune, through what has been a very difficult and I dare say often unpleasant time for you.'

While doing her best to look duly grateful as well as understanding, Lynne privately wished that her lawyer wasn't so long-winded. He really had no need because, as both of them knew, hers was a pretty straightforward case. Yet still he droned on about nothing very much in particular, so to escape from the monotony she allowed herself to indulge in a recap of the events via which she had come to find herself closeted in a stuffy, overheated, dusty and dreary office with someone as boring and embarrassed as her solicitor.

It had happened when she had gone away for two days' pampering, not as a self-indulgence but as the result of a surprise birthday present from her adored husband Gerry.

Have some seriously wicked days enjoying yourself at the Lakeside, my lovely. Pamper, pamper, pamper! And come back looking even more sexy – as if that were possible! A ton of love, Gerry xxx

So Lynne had turned up for her pre-booked stay at the Lakeside Beauty Spa, where, after being toned, massaged, plucked, pummelled, beautified and coiffured, she finally considered she'd had enough, not only thinking that the spa had done everything it could for her but also a little resentful of the staff's slightly high-minded attitude. She decided there was too much emphasis on the body's being a temple and not enough on life's being a bowl of cherries, the latter summing up a philosophy to which Lynne was more than a little addicted. So she decided to bail out early and return home to surprise her beautiful Gerry, a man she reckoned was just about the best and the sexiest husband a girl could have.

Full of good and loving intentions she stopped off in Bath to shop for Gerry's favourite food – fillet steak, which she'd serve with a Béarnaise sauce, baked potatoes and a tomato salad with mozzarella and follow with his addiction, chocolate mousse – as well as flowers, vintage champagne, and an expensive bottle of claret. With all her goodies packed in the boot of her blue sports car, she had driven smartly off home, easing down only when she reached their automated gates and remotely controlled garage doors, driving in as slowly and as quietly as she could in the hope that if Gerry was around she'd surprise him. The house was so designed that she could unload the shopping straight into the kitchen or if necessary into the deep freeze in the garage, yet another of the luxuries and blessings she thanked her darling husband for.

So, having happily stowed away her shopping, delighted to be home and feeling suitably primped and pampered, Lynne had gone looking for her husband, who she thought must be somewhere about because his car was also in the garage. Upstairs, she finally went along to their second-floor bedroom suite, with its brilliant yellow Cole's wallpaper and its balcony overlooking the garden – and surprised him.

He was in bed with her best friend Maddy, and they were all more than a little surprised. In fact it was hard to tell which of the three of them got the biggest shock.

Afterwards she had wished she'd been able to think of something crisp and cutting to say, but all she could do was stare in momentary horror before turning on her heel and fleeing back downstairs, her eyes flooding with tears.

She also found herself wishing she'd made a real scene, but unfortunately making scenes was just as much *not her thing* as finding something witty and crisp to say at moments of distress. She hadn't quite said that to Mr Morgan when he had asked her what her reaction had been. She just said she thought that since the deed had already been committed it was better simply to walk away from it in as dignified a manner as possible, although in fact her departure had been well short of that. During her confusion she had lost a shoe on the staircase, which caused her to slip and fall and slide the rest of the way down to the first floor on her backside. Then she had walked into the doorpost, and finally she had managed to engage drive in her car rather than reverse and put a serious dent in her front bumper before regaining her senses and reversing out of the garage, after which she had driven way too fast back into Bath and checked into a hotel in a quiet part of the city for a very long think. At first her thoughts, predictably enough, had all been the heartbroken *how could he?* stuff, self-pitying reflections that quickly turned to the angry *how dare he!* bit, and finally became quite practical as soon as she realised that there was no use in thinking that a man who had strayed once would not stray again, and at the earliest opportunity.

Her mother had always told her, drink in one hand and a cigarette in the other, that the rule was one strike and they were out. 'Believe me, Linnet,' she'd say. 'Believe me, girl, it's the only way.' And now Lynne – who privately had always thought her mother's creed to be a little unforgiving – found herself agreeing absolutely with this point of view: *one strike and out.* Most certainly did she not want to spend the rest of her life pretending not to notice that Gerry was at it again . . . and again. She'd seen quite enough, up front and very personal, of what infidelity could do to a woman. It had most certainly done it for her poor mother – spelt out in great big capital letters.

Being married to the two-timing so-and-so that was Lynne's

father had driven her mother quietly mad, no question about it. Possibly its most useful result had been the piece of worldly wisdom she had passed on to her daughter; it was her tragedy that she had learned it too late to put it into practice herself. A life spent always wondering where a man was and why, or whom he was with and why, or simply whether or not he had just told her the truth instead of yet another lie, had without any exaggeration made her mother paranoid. In the end she had not known which way to turn, whom to trust, what was the truth, or whether there was any security to be found anywhere, which was obviously why she had finally chosen to take what she thought to be the only way out.

'I still don't know why she did it,' Lynne's father kept saying at the funeral.

'You might not, Dad,' Lynne had replied. 'But everyone else seems to.'

'Meaning?'

'Meaning Mum got tired of covering for you, Dad, you know? She just ran out of that kind of energy – always making excuses for why you hadn't turned up for dinner, or were late back for my birthday, or, even missed your son's eighteenth *altogether*, know what I mean? People get fed up with it – worn out, if you'd rather – and it becomes too much. So you decide you can't go on, so you don't. Got it? But don't you worry, Dad. You're on your own now, and here's hoping you find out just what it's like yourself. And who knows? You might end up feeling just the way poor Mum did.'

Then she'd left him to it, all alone – turned on her heel and walked out of the graveyard and into a brand-new life of her own with Gerry.

A brand-new joke rather, she had told herself as she sat privately reflecting in the room she'd taken in the Bath hotel, and not exactly a good one. In fact it was a joke in the worst taste possible because even Lynne, who as she herself well knew was not exactly the brightest bunny on the block, now saw that within a few months of her mother's death she'd fallen into the trap. She had only gone and fallen in love with exactly the same kind of man as her mother had loved, in other words her father. She'd fallen for a two-timing so-and-so who obviously couldn't wait to get her out of the way so he could lay someone else. As she stared out at the hotel's fine gardens below her window, her normal resilience had suddenly vanished, the world turning into just one large room with only her in it, a room with no walls and no other people. She found herself sitting in the darkness of space.

But as the light faded and only the sounds of distant city traffic, punctuated occasionally by the wail of ambulance and police sirens, floated up to her room, she found her centre once again and steel entered her heart.

'Let's face it, Linnet,' she told herself, pouring herself a drink from the mini-bar. 'If and when push comes to get out, maybe it's better to get tough rather than angry. Being angry and staying angry's too bloody tiring.'

Getting tough meant resolving to take her husband Gerry not just for everything he had, but for everything he was even thinking of having. Lynne determined to skin him, skin him so badly that dear sweet little ex-best friend Maddy, she of the innocent eyes and ways and the little girl looks, wouldn't be able to get a postage stamp off him, let alone another pair of Janet Reger silk knickers.

So she had steered Mr Morgan's boat and steered it well, the end result being that her divorce settlement meant Lynne would never have to work at all, at least not in the remotely foreseeable future. The sum settled on her ensured she could not only afford to live, but afford to live very well, enjoying herself in more or less any way she wished. The world was not merely her oyster. As far as she was concerned, it was to be her playground.

'I have to say I feel that their final offer is really quite generous,' Mr Morgan told Lynne now as she studied the papers in front of her, getting up from his chair and coming round to Lynne's side of the desk as if to go through each point carefully with her, but really simply so that he could be that little bit closer to her.

'Generous, Mr Morgan?' Lynne laughed. 'It's fab.'

Mr Morgan nodded, and then sneezed, whipping out a spotless white cotton handkerchief, which had *Monday* embroidered on it, even though it was now Friday.

'You've done a great job, Mr Morgan, really good.'

'Really?' Mr Morgan replied, putting *Monday* away and looking down at her over the top of his glasses. 'Do you think so?'

'I really do. Straight up.'

'I'm so glad. Thank you, Mrs Fortune.'

'I think you've done such a good job, in fact' – Lynne folded the papers up and slipped them into her bag, shutting it with a snap – '*such* a good job that *I* am going to take you out to celebrate. You were dead right to go for a lump sum, Mr Morgan, really spot on. No haggling and no bargaining, just down and dirty. So come on. A glass of the bubbly certainly beckons.'

She turned and smiled, the first true and heartfelt smile she had given in months.

'It is a little early in the day for me, Mrs Fortune,' Mr Morgan said with a sad smile and a series of quick nods to indicate his regret. 'Still only a quarter to twelve.'

'Yes, well, time to live dangerously, Mr Morgan,' Lynne told him, on the move now and taking his arm. 'Now the harvest is in.'

Leading him past an astonished Miss Fanshawe and a couple obviously waiting for the next appointment, Lynne marched Mr Morgan smartly out of his office and across the road to a wine bar, where she ordered a bottle of their best champagne.

'You know what this means, don't you, Mr Morgan?' she asked him, as she sipped her drink, displaying even more leg than Mr Morgan had seen before, thanks to the height of the bar stools. 'It really means no more worries. It means I do *not* have to think about where next month's rent's coming from; it means I do *not* have to think I'm going to be forced to find me some rich old sod – sorry, I mean bod – some rich old bod to be nice to, just so that I can keep my head above water.'

'No, no – less of the *old*,' Mr Morgan chimed in. 'I feel perfectly sure that you will only attract the best, Mrs Fortune.'

Lynne gave him a quick glance, and then looked away, frowning lightly.

'What I meant to say—' he continued, too late, only to be stopped at once by his client.

'Think nothing of it, Mr Morgan,' Lynne assured him. 'As I was saying, this settlement, if it's as good as it looks—'

'Which it is, Mrs Fortune. Believe me. It most certainly is.'

'Provided, of course, that Gerry coughs up with the cheque a.s.a.p.'

'They're much stricter about this sort of thing nowadays, Mrs Fortune – he really won't be allowed to delay payment.'

'You have to watch Gerry. He's not someone to take your eye off. He didn't get where he is by playing soppy date.'

'He's certainly been very successful, Mrs Fortune.'

'I'm just surprised the way he's simply rolled over the way he has. I really thought he'd put up a bit more of a fight. I suppose he's so glad to be shot of me, he doesn't mind paying.'

Lynne sipped her champagne and looked over the top of her glass at Mr Morgan, hoping he might contradict her. He did not.

'You have half the value of the house, you keep your car, you have a generous settlement in consideration of your excellent record as a wife,' he said. 'So, as long as you take the right financial advice, you most certainly should remain more than solvent, Mrs Fortune.'

'OK, Mr Morgan.' Lynne checked her lipstick in her compact mirror. 'Fair dos. And now I think I might treat myself somewhere. After all, getting divorced isn't something you do every day.'

'I don't see anything wrong with that,' Mr Morgan agreed. 'Provided we don't go too mad.'

'Oh?' Lynne looked at him teasingly, wide-eyed. 'You coming along too, then?'

Mr Morgan smiled shyly back, turned a beautiful plum colour, and walked uncertainly back into the broad daylight of the street to return to his office.

Lynne stared at herself in the mirror behind the bar, all her put-on flirtatious manner gone, a sense of trepidation and muted excitement taking its place. She still had half a bottle of champagne to finish, and by the time she had done that justice she reckoned she should feel ready for the fray. After all, as she'd decided, this was the start of the rest of her life. This was her, herself, by herself.

She drank another glass of champagne and thought some more about the reality of her position. Until this moment there had still been half of her that believed this was happening and half that did not, yet now she knew it was in fact all true, one hundred per cent so. She really was on her own. *By* my own, as she used to say when she was small. *I don't want to be by my own.* Yet now, like it or not, she was indeed by her own, totally and utterly and completely. And because she was alone she knew she would be lucky if she didn't end up as some dreary divorcee with a backlog of hard luck stories about relationships that hadn't quite worked out, tales of near misses, of what might have beens. She knew, champagne or no champagne, that from now on she was going to need all the luck that was going. She looked into the face staring back at her in the mirror behind the bar and saw the former Mrs Gerry Fortune, looking a lot less poised and buffed and groomed than the happy young woman who had waltzed happily out of the Lakeside Beauty Spa, on her way home to surprise her gorgeous sexy husband.

Chapter Five

Back Across the Wather

He sensed the change; smelt it even. It was the tones of the voices of those who came to feed him, to look at his feet, to brush out his coat and mane, to check his legs. And he knew it because wasn't herself coming too often, bringing his favourite sweet things to eat, pulling his ears and resting her face on his neck before kissing him on his nose, the way she knew he liked it. More than that, he noticed that despite all this there were none of the words that were normal to her coming to him. Since he was hardly old enough to put his head over the door he had known it was her coming, for she would sing quietly to him as she went about her work, and ask him all the time, time after time, if he was all right then – which he always was. But not today. Today he was not all right. He was uneasy, walking about in the straw, holding his head away from her, standing at the back of his stable and looking into the corner. He sensed something was up, and not something good. Something bad was about to happen. He understood this from the tone of her voice and the sadness in her dark eyes.

'I shall try to come and see you, Boyo,' Kathleen told her horse, as if sensing his trepidation and seeking to reassure him. 'I don't know how, my love, and I don't know when, because it won't be easy, but I'll find a way. I'll think of a way of getting to see you, because if I don't . . .' She fell silent, as if reluctant to spell out the rest of her thoughts. 'You just make sure you're a good boy and behave yourself, Boyo. You'll always be mine, don't you worry.'

She pulled his ears and kissed his muzzle softly and gently.

'At least you'll have your friend Finoula with you,' she whispered. 'Some of the way, at least.'

Which indeed was the case, since their neighbour had sold the young filly who was Boyo's paddock playmate to a horse scout from England, arrangements having been made for the two horses to travel with a large consignment of other bought horses from the area.

A lad came in later, looked in Boyo's manger, then slapped the horse on the neck and asked him why he wasn't eating. In answer the horse just pushed him aside, turning his rump on him, ready with his hind feet. The lad was about to have a go but seeing the way the horse had laid his ears back flat thought better of it.

'Suit yourself so,' the lad said, taking his manger away but avoiding his hind quarters as he eased his way to the door. 'You're the one who's going to get hungry, not me, and you won't be getting much on your travels.'

Sensing something bad, the horse walked his box for the next two hours before finally sleeping. He woke at first light, but it wasn't the dawn that woke him. There were sounds in the yard, the sort of noise that he normally didn't hear until much later in the day. His stable door was thrown open and the tall boy came in, carrying the things they put on his legs when they took him to some different field to jump hedges with others like himself, things to protect his legs in the moving box. So perhaps that's what it was. Perhaps this was another of those times when they went and raced each other in another field somewhere, yet if it was, why was herself so upset? Why had her face been wet? And why wasn't she here now? Why wasn't she here now with him? It was always herself who put these things on him, not this skit of a lad who liked to hit his rump and slap his neck. So why was she not here?

So when they led him out to the moving box with the things on his legs and a warmer on his back he tried to get away. He stood up on his hind legs and gave the moving box a great whack with his fore legs; then he crashed down again and turned and turned and bucked and pulled. The great strip still had a hold on his head collar but he was red in the face and yelling at him fit to burst.

The noise brought herself down. She rushed out of the house, shouting at the lad and taking hold of the leading rope.

'What in hell do you think you're doing, boy?' she shouted. 'You get him stirred like this you'll never get him in!'

Now he stood still and looked at her, wanting her to tell him why she hadn't been there earlier and why she wasn't dressed to go with him in the moving box the way she always did when they went to another field. But she said nothing. She stroked him, gave him a carrot, stroked him again, and led him silently into the moving box. He went in. He would always go in for her. He would do anything she wanted. So he walked up the ramp and went in, and still she said nothing.

When he was in, she tied his head. He gazed at her, turning both his great brown eyes to her, looking to her for help. Still she said nothing. All she did was suddenly hug his neck, hug it tight, and then she was gone. *Why?* He gave a great cry. *What are you doing? Come back to me! Come back now! Come back! Come back!*

'Quiet!' the strip told him, checking his head rope to make sure he couldn't get free. 'And stop stamping those damned feet of yours!'

Then they led Finoula in. He didn't know she was coming as well, or going, whatever it was they were doing. Where were they going? No one had said where, but the little mare was standing beside him now, her own head roped to a ring, and she looked frightened. She had never been in the moving box before and had had to be manhandled and beaten before she would jib her way up the ramp. Finally she had relented and allowed herself to be installed and tied up, but she was scared. Boyo could see it in the way her eye was, with half the white showing. He whickered at her and she whickered back, but nothing it seemed could stop her trembling.

When they took them out, the horses found themselves in a very big barn. Outside, through the doors, Boyo could see something huge and dark, like another barn but much, much bigger, with enormous doors thrown wide to allow a line of wheeled boxes to enter, which they were doing, slowly, while people in brightly coloured coats waved and pointed at them. The huge barn seemed to be moving very slowly up and down, up and down, and on top of that he could smell and taste salt. A wind was blowing hard, swirling heavy rain about the large barn and drenching everyone who was standing between the two buildings. He and Finoula were made to wait in a small box with rails, with their heads tied and no hay or water, so Boyo stamped and shouted until Liam appeared with a bucket. He stroked his neck.

'It'll be all right, lad. I wanted to come with you all the way and so did Kathleen, but we can't afford that now, so we can't. But I'll see they take care of you all right.'

And then the two of them were put in a big box with other horses, but all their eyes talked of was fear, and then the big box moved, slowly, and there was a lot of noise outside the big box, the rumble of other boxes, and the slamming of doors. There were raised voices, the smell of fumes and a slow, sickening, rocking motion. Some of the other horses whinnied fearfully, and started to stamp, and someone moved among them tightening their heads, talking to them roughly.

Boyo knew that here was danger, and knew also not to make a sound. After a lot of darkness there was a long, slow shudder and the sound of something deep and low and powerful, a throbbing noise, and the clanging of a bell somewhere, and he could hear the rushing of water. Alongside him the other horses began to stamp and whinny, calling to each other, crying out, *What is happening, where am I?*

Now this new, more frightening box was moving, swaying from side to side, then plunging forwards and backwards. The deep throbbing had become louder and more powerful, while all the time there was the distant sound of thrashing, rushing water.

In the darkness Boyo could see Finoula's eyes grown even larger. She was pulling back on her head collar, whinnying pitifully, her eyes rolling white and huge, half sitting as she tried to break free. Boyo whickered to her; he whickered to show her that she would be all right if she stood but not all right if she went down. They were packed tight in the big box and it was hot and airless. If anyone went down they could really hurt themselves. They had to stand. They had to endure it, to stand together, to keep each other on their feet, although the big box was now dipping and climbing and swaying terrifyingly. The water could be heard now smashing on the sides of whatever huge thing they were in and the journey got rougher and rougher.

The little mare saw his eye, felt his breath on her, and stopped her tugging. Half down and half up she scrambled, her hooves sliding on the wet floor as she tried to get her hind legs up under her. But the box was swaying and plunging so much now that as soon as she was almost up another great drop downwards would make her lose her balance all over again.

He pushed his rump round behind her as best he could, standing there with his own hooves planted as firmly as he could manage. The mare felt his strength and pushed herself back against him, and then was safe, up on her own feet, shoving herself forward and regaining her balance. Her whinnying stopped and her eyes regained their proper look. They all calmed down as best they could, but after a long darkness the plunging and rolling became even worse and once again a panic broke out, and there was whinnying and stamping, neighing and snorting. He stood as steady as he could but it was so difficult now that he kept sliding sideways and almost falling over, his head and neck stretched out as he slipped and then wrenched as he lurched to one side. He had never known a feeling like this. And it was endless; endless, and so dark. Except for the dimmest light filtering in through the filthy windows of their big wheeled box, it was dark, and terrifying.

Some time on, the long and horrifying nightmare ended. The ground stopped heaving, the water stopped rushing, and suddenly there was a great flood of light and noise.

Boyo could hear the other wheeled boxes beginning to move, and finally their big box slowly but surely followed the others out into the daylight. There was still wind and rain, growing louder as the light in their box grew brighter, but underfoot it was firm, and the ground seemed to have stopped moving. In the calm that followed he looked around him at the other horses and saw that they were settling down as well, some beginning to pull at their hay nets even though the hay was dry as dust. He was thirsty too, but there was no water anywhere, just the dry and dusty hay to pick at.

It was a very long day and the wheeled box grew very hot from the heat of all the horses. But there was no respite and no refreshment. Even when the box stopped for a time, there was no water brought, although the dust from the hay was parching. A man came in and they all looked at him as best they could. They tried to tell him they must have something to drink but he ignored them, blowing smoke out of his mouth and nose as he picked his way through the packed box looking at them all. Then he was gone and the door was shut again. The heat built up more and more and to his horror he saw the little mare suddenly stagger and slip even though they were not moving. He tried to help her again, but she was too distressed to respond and fell heavily against the partition separating them. The others sensed the crisis and started to panic but no one came, despite the crescendo of stamping and whinnying. Then the box began to move again, on and on and on.

It was all but dark when the back of the box was finally lowered and a gust of fresh cold air blew in, making them all suddenly shake and shiver as the sweat dried on their steaming bodies. Some stamped again to get their blood running, others bowed their heads as if in hope of finding water, while others just stood trembling in every muscle. The box was full of the steam of their terror before they were all pulled out and led off to a block of stables. All but one. Finoula, his friend. The little dark mare was no longer moving, half held up by her head collar as if that was what had caused her death; as if she had been strangled by it. But she hadn't. She had died from terror, and thirst, and shock, and unable to fall to the floor hung there with her beautiful head twisted grotesquely to one side and her big pink tongue lolling uselessly out of her parched mouth.

As he was led away he heard them dragging her body out

and half turned to watch. The man leading him pulled roughly at his head collar but he was so much the stronger that he just pulled the man over as he turned to see the body of his dead friend being towed away behind a wheeled box, bumping and shuddering over the concrete of the strange yard, steam still rising from her skin. The one at his collar tried to pull him on, hitting him round the head, but he just butted him away, causing the man to make a noise and hold his face.

They were all put in a line of draughty stables with only the thinnest of beds to lie on, bedding that had not even been cleaned out after the other horses that had passed through the yard. They all wanted nothing more than to lie down, but the beds were so filthy and poor that most just stood disconsolately, their ears back, their lower lips sticking out in misery, with only half-buckets of lukewarm, dirty water within reach. Later they were given food, but it was old and worthless, dusty nuts that tasted of nothing, and a slab of stale hay chucked on to the floor to see them through the long darkness.

He stood in the corner of his box, resting his hocks against the splintered timbers behind him. He had no idea what was happening to him or why. All his life he had met nothing but kindness. He'd had to stand in the rain and the wind, he'd had to put up with the sun and the flies, but no matter, since every day he was brought into a stable and brushed and washed, and given fresh food and damp hay. And on the fine days they were all put out in a field with sweet grass and clean fresh water in a stream that ran down from the hills. But now all he knew was misery.

When it was light again another wheeled box came for him and two other horses. It took him on a shorter journey to another place where he was taken out alone, leaving his new friends behind. He looked around him. Stables, and the sense of another horse nearby, and a new human standing looking at him.

'There's not exactly a lot of him, boss,' Teddy said after he and Rory had unloaded the new arrival. 'I thought the guv'nor liked 'em tall.'

'He does,' Rory replied, walking round the liver chestnut to take a good look at an animal that seemed a good deal smaller than the one he and his father had bought in Ireland. 'And now he looks even smaller than he did over there.'

'Knowing the Irish they probably sent you another,' Teddy said with a shake of his head. 'And there really isn't a lot to him.'

'He jumps well,' Rory said defensively. 'He can certainly jump. That we do know.'

'He'd need to, boss. He'd need to stay as well.'

'Wash him down, Teddy, and give him a decent feed. The poor fellow looks half starved.'

Boyo shook himself thoroughly, from the top of his head to the end of his thick tail, and then took another look at his new surroundings. That done, he raised his head and shouted as loudly as he could; after a moment, from some distant field, another horse answered his cry. Boyo listened attentively, then gave another loud shout. Neither Teddy nor Rory could hear any response this time, but Boyo obviously did because he pricked his ears and whickered to himself quietly before allowing himself to be led away for a good hosing down.

Rory watched him walk away, noticing that even in his travel-weary state the horse moved well and easily. He was a long way short of what his father would call match fit, but there was plenty on his quarters, tissue that if Rory and his small team did their work right should soon build up into good racing muscle.

Once the horse was washed down and housed in the box

reserved for newcomers – a stable set well apart from the others just in case the incomer was carrying any sort of infection – Rory wandered back to his father's office. The horse's papers, including his passport, lay on his desk.

'That the new boy?' Maureen, his father's and now his secretary, asked, looking up from her paperwork. 'Not very big, is he?'

'Don't you start,' Rory replied. 'We have to find an owner for him, so as far as everyone here is concerned, he's a fine stamp of a horse. OK?'

'Got it.' Maureen smiled. 'As it happens I like small horses.'

'Then get one of those brown paper parcels out from under your bed, Maureen, and buy him.'

'I wish. What's he called? Is he named?'

'He must be, because they've already raced him. But I can't remember what they called him.'

'Small wonder,' Maureen said, rolling another letter page into her typewriter. 'It usually takes your father a good two or three days to recover from his Irish trips.'

'Small Wonder would be a good name, but he's called The Enchanted,' Rory announced, having consulted the horse's passport. 'That's apparently his given name, although what is enchanting or enchanted about him has yet to be seen.'

'Let's hope he's just that,' Maureen returned. 'And before I forget, Colonel Willoughby wants you to call him.'

Rory made the call immediately, the colonel being both one of his father's oldest friends and an owner.

'Any improvement, Rory?' the colonel wanted to know up front. 'Do hope so.'

'No change as yet, Colonel,' Rory replied. 'But he's no worse and that's good. I think they describe him as stable.'

'Glad to hear it. Keep me posted.'

'Of course.'

The colonel cleared his throat. 'Now this isn't easy, Rory. I prefer to do these things face to face. But fact is, don't have much option. Betty's fallen ill, I'm afraid, and is going to take a lot of looking after.'

'I'm sorry to hear that, Colonel. It never rains, does it? Has to damn well pour, as my father always says.'

'Absolutely so, Rory. Now, you know as well as I that when this sort of thing happens, one has to clear the deck somewhat. And, as you also know, certain people have been pressing me to sell Hardway Boy.'

'I know, sir,' Rory replied, his heart sinking at the realisation that they were obviously just about to lose the only class horse they still had in the yard. 'But before you do, Colonel—'

'Too late for that, I'm afraid. Don't want to sell him, you know that. We all think he could be a National sort of horse, but it's a question of needs must, and of course Betty comes first.'

'I quite understand, Colonel. If you'll just keep me informed as to when and where, and all that.'

'Naturally,' the colonel replied, and cleared his throat once more. 'And you keep me posted about your father.'

'Damn,' Rory said after he had put down the telephone. 'Damn, blast and every other wretched swear word.'

'I thought something was up,' Maureen said, typing away. 'He doesn't give much away, but there was something in his voice.'

'Not a good day,' Rory concluded. 'Out goes the only class horse in the yard, and in comes an Irish donkey.'

'You never know,' Maureen replied, handing him the letter to sign. 'Strange things do happen, particularly with horses.'

Chapter Six

The Odd Couple

Constance always chose the same ensemble for such occasions: a middle-length skirt in dark grey, black silk blouse with cravat, three-quarter-length black wool jacket and large-brimmed black hat. Looking at her image in the cheval mirror in her bedroom, she was forced to realise that really, give or take a few wrinkles on her hands, she was nevertheless remarkable for her age. She still had a good figure, her eyes were nothing less than brilliant – many remarked on them still – and her complexion was flawless.

Beneath the shade of her deeply brimmed hat she reckoned she could pass for a woman in her fifties rather than one of her real age, which she was far too vain to acknowledge, even to herself. This proved to be no misconception, she was very happy to discover, since the moment she left the house to walk to the bus stop two workmen high up on the scaffolding wolf-whistled at her, and a well-dressed gentleman walking along the King's Road nodded in her direction, or at least she thought he did. No matter. It was a good feeling to think that the opposite sex noticed you at all, and that for a change it wasn't just you noticing them.

The only thing that spoilt her growing good mood was the fact that she had to travel by bus, but since it was very unlikely that anyone else attending the service in St George's, Hanover Square would be taking public transport she assumed it was quite safe to do so, as long as the bus arrived promptly so that no one she knew saw her lingering at the stop.

She sat downstairs towards the front of the bus. It wasn't too crowded, since it was well past the morning rush hour; the conductor gave her a smile, there were riders and horses trotting through the Park, and flowers still blooming in window boxes even though they were now well into autumn. In all, Constance decided she liked the look of London that morning. It was a good place to be, a great city which still had a heart.

She alighted from the bus, and made her way slowly towards the church. It was only as she made her way up the steps that she realised she had forgotten the name of whoever it was whose life and times she had come to commemorate. Nor could she recognise the faces of any of the other people who were now arriving, alighting from taxis or out of very large and frankly, as far as Constance was concerned, somewhat vulgar motor cars.

She gave her engraved visiting card to the man on the door; then, as she always did on these occasions, settled into a seat halfway down the church, the right position for someone titled but not related, an acquaintance of the deceased but not necessarily a close friend. Constance enjoyed memorial services, attending at least two or three a month, carefully earmarking the date of any forthcoming event. She worked from information gleaned from the *Daily Telegraph*, naturally, yet there was something about the congregation gathering for this particular commemoration that bothered her. She knew she had the right day because it was obvious that a service was about to be held. But when she looked about her, as she felt increasingly free to do, she found there was no one there whom she could recognise, which was unusual to say the least. There was always someone who knew her, or whom she knew – but not, it seemed, today.

None the less, she would be able to identify the deceased from her programme – or *dance card* as she called it for her private amusement – just as soon as she had retrieved her spectacles from her handbag. She managed to find them after some initial difficulty, and having held them carefully at the end of her nose so that she did not have to disarrange either hat or hair she stared with some surprise at the name. *How very embarrassing*, she thought. She had absolutely no idea of who the deceased might be. She had never heard of him, in fact, nor indeed of any of the speakers marked down on her card. However, to judge from their names and the general look of those beginning to fill up the seats, the departed perhaps had been somebody from either the world of sport or possibly even the underworld, two things about which she knew absolutely nothing at all and cared even less.

As soon as the service began she found herself quickly able to reject the notion that the subject might have been a gangster, thanks to the innumerable references to scoring the goal of ambition, playing the game of life, and passing on to what was – it was to be devoutly hoped – the final round of a long and distinguished cup tie. All too ghastly for words, Constance decided, but sitting as she was in the very centre of her pew, hemmed in by both gentlemen and ladies carrying considerably more weight than she, she was quite unable to slip away early without causing offence. So she had to sit through what turned out to be a long and extremely tiresome service, with terrible hymns and embarrassing eulogies. As she listened to a large red-faced man in a shiny suit telling singularly unfunny anecdotes about the dead sportsman, Constance decided that, given the nature of a memorial service, in order to avoid total boredom at least a rudimentary knowledge of the deceased was an absolute necessity.

Finally the service began to draw to a close with 'I Vow to Thee My Country', a hymn that Constance at least knew and could sing. As she did so, she heard a rather fine tenor giving out right behind her, so, when able, she took a discreet peep to see who owned the fine, well-modulated, upper-class voice, hoping as always to see herself staring into the eyes of some handsome grey-haired patrician gentleman with whom she would at the earliest opportunity find something or perhaps even someone in common. Instead she found herself look-ing at the tall, slim, well-dressed figure of early-middle-aged Grenville Fielding.

'I think we know each other, but from where?' Constance asked at the end of the service, when she found herself lined up in the aisle beside Grenville as they queued to leave the church.

'Ah, yes – well, we live in the same square, Lady Frimley,' Grenville replied, having recognised her immediately. 'You walk your dogs in the gardens, and we have met once or twice at various things – last December, for instance, at the Belvilles' drinks party. They always have such a good party on the Sunday before Christmas, don't you think?'

'Oh, the Belvilles. It was there, was it? How interesting. They're in Eaton Square, of course. I know. And I think you shared my cab back, did you not?'

Grenville smiled politely, although the way he remembered it, it was the other way round, with Lady Frimley getting into the cab he had called, and sitting herself down even before she had asked him in which direction he might be headed, simply announcing that *they would share the cab*.

'Very interesting service,' he heard Lady Frimley continue. 'A close friend?'

'An acquaintance,' Grenville replied. 'I looked after his affairs for a while.'

'I am a complete dunce when it comes to sport.' Constance sighed. 'I don't even do the pools. Does anyone these days, I wonder?'

'Oh, I'm sure,' Grenville said, looking to see if he could spot a fast path out. 'Oop north and that. Old habits, right?'

'He was some sort of footballer, this chap, wasn't he?'

'Indeed.' Grenville nodded. 'Quite a famous one, as it happens.'

'Do you watch football?'

'No. No, it's not *actually* my game, Lady Frimley. Ours was purely a business relationship.'

They were now almost at the book of condolence, a landmark after which, Grenville knew, he could find freedom.

'On to the reception, Grenville?' someone asked from one side of them.

'Thought I'd opt out actually, Charles,' Grenville replied. 'Not really being a *familiar*. Thought I might stroll along to Claridges, and avail myself of one of their excellent dry martinis.'

'My thoughts exactly.' Constance seized the moment and turned to him with a smile. 'Why don't we stroll along there together?'

Constance drank champagne, while Grenville slowly sipped his cocktail, making it last as long as he could. He had already guessed who would be picking up the bill, and he wasn't sure how quickly he would be able to escape.

'Interesting title, yours, if I may say so.'

'An old title, *and* an interesting one,' Constance murmured, looking at him a little more closely now over her champagne flute and wondering as to his sexuality. Were he some twenty or so years older he really would have made the ideal walker. Nicely mannered without being too smooth, good-looking enough but not in a gigolo way, and well dressed without being a peacock. He also looked at people when they were speaking as well as apparently listening to them, appeared to mean what he said, laughed without showing all his teeth, or his gums; altogether he was very what the French called *comme il faut*. 'It wasn't always Frimley,' she continued. 'That is the modern appellation.'

'I always thought Frimley was a town in Surrey,' Grenville said. 'I never knew there was a title.'

'It has nothing to do with Frimley as in Frimley, Surrey. People always make that mistake. It is a medieval title, as I understand it, originally of course spelt entirely differently.'

Taken aback by this apparent non-sequitur, Grenville decided to let it pass.

'The title *hove* from a husband, obviously?'

'Certainly.' Constance sighed. 'It certainly *hove* all right. Some earldom or other granted during the Barons' Revolt way back when. Long before things began to matter.' She smiled. It was still the smile of a great beauty, which she had indeed once been, and she hoped this was a fact that her new friend appreciated.

'You are having another?' she quickly observed as Grenville summoned a waiter to their table. 'Thank you, then so shall I, thank you.' She nodded at her now empty glass and then at the waiter, while Grenville picked up the order of service he had put down and tapped it on the table.

'I suppose you go to quite a few of these things,' he said, having decided on a change of subject from titles.

'One sees so many very attractive men at memorial

services,' Constance replied. 'I do so prefer my men to be grey. They look *so* much more distinguished. Although there were perhaps rather fewer such gentlemen there today, alas.'

As fresh drinks arrived, Grenville once again searched for a safe subject, and found one.

'And how long have you lived in our square, Lady Frimley? It is the most charming location, do you not agree?'

'Our square?' Constance repeated. 'Whose square?'

'I see you walk your dogs in the garden.'

'They are not actually my dogs.'

'But you have a key to the garden.'

'I do have a key to the garden,' Constance agreed. 'The dogs too are residents.'

In spite of another conversational impasse, Grenville managed to smile politely and sip his cocktail, wondering which of them was going to make the first move to leave.

Moments later Charles Danby, the acquaintance who had first hailed him at the service, appeared with drink in hand.

'Ah, Grenville, excellent,' he said. 'I was looking for someone to drink with. Mind if I?'

'Oh. No. No, not at all, Charles,' Grenville said, half rising and immediately and thankfully effecting introductions.

'Are you going to Sandown tomorrow, Grenville?' Charles wondered, after the initial small talk was over. 'It's the opening meeting of the new NH season and my bro-in-law, who trains, as you probably know – he's got a runner. Says he rather fancies its chances.'

'That sounds fun,' Grenville replied. 'First place I ever went racing, you know. Because of course the family home's in Esher.'

'I adore Sandown,' Constance sighed. 'I haven't been there

for centuries, but I *have* always simply loved it. I know! Why don't we all go?'

'You don't have to if you don't want to, Allie love,' Millie was saying in a vague voice, turning back from the stove to where Alice was sitting at the kitchen table chopping carrots into neat julienne slices. 'I'll quite understand if you'd rather not.'

Carefully side-stepping round not one but five dog dishes of varying sizes, she went to a kitchen cupboard to take out some wine glasses, while from his perch Excelsior, her parrot, made a cracking sound with one of his new satisfactorily overlarge nuts, a bag of which had been a gift from Alice.

'Of course I'd like to,' Alice stated, trying to make the best of a somewhat ancient and wrinkled carrot. 'Why wouldn't I want to?'

She had no absolute idea as to what Millie was actually talking about, but since she rarely did she generally found it best to agree to whatever was being suggested, before Millie forgot what it was that she had proposed. It was their own particular way of going on, and had been for years and years.

'And by the way, you're looking better than ever.'

'Thank you,' Alice replied. 'But I still feel quite tired. In fact this morning when I looked in the mirror I thought I looked so exhausted that . . . well. I think it's when you stop everything that you feel at your most drained.'

'Children are very demanding, duck. Particularly old children.'

'It's really so good to be here, and for you to have me to stay, Millie. I can't thank you enough.'

'Stay as long as you like. It'll do us both nothing but good.'

'How does that poem go? Not waving but drowning? I've been treading water.'

'It's all right, you're out of the water now – and do get out of the way, Simpkin,' Millie grumbled, stepping round a tabby cat who was sitting washing itself on the kitchen floor. 'I'll break my neck tripping over you one of these days.'

'It was my fault really,' Alice continued. 'After Alex died, I had the blinkers on. Charged about like the famous bull in a china shop – so what I got was what I well and truly deserved.'

'You sound like my mother,' Millie laughed. 'After I lost Douglas she was always saying, *You people nowadays – you don't observe the mourning periods properly. Mark my words, you're only storing up trouble for yourselves.*'

'Well, she was right in her way,' Alice replied. 'I know mourning *is* old hat, and the Victorians *did* take it too far, et cetera. But there *was* a sort of sense to it all. A period of mourning *is* sensible. It's not just out of respect to the person you've lost – it's out of respect for your self and your *own* feelings. Nowadays everyone thinks you should be up and running within a couple of weeks of the funeral.'

'You're absolutely right, of course. As always.'

'It all changed with the First World War when the losses were so huge and came so quickly, there was literally no *time* for mourning. So all the old customs were thrown to the wind, and then when the Second World War came, well – same old, same old, really. Only worse. War isn't just about loss of life, though God knows that's horrific enough,' Alice continued. 'You lose so much more as well, as our parents did; and yet our generation always seems so cheerful. Despite the war and rationing and all that austerity, and bringing up our children with next to no money, as well as looking after our husbands full time, with no time off for good behaviour.'

Millie was about to reply when the parrot interrupted her. 'Hello, sailor!'

'Shut up, you, or I'll turn you into an oven glove,' Millie

grumbled. 'Anyway – to get back to what we were talking about. What *were* we talking about?'

'You were saying something about my not having to do something or other,' Alice replied. 'Though don't ask me what it was.'

'Oh, yes. I just wondered if you'd like to come racing tomorrow,' Millie said, removing a cheese sauce from the stove and pouring it over the chopped chicken and ham, before sprinkling it with grated cheese.

'Racing?' Alice frowned. '*Racing?*'

'It's perfectly legal,' Millie reassured her, straight-faced. 'Truly, a lot of respectable people do it.'

'I really know absolutely *nothing* about horses.'

'That goes for most people who go racing, sweetie. Particularly the trainers. Actually, that's why I'm going tomorrow. The Dear Departed had this rather useless horse with this very nice trainer. They were army bods together – and after the Dear Departed handed in his dinner plate I was going to sell said horse, but Anthony, the trainer, offered to keep the horse in the yard at *prix d'ami* which was jolly fair of him. Anyway, said horse is running tomorrow, at Sandown Park of all places. He usually runs at places like Catterick and Newton Abbot, so I just thought it might be a bit of fun. For us both.'

'I really don't know a thing *about* racing, Millie. I'll say all the wrong things, and do all the wrong things, and generally make an ass of myself.'

Millie laughed. 'You don't have to pass an exam at the gate, duck. No one's going to ask you testing questions – such as where would you find a fetlock, or what's the difference be-tween a standing and a running martingale, et cetera. It's not like the Pony Club. There are no tests, and you don't have to go to camp. Besides, I'll tell you all you need to know – *and* introduce you to the excitement of the Tote Double and the Dual Forecast.'

'Heavens above,' Alice said solemnly. 'And to think I was hoping that you might be about to start trying to lead Sam and me astray.'

'Listen up, sugar plum – the Tote Double can lead a nun astray.'

Chapter Seven

A Day at the Races

The following day was bright and dry, with a freshly raised zephyr changing the going on the racecourse from good to soft to good. As always there was a large crowd for this particular meeting, a mixture of visitors from the country and the regular racegoers.

As soon as they arrived Alice found her spirits rising, charmed by the setting of the lovely Surrey course, so well laid out in parkland that it provided possibly the best viewing anywhere in the country. Here was something altogether new and different. Walking from the car park to the course, as the mix of colours and the constant flow of people became a heady kaleidoscope of ever-changing patterns, Alice realised she had quite lost her feeling of being more than a little grey around the gills – or perhaps, almost shockingly, she realised just how grey about the gills she had actually become. Here, she realised, she was stepping into a shower of experiences that promised, over just a few hours, to make her a part of something both exciting and risky.

'Is this right?' Alice asked as Millie headed them towards the members' enclosure. 'I'm not a member, for a start.'

'If you have a runner you get free admission,' Millie explained, picking up her complimentary tickets. 'And I have a runner, remember?'

'This *is* going to be fun,' Alice decided.

'If you can still recognise fun,' Millie agreed, picking up on it. 'You've spent so much of your life making sure everyone else was all right, I bet you've quite forgotten what you actually like.'

'All too true, I'm afraid, Millie. I seem to have fallen right out of touch with myself.'

They had arrived at the rails and were watching the horses being led round.

'Goodness, aren't they a picture?'

'They'll look even more of a picture when you see your pick running up the hill clear of the rest of the field, with your quid about to become twenty.' Millie laughed. 'While on the other hand . . .'

'If the one you picked is trailing in last . . .' Alice said.

'Now looks like a dog, and you can't understand why you liked it. So, no taste in nothing as they say, sweetie, and racing's no fun without a little flutter, so what's your pick of the paddock?'

'I wouldn't know where to begin. Will you help me?'

'Of course.' Millie opened her racecard. 'First race, drop a finger, look at a name you like. Anything's as good as anything else when the sun shines.'

Alice hesitated before she even began to consult her own card. She hesitated because of the money she had been foolish enough to advance to Christian on the way down, and the cheque she had recently handed over to Georgina to help with the children. She hesitated as she thought of the gas bill, the rates, her weekly household expenses; and the more she thought the more she realised that the very last thing she could afford to do was to lose money on a horse, however small the sum.

And yet a second later she thought, *What the heck? This is not a race for the faint-hearted, and this is a one way ticket to ride. Above all, just remember – it's the soul afraid of dying who doesn't want to dance. So do it. Better to do something than to stay grey at the gills. What was it Alexander used to say – yes, 'Follow your bliss.'*

'Yes, of course,' she suddenly said a little too loudly, making Millie turn and stare at her. 'You bet I'm going to have a bet, or else – else I'll never be able. Of course I must have a bet, or else I shall never be able to face myself in the mirror again. OK – so what do we do? Lead on, Mrs McDuff.'

'God forbid a name such as that,' Millie sighed. 'I could not imagine being a Mrs McDuff, could you?'

'I'm beginning to imagine all sorts of things, Millie, do you know that? Up to and including winning this famous Tote Double thing.'

'You've got a little time yet, sweetie,' Millie informed her, steering her friend towards the Tote. 'First what you are going to do here is buy a ticket for however much you want to put on the horse – or horses – of your choosing. You can back them to win, or come into a place, or both. And the very best of British. I know what I'm going on.'

While Millie bought her tickets, Alice played eenie-meenie-minie-mo with the runners in the first race, coming up finally with two horses.

'You can back them separately, as I told you,' Millie informed her. 'Which I should do, seeing they're both decent prices – in fact why not do a forecast?'

'A forecast?'

'A dual forecast, for them to come first or second, in either order. One never knows, does one?'

Alice duly followed Millie's recommendations even though

she was still not sure what they meant, then went up into the stand to watch the race – or rather not to watch it.

'I can't bear it,' she said from behind hands shielding her eyes. 'I didn't know they were going to jump things.'

'Yours is ahead!' Millie yelled at her over the increasing din. 'Yours is only leading – and your other one too!'

'They can't both be ahead,' Alice replied, still not daring to look.

'Oh yes they can!' Millie screeched. 'In fact they're first and second! Oh my God! You have only got the first and the second!'

'What does that mean?'

'You had a forecast, yes?' Millie laughed, waving the tickets in Alice's astonished face. 'The winner was ten to one, and the second sixteen to one, so chances are you are going to be one rich bunny! Come on!'

Grabbing Alice's hand Millie tugged her all the way down the grandstand steps and back to the Tote, this time to the Pay window, where once the winner was weighed in the announcer declared the Tote dividends.

'What?' Alice cried in astonishment. 'That isn't me, is it? I can't have won that sort of money!'

But she had. The Tote paid out handsomely on the two long-priced horses, particularly when coupled in a forecast, which was how Alice found herself staggering away from the window with nearly two hundred and twenty-five pounds in her wallet.

'But how come it's this much?' she asked Millie in amazement. 'Really? You only put on – what? Two pounds or something for me, didn't you?'

'Two pounds fifty to be exact, duck. One pound to win on horse number seven, fifty pence each way horse number ten, and a one pound forecast the two.'

'Yes, but two hundred and twenty-four pounds?'

'The Tote's not the same as the bookies,' Millie explained in a patient voice, leading Alice off to a nearby members' bar and ordering them both whisky and ginger ales. 'All the money goes into a pool and you get paid out according to how many tickets were on what horse, et cetera. Obviously a lot of people didn't have horses seven and ten in a forecast, because that alone paid out over a hundred and fifty pounds.'

'I still don't understand,' Alice objected, trying to work out how she could possibly have come to win so much money for such a small outlay. 'Are you absolutely sure they've got this right?'

'Absolutely!' Millie laughed. 'In fact I'm so sure, you're going to buy the next round – while we choose the object of your next betting coup!'

Alice won again, this time at fourteen to one.

'I don't think I should bet any more today, actually,' she muttered after she had walked away from the Pay window clutching yet another handful of ten pound notes. 'What do they say? Always stop when you're ahead.'

'Nonsense,' Millie retorted. 'What sort of stuff are you made of, Mrs Dixon? You have the winning touch today, so to stop now would make the gods angry.'

'Seriously, Millie—'

'You can't lose, honey! If you keep betting only a couple of quid on each race as you've been doing, you're still going to come out way on top – so live a little! You're having fun, aren't you?'

'Well – yes. Yes, I suppose I am really,' Alice admitted. 'Yes, I am.'

'So go for it, as they say, sweetie. And have some more! Now I promised Rory I'd meet him at the saddling-up boxes, and since I have no idea where they are – why don't we ask that chap over there?'

Having been directed to an area adjacent to the paddock proper Millie soon found Rory Rawlins on his way to saddle up his runner. With little or no knowledge of what trainers looked like, other than a very occasional glimpse of one on television, Alice had formed the image of a red-faced middle-aged man dressed in tweeds and one of those heavy military-type overcoats. Instead she found herself being introduced to a young man who had more the look of a scholar or even an artist about him than of a racehorse trainer, a tall, slender, thoughtful and handsome young man, his dark hair worn at a length that showed under the baker's boy tweed cap he sported – instead of the sorts of battered brown trilbies worn by most of the other trainers around them – and his faded tweed coat cut with a decidedly dashing look to it. All in all, Alice decided, if she was going to use one word to describe Rory Rawlins it would be Florentine, and only the fact that he carried a saddle cloth and a racing saddle over his arm, and had a large, old-fashioned pair of racing binoculars slung over one shoulder, suggested what his profession might actually be.

As Millie introduced Alice he nodded at her, and put the saddle and number cloth down on the ground by the corner of an empty box. Then he turned to look at the rugged up horses who were being led round the pre-parade ring by their lads and lasses.

'He's got a bit of a chance at the weights,' he told Millie, his eyes running over the horse. 'Probably best chance he'll ever have. If he's ever going to win, or go close, today might actually be the day.'

'The sooner the better,' Millie replied. 'Otherwise we'll have to change his name to Also Ran.'

'As it happens,' Rory continued, as the horse walked past

them for a second time, 'he did a decent piece of work a couple of days ago. Galloped all over Goldenhawk who'd run a horse called Makeshift to a short head at Ascot a week before, and Makeshift's a decent sort of horse. So you never know. Funnier things have happened. And if you're in the betting mood, girls, Harry Jenks's horse is meant to go close in the next, but don't go putting all the housekeeping on it. Might be worth a bit each way. I'll see you in the paddock proper in about twenty minutes.'

Harry Jenks's horse did not in fact win. Under a sterling ride by the amateur Mr Theodore 'Tog' Ogilvy, it just failed to catch the Queen Mother's horse at the post, the two horses battling it out up the famous Sandown hill.

'I followed the trainer,' Millie sighed, tearing up her Tote ticket. 'Idiot that I am. How about you?'

Alice managed to look embarrassed. 'I don't know.'

'What do you mean, you don't know, love? What did you back?'

'I think I might have backed the winner.'

Alice showed Millie her ticket.

'Another winner?' Millie exclaimed, her eyes widening to their maximum as she looked at the ticket and heard the result and starting prices being announced.

'And I put five pounds on it this time.'

'You've not only got another winner, duck, but another long price one! Ten to one? What is it about you today? Come on, let's go and see how much the Tote are paying out.'

The Tote paid out odds of nearly fifteen to one, so for her five pound bet Alice got a few pence short of seventy-five pounds. Millie shook her head and laughed so much when she saw Alice's expression as she collected her winnings that several racegoers stopped momentarily to stare at the sight of two middle-aged women beside themselves with laughter.

'The gods of punting are smiling on you, Alice Dixon – they really are,' Millie avowed as they walked to the unsaddling enclosure so they could watch the horses coming in. They stood by the white rails in front of the weighing room, admiring the winner and the two runners up, the steam rising off them, their mouths flecked with white, their flared nostrils reddened and dilating while their lads expertly swung sweat sheets over their heaving frames, as the jockeys, having already unfastened their saddles, girths and weight cloths and swung them over one arm, tipped their caps to their connections and hurried off to weigh in.

'Time to go and see our horse,' Millie announced as the un-saddling enclosure emptied of people. 'See if they managed to screw all four legs on in the right order, for once.'

Even to Alice's unschooled eyes Millie's horse was an unpre-possessing animal, what would professionally be described as a lightly furnished chestnut with big floppy ears and an odd uneven gait.

'That's called stringhalt,' Millie explained as they walked into the middle of the paddock, a space reserved only for owners, trainers and officials. 'Funnily enough once he's cantering it disappears so it doesn't affect his racing prowess at all. Prowess? What am I talking about? Anyway, as a last resort Rory's running him in blinkers for the first time. Not that apparently he particularly believes in the *shades*, as they call them. But you know – any port in a storm.'

'I feel rather self-conscious standing in here,' Alice muttered. 'I mean, I don't really have any business being here at all.'

'Nobody'll notice you, honey,' Millie reassured her. 'They're all too busy pretending to look at the horses, but as everyone in racing knows, all they really talk about here in the ring is who did what, when and with whom.'

Rory arrived, looking nervously round at the opposition with an expression of near doom.

'Cheer up, Rory,' Millie said. 'Silly old horse has got his donkey look on, which usually means he's at the races, doesn't it?'

'At the races?' Alice frowned. 'So where else would he be?'

Rory smiled at her bewilderment.

'*Façon de parler*, Mrs Dixon,' he said. 'Racing jargon. Means he's feeling fit and ready to go.'

'Think he's got an each way chance, Rory?' Millie wondered.

'Don't see why not,' Rory replied, before departing to leg up an over-tall jockey who was standing by the horse, tapping his leg nervously with his whip. 'As I said, he'll never have a better chance. But don't put the mortgage on him.'

Yet in spite of his professed caution, and most unusually for him, Rory himself had placed a large bet to win only, a wager he could really ill afford given not only his own financial position but also the family situation. He knew that should anything happen to his father he would need every penny he had in order just to keep afloat, yet he had placed the largest bet he had ever made on a horse that had always been considered by everyone concerned as a no-hoper. But Rory had somehow convinced himself, the way those who back horses so often do, that the information he had as to how the horse had worked and how well he was in at the weights was enough to all but guarantee the animal's not only coming in first but easing up and still being, as they say, on the bridle. What he really couldn't afford to do, other than actually place the bet, was contemplate losing.

Despite her intention to stop when she was ahead, once again Alice found herself in the Tote queue behind Millie, who was about to put ten pounds to win and ten to place on her late husband's horse, currently at sixteen to one on the Tote.

'What does IRE mean? By the horse's name?' she asked Millie.

'Means that it was bred in Ireland. Or by an Irish stallion.' She looked down at her racecard. 'You fancy number thirteen, do you? The Gossoon? Didn't you see it in the paddock? It's about the size of a milk pony.'

'Does that matter?'

'It'd be better off running at the dog track.'

But Alice wasn't deterred. For some reason or other – and she knew not either – she had quite fancied the burly little horse, so instead of following Millie's example she put her twenty pounds on number thirteen. Then she hurried off to join Millie and Rory on the lawn in front of the stands.

It was a fierce gallop from the off, which made Millie groan.

'Too fast too soon,' she said. 'Always the way in these handicap hurdles. Particularly when Mr Pope has a runner.'

'The difference between hurdles and fences being?' Alice asked, needing reminding.

'Hurdles are much smaller than fences and you can knock them over,' Millie replied, still watching the race through her binoculars. 'Although it's not particularly advisable. But you can do and get away with it.'

'They really are going awfully fast,' Alice observed as the field thundered past them for the first time. 'I never realised they went that fast.'

'Our chap's pulling the jock's arms out,' Millie muttered. 'He's taken a hell of a hold, Rory.'

'He's all right,' Rory muttered from behind them. Too nervous to watch the race, he was staring up at the sky and following what was happening via the commentary. 'It's OK – he likes to front-run.'

And so indeed it seemed, since as they headed for the hill and for home with only two hurdles to jump, their horse Trojan Jack was a good ten lengths clear of the field and still going strong, while the rest of the runners behind had wilted, as was obvious from the desperate thrashing of whips and kicking from their beaten jockeys. The only danger was The Gossoon, who was still on the bridle, going easily, and in between the two last hurdles now starting to mount a challenge.

'Come on, Trojan Jack!' Millie urged, finding herself suddenly in full voice as she realised her horse was probably going to win. 'Come on, our lovely boy! *Come on!*'

Torn between shouting for her friend's horse and the horse moving up so smoothly on the outside, Alice chose instead to keep quiet and watch, which was more than Rory could do. Hearing what he could not believe and then seeing it, he had now turned his back completely on the action, closed his eyes and put his head in his hands.

'Come on, Trojan, my love!' Millie was shouting. 'For God's sake, horse! Come on! *Come on!*'

But it seemed that The Gossoon might have him, so easily was he going, his jockey not having had to make a move other than give one shake of the reins. Coming to the last Trojan Jack was still two lengths to the good, but with the Sandown hill still to contend with the little dark bay had him, and that was for sure, even to Alice's inexperienced eye.

'Come on, The Gossoon,' she said quietly to herself, quite unable to believe her luck. '*Come on.*'

The race was the little dark horse's bar a fall until his idiotic jockey tried to organise him at the last hurdle, shortening up and kicking him into a stride. Consequently the animal half checked, put down, and hit the hurdle hard. Thanks to the blinkers Trojan Jack had been unaware of the horse that had been mounting such a challenge to him, although he must have sensed that he had a fight on his hands, because he stood well off the last hurdle and flew it as consummately as he had flown every previous one, landing running and pulling a good five to six lengths clear of The Gossoon who, although now clearly beaten, somehow remained on his feet.

'He's won, Rory!' Millie shouted, turning to her trainer, who still had his head in his hands. 'You've only gone and done it! He's only gone and blasted well won!'

Rory put up his glasses at last, just in time to see his horse gallop past the winning post with The Gossoon four lengths behind in second.

'I don't believe it,' he said, pushing his cap to the back of his head. 'I just do not Christmas Eve it.'

Millie turned and threw her arms round her trainer's neck and kissed him on both cheeks, while for the first time in what seemed to him to be a very, very long time Rory found himself smiling.

'Amazing,' he said quietly. 'Amazing. Well, well, well.'

'Well done, well done indeed,' Alice said, putting her hand out to shake his. 'What a very good race. Really well done.'

'Thank you,' Rory replied. 'Thank you very much.'

Alice smiled at him, then looked out on to the track where a couple of officials had gathered just by the winning post. She pointed towards it with her hired binoculars.

'I don't suppose it matters that something dropped off just before the post, does it?'

Rory stared at her, hoping he had not heard right.

'Dropped off what?' he asked anxiously. 'Off what? Dropped off the horse? My horse?'

'Yes. I thought I saw something drop off him just there.' Alice pointed to where the two officials were standing, one of them holding something that the other was inspecting.

'Looks as if a weight cloth just dropped off someone, Rory,' a fellow trainer said, as he began to leave the stands. 'Hope it's not yours, dear boy.'

'And if it is our weight cloth, Rory?' Millie asked, faintly, even though she already knew the answer.

Rory didn't reply. He had his race glasses up again, observing in close-up as one of the two men now held up what was quite clearly a weight cloth for another official who was hurrying to the scene to see.

'It's a weight cloth all right,' Rory muttered, putting his glasses down. 'And I have a terrible feeling that it's Jack's.'

'What difference should that make, Millie? I don't understand,' Alice wondered as Rory hurried off to the unsaddling enclosure. 'Your horse won fair and square, surely?'

'If his weight cloth fell off I think the rule is that the horse didn't finish with the correct weight, which means Jack will be disqualified.'

'Even though he was first past the post?'

'That's the rule, duck,' Millie replied, looking tight-lipped and starting after Rory. 'I'm very much afraid.'

The result was announced over the tannoy. Trojan Jack was disqualified for failing to finish the race with his correct weight which meant that The Gossoon was automatically promoted to the winning spot.

'Oh, that really is terrible luck,' Alice sympathised, taking Millie by the arm. 'Come on, let me buy you a very large double something or other.'

'One man's bad luck,' Millie said resignedly. 'It means you won.'

'Oh.' Alice stopped and thought for a moment. 'You mean the horse I backed – The Gossoon? I see what you mean. Yes, of course, I see what you mean.'

'How much did you have on it?'

'Twenty pounds. I think. Ten to win, ten to place.'

'And this from the girl who wasn't going to bet.'

'I'd far, far rather you'd won,' Alice said, pulling a face. 'Talk about turning to dust in your mouth.'

Millie shrugged her shoulders. 'That's racing, Allie. Come on – let's go and collect your winnings and have that double something or other.'

They walked off to the Tote window, and Alice began to search through her chaotic handbag for her purse. 'I don't believe it,' she said. 'I think I've lost the ticket.'

'You can't have done. What about your jacket pockets?'

More searching revealed no winning ticket, just as the results of the dividend were being announced over the tannoy.

'What can I have done with it?'

'Maybe you dropped it,' Millie replied. 'If so, we are going to have to find it. Did you hear what they're paying out? Eleven to one your horse! So we are going to have to find that ticket.'

Millie marched Alice back over the way they had come, retracing their steps up to the place on the lawn where they had watched the race. Alice looked about her at the sea of dropped tickets. 'You'll never find it, Millie. Not in a month of whatevers.'

Millie looked up at her. 'I might not. But you and I might, so you do the lawn while I look on the steps here.'

Reluctantly Alice began sorting through the discarded litter that lay on the grass while Millie started sifting through the trash lying on the steps. As they searched, they were observed by a couple of older gentlemen racegoers who stopped to watch.

'I'll say this for Sandown,' one of them remarked. 'It attracts an altogether better class of bag woman.'

'Thanks for that,' Millie muttered. 'That's all we need.'

'Got it!' Alice suddenly cried.

'You sure?'

'Absolutely. Look!' Alice waved the winning ticket from the lawn. 'It must have dropped out of my handbag when I got a hankie to clean my binoculars.'

After they had walked away from the Tote window, with Alice stuffing into her already packed handbag another large wad of money, they went looking for Rory. They eventually ran him to earth in the trainers' and owners' bar, standing up in the corner staring darkly into a very empty glass.

'Cheer up, Rory,' Millie said. 'It wasn't your fault.'

'Kind of you to say, but of course it was my fault. I saddled him up.'

'Was that what it was? A saddling-up error?'

'The jockey insisted on using his own numnah.'

'That's the thing that goes under the saddle,' Millie explained to Alice.

'I saw it,' Alice returned. 'That sheepskin thing.'

'It shouldn't have been,' Rory said. 'Should have just been a cloth, but Dennis had a fall yesterday and hurt his – whatever that bone is at the bottom of your spine.'

'Coccyx,' Alice said helpfully. 'Least I think that's what it's called.'

'If only,' Rory sighed. 'I shouldn't have let him – then the bloody saddle wouldn't have slipped. And et cetera.' He raised his eyebrows helplessly, which made him look even more tragic, and to Alice even more Florentine. She felt like taking him into her arms and giving him a hug, and then remembered her age.

'Did you have a bet, Rory?' Millie asked, as Alice disappeared to order some drinks.

'Better not go there, Millie,' Rory replied. 'Don't go anywhere near there.'

'OK.' Millie grinned, nodding in Alice's direction. 'But if

you need a loan, ask Mrs Midas. She's hit just about every winner so far. If she goes on like this, she'll be warned off.'

'I'm going to need more than a loan, Millie,' Rory said. 'I'm going to need a miracle. The yard is in something of a mess.'

Alice returned from the bar carrying a tray with three glasses of champagne.

'Not in celebration,' she said. 'In commiseration.'

Millie looked at her friend and decided that this was very much *not* the person she had brought racing. Gone was what she thought of as Alice's startled rabbit look and in its place was an altogether different person. In fact if Millie hadn't been with her all afternoon she would have sworn that her best friend had just fallen in love.

'What is it they say about champagne?' Alice wondered, setting the glasses in front of them. 'I read it somewhere. About the best time to drink it. I can't remember what it was for the life of me. Any time, that was it. The great thing about champagne is that it can be drunk at any time – for anything.'

'Last glass I'll be having for a while,' Rory muttered. 'Of all the things to happen. Wait till the old man gets to hear.'

'How is he?' Millie asked. 'Is he back with us yet?'

'Sort of,' Rory replied. 'I mean he's come round, thank God, and they don't think there's any – any brain damage or anything. There certainly will be if he gets to hear about my performance today.'

'You're being awfully hard on yourself, if I may say so,' Alice chimed in. 'My husband always maintained there are such things as *accidents*, pure and simple. And that the sooner we recognise that fact the better able we shall be to cope with them. It was an *accident*.'

'You're really very kind, Mrs Dixon.'

'Alice, Mr Rawlins.'

'OK, Alice.' Rory nodded. 'And I'm Rory.'

'I know.' Alice smiled.

'The trouble is I compounded the felony – or accident as you so kindly have it – by placing a rather large bet on the horse, with money I simply do not have.'

'I'm sorry to hear that.'

'I said you'd see him right,' Millie joked.

'Of course,' Alice agreed. 'If you really are a bit stitched, Mr Rawlins – I mean Rory—'

'If the seat were hanging out of my trousers, Alice,' Rory said quickly, 'I wouldn't take a penny.'

'I'm serious.'

'I'm sure you are. And so am I.' Rory smiled at her then took a drink of his champagne. 'Of course you could always buy a horse and put it in training with me.'

'Could I?' Alice's frown deepened.

'That was a joke,' Rory said. 'And not a very gallant one either. Sorry.'

'But I could buy a horse, could I? When we've all stopped joking.'

'You won that much?' Rory laughed. 'Sorry – there I go again.'

'Depends how much a horse costs,' Alice said. 'Anyway. What I have in my handbag isn't all I have.'

'Alice?' said Millie. 'Steady.'

'I'm being serious, Millie,' Alice insisted. 'Anyway, this is your fault. You brought me here, and if you really want to know, other than your poor horse losing so unfairly, I don't think I've had as much fun in – well, actually I don't remember when last I enjoyed myself so much.'

'You're not a regular then?' Rory asked. 'You don't do this – go racing – this isn't something you do?'

'This is my first time on a racecourse. And it certainly won't be my last. I'd love to come and see your stables. That's somewhere else I've never been. A racing yard.'

'There are better yards to see,' Rory replied. 'It might put you off.'

'Nonsense. Perhaps Millie and I – I'm staying with her at the moment.'

'If you really want to,' Rory said. 'But as I said, it's not exactly Lambourn.'

'The Newmarket of jump racing,' Millie explained once more.

'Thank you,' Alice said. 'Actually I think it might be rather fun.'

'Visiting the yard?' Rory said with a frown.

'Having a racehorse,' Alice replied. 'And visiting your yard, of course.'

Before the matter could be taken any further a slim, beautifully if traditionally dressed man stopped by their table, putting a consolatory hand on Rory's shoulder.

'Rory,' Grenville Fielding said. 'I say. *Such* hard luck, really. Of all the things to happen.'

'That's racing, as they say, Grenville,' Rory said, before introducing the visitor to Alice and Millie.

'Sorr-ee,' Grenville said when he realised everyone's attention was being drawn to one of the people with him. 'Yes. This is – this is a *friend* of mine,' he continued, hoping there was enough uncertainty in his delivery to indicate that the person in question was an acquaintance rather than a bosom buddy. 'Let me introduce you to Lady Frimley.'

Constance looked round from one face to another, and as she did so she had the same pleasurable feeling she experienced standing by a nice, warm fire.

'How do you do?' she said as she shook everyone's hand. 'How very nice.'

When Alice was introduced the two women smiled at each other, Constance because she found herself immediately taken by what she saw as the kindness and honesty in Alice's eyes, and Alice because she found herself privately approving of the older woman's style, pleased that at least some people still bothered to dress up when going out for the day, rather than wearing clothes that made them look as though they were living in what Evie always called a Fifth World country.

'I do like your hat,' she told her, after the introductions. 'I wish more people wore hats nowadays.'

'Some of the men could do without them altogether,' Constance replied, narrowing her eyes. 'That ghastly little man Grenville was talking to—'

'A steward, Lady Frimley,' Grenville interrupted with a helpful smile. 'One of the stewards.'

'Got a hat like a scoutmaster's,' Constance continued. 'Looks like an old pixie.'

'My father had a hat very like that,' Grenville told her. 'Used to actually steam it into that shape.'

'Backed any winners?' Millie enquired. 'Alice here has absolutely emptied the Tote.'

'I only ever bet on the Tote,' Constance replied. 'I cannot abide bookmakers. One thing the French have got right. I used to adore going racing in Deauville. But of course France is no longer the same, one just has to face it. You have to say the Revolution was the worst possible thing for the wretched French, you really do.'

'I did tell her to back The Gossoon,' Grenville informed the company. 'With respect of course, Rory.'

'I couldn't possibly back a horse with such an absurd name,' Constance retorted, now seated and fishing out of her handbag a small cheroot which she lit with a large old-fashioned silver table lighter, also produced from her bag. 'I cannot stand all these foreign names they keep giving these poor creatures.'

'I really thought Trojan Jack ran an absolutely splendid race, Rory,' Grenville said, sitting down beside him. 'And how's your father? Rory's father used to train for mine, do you see?' Grenville continued, enlightening the rest of the company. 'They were in the army together.'

Rory put Grenville in the picture regarding his father's current condition, about which Grenville was immediately considerate and sympathetic, assuring Rory that as soon as Anthony was well enough to receive visitors he would be there.

'Actually though,' Grenville said after a moment of further reflection, 'actually this could be karma, or whatever it is they call it. Seeing you here. Meeting you like this, because I was thinking only the other day I should get myself a racehorse. Now the old man's gone AWOL I rather miss having an interest.'

Rory nodded but said nothing. Much as he would like to sell the donkey that had just arrived from Ireland, given Grenville's family background and racing experience he saw little chance of persuading him it would be just the sort of horse for him. Anyway, even if Grenville Fielding were to visit the yard his eye would hardly be taken by an animal that hadn't eaten an oat since its arrival from the Emerald Isle, a self-imposed starvation diet that was beginning to cause everyone at Fulford Farm a considerable degree of worry.

'So how *are* things at the yard?' Grenville wondered, as Rory finished his drink and began to think about leaving.

'On hold a bit, really.' Rory pocketed his racecard and started winding the strap round his race glasses. 'We're keeping things ticking over, but with my father in hospital and not knowing what sort of recovery he's going to make . . .'

'So not a good time to come and have a look-see then. Got you.'

'There's not exactly a lot to have a look-see at, Grenville.'

'Thought you said earlier about some horse or other you'd just brought over from Ireland,' Millie remarked. 'Didn't you?'

'Did I?' Rory muttered. 'Oh yes, that's right. But there's somebody coming to look at him.'

'Really?' Grenville asked, pricking up his ears. 'Got any form, has he?'

'The person coming to see him? Don't really know.'

'The horse, old chap.'

'Not a lot.'

'Unexposed?'

'Sort of. Now if you'll excuse me . . .' Rory made to get up and take his leave.

'Worth coming to take a look?'

'As I just said, someone else is already interested.'

'Even so,' Grenville smiled. 'If someone's already *interested*, someone else might also be interested. Look – I have to come down west on some business, so why don't I pop in and take a shufti? Nothing ventured as they say, eh?' He produced his pocket diary and consulted it. 'I could in fact come down quite soon, as it happens – this business thing being a movable sort of feast. Why don't I call you when I get back to town – when I've sorted out the old diary? Right?'

'We might see you there,' Alice said with a smile, as she too began to take her leave, prompted by Millie who wanted to watch the last race. 'Millie and I are planning a visit to the stables as well.'

'Then why don't we all make a day of it? I should be charmed,' Grenville said, standing and raising his hat to Millie and Alice. 'I shall liaise with Rory here.'

'Nice man,' Alice remarked as she and Millie returned to the grandstand. 'Lovely manners.'

'I thought the woman with him was his mother,' Millie remarked, putting up her glasses to watch the horses at the start. 'He looks the sort of man who'd take his mother racing.'

'Unlike my son,' Alice said with a wry smile. 'The only place Chris takes me is to the cleaners.'

'They're off,' Millie said. 'Last chance saloon.'

The race was won by yet another long shot, a victory greeted in near silence by the few dogged punters determined to see the end of what had turned out to be an expensive afternoon for backers.

'Don't tell me you had it or I shall scream,' Millie said to Alice, consigning her worthless ticket to the litter bin.

'Not exactly,' Alice replied, looking at the slip in her hand. 'Only on that thing you said I should do.'

'The Tote Double? That's been and gone.'

'Oh. Then what's this?' Alice handed Millie the ticket for her perusal.

'The Tote Treble, duck,' Millie informed her, then widened her eyes. 'You did the Tote Treble?'

'Apparently.'

'And?'

'They all seem to have won.'

There were three winning tickets and the Tote paid out seven hundred and ninety-eight pounds exactly.

Coincidentally Lynne had also been to Sandown races. She had been out shopping first, her newly gained money already burning holes in her pockets, and among other items she had bought she was extremely pleased with the outfit she was wearing, a silk dress in a particularly fashionable Matisse blue, with big shoulder pads, and a wide, tight belt, teamed with a particularly outrageous pair of pink shoes. She also wore a well-cut middle brown suede top coat with a pale cream fur lining, which came to just below the knee and was very flattering. When she got to Sandown Park and remembered that this was a jumps meeting, not a flat one, she immediately buttoned up her coat, and wished she had chosen the sort of sensible racing outfit being sported by the other women racegoers.

Happily, since everyone seemed to be caught up in their own little worlds, Lynne seemed to attract little undue attention. However, one man whose attention she most certainly grabbed was Rory Rawlins, for the good reason that Lynne quite literally bumped into him as he was backing out of the building she was walking past, his arms full of saddles and bridles. Lynne had been looking round at a couple of young men who had given her the full up and downer. The next thing she knew she had knocked someone flying.

'Oh, God, sorry,' she exclaimed, immediately helping the man she had knocked over to his feet. 'I really am sorry.'

'No, no – my fault entirely,' Rory replied. 'I really should look where other people are going.'

'All your stuff, it's gone everywhere,' Lynne said, picking up some of the spilled tack. 'Oh, I just love the smell of leather. I used to think if I had the money I'd have a tack room just for the *smell*. Actually – what the hell.' She laughed. 'I've got the money now, so who knows!'

'Sorry – I have to go and saddle up a horse,' Rory said, retrieving his racing saddle.

'Right,' Lynne replied, standing up. 'That what you do?'

'In between training horses,' Rory replied. 'Or rather trying to train horses.'

'OK,' Lynne said, nodding. 'I'd heard it was a tough job. A friend of ours – well, that's when there was an *ours* – this bloke we knew was a trainer but he found it so tough he took to burglary.'

'Thanks,' Rory said, having now collected the rest of his tack and standing back up. 'That's just the steer I needed.'

'No, seriously. He lives in a huge villa in Marbella all year round now. So it doesn't have to be all bad.'

By now Rory was taking a good look at the beautiful young woman who had just knocked him for six. She was handing him the last piece of recovered tack, smiling and regarding him with a pair of blue eyes that were quite literally the colour of her dress.

'Got a runner then?' she asked.

'Yes,' he said, feeling himself lightly blushing, which was certainly not a habit of his. 'Trojan Jack in the handicap hurdle.'

'Worth a couple of bob?'

'That's what they tell me.'

'Even though you're the trainer?' Lynne raised two perfectly shaped eyebrows.

'Next to owners, trainers are the last to know anything.'

'Seriously. Should I back him?'

'He's very well,' Rory muttered, hugging his tack to him. 'He could go close.'

'Then I certainly shall back him,' Lynne said. 'And if he wins I shall find you and buy you champagne.'

'Date,' Rory said with a nod to indicate he was on his way.

'Date,' she called after him. 'Good luck!'

When she heard the announcement telling racegoers that Trojan Jack had failed to win his race because of his lost weight cloth, Lynne remembered the handsome young trainer and went in search of him, thinking she might buy him a drink to console him. She saw him in the distance by the unsaddling enclosure, but just as she was about to approach him she saw someone else, too – her now ex-husband Gerry, with one arm draped round her now ex-best friend Maddy's shoulders. As The Gossoon was proclaimed the winner, Gerry punched the air, kissed his mistress, and turned in Lynne's direction. Before he could spot her Lynne took evasive action, hiding herself behind one of the large trees that stood nearby and shifting carefully round its great trunk as Gerry and Maddy crossed close by. When they were past, Lynne trailed a safe distance behind them until she saw where they were headed, then she took her dark glasses out of her handbag and set off in the opposite direction.

She could have kicked herself when she realised how stupid she had been. Why wouldn't she bump into Gerry taking Maddy to the races? After all, he had taken her racing often enough when they were married, so there was every possibility that he would now take Maddy. Had Lynne been with someone else she might possibly have had enough confidence to see her through the afternoon, regardless of whether or not she bumped into Gerry. But by herself she felt exposed and vulnerable, and yet determined not to be put off. She would not, absolutely would not be scared away. Lonely, friendless, but not scared. Besides, it was becoming a kind of duty to spend Gerry's money, even lose it, and she proceeded to do so on a procession of horses.

Just before the last race she saw them leaving and breathed a sigh of relief, deciding to treat herself to a drink to celebrate their departure.

Rory passed her going out as she was coming in.

'So there you are,' Lynne said when she saw him, as if she had been spending her time looking for him rather than hiding from her ex-husband. 'That was such tough luck about your horse. Maybe I could buy you that drink I promised, even though for a rather different reason?'

There was nothing Rory would have enjoyed more at that moment than to have a glass of champagne with this particular young woman, but whether he liked it or not he had a job to do.

'Thank you,' he said. 'But I have to see my horse loaded and get him home.'

'Oh,' Lynne said, trying not to let her disappointment show. 'Right. Some other time, perhaps.'

'You bet,' Rory agreed. 'Sorry.'

In two minds whether she should stay or go, Lynne found herself hailed by someone else who recognised her.

'Mrs Fortune?' a voice from across the bar called. 'Mrs Fortune.'

When she turned Grenville Fielding was at her elbow, doffing his brown trilby hat.

'I thought it might be you,' he said. 'Grenville Fielding. I had dinner with you and your husband not long ago. Last year sometime. At Cappelli's, wasn't it? I thought it was you.'

With his hat off Lynne just about remembered him from a rather overlarge dinner Gerry and his business partners had thrown in a restaurant to celebrate some company coup or other.

'Sorry,' she replied with a smile. 'There were rather a lot of people there.'

'I sat next to you,' Grenville reminded her. 'We talked about the house your husband was thinking of buying in Provence.'

'Of course. Sorry. It's just that since the divorce—'

'You've got divorced?' Grenville frowned at her. 'I am *so* sorry. I had no idea.'

'It's OK,' Lynne replied rather too brightly. 'It's not as if someone died.'

'No, I am *so* sorry,' Grenville said again. 'I had no idea.'

'Why should you? Hardly page one stuff.'

'Can I buy you a drink, Mrs Fortune? I'm with some people over here, and we'd be delighted if you joined us.'

Lynne glanced over at the man and woman sitting at the corner table and, seeing no danger, agreed. Grenville introduced her to Constance and to Charles Danby before going off to buy more drinks.

'You look very colourful, my dear,' Constance said, lighting a cheroot. 'That blue doesn't look good on everyone.'

'Thank you,' Lynne replied, pleased at being complimented by an older woman, particularly one as stylish as Constance. 'I like your hat and all.'

'Of course,' Constance said with a regal smile. 'You're acquainted with Mr Fielding, then.'

'Well – yes and no. He's a friend of my ex – least, I think he is. Business friend, that is.'

'Your ex?' Constance puffed her cheroot. 'You are *divorcée, alors.*'

'You got it.' Lynne nodded. 'Hole in one.'

'It happens to the best of us,' Constance said. 'It happened to me all over the place.'

'Right,' Lynne agreed. 'So let's just hope it might also be the best thing to happen to us.'

'I like that,' Constance replied. 'I think I like you, too.'

The crowd was dispersing fast as Grenville returned to the table bringing glasses of champagne for Lynne and Constance, and gins and tonics for Charles and himself, but before the party broke up he discreetly managed to get Lynne's current telephone number while Constance had disappeared to the loo – as she informed the company with a perfectly straight face – to shed a tear for Lady Hamilton.

Chapter Eight

Irishitis

Kathleen had not been herself since Boyo had gone. A restlessness filled her being, and nothing that would normally give her happiness held much interest for her. Her father and brother seemed too human, and the dog too canine. The sea lacked impact without the image of a horse coming out of it, and the skies, whatever their colour, were merely patchwork pieces above her head when she could not hear the sound of her beloved horse cantering towards her. She knew that they had been too close, as an animal and a human being often can be. His feelings had become her feelings, and she knew before he knew it if he was sick. So now, even in her restlessness, she felt that he was ill, and yet she also had no way of knowing whether she was right. If only they had not had to sell him. If they had had just a little more money they would have been able to keep him, but they were poor and every penny counted, so it was inevitable that every horse born on their little farm would always finally be sold.

If only things had been different, Kathleen would often sigh. If only her mother hadn't died so young – if only her uncle hadn't swindled her father out of his inheritance, which small though it was would have surely been enough to pay for rebuilding the yard. If only, if only. If only her Auntie Aileen had wheels sure she'd be an omnibus, she would scold herself. And sure with a big enough *if* you could even put Dublin in a bottle.

'You're not yourself, girl,' her father chided her one morning when he found her sitting at the table with her chin in her hands, her tea undrunk. 'You're looking as pale as a winding sheet. 'Tis a grand morning, so take out auld Batty Boy for a spin. You like riding auld Batty Boy, so you do.'

'Boyo isn't well, Da,' Kathleen stated, not looking at him.

'Ah, and why shouldn't the horse be well? He's gone to a good enough yard, so why shouldn't he be well? You and that horse. You and your imaginings. We've got enough to deal with here without your imaginings. The horse is fine. So now you go out riding.'

'You know what happens to horses when they leave Ireland, Da. You told me so yourself. They often get sick. I know Boyo's sick.'

'And if he is, there is nothing you can do about it from here, Kathleen. They have veterinaries over there, and men of the stamp of Mr Rawlins look after their horses. If a man pays for a horse himself he'll keep it well, so he will. There's no point otherwise.'

'I'll ride Batty Boy out for you, Da,' Kathleen said, fetching her oilskin coat and taking down her boy's cap. 'But only because there's little point in doing anything else.'

It was a fine and breezy day with the rain keeping well off and a weak autumn sun shining down, the distant hills still blue and the valleys green though the countryside was about to give way to winter, yet even though Batty Boy was as good to ride as ever, striding out strongly with his tail held high behind him and his ears well pricked, Kathleen rode with a heavy heart. She knew her horse was ailing.

Every anxiety ran through her. She could see what might happen. The new owner might become so dismayed by the horse's lethargy he would sell him on. Boyo might find himself in some inferior yard where they would do all manner of things to him in order to get just the one race out of him, so they could recover some of the cost to themselves before selling him on to some rundown riding school, or worse.

'There's only one thing to do, Batty Boy,' she yelled to the horse as she galloped him up the grass track. 'He needs me so I must go to him, God help me!'

After she had mucked out, groomed and fed the horses, she found her brother and told him he must look after everything.

'And what am I to tell Da when he finds you gone?' Liam asked.

'You play the dumb one,' Kathleen replied. 'You're good at that. Put back that old cap of yours, scratch your head and say, *Jesus, Da, I didn't know she'd gone anywhere – but if she's gone at all sure she won't be long for she never is.* Anyway, it's market day tomorrow, which is why I've chosen it. So if he notices it won't be till he's home, and when he's home after market he's always late and always drunk, so the chances are he won't know I'm gone till the day after.'

Kathleen smiled at her brother, kissed him fondly and hurried to her bedroom, where she took a small tin box from inside her mattress. Out of the box she lifted her trousseau money and counted out what she would need for the journey, then returned what was left to the box and the box back to the mattress.

'The bus, the train, the ferry,' she said to herself. 'Then a train again and possibly another bus. Then a bus, a train and the ferry, then a train and then the bus.' She regarded the cash she was holding. 'That'll never be enough – not when you account for refreshments and emergencies.'

She withdrew the box again, took out some more money and stared at it.

'Ah, to hell and high water anyway.' She sighed. 'Might as well be hung for the sheep as well as the lamb. And wi... ...... If Boyo needs me I most certainly don't.'

The train to Cork was overcrowded, and the ferry to Fishguard full of nuns and people returning to what they liked to call the mainland. Kathleen avoided the bars, and sat with the nuns who, when they heard the reason for her journey, offered prayers to St Francis for her little horse. Then, after another two long and crowded train journeys, first to Bristol then on to Salisbury, and finally a taxi ride, Kathleen finally arrived at Fulford Farm.

'I'm looking for Mr Rawlins,' she informed a curious Teddy, who was leaning on his broom when she walked into the yard. 'Would you know where he might be, please?'

Teddy continued to stare for a moment at the apparition before him. Her clothes might be poor, but he couldn't remember ever seeing a more beautiful girl than the one standing staring at him so solemnly.

'You could try the office, miss,' he finally advised, after a small pause during which he wondered if he had ever seen a greener pair of eyes, or a darker and more lustrous head of hair. 'Shall you wish – that is, shall I take you – I mean, show you?'

'You're so much more than kind,' Kathleen replied, picking up her small suitcase. 'Thank you.'

'It's nothing, miss. Let me carry that for you.' He took her case and with a doff of his flat cap and a quick shy smile he led the way to the guv'nor's office. They found Rory sitting staring into space, having just come off the telephone to his bank manager.

'What is it, Teddy?' he asked, seeing just the lad standing in the doorway. 'Didn't anyone tell you it's rude to interrupt a suicide?'

'There's someone here to see you, Guv,' Teddy replied. 'A young lady.'

'Wouldn't make much difference if it was Julia Roberts, chum,' Rory told him. 'Altogether in the altogether.'

'It isn't she, Mr Rawlins,' a soft voice said from behind Teddy. 'I'm quite fully dressed, too.'

Rory looked up and could hardly believe what he saw.

'Miss Flanagan, isn't it?' he said incredulously. 'Miss Flanagan? Surely not.'

'I should have telephoned you,' Kathleen said, her well-prepared excuse at the ready. 'I would have done too,' she lied, 'had the lines not been blown down in a terrible storm.'

'So, what – what can I do for you?' Rory was almost at a loss for words as he stared at the beautiful young woman standing in front of him. 'What are you doing here?'

'I've come to see the horse,' Kathleen replied. 'That's why I'm here.'

'You – you've come all the way from Ireland just to see your horse?' Rory stammered, finding himself reduced to the help-lessness he used to feel as a boy when confronted by pretty girls.

'I have, Mr Rawlins. If you've no objections.'

'Nobody from here – nobody telephoned you, did they?' Rory suddenly remembered the new incumbent's present ill health. He turned to his secretary, who was busy at work in the other corner of the office. 'Maureen—'

'No one has called anyone in Ireland from here, Rory,' she replied. 'At least not to my knowledge.'

'No good looking at me, Guv,' Teddy said. 'I wouldn't know who to ring.'

'And why should they, Mr Rawlins?' Kathleen asked, all innocence. 'Is there something wrong?'

'No,' Rory faltered. 'I mean, yes, but nothing really wrong as in the horse being ill. It's just – it's just he's not eating. We can't get him to eat.'

'Not at all?' Kathleen asked, concerned.

'He's barely gone near his manger for a week. Is he prone to this sort of thing?'

'He never left an oat at home, Mr Rawlins. Always got to the bottom of the pot.'

'The vet can't find anything wrong.'

'He wouldn't. The horse is homesick.'

'Homesick?' Rory repeated in astonishment. 'Did you say – did you say homesick?'

'I did so,' Kathleen assured him. 'Do you find that so astonishing? It happens all the time, bringing horses over here. They call it Irishitis. Or rather you do. We don't. We call it homesickness.'

'Really.' Rory half got up from his seat then sat back down again with a deep frown on his face. 'Really.'

'Horses have feelings, Mr Rawlins. Same as you and me. I wonder if I could see him? I don't have a lot of time. I'd like to be back home again by tomorrow morning, before my father finds me gone.'

Rory shook his head and frowned even more deeply, utterly thrown by this turn of events.

'I can't b-b-believe you came all this way on a whim. J-j-just to see your horse.'

'It wasn't a whim.'

'Well – what-what-whatever,' Rory said, gritting his teeth and closing his eyes against his suddenly returned stammer, an affliction he had thought he was by now well rid of. 'Yes, of course you can see the horse – your horse. Yes, of c-c-c-course you ker-ker-ker-ker—' He stopped and clicked his finger and thumb together, as taught by his therapist. 'Of course you can,' he said slowly. 'I'll show him to you myself. Not that I think you'll learn much by l-l-l-looking.'

'No, Mr Rawlins,' Kathleen replied. 'But he might learn something be seeing.'

The horse was standing in a back corner of his box, facing the wall as if he was a dunce with a cap on his head. Kathleen watched him for a moment from the door, noting how tucked up he was and out of sorts with himself. After a few seconds, as she knew he would, the little horse turned his head slowly to look at her, which was when Kathleen put her hand over the top of the door and held it out, palm upwards.

'Doubt if that will work. He's been refusing treats all week,' Rory assured her.

'I'm not offering him a treat,' Kathleen replied. 'Just my hand. Just me.' She kept her hand outstretched and the horse returned to staring into the corner.

'This is how he's been for days,' Rory said. 'Won't go near anything or anyone.'

'Boyo?' Kathleen called quietly, then spoke to him in Gaelic. Still the horse didn't move.

'S-see what I mean?' Rory said.

'I think we have to be patient, Mr Rawlins. Really we do.'

A few minutes later the horse slowly swished his tail, after Kathleen had spoken to him some more in Gaelic.

'I don't speak any Gaelic so you'll have to help me out here,' Rory muttered. 'About all I know is Aer Lingus.'

'Sure even if you did, you mightn't know what to say to him.

He's far from himself, you can see that. Look. Look into his eyes for yourself now – look at his sadness.'

'His – sadness?' Rory repeated. 'Do horses get sad?'

'And why shouldn't they now?' Kathleen chided him. 'The horse is pining. Perhaps if I could fetch him a fresh feed he might just eat. Particularly if I put some of this Guinness in it. I didn't know whether you would have any so I brought some over with me just in case,' she added, taking a bottle out of her overnight bag. 'Might I use your feed room?'

Rory showed her the way, and she prepared a mixture exactly to her recipe, adding the Guinness last of all.

'He likes a drop of stout,' Kathleen told Rory, carrying the manger back to the stable. 'He always has, ever since he was a nipper.'

As Rory opened the stable door, for the first time the horse turned right round and came over to greet Kathleen. Kathleen at once put up a hand to touch him and to stroke his neck, and when she did so the horse pricked his ears and shook himself thoroughly, as if awakening from a sleep.

'At least he can still walk,' Rory said. 'He's hardly m-moved for a week.'

'He's a sick horse, Mr Rawlins. Think about it. It's a big thing, leaving the place where you're born, being shoved in a lorry and then on a boat – things you know nothing of, with people and horses not known to you. Wouldn't you expect him to get sick?'

The horse now lowered his head slightly, both eyes watching Kathleen. She put one hand up to pull one of his ears. After a moment he took a deep breath and seemed to sigh. Then he shook himself again, slowly at first, but then faster and faster until it seemed to turn into a full-scale tremor.

'That's better, Boyo. You'll be better now,' Kathleen told him as she walked round him and put his manger in the corner holder. 'So now you be a good boy and eat up every last bit, you hear me? Every bit now.'

'Or else,' Rory said, trying to lighten the mood, 'it's s-straight to bed and no ster-ster – no *story*.'

'You may laugh, Mr Rawlins, but it's not funny really, what they like and don't like,' Kathleen said, coming out of the stable, closing the half-door and bolting it. 'Let's leave him now. He likes to eat in peace.'

Rory frowned again, giving her another away-with-the-fairies look behind her back, yet he did as he was bidden, following Kathleen away from the stable. He couldn't, however, resist a look over his shoulder to see how the horse was doing.

'You shouldn't,' Kathleen warned him. 'You'll put him off, I promise.'

'He's eating.'

'He'd rather be left in peace, really he would. And if it's all the same to you, I wouldn't say no to a cup of tea. I haven't had a thing since I changed at Bristol.'

'I don't know wh-what I was thinking,' Rory said, finding to his dismay not only that he had started stammering again but that the blush he had suffered at Sandown was not a one-off. 'In fact, why don't I get you something to eat? You must be ster-ster-ster—'

'I am,' Kathleen said with a smile. 'Not even half starved. Totally.'

Rory nodded and led the way into the house, where he made not only a cup of tea for both of them but a cooked breakfast of eggs, crisp bacon and fried potatoes for Kathleen. She ate in near total silence.

'If you feed your horses as well as you fed me, won't you be winning everything?' she told him when she had finished, gratefully accepting a second cup of tea.

'Yes, but I'd love to know what really brought you over, Miss Flanagan,' Rory said as Kathleen got up and started to clear away. 'And you can leave that, really you can.'

'I wouldn't hear of it,' Kathleen replied. 'The mess you make you clear. And didn't I tell you? I came over to see the horse.'

'Ber-ber—' Rory stopped and scratched his head. 'Because?'

'You'd laugh if I told you, so I won't. Where do you keep your tea towels, please?'

Rory handed her one automatically, then scratched his head again.

'Did you know something was wrong?' he finally wondered. 'You wouldn't travel all the way over here – you'd her-her – *hardly* come all this way and at great expense just to s-see the horse. Would you?'

'Don't you ever have feelings, Mr Rawlins?' Kathleen wondered, turning round and looking at him directly with the brightest pair of green eyes Rory had ever seen. 'Some people do, you know. They have feelings – and that's exactly what I had.'

'A f-feeling? A pre-pre-premonition?'

'I said you'd laugh.'

'I'm not laughing.'

'You're smiling. The overture to a laugh. Yes I had a feeling Boyo wasn't right, and you can make what you will of it.'

'You could have written,' Rory argued. 'If the telephone lines were down—'

'Which indeed they were,' Kathleen said in quick defence.

'I'm just trying to save you money, Miss Flanagan.'

'It's a little late for that, Mr Rawlins. Anyway, I consider it well spent. And talking of that, I have some trains and boats to catch,' she added, glancing at the kitchen clock.

'I think it was mer-mer-mer—' Rory stopped and snapped finger and thumb behind his back. 'I think it was very good of you to come over. I think it was a terrific thing to do.'

Kathleen looked at him with her head on one side, then nodded.

'Thanks,' she said. 'But you see, if I'd written and say you hadn't written back because you thought the horse just wasn't eating and would get over it—'

'Which he would have done, eventually.'

'You can lose the best part of a season, Mr Rawlins. While a horse – while it acclimatises itself.'

'So it was just as well you came,' Rory agreed. 'I really do believe that.'

'OK. Right. Would you ever run me to the station, please?'

'I'll take you back all the way if you like,' Rory offered. 'To F-Fishguard if you want.'

'That's really kind, thank you, but I have my tickets.'

'Let me at least run you to Bristol. Save you that change at least.'

'OK. Right. Thanks.'

Before he left he put his head round the office door to tell Maureen where he was going.

'If anyone rings,' he added, 'tell them I'll be ber-ber-ber-ber—' He stopped and closed his eyes, waiting for the block to pass. When he opened them he found Maureen frowning at him.

'I know,' he said. 'It's just come back. Don't ask me – I don't know. It'll go away again. I don't know what b-b-b-brought it on. Anyway, tell anyone who rings or c-calls I'll be back in a couple of hours. Say three. OK?'

Maureen agreed. After Rory had gone she glanced out of the window that overlooked the yard and when she saw Kathleen waiting for him, Maureen nodded to herself, taking a pretty good guess as to why Rory's long-absent stammer had so suddenly returned.

'I'm sorry about your mother,' Rory said to Kathleen in the car as they began to talk. 'Must have been very hard, her dying when you were that young.'

'Two's no age to be an orphan,' Kathleen replied, but without an ounce of self-pity. 'No, it was hard on everyone. Particularly the da. My father. They were childhood sweethearts.'

'I thought my father would never get over it – when my mother died. She died in a train accident eight years ago.'

'Jeeze,' Kathleen said, looking round at him sharply. 'Losing someone like that, in an accident – it's unthinkable. Do you have brothers and sisters?'

'I've a sister,' Rory replied. 'An older sister.'

'Right,' Kathleen agreed. 'But nothing really helps, does it? Not that I'd know, because I don't remember my mother. But my brother does and it hit him hard. And now there's your father lying in hospital—'

'At least he's back with us,' Rory said, stopping at some traffic lights beside a cider factory. 'The der – the *doctors* thought he wasn't going to make it, but then they don't know how tough the old man is. Take more than a couple of heart attacks to see him off.'

He turned and smiled at Kathleen but she wasn't looking at him. She was staring far into the beyond.

'I'll have a Mass said for him when I get back,' she said as Rory moved the car off from the lights.

'That's very good of you. Thanks. Really.'

'Anyway,' Kathleen continued, now giving Rory her full attention. 'We got Boyo eating all right.'

'You did.'

'He'll be fine now,' she assured him. 'Did you see he has the prophet's thumb on him?'

'That impression, you mean, on his neck?'

Kathleen nodded. 'You know about the prophet's thumb, right? The prophet was said to have marked all the best horses with his thumb, which is why horses with the prophet's thumb always win. Which they do.'

'As long as they don't stop eating again,' Rory returned.

'He won't,' Kathleen told him. 'Particularly if you put this on – I near as anything forgot.'

She produced a tape from her bag, pushed it into the cassette player and turned it on. Moments later the sound of a lyric Irish tenor filled the car.

'Who's this?' Rory enquired. 'And why?'

''Tis only John McCormack, our most famous tenor. I near as anything forgot to give it you. You're to play him this now—'

'By him I t-take it you mean your horse?'

'Your horse, Mr Rawlins. Yes, you're to play him this,' she continued as factually as if she was telling Rory what food to give him. 'You're to play him this continuously and he'll think he's back at home. My father's forever singing John McCormack in the yard.'

'I suppose I'll be lighting peat fires next.'

'Do you have an Irish lad on the place?'

Rory shook his head but more to stop himself from laughing in delight than in disagreement. 'I've a Welsh one,' he said. 'Think the horse will know the d-d-difference?'

'Don't be silly, with all due respect, of course he will.' Kathleen sighed. 'I'm serious now. Horses are no different from us. They miss the sounds of home as well. So make sure he gets a good daily dose of John McCormack and you won't look backwards again.'

Rory just drove for a while, happy enough to be in Kathleen's company and perfectly content to listen to the music of the greatest Irish tenor of all time.

'If you ever want a job over here,' he finally said when the cassette had finished playing the first side, 'I mean I know you're wanted at home—'

'No, I'm needed there, Mr Rawlins. As you know, we're not exactly overstaffed, and I'm afraid I'd be missed. But thanks for the offer, OK?'

'Well, if anything changes,' Rory concluded, 'you know where we are. And where the horse is.'

'Don't you worry yourself now.' She laughed, tossing back her head of lustrous dark hair. 'I shan't ever be out of touch with Boyo. Not ever.'

They heard the train long before it pulled into the station, heralding its approach like a bad guest arriving full of his own importance. Rory handed Kathleen her overnight case, and, noting how battered and worn it was, realised how much she must have spent to come over and see what might be wrong with the horse. 'Can I give you something towards the cost of your journey?' he asked.

'You most certainly cannot,' Kathleen replied smartly. 'Coming over here was my idea, not yours.'

'I just thought it might help.'

'And there's nothing wrong with the thought so you don't have to look so tragic about it.'

'I'm l-looking tragic?'

'As if you're being sent off to war. Now don't forget the music, and don't forget to give me a call if anything else goes wrong,' Kathleen said as Rory held the carriage door open for her.

'I won't,' Rory assured her. 'And I'm awfully ger-ger – I'm

awfully ger-ger-ger—' He stopped, half closed his eyes and clicked a thumb and forefinger.

'Me too,' Kathleen said with a smile which through his half-closed eyes Rory missed seeing. 'I'm awfully glad I came over as well. 'Bye now.'

Then she was gone, disappearing into the rapidly filling train, turning to wave to him once she had found herself a seat by the window, then suddenly remembering something and sliding a window open to beckon to him.

'One other thing,' she said when Rory had hurried to stand below the open window. 'He has a very soft mouth on him, and he won't be hit.'

'Right,' Rory called back. 'I'll remember that.'

'Never.'

'Not once.'

He watched the train leave the station, waving once or twice at the girl who could no longer see him and feeling at long last as if all the hurt had now gone from the past, although on the drive back he wondered if it was just the beginning of yet another heartbreak. He put any such thoughts from his head and instead played the second side of the John McCormack tape, listening to the great tenor singing 'Bless This House' and finding his mind straying straight back across the sea to Ireland.

Chapter Nine

Moving On

Millie had decided for them both. They would keep looking at cottages and small houses until they found something near to Alice's idea of where she might now like to live. In the short time she had been staying Alice had already been taken to see the outsides and some of the insides of near twenty properties, but, as she said, there was always a snag.

'They're either right on a road, just under a huge great pylon, slap bang next to a pub, or next door to a quarry,' she had observed.

'Which is why they're still on the market, and stuck,' Millie had replied. 'It's very difficult to find anything round here because everything nice gets snapped up before it's even advertised. We're just going to have to pray to whoever the patron saint of estate agents is—'

'Croesus, perhaps?'

'—or hope that I hear about something before it hits the market.'

But they drew another blank that morning, finding something very wrong with each of the three properties they viewed. On top of that it was pouring with rain, which made the somewhat down-at-heel cottages look even more dismal as well as helping to compound Alice's belief that this was a wild and miserable goose chase.

'Come on,' she finally urged her friend. 'Take us to that nice pub near you and I'll buy us a cheery lunch.'

'You're on,' Millie replied. 'Then after that I'll drive us over to Rory's. He wants to run Trojan Jack again next week at Wincanton, so we might as well go and see how the old horse is. We promised we'd look in anyway, remember? When we were at Sandown.'

Just as Millie and Alice were disembarking outside the Cross Keys prior to enjoying the excellent lunch that was always available in the pub, Grenville Fielding was also about to eat. He was in the bar of the Wellington, one of his favourite lunchtime haunts, a small but smart hotel tucked away in a side street in Knightsbridge just behind Harrods, a venue that suited him not only because it served one of the best lunches in town, but also because it meant ease of shopping. Being a man, Grenville liked to be able to stroll into a store, buy everything he needed and then stroll off to lunch in the immediate vicinity. He had never been able to understand how women shopped. Pell-mell, rushing from one shop to another, and very often back again, never seeming to have a clue what it was they were meant to be buying.

Grenville's way was always to make a list before going on a shopping trip, often taking the extra precaution of telephoning the store in advance to make sure they had what he wanted in stock. It was only sensible. It saved time. It saved boredom. But women seemed to like to waste time; they even seemed to like boredom. Today, however, he had been too excited to visit any of his usual haunts. He was having lunch with Lynne.

He arrived at the Wellington a little early so that he might enjoy a quiet and private early gin and tonic to settle his nerves. Even as he was sipping from his glass in that rather surreptitious manner that lone drinkers develop, he found himself wondering how he had plucked up the courage to ask such a beautiful young woman out. It seemed to him it was as if he had been propelled by some unknown force. It had never happened before. He had never asked someone he had barely spoken to actually out on a date, as it were. After all, they had hardly exchanged more than a few words at the races, nothing more than the briefest of conversations, and yet within hours of wishing her *au revoir* he had found himself picking up the telephone to ask her out.

'I'm sorry, I don't know what you mean? You want to go on a date?'

'No – no, well yes, at least what I was wondering was whether we might have lunch? Pick up where we left off?' He cleared his throat. 'I could help you with your affairs, perhaps?' he added lamely.

'What sort of affairs?' Lynne had asked him, pretending to be shocked. 'A bit fresh, isn't it? I mean I've only been divorced a couple of minutes.'

'No, look, I'm sorry, that's not exactly what I meant.'

'It's all right. I'm only joking.' She must have guessed how disconcerted he felt, because her next words sounded part maternal and part contrite. 'Of course I would like you to look after my affairs, and have lunch.'

As he put down the receiver Grenville found himself smiling in a way, now he looked back on the moment, he might not have ever smiled before, except perhaps when he was given a bicycle on his sixth birthday. She had accepted his invitation, and he knew he was done for, perhaps for ever.

But now she was late.

He tried not to look at his watch. Of course ladies were

always late, and he had half expected she might be, because even with his limited experience with members of the opposite sex he prided himself on spotting the sort of person they might or might not be, and he had certainly marked this particular card down as *perhaps a little disorganised*. So he wasn't surprised. Of course not. He just wished that she would arrive.

He stopped looking at his watch, and settled for staring at the clock behind the bar. She was now nearing his maximum patience point, and that was half an hour late. Half an hour was the very longest time he could be expected to remain waiting for a guest.

He ran through the telephone conversation in his head. She had seemed to have accepted his invitation not only readily but happily, so to have been stood up made him feel not only rejected but dejected. It had meant nothing to her.

Someone arrived by his side. A waiter.

'Mr Fielding? A young lady has just telephoned to send her apologies and to say that unfortunately she will not be able to meet you for lunch.'

'I see. Thank you. Did she happen to say – did she happen to say why?'

'No, sir. She simply asked me to convey her apologies.'

Grenville leafed through his diary, found her number, and went to the public box in the hall to telephone her. He got her answering machine. Without leaving any message he returned to the bar and immediately ordered another gin and tonic.

She had been at the doorway of her flat and just about to leave when the panic had set in. It had been as unexpected as a sudden spasm of pain, hitting her without warning as she was just about to pull the door closed behind her. The next thing Lynne had known, she was sitting trembling in a chair with her head in her hands. Later she would vaguely remember making a telephone call but at that moment she could think of nothing other than trying to control the deep and totally unreasonable fear that had her in its grip. She thought she heard the telephone ringing and her own muffled voice saying something as the answerphone kicked in, but she was totally incapable of getting up to answer it herself. All she knew was that somehow she had to pull herself together and try with all her might to return to her previous state of perfect sanity.

She could recall perfectly standing in front of the full length mirror fixed inside the wardrobe to check how she looked before going out; she remembered looking into her handbag to make sure she had enough money and her door keys; she knew she had taken one last look at herself in the small mirror hanging in the hallway and smiled at herself because she thought that she didn't look at all bad, that in fact she really did actually look on top of it all; but that was all. She couldn't remember with any definition at all what had happened after that, in the moments that had taken her from standing at the door of the flat to sitting in a chair, for some reason frightened out of her wits.

Had someone been outside? Had she seen something dreadful or had someone perhaps threatened her and she had fled, banging the front door behind her and locking herself in for safety? She took her hands from her eyes and stared round the room and then out into the hallway, where she saw that far from being locked closed the front door was wide open. Lynne sat looking at the open door knowing that she should get up and shut it but unable to move, still petrified with fear. *But why?* she wondered. Why was she panic-stricken? Was the person she had seen, this someone who had obviously frightened her, inside the flat? But if so, why was the door still open and why was she free? Surely if someone was attacking her or robbing her they would have shut the door and rendered her helpless, instead of leaving her sitting in a chair with an open door in sight? There seemed to be no sense to it at all, no rhyme, no reason. What could have happened to her in the moments between opening the door and finding herself sitting shaking and nauseous in this chair?

After a long time, a length of time that Lynne couldn't possibly quantify, she found she had come back to her senses, seemingly as suddenly as she had lost them. She knew what had happened – she had panicked. In fact, she thought to herself, I think they even have a name for it now. A panic attack. She'd suffered a panic attack, in exactly the same way as the people she had read about only recently in some paper or magazine or other. She had been on her way out to lunch, something to which she thought she had been looking forward, when all at once she knew she just couldn't go through with it. She remembered standing in the open doorway suddenly feeling sick and dizzy and unable to do anything else except go on standing there feeling sick and dizzy. Someone had walked by her to the lift, a total stranger who Lynne remembered had just stared at her, saying nothing. The woman had kept throwing curious glances back at Lynne, still standing marooned in the door of her flat, as she waited for the lift. Then the lift had arrived and the woman had disappeared, which was when Lynne had finally summoned up enough strength to go back inside her apartment and lower her shaking frame into an armchair.

'Come on, girl,' she now found herself muttering. 'Come on – this won't do at all. This won't do one bit. Where were you going anyway? What was it that made you feel like this? You were only going out to lunch. That's all you were doing,' she repeated slowly. 'You were only going out to lunch.'

That was when she remembered making the telephone call. Lynne turned her head to stare at the telephone as if in hope that somehow the instrument would help unravel the next part of the mystery.

'My God,' she whispered miserably as another piece fell into place. 'Grenville. It was Grenville, poor bloke. Oh, poor Grenville. He deserves better than that. No way does he deserve to be stood up.'

Yet there was no way that she could have kept her date, not feeling like this. If by some miracle she had actually managed to get as far as the restaurant she knew she'd have only made a fool of herself, either by bursting into tears or by collapsing, which was not like her at all; but she knew something like that would have happened because whatever had been holding her together wasn't doing the trick any more. The elastic had suddenly snapped and gone.

Lynne spent the next few minutes sitting breathing in and out as deeply as she could, which was something she remembered being recommended in the article she had read about this sort of anxiety attack, and then, once she had all but stopped trembling, she went and made herself a cup of strong coffee.

'Poor Grenville,' she thought aloud once more. 'What can he be thinking? What could I have been thinking? Of all the people to stand up.' She shook her head sadly as she took her coffee back into the living room. She'd been looking forward to having lunch with Grenville, had been flattered when he'd asked her so unexpectedly to have lunch with him after they had met at the races. She'd never gone out with anyone of Grenville's class before and she sensed that he would treat her very well, in complete contrast with the way Gerry had treated her. Gerry had always behaved as if Lynne was the lucky one, lucky to be there, lucky to be part of Gerry's world, to be allowed to share certain moments of his life, and most lucky of all to have been allowed to be Gerry Fortune's wife.

There'd been no give and take in their marriage – at least, there had been, but it had always been Lynne doing the giving and Gerry doing all the taking. She sensed that Grenville was absolutely not that sort of man; that he was the very opposite, in fact, which was why she had been so looking forward to their date, particularly because she knew Grenville was the sort of man whom Gerry would take one look at and write off as *a bit of a ponce*.

As she sat drinking her strong black coffee and trying to pull herself together, she reflected on quite how hard she had been hit by Gerry's infidelity. She had felt humiliated, deceived, betrayed and cheated and those, she decided ruefully, were not good feelings. She had loved Gerry. She knew he could be mouthy, and she knew he could get a bit rough sometimes, but when he wanted to be, Gerry could be fun, and that, Lynne decided, was what made his treachery even worse. The fact that they had had fun together. But the fun ended the day she caught him with Maddy, when she finally discovered the real Gerry, a man who could obviously lie about anything and everything. And that meant, to her way of thinking, that when he had said he was having fun with her he might just as well have been lying. And when he had said that he loved her, that he really fancied her, that she was just the greatest and most gorgeous thing on two legs, he could have been lying as well. Everything about him and everything to do with their life together could have been a lie, and if he were to deny it now and tell her to her face that it just wasn't true, who was to say that he wouldn't be lying then as well?

After her divorce had been granted Lynne had felt a sense of euphoria, but that had quickly evaporated and she had found herself starting to suffer from what she understood others called *the come-down*. She'd learned that dealing with a divorce was very like dealing with a death – not of someone but of something, a trust, a love, a union. She had read that when people got divorced the innocent party often went through exactly the same range of emotions that people go through when they lose a loved one – release and a sort of euphoria, the process of depression and guilt, then anger and helplessness before they start to rebuild. Now her own marriage was over Lynne was beginning to see how much truth there was in this theory.

'Fine,' she suddenly announced out of the blue. 'But that's all done and dusted now, and you are certainly not going to sit here feeling sorry for yourself for the rest of your life, my girl. What's done is done and where you are right now you do not want to be. So take a deep breath – and get on with it! You have got to get *on* with your life, and getting on with it starts right here.'

With that she went and repaired her make-up, left the flat, hailed a taxi in the Brompton Road and ordered it to take her to the King's Road, where she shopped almost until she dropped. On her return home, with designer bags full of yet more new clothes and shoes, she poured herself a glass of cold white wine, took several more deep breaths, then made a telephone call.

She also got an answering machine, but unlike the man she had stood up she left a message.

'It's me – Lynne – and please listen. I am terribly sorry about lunchtime, Grenville. But I can explain, and I'd really like to – so look, why don't you let me buy you lunch in return for standing you up, and maybe we can start again. If you don't want to I'll quite understand, fair enough and all that, but if it's all right then give us a ring back and we'll make a date.'

Her phone rang almost as soon as she replaced the receiver and Grenville and she made a date not for lunch but for dinner that very evening.

*   *   *

'You couldn't have come at a better time, actually,' Rory said, when he greeted Alice and Millie in the yard that afternoon. 'As you know, Millie, we generally work the horses in the morning, but the farrier was late this morning – had a shunt in his car – so everything was put on hold.'

'Why does that make this a good time?' Millie asked.

'Because we're just about to work old Jack now, so if you hop in the back we'll go up to the gallops.'

'Just don't forget I have a train to catch,' Alice murmured to Millie as they dutifully climbed into the back of Rory's old Range Rover and took their seats alongside his dog Dunkum, among an assortment of old racing papers, sweet wrappers and much other ancient detritus.

'If the balance of your mind really is still that disturbed, I will try to remember,' Millie replied, giving her a look.

'I'll be back as soon as maybe. I was strong-armed into it. You know that.'

Actually they both knew it. Georgina had rung every day to work on her mother to come back up to Richmond to babysit for her, and finally, as always, Alice had relented.

'Anything for a quiet life,' she'd sighed, giving Millie a craven look when she'd finally had to confess she had conceded. 'You know how it is. If I don't agree, I shall rue it for the rest of the year, or possibly even the century. She'll stop me seeing the grandchildren, or move to Albania, or something!'

'The sooner *you* move down *here*, the better . . .'

'Your horse did a good bit of work two days ago,' Rory now said to Millie, as they drove up the steep track that led to the gallops. 'If he doesn't do anything too stupid this afternoon, I'd say we really should run him again at Wincanton.'

'You're the boss,' Millie said, doing up her coat tightly in preparation for braving the elements on the hill, as Rory slowed the car to a halt. 'Who's that?' She pointed to a tall patrician figure standing with another man, both of them with race glasses hung round their necks. 'Some of your other owners?'

'Someone who rents the gallops,' Rory replied, getting out of the car. 'Trains near by.'

As the three of them walked across to where the other trainer was standing, they heard him calling to his owner.

'Here they come now!' he was shouting, pointing to a line of horses just cresting the hill, still some quarter of a mile from them. 'They'll be coming up and past. Yours should be leading, and if he's not there will be questions asked.'

Everyone watched in interest as the line of horses drew nearer. The air that had been absolutely quiet except for the sighing of the wind became full of the thunder of horses' hooves, a noise that grew louder and louder as the line of galloping racehorses came up to where the five of them were standing and pounded past them, rugs flapping in the wind, work riders crouched over their mounts' necks, reins threaded lightly through skilled fingers, balance perfect, half standing in their irons with their eyes fixed firmly on their chosen point, and then they were gone, the horses' hooves fast becoming a faint and distant rumble.

'Jolly good,' the trainer said, a hand cupped over his eyes to shield them from the afternoon sun. 'Looked good, your chap. Strode out nicely, I thought. We'll go and hear what his lad has to say.'

Sticking a cigarette firmly back in his mouth, the tall, hawk-faced man was about to return to his car, parked just behind him, when he was stopped by a shout from a man coming up fast on horseback.

'Henry?' cried the rider, a small man in riding-out clothes, with an uncovered race helmet strapped under his chin.

'Sorry about that, chum! I sent my string up first because one of yours has got loose and is still about at the bottom of the gallops on the road! Hope you didn't mind!'

Then he was gone, cantering off after his string on his old hack.

Alice stared after the retreating male figures as Rory and Millie turned away, their shoulders shaking.

'I don't understand,' she began.

'It wasn't his string,' Millie replied, poker-faced. 'He was watching another trainer's horses.'

'Easily done,' Rory added, shaking his head. 'When I began helping Dad, I tried to saddle up the wrong horse at Fontwell once. Two greys, couldn't tell a spit of difference between any of them. At least I couldn't. Ah. Here come ours – at least, after all that, I hope they're ours!'

Rory pointed to a distant line of horses thundering up the gallops and raised his glasses to watch the horses go past, all except one which cantered by about a dozen lengths or so adrift of the others.

'Wasn't that Jack?' Millie said, pointing at the straggler who was now pulling himself up, opting to stop and eat grass rather than bother with any more work, in spite of his rider's clearly strenuous efforts to get his head back up off the ground.

'There is a possibility,' Rory admitted. 'He doesn't always put his best feet forward up the hill. A morning glory he is *not*.'

The three of them wandered over to where the unwilling horse was still happily grazing, ignoring all the slaps Teddy was delivering to his rump.

'OK,' Rory said as he came alongside the horse and rider. 'So did he do anything right?'

'Not a damned thing, boss,' a still out of breath Teddy replied. 'Got one of his stay abed days on. Come on, you idle bugger! Stop eating that grass!'

Again, in spite of the directions and reminders he was getting from his pilot, Trojan Jack remained happily grazing, until, unable to put up with any more rib-kicking and rump-smacking, suddenly and without any notice whatsoever he put in a massive buck, ejected his pilot and with a flash of flying hind feet bolted off in the wake of his distant stablemates.

'I think I'll take up rocket science instead,' Rory said, turning away with a shake of his head. 'It has to be easier than this.'

They arrived back in the yard well ahead of the string, which was being walked steadily back from the gallops. Alice asked permission to wander around the yard while Rory and Millie tried to form some kind of game plan concerning the errant Trojan Jack. She declined Rory's offer of refreshment, as she was anxious not to miss her train from Salisbury.

With an anxious glance up at the stable clock, Alice decided to fill in the time before leaving by looking round the top yard. As she walked into the yard she heard the sound of music from somewhere and traced it to a cassette player that was hanging outside one of the boxes. Curious as to who might be listening to this fine Irish tenor she looked into the stable and found herself being stared at by a small lop-eared horse that was standing to the side of the door munching contentedly on a mouthful of hay.

'You like this, do you?' she said, as the tenor began to sing 'The Star of the County Down'. 'This is your sort of thing, is it?'

The horse continued to watch her, still chewing slowly.

'You have lovely eyes,' Alice murmured to him. 'You really do have the most lovely, lovely eyes.'

After more mutual staring the animal slowly laid back his ears and equally slowly curled back his top lip, as if giving her a smile. Alice laughed in delight, taking the expression at face value, whereupon the horse curled his lip back even more, revealing a large expanse of bright pink gum, a sight so comical that Alice found herself laughing even more. The horse immediately disappeared back into the darkness of its box, and Alice stopped laughing, afraid that her laughter had upset him. Not a bit of it, it seemed, since the horse reappeared as quickly as he had disappeared, with a new slice of wet hay which he then proceeded to shake so thoroughly that drops of water as well as loose bits of forage flew all over Alice.

'Where's the party?' Millie enquired from behind her, having come to look for her. 'You found a new friend?'

'Just look at this horse, Millie.' Alice sighed. 'Isn't he lovely?'

'Could be a she.'

'He isn't. He's a he. Isn't he lovely?'

'He's certainly not enormous.'

'Looks big enough to me.'

'Yes, but then you're not exactly tall, ducks. Come on – we have a train to miss.'

'I think there's something rather special about him, don't you?' Alice continued, staying when she should be moving on. 'He's got very wise eyes. And any horse that listens to John McCormack has my vote.'

'Is that who this is?' Millie was looking up at the cassette player. 'I thought it was that man who used to sing on the TV in a cardigan.'

'You have such a tin ear, Millie. But then you always did have, even at school. I wonder who actually owns this fellow?'

'Ask Rory – here cometh the man now.'

'No one owns him,' Rory told them. 'Yet. He's a newcomer.'

'You mean he's for sale?' Alice asked.

'I think I'm probably going to end up having to give him away.'

'Why? Isn't he any good?'

'I don't know how good or how bad he is,' Rory replied. 'He's a long way off any serious work. He can jump, though. That I can vouch for.'

'So how much would a horse like this cost?' Alice persisted.

'Your train, sweetie?' Millie said, touching her arm.

'Seriously, Mr Rawlins.'

'Rory.'

'How much would he cost, actually?'

Rory looked at her, frowning, not thinking for one second that Alice could be seriously considering buying herself a racehorse, but even so, he knew that when it came to owners he had to watch what he said. If he named too low a price she might repeat the figure to someone who *was* thinking of buying a horse. There again if he quoted too high a price the same thing might happen, but this time it might deter any potential buyer.

'As he stands, that is as an unknown quantity – although he's young so he's got all that going for him, as well as having no miles on the clock – we certainly wouldn't ask anything less than fifteen thousand.'

'Fifteen thousand. I see.' Alice nodded, trying not to look either shocked or surprised. 'But then that's quite cheap for a racehorse, isn't it? Not that I'm thinking of buying one, of course.'

'Alice,' Millie reminded her. 'Not that I mind if you miss your damned train, but just in case you do, by my reckoning it is about to leave the station.'

'I read that some sheikh or another only recently paid over a quarter of a million pounds for a horse.'

'Guineas,' Millie told her in a kind voice. 'And that was for a stallion that had some rather good races. Now come along.'

'I was only asking, Millie,' Alice protested as she found herself being bundled into the car. 'There's really no harm in asking.'

All the way up to London Alice found herself thinking about the little liver chestnut horse she'd just seen. Not that she herself actually thought of him as being particularly small, since she didn't really know what size racehorses were meant to be, but she did think him odd; this was not anything to do with his conformation or appearance in general, but it most certainly had something to do with his appearance in the particular. It had to do with his eyes, the eyes that had watched her so closely, the eyes into which she had stared and by which she had found herself transfixed.

I know what it is, she suddenly said to herself. *Of course. I know just what it is. He's been here before. He's been here – before.*

The delight of her fanciful notion carried Alice through her babysitting, not that she needed any such mental distraction as far as her grandchildren were concerned. She adored them wholeheartedly, although like so many other women of her generation she privately considered that they were allowed to spend too much time in front of the television. As usual she turned the set off as soon as Georgina and Joe had left the house for the evening, and in spite of Will and Finty's protests she read to them instead. After only a few minutes their tantrums abated, thumbs and sucky blankets went into mouths and they happily listened to nearly an hour of stories before drifting off into blissful sleep. Nothing more was heard of them all evening. Alice checked them before turning in herself, but the two children were still sound asleep.

*   *   *

'What's that tie you're wearing, Grenville?' Lynne wondered, as she finished her smoked salmon first course at dinner that evening. 'Were you in the army?'

'MCC,' Grenville told her, trying not to smile. 'The Marylebone Cricket Club.'

'Really? I didn't know they had a club,' Lynne said with a frown. 'Where do they play? Down the High Street?'

'Oh, very good.' Grenville laughed, seeing it as a joke, while all the time trying to come to terms with the fact that it was actually Lynne sitting opposite him and not some illusion. He had already noted and been pleased to see the envious looks on the faces of several of the other male diners when Lynne had swept into the bar, looking like something that had just stepped out of a fashion magazine.

Maybe not quite Vogue, Grenville thought as he assessed what she was wearing. *Maybe a little bit more* Cosmopolitan *than* Vogue, *but who am I to criticise?*

'No, the MCC do not play down Marylebone High Street, Mrs Fortune,' he said with a smile.

'Lynne,' she interrupted him. 'Anyway, I'm not Mrs Fortune any longer. I'm back to being plain Miss Faraday.'

'Never plain and Miss is lovely. Just as long as you don't become Ms. Sounds like an abbreviation for miserable.'

'What do you do exactly, Grenville? If you don't mind me asking. I remember you saying you were helping Gerry with something to do with business, right?'

'I'm an investments manager, Lynne. In the private sector. Nothing to do with banks or anything. I work purely for myself, for my clients.'

'You managed Gerry's money, then?'

'I was helping him build a portfolio. But he . . . he didn't see it through.'

'Hope he didn't short-change you. He's pretty good at that. I shouldn't have said that, I suppose. Sorry.'

'You don't have to be sorry.'

'Sorry,' Lynne said, yet again. 'Anyway – you were saying you were going to help Gerry with his car businesses.'

'I was going to help him invest some of the proceeds, Lynne,' Grenville said, remembering how long Gerry had kept him waiting for his cheque, a cheque that when it finally arrived was a couple of hundred short. 'I think he simply decided to put his money elsewhere.'

'Right.' Lynne nodded, and sipped some champagne. 'Actually, I wouldn't mind some financial advice.'

'You have money to invest?'

'I have some money, Grenville. But I don't know about investing it. I quite enjoy spending it.'

Grenville nodded, took his glasses off and in order to buy a little time began cleaning them with the silk handkerchief from his top pocket. He knew plenty of ways to invest Lynne's money, mostly ways that would be highly advantageous to him, yet he found himself resisting for the first time ever.

'For the first time ever,' he said out loud.

'Come again?'

'Sorry,' Grenville said, replacing his glasses. 'Just thinking out loud. No, look – look, if you're enjoying yourself, provided you always leave yourself what my father used to call the rainy-day reserve for the times you may need a bit of money, if I were you I'd go on enjoying myself. After all, as someone once said, this life is not a dress rehearsal. I rather like that. Life's not a dress rehearsal. Rather good, that.'

'That's a bit what I feel now, Grenville,' Lynne admitted. 'I mean I was all over the shop when it happened, the divorce – you know. It was just something I wasn't prepared for.

Something I just hadn't imagined happening, fool that I was, and probably still am. But I'm sort of trying to get it together now and everything, and since I have I've started to think sod it – sorry. Sorry. I meant – I meant to hell with it. 'Cos just like you just said, this isn't some blooming dress rehearsal. I don't want to go through the rest of my life regretting not the things I've done but the things I haven't done. Know what I mean?'

'I do indeed, Lynne.' Grenville nodded solemnly. 'As they say nowadays, I hear what you're saying.'

Lynne gave him a shy smile, wondering how she was doing. She hoped she was keeping the ball in the air and convincing the man opposite her that she was one altogether together young woman, and not someone who was becoming increasingly certain that she was busy falling to pieces inside. If she could get him to believe that she was as fine as she knew she wasn't, then there was every chance she would convince herself.

The next morning, while their parents slept in after their late night, Alice got her grandchildren up, fed them their breakfast – which, strictly for her sake, she knew, they ate at the table – and knocked on Georgina's bedroom door to tell her she needed to be taken to the station to catch her train.

'Oh, listen,' a weary voice answered. 'OK if you take a taxi? We didn't get in till three, Mum. There's some money on the hall table.'

'What about the children?' Alice asked. 'They've had their breakfast.'

'Fine,' Georgina called back. 'Just give them each a bag of Cheerios – they're in the larder – and stick them in front of the telly. They'll be fine. Oh – and make sure you pull the front door shut behind you.'

'If that's what you want.' Alice pulled a face. 'As long as one of you is up and about to check them.'

'Mum,' came the familiar cry from the bedroom.

'OK. I have to go, Georgina.'

Having made sure there was something suitable for her grandchildren to watch on the television, Alice kissed them goodbye and took a taxi to the station, praying every inch of the way that no harm would come to them while their parents remained in bed sleeping off their late night. In the train she sat by a window watching the landscape gradually changing from urban to rural, and found herself enjoying the reverse of the feelings she normally experienced on such journeys: instead of leaving home to go somewhere, she now felt she was leaving somewhere to return home.

She thought about her family and wondered how she had come to let herself be persuaded to make such a long and tiring journey just to babysit, knowing perfectly well that Georgina could have easily found someone else. So why, she wondered, had Georgina insisted that Alice come up to babysit all the way from deepest Dorset? There could only have been one reason for the summons from Richmond, and that was that her daughter had *wanted* to interrupt Alice's holiday, just out of pique. She still wanted her mum at her beck and call.

Alice sighed, but it wasn't really a sigh of regret, rather one that could be taken to mark the end of something, a sigh of punctuation, the mark of coming to the end of a particular chapter, or perhaps even a book; and now she had finished that chapter or book she sensed there was a new one on the way.

An eye was looking into hers, a large round brown eye, and in it she could see a land under the sea. The waves were high above her, with a bright sun shining through them, while first one horse then many swam through water which was as clear as crystal with the most beautiful people she had ever seen riding them. They rode bareback and without bridles and now Alice was riding as well, through an underwater palace whose walls were hung with gold drapes and harps and swords that rested in jewelled sheaths. As she rode silently through the ocean there was nothing but a sense of peace and a fine voice singing a song in a tongue she didn't know, yet she thought she knew what the song was saying.

Her horse looked round at her and she saw herself in its eye, young again, a little girl in a gingham dress with her hair in plaits just the way she used to wear it, and on her feet red shoes that sparkled in the sunbeams.

She woke up just in time for Salisbury. People were already getting up from their seats in preparation for the train's pulling in to the station, but Alice just sat there, remembering the dream, determined never to forget it.

The two days of rain had stopped, so Millie and Alice drove through a rolling countryside warmed by late autumn sunshine, with a strong breeze making the clouds scud so that shadows flitted across the dark green hills. There was no traffic on the long sweeping road that went down into a valley then up and round a long barrow in front of them, so for a while it was as if they had both been transported back to a time when there was just the land, and the sky and the unseen sea beyond the hills. They drove in silence, hushed by the elegant majesty of the landscape.

Finally they found themselves not in Millie's hamlet but in the neighbouring picture-postcard village of Chalfont Magna.

'Hold your horses!' Millie stopped her car as she saw a man coming out of a thatched cottage at the top of the lane. 'I think I know him. Yes I do – and it's just the man we've been looking for – Mike? Michael?'

Seeing Millie becoming involved in talking to her acquaintance, Alice decided to stretch her legs, and take a better look
round the village. As she peered over garden walls and the
tops of gates it seemed to her to be an idyllic spot if not the
ideal one, peaceful and quiet, well away from any main roads
and miles from any flight paths. In fact every property she
saw seemed to be just the sort of small house or cottage for
which she had been searching, particularly the one she finally
found herself standing outside, the one up whose path Millie
stood talking to a short red-faced man in a lovat green tweed
suit.

'Of all the luck,' Millie said as she rejoined Alice in the road-
way. 'The man I've been talking to? He's only the bloke who
sold me *my* house, would you believe? And as luck would have
it he's just been taking instructions from the man who owns
that drop-dead-lovely cottage. Not only that, ducks: no one,
but no one else has seen it yet – and what is more and what is
best of all, we are allowed to look round it, right now!'

The old stone-built cottage was as lovely inside as it was
pretty outside, with plenty of exposed beams, open fireplaces
with fine old carved stone surrounds in the sitting and
dining rooms, a flagstone-floored kitchen with an Aga, four
surprisingly light and airy bedrooms, all of which enjoyed
views over the unspoilt rolling countryside, and a beautiful
acre of gardens that were laid to roses and lawn.

'You are going to have to buy it,' Millie whispered as they
walked round inspecting the outside. 'Because if you don't the
next person up the path most certainly will. It is *perfect. Quite
perfect.*'

'I'm about to do just that,' Alice assured her. 'Buy it, that is.
I think I'd be mad not to.'

'Bonkers,' Millie said with a broad smile, taking Alice's arm
for one more stroll around the gardens. 'And I would give

good money to see the look on your children's faces when you tell them.'

'But I'm only doing what they're always nagging me to do,' Alice replied. 'What is it they say? Getting a life.'

'Right on, sister.' Millie laughed. 'Let's hear it for the biddies.'

A brief discussion with the agent and the owner was all that was needed for parties to make their resolutions clear. Alice agreed to buy the cottage at the asking price, and would put down a deposit to secure it as soon as was necessary while she issued instructions to put her London house on the market. On learning exactly what sort of property Alice owned and its location, the estate agent told her his firm's London office would happily handle the sale, since they had a list of buyers looking for houses in that particular part of Kensington.

'Couldn't have worked out better,' Millie remarked as they drove away. 'It was as if it was meant.'

'So all I have to do now is to break the news to the family.'

'Any time, duck. There's no obligation, you know.'

'You're right.' Alice sighed. 'I still think of them as depending on me.'

'While they dread the likes of us depending on them.' Millie laughed. 'So come on – let's go and have a drink to celebrate. After all, it's not every day you get to turn your life around.'

Alice agreed, unable quite to believe the change in her fortunes, while all the time wondering whether the strange and wonderful dream she'd had on the train might in fact have more significance than she thought; that in some way it had told her about this very moment in her life.

Chapter Ten

Himself

Grenville arrived first. Rory found him wandering around the yard looking into the stables, gloved hands clasped behind his back, trilby tilted down to the edge of his spectacles, in the company of the glamorous young woman who had literally knocked Rory for six at Sandown.

'Could do with a few more residents, old man, yes?' Grenville remarked when accosted. 'Not that it's any of my business.'

'Correct,' Rory replied. 'Want to go on to the next round?'

'Seriously, Rory. With the old man laid up – how is he, by the way?'

'Making progress.'

'Good. Good. I'm sorry – allow me to introduce you to Mrs Fortune. Or rather Miss Faraday, as she wishes to be called now.'

Lynne turned round from her inspection of the horse stabled in the box in front of her and put a hand out to Rory.

'We've met. Hello again, Mr Rawlins. Great yard.'

'Nice of you to say so,' Rory replied, shaking the offered hand. 'But it's not really looking at its best.'

'Long as the horses are happy, that's all that matters. And they certainly look happy enough.'

'To get down to business, Rory,' Grenville chipped in, anxious to get to the point. 'And racing is a business. With the old chap laid up, Rory, you could really roll up your shirtsleeves and get to work here. First of all, you could have an Open Day. You know, let Joe Public in to ooh and aah. Never know what the tide might bring in.'

'With the number of horses we have in training, Grenville, they'd be here for all of five minutes.'

'Do what some of 'em do over at Lambourn, in that case.' Grenville lowered his voice. 'Borrow a few nags from your neighbours and pretend they're yours. Fill the yard and say they're all spoken for, then along comes Bob your famous uncle. Shove a few geraniums about the place, couple of hanging baskets, you can even borrow some staff from your chums, too. Works wonders. Appearances are everything, as you know, old chap. Even if they do turn out to be mirages.'

'Not exactly my style, Grenville,' Rory replied. 'And can you imagine if my father found out?'

'Just a thought,' Grenville said, taking his hat off and carefully removing a small piece of straw from the brim. 'What about this famous horse, then? I like the look of that big bay in the second box.'

'That's not him, Grenville. That's Tiger Talk. And as a matter of fact I'd far rather you saw the horse when he's fitter. He's only just arrived and we're – we're still acclimatising him.'

'Do I hear music?' Grenville wondered, looking round. 'Who's that singing somewhere? Sounds like John McCormack.'

'The lads play the radio when they're doing the grooming and mucking out,' Rory said quickly. 'They say the horses like it.'

'My mother *loves* John McCormack.' Grenville smiled. 'Daddy did as well. But look. Look, now I'm here and since I've come all this way, you might as well let me just have a quick dekko.'

'I thought you said you had to come down this way anyway,' Rory said, continuing to try to stall him. 'I'd quite like a cup of tea, and I'm sure you both would as well, then perhaps I'll give you a guided tour afterwards.'

'I'd love a cuppa,' Lynne put in quickly, sensing that Rory wanted to tread water for a little.

'Of course,' Grenville replied politely, offering Lynne his arm. 'But I really would like to see what you've got afterwards, Rory. Now I *have* come all this way.'

'Teddy?' Rory hissed at his head lad, dropping back as the others made for the house. 'While we're inside, pile the little horse's box as high as you can with fresh straw, and don't ask why. OK?'

'He's just had a fresh bed, boss,' Teddy replied. 'I only just skipped him out.'

'That's not what I'm saying, Teddy,' Rory insisted. 'What I'm saying is bulk the horse's bedding up as high as you can.'

'Ah,' Teddy said with a nod. 'I hear you, boss. Gotcha.'

'What one would dearly like is what's known in the trade as a *fun* horse,' Grenville said as they sat having tea in Rory's seriously untidy kitchen. 'A horse that will provide the necessary entertainment without necessarily breaking the bank.'

'Really?' Lynne said, dropping two sweeteners into her mug of tea. 'I'd have thought if you were getting a horse you'd want one with a blooming good chance of winning. Sorry, but I mean that's what I'd want.'

'I didn't know you wanted a horse, Lynne?' Grenville looked vaguely unsettled, as if she had been keeping something from him. As far as he could make out Lynne had only accepted his invitation to come down to the country because she wanted to look at some apartments that were for sale in a large country house that had recently been converted into flats.

'I don't,' Lynne replied. 'That was – what do they call it? A something or other.'

'An hypothesis?'

'If you say so. Who knows what I might buy next?' Lynne looked at Grenville, before starting to sip her tea. 'The world is my oyster, right?'

When they had finished their tea and Teddy had done the bed, Rory took the two of them round the yard and showed them three of the horses he knew the owners were keen to sell. Grenville failed to be taken by any of them, spinning all three for elaborate reasons that smacked to Rory of being straight out of the a-little-knowledge-is-a-dangerous-thing school of equine thought.

Finally, he showed them The Enchanted.

'The Enchanted?' Lynne said, taking an interest for the first time. 'What a great name for a horse. You call him that?'

'He was named that when my father bought him,' Rory said. 'Something to do with some old Gaelic myth or other.'

'The Enchanted,' Lynne repeated, looking over the stable door at a horse that thanks to Teddy's constructive bed-building looked considerably taller than he had before. 'I think that's a winning name.'

'There's not exactly a lot of him, is there, Rory?' Grenville turned back to look at the trainer. 'Hardly an Aintree type.'

'But then he was hardly bought for that,' Rory said defensively. 'Although a horse that won the National just before the last war – Battleship, I think it was – was only just over fifteen hands, my father said.'

'Can we see him out of the box?'

'Yes, of course, I'll have him taken out for you,' Rory replied, unable to think of a good reason to refuse. 'If you go and stand in the school over there I'll have the girl lead him round.'

'What? Over there?' Grenville said. 'I'd quite like to see him led out from here.'

'He's still a little skittish,' Rory lied, crossing his fingers. 'I'd hate to see him take a lump out of Miss Faraday here.'

'He moves well enough,' Grenville observed as Pauline, the most diminutive of Rory's skeleton stable staff, trotted the horse up and past them. 'Gets his hind legs under him.'

'I don't understand. Where else would he put them, Grenville?' Lynne puzzled. 'Bit odd if he got them over him.'

'It's an equine expression, Lynne,' Grenville explained. 'Like the way this horse covers the ground, do you see? For a smaller sort of horse he walks out well and covers a lot of ground. You want a horse that covers the ground well, and picks his feet up, as this chap's doing. He's nice and short-coupled, too, and not over at the knee.'

'All Greek to this lady,' Lynne said with a shake of her head. 'You are speaking complete Greek to me.'

'Let's see him stand up, if we may?' Grenville called out to the lass. 'If you could stand him up just there, please – I'd like to come and pick up his feet, if that's all right, Rory?'

'Your call, Grenville,' Rory replied. 'Just watch the sharp end.'

'I understand that bit all right,' Lynne said. 'Hope you know what you're doing, Grenville.'

'I was brought up with horses, Lynne,' Grenville assured her. 'No worries.'

He went up to the horse, which was standing eyeing him with half-flattened ears. He walked round him twice, nodding to himself, then walked round him twice in the opposite direction. Behind his back the horse kicked out, narrowly missing him.

'Change of rein there, I see,' Rory called out. 'Even a change of leg perhaps.'

'Got a good shoulder on him,' Grenville called back, ignoring the tease. 'Stands into himself well.'

Rory winked at Lynne, who smiled back at him.

'Nice and high in the wither as well,' Grenville continued, bending down to pick up and flex one of the horse's fore legs. When he replaced it he ran one hand down the back of it as he had often observed horse people doing when inspecting possible purchases.

'Find anything?' Rory called out.

'Got plenty of bone as well.' Grenville nodded. 'What's he got, Rory? Seven? Eight inches?'

'Haven't measured, Grenville,' Rory replied, exchanging another look with Lynne, who came over to stand beside him.

'I think he's a smashing little horse,' she said. 'Just gorgeous. Not that I know a thing about horses.'

'Long as you like him,' Rory returned. 'But a little less of the little, if you don't mind.'

'I only mean that affectionately,' Lynne said, taking him seriously. 'I haven't a clue what size a horse should be. I just think there's something about him.' She blushed a little as Rory turned to look at her. 'I mean it. He's got sort of – I don't know what they call it. When a horse looks a bit special.'

'The horse has presence.'

'That's it exactly.' Lynne nodded. 'That's exactly what this horse has got. Presence.' She looked back at the horse and found she was being stared at in return.

'I'd say the feeling's mutual,' Rory told her, nodding towards The Enchanted.

'Is he cantering, Rory?' Grenville asked, still walking round the horse.

'Not at the moment, he isn't,' Lynne muttered, with a sideways smile at Rory.

'He's in light work,' Rory called across to him. 'And he's working fine.'

'And he's really done relatively nothing?'

'Hardly any miles on the clock at all. Run in a point and a hunter chase – both of which he should have won, apparently.'

'Ah.' Grenville nodded, coming to join Rory and Lynne. 'That old that-old. Ah.' Grenville took his hat off, wiped his brow, nodded again, then replaced his hat. 'Fine. No, I think I'll pass on this one, Rory, thanks – if it's all the same to you.'

'Your choice,' Rory said. 'You're the expert.'

'Even so.' Grenville smiled, nodding once more. 'I think I'll pass just the same.'

'Well, if you don't want him, I think I'll buy him,' Lynne said suddenly.

'Lynne?' Grenville turned and attempted a businesslike look. 'What did you say?'

'Hang on, Grenville,' Lynne said, turning to Rory once more. 'Just for fun – if I was to buy him, just for fun, what would it cost me?'

'Lynne?' Grenville tried again, but Lynne wasn't listening.

Rory paused, cleared his throat and looked into the pair of bright blue eyes that were looking into his. Again he found himself between the notorious rock and a hard place. If he said too much he might put her off, whereas if he asked too little away would go the profit all trainers must make when selling on a horse.

'Just for fun?' he wondered, buying a little time.

'Just for fun. How much would a horse like this cost?'

'Fifteen thousand.'

Grenville gave a small but significant whistle while Lynne's eyes widened to the full.

'Fifteen thousand – what, fifteen thousand pounds?' she echoed. 'God, I'm a right charley. I thought a horse like this in a place like this would cost, I don't know – a couple of grand, tops.'

Rory shook his head sadly and heaved a deep sigh. 'It's fifteen thousand guineas. And you could hardly buy a decent riding horse for two thousand now,' he said.

'Right,' Lynne agreed. 'I said I was a charley. Oh well.' She shrugged and buttoned up her coat as if that was the conclusion of any possible further business. 'A girl can dream, I suppose.'

'There's more than one way of skinning the famous cat,' Rory said lightly, sensing her very real disappointment. 'You could get up a partnership. That's what a lot of people do. Buy a leg, as they say. Find three others to come in with you – to buy the other three legs. That's what a lot of people like yourself do to have a bit of fun, to have an interest, as it were.'

'Really?' Lynne's blue eyes came alight once more. 'I see. You mean sharesville?'

'Sharesville. Precisely. And a lot of people do it.'

'Lynne?' Grenville said in a tone with a distinct warning note. 'Lynne?'

'Go on, Mr Rawlins,' Lynne continued, ignoring her escort. 'So what would that mean?'

'If you were serious,' Rory replied, 'and if you could find three other people, and if, say, I let you have the horse for twelve K, that would be three thousand one hundred and fifty guineas a leg, plus training and racing costs.'

'Which costs will run out to at least a hundred guineas a

month per share,' Grenville chipped in. 'So you would have to think *pretty* carefully, Lynne.'

'I think I could afford that, Grenville. Easily, in fact. Particularly since it would be fun, which is something I have been a bit short of recently. Wonder who else would go sharesville?'

Both Rory and she pretended to think deeply; then they both turned to look at Grenville.

'Now wait a minute, one and all . . .' he stammered.

'All that stuff you were saying just now?' Lynne asked him overseriously. 'About how he covered the ground so nicely, and got his legs under him, and stood up to his withers and all, and how he's got these huge bones—'

'We'd still have to find two other people, my dear.'

'But you just said you were thinking of buying a horse. I mean otherwise why did you come down here? You just said you wanted to buy a *fun* horse, wasn't it? Right?'

'Yes,' Grenville said uneasily. 'But I just spun this one.'

'Spun?'

'Said thank you but no thank you, Lynne.'

'We won't hold it against you,' Rory said. 'In fact we'll pretend you never said it.'

'That's right, Rory,' Lynne agreed. 'That's what we'll do.'

'Good,' Rory said. 'That's exactly what we'll do. While if you refuse, Mr Fielding . . .' Rory teased, wagging a schoolteacher's finger at him.

'Right,' Lynne said with a grin, following suit.

Grenville smiled weakly back and nodded once again. He found himself in a dilemma. By now he was so taken with Lynne that the last thing he wanted was to lose the pleasure of her company. Since the horrendously painful experience of his broken engagement to Jane some twelve years earlier he had never enjoyed any sort of medium- let alone long-term relationship with a member of the opposite sex, and not even a short-term one with a member of the opposite sex as gloriously attractive and glamorous as Miss Lynne Faraday. If he were now to refuse a share in this little racehorse with which she had suddenly become so enamoured, he knew it could easily spell the end of any chance he might have of extending this burgeoning friendship, particularly if she went ahead and formed a partnership to buy the horse, since chances were she might well meet someone else infinitely more attractive and personable than he. Yet as he knew – something of which he now felt properly ashamed – he'd only really brought Lynne down to Rory's yard to try to win a few Brownie points, or in other words to show off, hoping that by airing his knowledge of the horse world but spinning anything Rory might have to offer he would succeed in impressing her.

But now it all seemed to have backfired, and to such an extent that he was going to have to dig deep into his pockets to finance a quarter-share in a horse that he considered had as much chance of winning a race as he had of landing a Hollywood contract.

'Look,' he said finally. 'This is lovely. A lovely idea altogether, but one we should perhaps talk over between us.'

'Why?' Lynne wondered. 'I mean, sorry, but it's not as if we're contracted to each other in any way. My money is my money to do what I like with, if you know what I mean. No offence and everything, but really, if I feel like blowing it all in one sort of great big spending spree, then the only person I've got to answer to is me. Really, isn't it? Sorry. But you know what I mean.'

'I do,' Grenville agreed, feeling himself beginning to redden under the collar. 'I was only trying to help. Explain all the ins and outs. Owning a racehorse is not as easy as it sounds. Perhaps on the way back to town I can explain exactly all the whys and wherefores.'

'Well of course you can, Grenville, because that's something you're good at.' Lynne nodded seriously. 'But I doubt it'll make much difference 'cos this is something I really think I might like to do. OK? So when you're ready and everything, you promised me we could have a look at those apartments on the way home.'

With one last look at the new object of her affection, who was standing nearby pushing his groom in the back with his muzzle, Lynne said goodbye to Rory and walked off towards Grenville's car. Rory followed them, saw them off, instructed Pauline to put Boyo back in his stable, and prepared to leave for the hospital to visit his father, unconvinced by anything that he had heard. Lynne was obviously a nice young woman at a loose end, and Grenville was clearly besotted with her, but he would talk her out of it on the way to see the flats. Rory was quite sure of it, which, he thought ruefully later, once again only went to show how little trainers know not only about their horses but about those who own them.

Constance Frimley was walking her neighbour's dogs in the square when Grenville finally returned from his day in the country, having dropped Lynne off at her London rental. Contrary to Rory's belief, Grenville had been completely unsuccessful in talking Lynne out of buying the horse, or forming a partnership. In fact the more he had told Lynne about the ups and downs of racing, the more fun she declared it sounded. Even her decision to rent the apartment in the large house she had inspected on the borders of Hampshire and Wiltshire after leaving Rory's yard had not deterred her. On learning roughly what the rent on the large, unfurnished apartment might be on the pretext that a relative of his was looking for exactly the same sort of accommodation, Grenville had hoped the cost of the place might finally dampen her enthusiasm, but since this was not the case he could only conclude that Lynne must have more money than sense. Furthermore, she had given him every indication that if he didn't want to join the racing partnership he would have to expect to see very little of her, because she would be spending so much time on the gallops and going racing. Although that had been more of a tease than an ultimatum, Grenville reflected as he locked up his car in his resident's parking bay, if he wanted to continue to see the gorgeous Miss Faraday it looked as though he would have to declare himself in and put his winter skiing holiday on hold for at least a year.

'Good evening, Lady Frimley,' he greeted his neighbour politely, having every intention to hit and run. 'Bit of a chill about it, alas.'

'Been racing again, Mr Fielder?' Constance remarked, having noticed the binoculars slung over one of Grenville's shoulders. 'Quite the sportsman.'

'No, no, Lady Frimley, been down to my trainer's,' he replied. 'Down to watch gallops – and it's *Fielding*, Lady Frimley. Not Fielder.'

'We galloped, Dick galloped, we galloped all three,' Constance replied vaguely, reining in her two small canine charges. 'We had racehorses, once upon a once. In the dim and distant.'

'Did you now?' Grenville wondered, suddenly interested, seeing a window of opportunity open. 'Do well? Were they any good?'

'Arthur Budge-Thomas used to train for us.' Constance avoided the question. 'Frightfully nice man, if I remember correctly.'

'Hence your interest in the horse, obviously,' Grenville continued, falling into step alongside Constance as, having locked the garden gate behind her, she began to head for home. 'Something that never leaves one, yes?'

'I dare say, if you say so,' Constance replied. 'I find the older I get the less need I have for opinions.'

'True, Lady Frimley, very true.'

They stopped when they reached Constance's front door, and she handed him the two dog leads while she fished in her bag for her key.

'I'm off racing on Thursday, as it happens,' Grenville said carefully. 'A friend's got a runner at Wincanton.'

'Never been there,' Constance said, having located her key. 'Wouldn't even know where it was.'

'Charming course in the west country. Perhaps if you'd like another day out, Lady Frimley . . .'

'Perhaps.' Constance nodded. 'Thank you. But only if you don't drive too fast. You know how I cannot abide this modern habit of driving at absurd speeds.'

'Once again I shall be a maiden aunt behind the wheel, Lady Frimley,' Grenville assured her. 'Shall we say ten o'clock?'

It was raining heavily at Wincanton, sheets of water being driven across the course by the prevailing westerly directly into the faces of any racegoers brave enough to take the grandstands. The less courageous had sought refuge in the bars or were sheltering on the eastern side of the Tote building, trying to catch sight of the horses in the paddock directly in front of them where connections for the first race stood in miserable huddles, some of them occasionally testing the ground with the heel of a shoe or the point of an umbrella. Others, their coats dripping with rain, hunched their shoulders and narrowed their eyes the way people do when exposed to remorseless torrents sluicing down from windswept skies.

Millie and Alice had sought refuge in the owners' and trainers' bar, a charming but ramshackle building packed with trainers in gently steaming Barbours and owners in saturated tweeds. Several badly tuned televisions were broadcasting highly coloured pictures of the action from Wincanton and two other racecourses.

'This is the downside of winter racing,' Millie said. 'Weather like this on courses as exposed as this.'

'I don't mind at all,' Alice replied. 'It sort of adds to the fun, really. It's better than sitting inside staring at the rain pouring down the windows.'

'I forgot to ask you. What news about your house? That call you had before we left – I've been so busy talking about Jack's chances, I quite forgot to ask.'

'Yes, I put it out of my mind as well, isn't that odd? I was so excited about coming racing again. Anyway,' Alice continued, 'it seems they have someone definitely interested and so it's really a case of fingers crossed. I could be moving in a month.'

'And you're really not going to tell Georgina?' Millie smiled. 'I mean until it's a *fait accompli?*'

'I don't really see the point, Millie. It's really got nothing to do with her or Christian. They know something's up, I'm sure, but I'm dashed if I'm going to tell them what.'

'Right on, sister.' Millie laughed, clenching one fist.

'Hello,' Rory said, returning from the bar with drinks. 'Not another outbreak of white power?'

The door of the bar was once more pushed open as three more refugees from the weather came in.

'Here we are,' Grenville announced to Lynne and to Constance, who was still trying to hold an enormous and totally unsuitable picture hat in place even though she was now well out of the wind. 'Soon dry out in here.'

'I'm not sure I know anyone here,' Constance said, looking round the crowd. 'In fact I couldn't possibly.'

'Rory?' Grenville called, spotting the trainer seated at a corner table with Millie and Alice. He led his charges over. 'Well, well, so here we all are again. The Rawlins Racing Club, perhaps we should call it. Mrs Brandon, Mrs Dixon, may I introduce Miss Faraday?'

'I've never been to wherever this is before,' Constance said, sitting down on the chair Grenville had pulled out for her while Millie and Alice exchanged greetings with Lynne. 'I must say the climate is most incontinent.'

'This is nothing,' Rory said, as Grenville went to get drinks for the newcomers. 'You want to try one of the February meetings. There's nothing between here and the Urals.'

'It is a bit pissy, isn't it?' Lynne said, taking off her Mrs Miniver hat and shaking the rain off it. 'I think we should have come dressed as frogmen.'

'I hear you have a runner today,' Grenville said to Millie on his return, producing his racecard. 'Trojan Jack again, yes? Must have a squeak after that good run at Sandown.'

'He'll like this ground,' Rory said. 'Got just enough cut in it. He really doesn't like the soft, not a bit.'

'Might have a little interest then, Rory,' Grenville decided. 'That was *such* rotten luck at Sandown. Now then – how's our horse then?'

'Grenville has just bought a horse,' Rory said in response to Alice's quick look of concern. 'Or rather Lynne has and Grenville might well be.'

'Which horse have you bought?' Alice enquired of Lynne. 'One of Rory's? Please not the one with the big floppy ears who likes to listen to Irish songs.'

'The *very* one.' Grenville smiled.

'Put the sock back under the bed, duck,' Millie murmured, turning to Alice. 'It's sold.'

'Please not?' Lynne repeated, picking up. 'You hadn't got your eye on it, had you? Seriously?'

'Well, yes,' Alice replied. 'Yes and no, really. Yes when I saw him, and no when I found out how much he'd cost.'

Everyone fell silent for a moment, during which Rory finished his drink and stood up to take his leave.

'I'd better go and see how everything is with Jack,' he said. 'Don't want anything falling off him today. If you'll excuse me.'

'You really have bought that horse?' Alice asked Lynne. 'You and Grenville?'

'So it seems,' Lynne replied. 'Actually Grenville's still hovering, but I think he'll come in.'

'He will if he knows what's good for him,' Constance observed, straightening her hat.

'No, no, I'm definitely in,' Grenville said quickly. 'I was just kicking the tyres on this one, that's all, do you see.'

'Whatever *that* may mean,' Constance said.

'It's not all writ in stone,' Grenville continued, trying again. 'So if you really *are* interested . . .'

'It'd be great if you came in,' Lynne said, putting her hand on Alice's. 'I mean it really would be fun.'

'I'm not sure what it would entail,' Alice said, turning to Millie for help. Ever since she had seen the horse she had thought about little else except how it might be possible to buy him, and even when she realised there simply was no practical or indeed sensible way she could do it, she had still been unable to put the idea out of her head. Yet now it seemed there might be a way, although before she allowed herself to get her hopes up she needed to know the nuts and bolts of the situation. The matter had become vitally important to her and up until today she hadn't been quite sure why. Now, as she sat in the warm fug of a bar at a small rural racetrack, she began to understand. It was as if she was beginning to discover herself – the person who had disappeared during her marriage to a man whom she had loved but for whom she had sacrificed the greater part of her personality. But now, today, she felt a stirring in her soul, a reawakening of the person she had once been, of her younger self.

Millie was telling her how partnerships worked in racing and what a wonderful thing they were for small would-be owners, giving them a chance to enjoy all the excitement of owning without having to pay out the sort of money that only big business or the rich could afford.

'Then there are all the extras,' Millie was saying, in conclusion. 'The shoeing, the vet, the insurances, the entry fees, et cetera, but again in a partnership you are only paying a quarter. And if the horse you buy is any good and you want to go on racing it, you take it in turns to have it carry your colours.'

'Your colours?' a wide-eyed Alice repeated, since such a notion had never occurred to her. 'But I don't have any colours.'

'You design what you want, duck, and if they're available you pay an annual fee and they're yours.'

But before any real and businesslike conclusions were made there was Trojan Jack's race to be watched. When they all went to look at him in the paddock Millie remarked that he had one of his cross days on, since he looked moody and restless, swishing his tail as he walked and laying back his ears. Grenville commented that it might well be due to the increasingly inclement weather, to which Millie replied that it was the same for all the horses and none of the others seemed to be minding. There was certainly little confidence in her horse in the market, his opening price of two to one having drifted to nine to four, then to three to one, finally to settle at an uneasy nine to two.

'Not as uneasy as Herr Trainer,' Grenville observed as they saw a rain-sodden Rory scuttling across the paddock towards them, beetle-browed. 'Something amiss, guv'nor?'

'Only forgot to declare the blasted blinkers,' Rory muttered as he joined the party, now up in the grandstand as the horses went to post. 'My own damned fault.'

'What does that mean?' Alice wondered.

'Means he can't wear them, Alice,' Grenville explained. 'You have to declare the fact you want to run your horse in a blindfold. Which would explain why he's taken a walk in the market.'

'A walk in the market?' Alice sighed. 'This is all way over my head.'

'The way his odds have drifted,' Millie said. 'He really should be favourite, given his last run, and the fact he hasn't gone up notably in the handicap.'

'He's now five to one on the Tote,' Grenville said, looking at the show of the approximate Tote odds.

'Why would he need blinkers?' Alice asked. 'I thought only milk ponies wore blinkers.'

'It's meant to make them concentrate,' Grenville said. 'Stop them becoming distracted by other horses. Lot of horses stop racing altogether when they see another horse drawing up alongside to challenge. They simply throw in the towel.'

'Like this one,' Rory said. 'And as if that's not bad enough, our pilot's just taken a bang on the head. Or on what passes for his head.'

'Then he won't be fit to ride, surely?' Grenville said in astonishment. 'He won't pass the MO, surely?'

'The doctor won't have known about it. They were horsing about in the changing room, playing piggy-back jousting or some such idiotic game as played by people with size three hats, and our jock banged his head on the lockers. When I was briefing him in the paddock he thought he was at Chepstow.'

'Can't you get another rider?' Alice asked.

'Bit late now,' Rory replied. 'Trouble is he knows the horse and he also happens to be a good pilot. So let's just hope his wretched concussion is only temporary.'

'I'm sure it will be fine once they're off and running,' Millie said. 'Jack's such an old hand I could ride him round here.'

'Now why didn't I think of that?' Rory said. 'As it happens, it's not much of a race. The two good horses have been withdrawn because of the change in the going, and so if only I'd remembered the blasted shades—'

'They're off, old sport,' Grenville announced, putting his race glasses up. 'And your chap's gone straight into the lead.'

It was a handicap hurdle race over two miles, the same as at Sandown but of a lower standard. This was perfectly apparent because as they passed the stands for the first time, having only jumped two flights of hurdles, half a dozen of the field of ten runners looked to be tailed off already, the two back markers already receiving hefty reminders from their pilots that there was still work to be done.

By the time they turned out of the back straight Jack was still ten lengths in the lead, and cantering, his jockey sitting still as a mouse.

'Bar a fall, Rory,' Grenville announced, glasses fixed firmly on the action.

'Just wait and see,' Rory muttered in return. 'Early days. Jack has a sleeve full of tricks.'

With two flights to jump, breasting the sharp rise in the track, Jack could be seen making his way to the far side of the run-in, his pilot having obviously decided to finish with the help of the running rail.

'Wrong,' Rory announced. *'Wrong move.'*

'He's still five lengths ahead,' Grenville said, watching the horse clear the penultimate flight with ease. 'And going easily.'

'But look at this other horse coming at him!' Rory shouted, slapping his head with his rolled up racecard. 'I told him to come over on the stand rails! To avoid exactly this! Seeing another horse coming at him! Kick him, Derek! Kick him on, for goodness' sake!'

But as he landed over the last flight, even though he was still a good three to four lengths clear, Jack's head went up as he became aware of another horse at his quarters and he started to look round. Even when the challenging horse was within three-quarters of a length of Jack, he was not really catching him, so if Jack just kept galloping, which he could well have done, so full of running was he, he would still have the race at his mercy. But the moment he sensed and then saw a rival out of the corner of his eye, he simply downed tools. He didn't just slow up and get caught: he all but stopped dead, his tail swishing round furiously and his head sticking up high in the air. The jockey did his best to regalvanise him, kicking him and hitting him, but the horse was having none of it. He simply planted himself a hundred yards from the winning post and let the second horse labour past him, and then the third and finally the fourth, the rest having pulled up. Finally, as if at last completely sure there was no danger from any other passing horse, Jack picked up his bit again and galloped happily past the post, barely out of a sweat.

Rory refused a consolatory drink, excusing himself on the score that he had to go off and shoot the jockey, while the rest of the party hurried back out of the rain and into the owners' and trainers' bar.

'That was dastardly,' Constance said, pressing Lynne's hand. 'Snatching defeat out of the jaws of victory, yes? What hard luck, my dear. Better luck next time.'

'Thanks,' Lynne replied. 'But it's not my horse, Lady Frimley. Sorry. It's Millie's.'

'I imagine you must feel a bit like the Queen Mother when that horse of hers did that silly thing it did,' Constance said, linking arms with Millie. 'The horse that writer chappie rode. Now come along, you need a good stiff drink. Glanville? Millie here needs a stiffie.'

'Of course, Constance, just coming.' Grenville sighed. 'And it's Grenville, not Glanville.'

'As if it matters,' Constance retorted. 'Just get this poor creature a large brandy. Really. Did you ever. The manners of the young nowadays.'

As Constance took herself off to the ladies, Alice sat down by Lynne while Grenville was busy at the crowded bar.

'The horse,' she began. 'There are to be what? Four partners?'

'So I'm told,' Lynne replied. 'And so far there's Grenville and me. So seriously, if you do want to come in, apparently it's three thousand, one hundred and fifty guineas, plus training, and all the bits and bobs.'

'Three thousand,' Alice repeated, more for her own ears than Lynne's. 'Still, that's a bit less than the fifteen thousand Rory was asking.'

'You'd have got him for twelve.'

'I couldn't have afforded that!' Alice exclaimed. 'That is an awful lot of money.'

'Yeah, me neither,' Lynne agreed. 'Well actually I suppose I could, but I didn't think I should. No – no, this seems to be the way to go, right? We'll have fun. Life's too short, Alice. So maybe let's try and have a bit of fun while we still can, eh?'

'Absolutely,' Alice agreed with a nod. 'After all, and as they keep reminding us, we all only pass this way once. Three thousand, one hundred and fifty guineas. Millie?'

'It's your money, duck,' Millie returned. 'And since it looks as though you've sold your house, and compared to what you're paying for Cherry Tree Cottage – if I were you, why not? Go for it. Why ever not?'

'We'd still need one more partner, to make it viable,' Alice said. 'Will you come in, Millie?'

'I'd love to, but I can't really, angel. Least not while I've still got old Jack to pay for. But really, it shouldn't be that hard to get the last leg. Perhaps Rory will take it, except I don't think so. Not given the precarious state of his business.'

'Hello,' Lynne said with a grin. 'I think Connie's scored.'

The other two women looked over to where Constance now was, having reappeared from the ladies, and saw she was being chatted up by a short red-faced man in a bright tweed suit who was holding an opened bottle of champagne up by way of invitation. After a moment's hesitation Constance allowed herself to be almost frogmarched off to a table in the far corner of the bar.

'Not really her type, surely?' Millie remarked. 'She told me she only likes tall men with silver hair, not short tubby bald oranges.'

'Well anyway,' Alice decided, 'I'm in. You can definitely count me in.'

'Great,' Lynne said. 'Grenville's doing all the paperwork. I reckoned he should look after the partnership since he seems to know all about it. Horses, I mean.' She added a shy smile before raising her glass to celebrate their forthcoming partnership.

'Alice is in,' she told Grenville when he returned with Millie's drink.

'Good,' Grenville said. 'Excellent. But I thought I was going to sharp-end it, as it were?'

'You are,' Lynne replied. 'I just invited her in, that's all. You can do all the dotting and crossing and all that.'

'Here's poor Rory,' Alice said, opening her bag. 'Rory, let me get you a drink – and I insist. What would you like?'

'A large hemlock would do nicely, Alice,' Rory said as he sat down. 'And if they can't do hemlock a brandy and ginger would do the trick. Thank you.'

'Well?' Millie said.

'I don't know what to say.' Rory sighed. 'What can I do to get this wretched horse of yours first past the post?'

'A one-horse race, maybe?' Grenville laughed. 'Find a nice walkover somewhere?'

'I wouldn't be too sure,' Rory replied. 'Knowing Jack he'd find a way to lose a walkover as well.'

'Quickly, one of you,' Constance hissed, quite suddenly re-appearing at their table at considerable speed, pursued by her claret-faced, bright-check-suited suitor. 'One of you say you're my husband. Quickly!'

'I think this had better be one of you two,' Millie said with a smile at Rory and Grenville.

'Perhaps I could be your son?' Grenville wondered *sotto*. 'Would that be any help?'

'Darling,' Constance sighed, putting her hand over Grenville's, as her admirer arrived equally hotfoot, bottle of champagne still in hand. 'Have you seen that great big strapping husband of mine anywhere?' She fixed Grenville firmly with her eye and waited, while her beau came to a stop behind her chair, wondering whether or not to pursue his suit.

'When last seen he was just putting some welshing book-maker to flight,' Grenville replied. 'Not a pretty sight.'

He turned to smile at the small bald man behind Constance, who was now obviously having very visible second thoughts. A moment later he withdrew and hurried away.

'He's gone,' Grenville said, reclaiming his hand. 'All clear.'

'What a perfectly dreadful fellow,' Constance said, straightening her skirt and adjusting her hat. 'Owns supermarkets and wanted me to go up to Blackpool. Imagine.'

'I've always thought it was a pity about Blackpool,' Grenville mused. 'Among the best sands anywhere. Be quite a different proposition in the south of France.'

'Thank you, Glanville,' Constance said, blowing him a little kiss with one gloved hand. 'What's that they say nowadays? I owe you one.'

'And I think I might just have the answer to that, Lady Frimley,' Grenville replied. 'And it's Grenville, remember?'

'Yes, yes. You do make such a fuss, you men. So what is your answer to everything, young man?'

'Let's discuss that on our journey home, Lady Frimley,' Grenville smiled. 'Or may I call you Cynthia?'

Almost caught, Constance looked at him sharply, then saw the smile in his eyes. Opening her bag, she took out her cheroots and lit up once more with the help of her table lighter.

'What you may do, Grenville,' she said carefully, 'is get me a nice large gin and It.'

'Hope you're feeling flush, Connie,' Millie remarked after Grenville had gone to the bar. 'I think your so-called son has plans for you.'

Chapter Eleven

A Sickness

Boyo wasn't at all himself. The day before he had relished every mouthful of his food, but this morning he couldn't even stand the smell of something he generally found delicious. Instead he stood with his head hanging down in the corner of his box, his nose running, giving the odd shiver.

Then he coughed.

'I don't believe what I just heard,' Rory groaned as he did his morning rounds, having just passed by the horse's box and now turning back. 'Don't tell me that was you, matey,' he told the backside that he saw facing him. 'Because if it was, that's all I something well need.'

Drawing the bolt on the lower door back, Rory entered the stable and saw the full manger of food. When he did, he knew the worst.

'Teddy?' he called in despair as he returned to the yard. 'Teddy – fetch the thermometer. This horse is coughing.'

'Never,' Teddy said, wide-eyed.

'No, of course he's not,' Rory replied. 'I'm just joking. You know it's the kind of thing that has me rolling about the yard holding my sides. He's coughing – and he hasn't touched his grub.'

'Typical,' Teddy sighed, dumping his pitchfork in the muck barrow. 'Just as I was getting some condition on him.'

'It might be nothing,' Rory said, without much conviction. 'It might be just a bit of dry food stuck somewhere. Though if it is I'll eat your hat.'

Just when he'd been getting the horse right and ready, Rory mused as he headed towards the office to ring the vet just in case of trouble. Since Kathleen's visit the little horse hadn't looked back. He had put on condition so fast that Rory had been forced to revise his training schedule, curtailing his road work and getting the animal cantering much earlier than anticipated. In fact so well had the horse come on that Rory had even managed to get a good fast piece of work under his belt, and had been well pleased with the result.

And now the little horse was coughing.

When he got into the office he noticed that Maureen had her bad-news look on.

'Now what?' he groaned. 'Don't tell me – someone else is taking their horse away.'

'No. That was the hospital, Mr Rawlins,' Maureen replied. 'They want you to call them.'

Rory bit his lip in anguish, as if to swallow what he had just said. As far as his father's health went, everything was going so well that Rory had simply assumed that any day now his father would be discharged and returned home all but fully mended. But when he spoke to the hospital he learned this was far from the truth.

'It's just one of those things, Rory,' said the doctor, a man with whom Rory had become friends, so much respect had he for the care he had taken over his father. 'These secondary infections catch us all out. We took every precaution we could.'

'I know that, Dan,' Rory replied. 'I know what care you've all taken.'

'The good thing is he was beginning to make such headway that the possibility is he'll be strong enough to resist the infection, which certainly would not have been the case a couple of weeks ago.'

'Can I come in and see him?'

'Of course. We've isolated him, naturally, but there's nothing to stop you coming in and showing him your cheery mug.'

'I'll come in now,' Rory said. 'I just have to call the vet and then I'll be on my way.'

He rang Noel, the stable vet, immediately.

'Yes,' the lugubrious Noel sighed. 'I'm not being surprised here. There is an awful lot of this about, young man.'

'I don't have any other horses coughing,' Rory replied. 'I've isolated him, but I'd like you to come and have a look at him as soon as you can. One good thing – his temp's only half a point over normal.'

'They don't always run a high temp with this thing. And I'll be there as soon as I can.'

'I have to pop over to the hospital to see Dad, but I won't be gone more than an hour.'

Ten minutes after Rory left the telephone rang again.

When she answered it Maureen could barely hear the person on the other end of what was obviously a very bad line.

'I'm sorry,' she said. 'I didn't catch who this is.'

'Leen,' was all Maureen could hear. 'Leen Lanagan. Peek to Mr Rawlins?'

'I'm afraid Mr Rawlins isn't here at the moment. Can I help you? This is a very bad line, I'm afraid.'

On the other end of the phone Kathleen missed that information altogether. This time Cronagh really was suffering the aftermath of a severe storm that had brought most of the country telephone lines down. She was making her call from one of the few lines still available, the one in Finnegan's Exclusive American Cocktail Lounge.

'I was just ringing to see how the patient was,' Kathleen said, raising her voice against the interference that she could now hear. What she didn't say was that the night before she had experienced a very vivid nightmare in which the horse was found sick and starving in a field. It had been such a disturbing dream that, unable to get it out of her head all morning, she had felt compelled to call his trainer, as Rory had told her she could.

'The patient?' Maureen repeated, having heard that question clearly enough and raising her own voice even more in reply, although misunderstanding the enquiry. 'I'm afraid it's not good news. He's had rather a bad setback and is suffering from a quite serious secondary infection. Mr Rawlins is with him now.'

'How . . . he?' the caller asked, now all but drowned in atmospherics.

'You'll have to repeat that, I'm afraid. This really is a terrible line.'

But all Maureen could hear was appalling interference on the line.

'Hello?' she called. 'Hello?'

But since it seemed she had lost her caller Maureen hung up, thinking that if the woman wanted to know more she would ring back when the lines were better.

'Hello?' Kathleen said in desperation at the other end, hearing Maureen well enough now, but then realising that she herself could not be heard. 'Hello – hello!'

But the line had gone completely dead. Kathleen tried going through her friend the local operator, but could get no joy there either.

'Sure the lines are down all over the place, love,' the operator told her. 'That was a heck of a storm and you were lucky to get that line out at all. I had to put it through on Father Leroy's line.'

The last time all the lines were down after such a storm they had stayed down for nearly a fortnight, all but cutting off the entire area from Cronagh to the Atlantic coast itself. Fearing the same thing might happen again, Kathleen knew what she must do. Somehow or other she would have to cross over to England again and go and see her beloved little horse, who she was now convinced was dangerously if not mortally sick, although how she was going to be able to afford the trip had not yet occurred to her.

Rory was back from the hospital in time to catch Noel before he left.

'I've taken some blood, and I scoped the horse as well, young man,' the vet told him. 'I'll call the moment we have the results. Been making any noise at work?'

'Not a sound,' Rory said, shaking his head. 'He's completely clean-winded.'

'I know it's little consolation, but there really is a lot of this about. Nick Granger's had to shut up shop.'

'Thanks for that, Noel.'

'Keep an eye on his temperature,' Noel advised, closing up his bag. 'You're right. It is only half a point up so it might be just a dirty nose.'

'And pigs might do aeronautics.'

'Not much of him, is there?' the vet remarked with a backward nod of his head as he walked away from the stable. 'Got quite decent quarters, but there's not really a lot of him.'

'Stand by for surprises,' Rory said. 'This horse has got a motor.'

'What were you saying about flying pigs?' Noel returned, getting into his cluttered car. 'Anyway, since he is coughing, I wouldn't go entering him up for a while.'

'Shall I move Boyo to one of the bottom boxes, boss?' Teddy asked, when he heard the news.

'I wouldn't bother, Teddy,' Rory replied, trudging back towards his office. 'If I were you I'd just start looking for another job.'

Certainly as far as Rory was concerned, had today been a fish, as he remarked to Maureen, he'd have thrown it back. Maureen told him about the call he'd missed without being able to enlighten him any further and in return Rory told her about his father.

'He looked better than I thought he would,' he said. 'All those awful tubes and feeders are out, or most of them, at any rate. He's still on a drip because of the infection, and he's also got one of those newfangled oxygen things. But still – he looks a better colour, and he even managed a cheery wave or two. The problem is that they think the infection might have gone to his chest, which is just the place they don't want it to go.'

'I'm so sorry,' his secretary said. 'Everyone's so fond of your father.'

'Right,' Rory replied. 'Me included. And now on top of everything, just as the little horse was coming to hand, he goes down.'

Rory made himself a cup of coffee and then sat at his desk to do a bit of metaphorical head-scratching. First of all he consulted the list of entries he had already earmarked for the horse and wondered whether he should just throw in the towel and forget about them, since if Boyo really did have the cough he wouldn't be seen on a racecourse for at least two months, or whether he should select a few choice entries just in case it was nothing serious. Then there was the problem of how much he should tell the new owners, if anything at all. Like his father Rory believed that owners had a right to know everything about their horses, good and bad, and that they should be part of the decision-making process, because they owned the animals and paid the bills for their keep. Yet because this partnership was not yet fully and officially formed he could see a reason for not letting them know just yet, not because he was afraid of losing them as potential owners but because he couldn't quite see the point since they hadn't yet paid out anything. Then if the horse was found to be suffering from something minor – which Rory still believed was possible since no one else was coughing in the yard – they could simply carry on from where they had left off, which was three legs in and one to go.

In that case, Rory told himself, he would make some select entries, which at least would look good on the cards he would then send out to his new but still nominal owners, and might even encourage someone to buy the fourth leg since as soon as entries were made attitudes changed immediately. It was the moment when reality took over from fantasy.

As it happened, as far as filling the partnership went, reality had all but been achieved, thanks to the sales pitch Grenville had delivered to Constance on their return journey to London from Wincanton. He had used Lynne as his unwitting accomplice, discussing with her how much fun and excitement they were going to have as owners, over-egging the pudding as much as he dared by even going as far as to suggest that if the horse was anywhere near as good as Rory said, he could see them ending up at Cheltenham being presented with some cup or other by the Queen Mother. Since he also made sure that the speedometer never went over forty miles an hour, his sales pitch had of course – just as he had hoped it would

– finally proved irresistible to Constance, while his driving speed had – as he had feared it might – totally bewildered not only Lynne but any motorist unlucky enough to get stuck behind him on the narrower parts of the A303.

Even so, by the time they reached Knightsbridge, Lady Frimley had declared herself to be the buyer of the fourth leg in the now perfectly formed racing partnership. Grenville's only remaining concern was how exactly he was going to extract any monies from the most senior partner.

'All my money is tied up in some wretched trust or other in one of those equally wretched islands or other,' she had told him when he invited Lynne and her up to his flat for a celebratory glass. 'It's an utter bore since it only allows one a certain amount of loot at a time, but then I'm such a spendthrift it's probably a very good thing, all told.'

Grenville had pulled a private face to himself, remembering Constance's taxi tactics. Her latest scam, having agreed to come into the partnership, was to promptly delegate Grenville to run her share of the affair, indicating that all telephone calls and any petty expenses incurred should be handled and met by Grenville. So be it, Grenville had privately decided between equally privately clenched teeth, if it meant that they were finally up and running – a situation he desired not because he had ever been really serious about owning a horse, let alone a share in one, but because it would give him free and constant access to his adored Lynne. No more could she threaten him with exclusion: their lives were now going to be permanently intertwined, thanks to their involvement with their new purchase. So if Constance proved to be a late or a bad payer, it was something with which he would have to deal – and most certainly would, because if there was one area in which he could steal a march over Constance it was in the running of any affairs of business. Most of all he knew that if she did prove a thorn in all their sides, or if she did indeed fail to meet her dues, then they would simply dump her overboard and find another sharer, something that he reckoned would not be very hard, provided that the horse when finally in action performed even reasonably. If the animal showed any real potential, the plus point was that they might even make some money buying Constance out.

The following evening he called Rory to tell him the good news.

'You don't sound very happy,' Grenville remarked when he heard Rory's tone. 'I thought you'd be greatly cheered, old chap.'

'I am, Grenville,' Rory replied. 'My apologies. It's my father. He's had a setback.'

Rory explained and Grenville listened sympathetically, saying that if there was anything at all he could do, Rory was to count on him. Touched, Rory thanked him and put down the telephone, feeling terrible. He had just had confirmation from the vet that the horse's blood was wrong, and he had said nothing at all about it to Grenville.

But as it so happened, his saviour was just about to make her way to him, once she had finished with what was to become known as the Cronagh Syndicate.

Those in that small Cork town who had seen The Enchanted run in both his Irish races were convinced they had seen something special, but then such normally is the case in that part of the world, and in particular in the environs of Cronagh, both rural and urban. Now they were waiting for his first run in England, and since they knew that Anthony Rawlins's small racing establishment must be a betting yard (for, as they all asked, how else do small trainers keep in business?) they were ready to note the horse's entries and then to take advantage. In order to get the best price, they knew to a man that it would have to be a well-organised coup, the money to be placed simultaneously with various bookmakers, spot on the dot of the chosen minute of the designated hour because none of them wanted the odds to shorten before the money was down. Absolute secrecy and total discretion were the prime requisites.

'Now something is afoot,' Michael Doherty declared when they were all met late one evening in the back bar of Finnegan's Exclusive American Cocktail Lounge. 'Here we have a horse entered up all over the shop yet not running, so we can only assume our man is waiting for *the right race*. So as soon as we see him declared as a certain runner, that's when we know, and that's when we move in. What would really help of course is if we had a spy in the camp. For not only would we know how the horse is doing in his home work, we'd know well in advance when he was running, and then we could get the money down early.'

'We've no way of tellin' who the work rider is, I suppose,' Napper Reilly wondered, himself a retired jockey and now a small-time bloodstock scout for a small-time British trainer.

'Pity about the auld leg,' Padraig sighed, tapping Napper's prosthetic with his hawthorn stick. 'Or we'd have you on the first boat over.'

'There's someone all too willing to go over, Padraig.' Yamon spoke up from the darkness. 'And they're family too.'

'God, man,' Padraig groaned. 'Aren't I short-handed enough?'

'Maybe so, but ye'll be looking at poor men for the rest of your days,' Michael warned him. 'Get that streak of a boy of yours to work double for a while.'

Padraig looked at Michael, shook his head, then drained his glass, pulled the collar on his old brown overcoat up round his ears and walked out into the cold night air, knowing that what his friends had said was true and that it was sense to do as he was advised.

When he got home, as if ordained by the gods, he found Kathleen sitting on top of a packed suitcase, trying to squeeze it closed.

'How's this, then?' he asked. 'Off on your travels again, my girl?'

'What travels?' Kathleen was surprised. 'I don't go on travels, Da.'

'So you're off on no travels, then.' Padraig nodded, sticking his pipe in his coat pocket. 'Just like the no travels you went off on before.'

'See, I have to, Da,' she replied after a while. 'I know the horse is sick.'

'You do so?'

'Yes, I do. I really do.'

'But how are you affording it? Sure you can't keep financin' this sort of thing.'

'I still have a bit left in the trousseau tin.'

'You think I'll countenance that sort of palaver?' Padraig growled. 'What sort of father do you think you have who'd allow his daughter up the aisle in her wedding gown with only some tired old chemise under it? What sort of father would that be? I'll hear of no such thing. So if instead I were to give you your wages for the next month—'

'No, Da!' Kathleen protested. 'You can't afford that. I'll be fine. I'll manage.'

'If managing means standing be the side of the road hitching your skirts I'll not hear of that either,' her father replied, taking a sheaf of notes from the top inside pocket of his trousers and counting some out. 'Sure we made a bit on the horse, so why not invest a bit of what we made? Besides that, you can be of use to us all, girl. And not only in getting the horse right, if you mind me.'

'I'm minding you, Da,' Kathleen said. 'When did I ever not?'

'Just when you get there, when you reach Mr Rawlins, offer him your services but do it for free, saying you have to be near this horse of yours. He'll not refuse you. What sensible man could?'

Padraig handed her some money, then, his pipe back out, lit it, not taking his eyes off his daughter.

'Ah, you want a spy in the camp, don't you?' She laughed. 'You're a wily old article, so you are.'

'We only need to know how the horse is working and when he's entered up, and who better to tell us than she who knows him best? Than she who rides him best?'

'So it's riding him I am now?'

'He's seen how you ride, that young man, and weren't his eyes out on broomsticks? You'll be riding him out in no time.'

'I have first to make sure of his health, Da. The woman on the phone said he was bad.'

'So go see, girl. If anyone can get him right, 'tis yourself.'

Rory was waiting for Noel to arrive when he caught sight of a figure carrying a small suitcase making its way up the long tree-lined drive that led to the farm and the yard. He thought he knew who it was from its size, and from the way it was walking, but then he dismissed such a notion as fanciful or maybe even wishful thinking, for he'd been in two minds as to whether or not to put a call in to Cronagh later in the day, particularly when he had heard the news that the horse was in the vet's opinion definitely suffering from the current equine virus. Not that he thought the call would do any definite good, because the virus was the virus. He had just thought about making the call because he thought he would very much like to hear Kathleen Flanagan's voice again.

Now he could see his visitor more clearly, and he felt a tug on the string of his heart, because unless his eyes and reason and understanding had all completely failed him his visitor was indeed none other than Kathleen.

'Kathleen?' he said, hurrying to greet her and to take hold of her suitcase. 'Do you know, I thought it might be you and, good heavens, it is.'

Relieved of her case, Kathleen straightened herself up and then extended her right hand.

'Look,' she said. 'Look, I was just passing so I thought I'd drop in.'

'You must have heard the ker-kettle,' Rory replied, falling into step beside her, and closing his eyes as the stammer returned – a hesitation that had completely disappeared since he had seen the girl by his side off on the train from Bristol.

'The Irish,' Kathleen said, 'can hear a kettle going on in another county.'

'So,' Rory continued, walking towards the house. 'So you were just passing through, on your way ter-ter-to . . . ?'

'Just on my way through.'

'Of course,' Rory agreed, pushing open the front door with his foot. 'And I'm right on the route.'

'Hello, dog,' Kathleen said in surprise to the large lurcher who was greeting them both. 'I don't think we've met.'

'This is Dunkum,' Rory told her as the huge dog suddenly jumped up to put both front paws on Kathleen's shoulders. 'And if you w-want to know why he's called that it's because of how he likes his teatime biscuits. You'll also need to – to – to *watch* your things, because he's also a full time ker-leptomaniac.'

'I'll do that,' Kathleen agreed, trying to keep up the pretence of the casual visitor. 'So how's everything?'

'So-so,' Rory replied. 'Unfortunately my dad's not too good at the moment.'

'God, no,' Kathleen said, her face suddenly serious. 'God, now, I'm real sorry to hear that. But he's going to get better?'

'If I have anything to do with it he will.'

'The right and the best attitude to have. And everything else about the place?'

'Your horse isn't too bright at the moment,' Rory said carefully, keeping an eye out for her reaction.

'He isn't working too well? Or what? What exactly?'

'What exactly is – he's been coughing.'

'He has to have his hay well soaked, but then you know that.'

'The hay's always soaked,' Rory replied. 'All the hay. It always is. The vet thinks he's got the v-v-virus.'

'The virus or a virus?' Kathleen wondered. 'I never do understand why vets always call these things *the* virus, as if there's just the one.'

'You can ask him yourself,' Rory told her. 'He'll be here shortly. Look. Look, I was just about to have a drink. Can I get you one?'

He got them both a drink, orangeade for Kathleen and beer for himself.

'I see you have a case,' he remarked as he handed Kathleen her glass. 'Are you staying with somebody?'

'Depends on what's required,' Kathleen replied, raising her glass, determined not to give away too much, reminding herself that, after all, it had only been a dream. '*Sláinte agus táinte.*'

'Your good health, Miss Flanagan.'

'If it's a virus, Mr Rawlins, I suppose you'll be shooting him up with antibiotics, then?'

'I suppose I shall have to do whatever the vet advises, Miss Flanagan.'

'I wonder if I could see the horse, Mr Rawlins? Before I go on, that is.'

'Go on as in passing through, do you mean?'

'I might. Would that be possible?'

'Of – of – of *course*, Miss Flanagan,' Rory replied, clicking finger and thumb behind his back. 'Soon as we've finished our drinks we'll go. We'll go as soon as we finish our drinks.'

'I got you the first time round, Mr Rawlins,' Kathleen said, eyeing him over the top of her glass. 'And I've finished mine.'

Rory nodded, downed his beer and led Kathleen out to the yard.

'I don't see him,' she said, looking at an empty stable.

'We put him in the lower case. Just in yard. We put him in the lower yard, just in case.'

'Has he been coughing much?'

'As far as I know, a horse doesn't have to cough much, Miss Flanagan, to be deemed to be coughing.'

'Sure I know that well enough.'

'He's been coughing enough to cause anxiety.'

Kathleen looked over the horse's stable door and saw him standing the way he always stood when something was amiss, with his head stuck in one corner, his ears flat and his tail tucked between his back legs. Kathleen didn't even have to call his name. The moment she put her hands on the top of the half-door he swung his head round and looked at her.

'He looks well enough, Mr Rawlins,' Kathleen observed. 'Looks the business, so he does.'

'He's a good doer, now he's back eating. Never leaves an oat – thanks to his personal serenader, Mr McCormack.'

'He's eating his bedding,' Kathleen said, having noticed the horse taking a mouthful of the straw on the stable floor.

'Horses do,' Rory replied. 'That's one of their th-things.'

'OK – fine,' Kathleen persisted. 'So where do you get your straw?'

'Off the farm.'

'And is it sprayed, maybe?'

'Maybe,' Rory said with a shrug, followed by a frown as he saw where this might be headed. 'I don't run the farm, and anyway everyone sprays their crops. Don't they?'

'If they do,' Kathleen said, 'they shouldn't give it to their horses as bedding. If they eat it what they get is a gutful of chemicals.'

'Sort of like us, I suppose,' Rory offered somewhat hope-lessly.

'Is that the right example, I wonder? With the greatest respect, I'd hardly take us for yardsticks, Mr Rawlins. Besides, horses have a completely different way of ingesting things and who knows what the chemicals do to them, the poor creatures. We only ever bed ours on straw we've grown or that we know hasn't been sprayed.'

'I was thinking of putting him on shavings,' Rory said out of the silence that had fallen. 'I was thinking of p-putting all the horses on shavings. But with my father in hospital . . .'

'Sure I know,' Kathleen consoled him. 'Isn't it one of those things you can do tomorrow? So now let's see how else he is.'

Kathleen entered the stable. After she had given the horse several long strokes down his neck, put a hand on his muzzle and pulled his ears, she gave him a thorough physical, paying particular attention to the area at the top of his neck and the bottom of his jaw.

'I'd say that the reason Boyo's been coughing, Mr Rawlins,'

she said, coming back out of the stable, 'is because the glands in his neck are up. Not desperately so, but they're definitely larger than they should be.'

'So he has got an infection, then,' Rory said, as if that would close the door on it.

'It could just be a reaction, on the other hand,' Kathleen replied, looking at him sideways on. 'To something that's disagreed with him.'

'The point is, surely – whatever the reason – the point is if he does have an in-in-in-*fection* he's going to have to have an antibiotic, which in turn means even if it's a short course we won't get him on a racecourse for at least a month. He can't run, as you know – well, of course you do. He can't run with antibiotics in his system.'

'You could perhaps try something other than antibiotics.'

'Aspirin, perhaps? Have him gargle with TCP?' Rory enquired facetiously, immediately regretting his tone. 'Sorry. What else is there? For horses, that is.'

'If you want your horse racing, I'd try some bryonia,' Kathleen replied. 'I might put him on some ignatia as well, in case he still hasn't quite settled – and I'd certainly take all the straw out of his box and fumigate the whole stable. And before I forget it, his teeth need a rasp as well.'

Silence fell. For a moment Rory just stared at the ground, hating having what he considered to be his incompetence discovered, as well as not knowing what to say regarding Kathleen's suggestion that they try the horse on homoeopathic medicines for whatever infection he might or might not be suffering from. He stuck his hands deep in his pockets and continued to stare at the ground while he tried to work out how to deal with what was being suggested – whether to allow Noel to shoot the horse up with antibiotic, which was the standard and most practical procedure, or to fly in the face of veterinary advice and expect a dilution of some weird herb or other to do the trick.

'If I may say so, one of the main reasons he's not eating up is because his teeth need seeing to.' Kathleen broke the silence. 'Has he been quidding? You know, dropping food at feed times?'

Rory nodded, remembering this was something he had indeed noticed but not paid much attention to, thinking the horse's carelessness at the manger was simply the result of sloppy eating habits. He coloured slightly at the illustration of yet another instance of his apparent equine mismanagement.

'The dentist's due in sometime this week,' he lied. 'He's been on holiday.'

In another ensuing silence he continued privately to berate himself for imagining he could simply take over and run the yard with as little experience as he'd had so far in training and managing thoroughbred racehorses. It had been easy enough when his father was around, particularly since Anthony always made it look quite straightforward. Consequently he had thought all he had to do when his father was taken ill was follow the daily routine. He realised now that he had never known for one minute what the full and proper protocol really was.

'Suppose I did – suppose we did try what you're saying we should try,' he suddenly asked. 'What would I say to Noel? To my vet? Who is probably going to appear in the drive any moment now.'

'You must only do what you think best, Mr Rawlins,' Kathleen replied. 'But if he does suddenly appear and you still don't know what to do, just give us a broom and an old cap and I'll say you're not here. That you had to go back to see your dad maybe, that the horse has stopped coughing and that you want to take a bit of a pull until you see if maybe the old infection will clear itself up.'

Rory took another long look at her, and realised that if this absurdly beautiful young woman with the bright green eyes told him to go and jump off a cliff because it was good for him he'd do it, willingly.

'OK, yes,' he muttered, frowning deeply and staring down at the ground again. 'But if we did – if we were to do this, you know. Where do we get this whatever it is – this homoeopathic stuff, whatever it is.'

'You have a big town near here?'

'We have a city. Salisbury. About half an hour away.'

'Then there's bound to be homoeopathic chemists. And if you're still anxious, let me tell you about the horse of Tim Milligan's that won at Cheltenham this year. He was said to have had the virus but they wouldn't treat him with antibiotics. Tim Milligan said if you do that you might as well put the horse away for the rest of the season. That horse won the Mildmay without going near the antibiotics.'

Rory listened and nodded. He knew what she was saying was perfectly right, not necessarily about homoeopathy, about which he knew less than nothing, but certainly about the effects of a course of antibiotics on a horse. He remembered one of his father's owners who happened to be a doctor saying that antibiotics remained in a horse's system for much longer than people believed or indeed than it showed on blood tests, which was why whenever one of his horses was treated that way he insisted they came out of training for at least three months.

Besides that, what was influencing Rory was the fact that he was starting to feel that he might actually have the sort of horse that, while not exactly projecting the stables into the big time, might well be capable of winning enough races to kick-start Fulford Racing Ltd back into proper business. The little horse that he had initially considered useless, first when his father had decided to buy it and particularly when it had arrived in the yard looking like something on its way to an equine rehabilitation centre, had now caught his fancy, not necessarily because of the little bit of faster work that he had seen but because of the animal's aura. There was not only something businesslike about the animal, but something almost mystical. By now Rory knew the characters, foibles and idiosyncrasies of all the horses in the yard and while he was fond of all of them, including the bad-tempered and dispiriting Trojan Jack, none of them had the presence that The Enchanted seemed to have. And although he was an artist and so blessed with an imagination, Rory knew that his instinct about the little Irish horse had nothing to do with imagination. He was like a star performer, in fact, he had *It*. Your heart raced a little faster when you saw him work.

Of course if the little horse did come up trumps the stable fortunes would take a turn for the better. A winning horse always catches owners' eyes, and since his father always maintained that there was nothing more a certain type of owner liked than to stable-hop in the hope that a new and winning trainer could turn their goose into a swan, every stable winner brought the chance of new owners.

And there was nothing that Fulford Racing Ltd needed more than new owners, unless it were a new *owner*. So the sooner Rory could get the little horse fit and ready to race, the better their chance for survival, and the only way to do that was to take a chance that Kathleen was right. QED.

'You've been away a long time,' Kathleen remarked, as Rory came back to earth.

'Things to think about,' he replied. 'Now you write down what I've got to get from this homoeopathic chemist place and I'll go and get it, because at the same time I can pop in and see my father – and you can do as you suggested, when the vet arrives.'

'OK,' Kathleen replied, with another toss of her dark hair. 'You won't regret it.'

'Guaranteed?'

'Absolutely.'

But as they turned away from each other, both of them knew nothing was absolute, other than real belief.

Chapter Twelve

Fast Work

'I'm moving to the country,' Alice said, closing her eyes and waiting for the explosion on the other end of the telephone line.

'I can't have heard right, Mum,' Georgina said after an ominous silence. 'Did you say you were moving to the *country?*'

'I think that's what I said, Georgie. Yes.'

'You're a townie, Mum.' Georgina sighed. 'You wouldn't work in the country.'

'Oh, I think I might.'

'Come on – you'd be bored stiff in a minute. There's nothing to *do* in the country. Not at your age.'

Alice was on the point of telling her about the horse but managed to button her lip in time, knowing that if Georgina got hold of that piece of information the fun would go out of it all, and it would lead to yet another litany of questions and accusations, such as:

What on earth did she think she was doing?

Had she *completely* lost it?

Did she *ever* think of anyone else but herself?

Like, did she *never* think of her family?

And much as she loved Georgina, which she did with all her heart, Alice couldn't face it.

It had obviously been a mistake to tell her and Joe that she was moving to the country. She should of course have waited until she had actually gone, because that way nobody would get the chance to spoil it, but unable as always to keep herself to herself she had proceeded to spill the beans.

'What about your grandchildren?' Georgina was now wondering. 'When are you going to see them, and them you – stuck miles away somewhere in the country? I suppose we'll be expected to hump all the way down there at weekends, just when the traffic is *really* at its loveliest.'

'Rather than me "humping" all the way up to you when I'm down in the country enjoying myself.'

'Meaning?'

'Meaning exactly that, Georgina. You'll all be more than welcome to come and stay once I'm settled in.'

'Joe's allergic to the country. It brings him out in depressions.'

'That's just too bad. The point is I've bought the cottage and I'm moving in next week.'

'Is this some sort of very late mid-life crisis?'

'No,' Alice replied as evenly as she could. 'It's just something I want to do.'

'You won't last a minute down there. Really, Mum, you're out of your mind. You really won't be able to hack it.'

'So you keep telling me.' Alice stroked the dog on her knee and then eased him to the floor, deciding it was time to end this conversation, in line with one of her new resolutions, rather than let her daughter hang up first, which she always somehow managed to do. 'I have to go now, Georgie dear – Sammy needs a walk. Goodbye, darling. Love to the children.'

Alice was sure she heard her daughter giving a slight gasp just before she put down the receiver, but that was just too bad. She was back to being herself. She'd found her voice again, young Alice's voice, the voice of the woman who had stood up to her parents and everyone else who had tried to stop her marrying the love of her life.

Lynne was also on the move, heading out west ahead in her recently acquired second-hand silver Mercedes SL sports car. All she had awaiting her in her new apartment in Brook House was one single bed and an armchair purchased and dispatched from Peter Jones, but as far as Lynne was concerned that was more than enough. What mattered was that she was making a brand-new start in a brand-new home, and for once she was not going to be rushed and bullied into buying not what she wanted but what someone else did.

Fortunately the newly appointed apartment came already fitted with an expensive kitchen and bathroom and the latest and most efficient form of central heating, as well as something Lynne considered the very height of luxury: a central vacuuming system. She would buy everything else she needed at her leisure, taking as much time as she liked to find exactly what she wanted. She didn't care how long it took her, because after all she only had herself to worry about.

'Blow you, Gerry Fortune!' she said to herself as she moved out into the fast lane. 'Who needs ya, baby?'

Brook House was a very large Georgian house that had once apparently been the country seat of some local earl or other, Lynne had gathered when being shown round the conversion. Then it had become a hotel, and then a girls' public school of doubtful repute, finally being purchased by a developer and turned into what was described as the ultimate concept in modern country living. At the end of the day, Lynne decided after her tour of inspection, what this meant was living in a nice new and very spacious apartment overlooking parkland instead of trying to hack it in a cramped two-bedroom flat overlooking some noisy and generally gridlocked road feeding central London, and for considerably less money. The ultimate concept in modern country living was fine by her. They could call it what they liked – to Lynne it couldn't matter less. What mattered was that it was hers and hers alone, and that she was free.

On her second visit Lynne had met a couple of people who'd already moved in, and since they seemed about the same age as her, the one fear she had nursed, that she might be moving into some sort of upmarket retirement home, had been quickly dispersed. In fact judging from some of the expensive machinery parked at the front of the large stone-built mansion the very opposite was possibly true.

Singing happily to herself she locked up her Mercedes and gave it an admiring glance, relieved that she had obviously bought the right sort of motor to go with her new home. Then she took the lift to the apartment on the second floor, which as the brochure had put it *enjoyed fine and uninterrupted views over some of the most unspoilt land in west Hampshire.*

'I'm home,' she said to herself as she put a bottle of Dom Pérignon in the fridge to chill. 'I have finally come home.'

Chapter Thirteen

Blaze

Returning to the yard after his trip to Salisbury, where he had managed to find the homoeopathic chemist as well as look in on his father, Rory presented Kathleen with the chemist's bag.

'Interesting,' he said. 'What the Alchemist had to say. Seems every horse he can name has been miraculously cured by one of these m-magic potions.'

'Might your second name be Thomas, Mr Rawlins? You're a born doubter.'

'I prefer to think of myself, if I think of myself at all, as a bit of a realist actually, Miss Flanagan.'

'And where did realism ever get anybody? Into the alcoholic ward, that's where. And I really don't mind if you call me Kathleen.'

'If you call me R-Rory.'

'Thanks, but how could I do that when I'm working for you? How was your father?'

'No better, I'm afraid. But then he's no worse either, and his doctor says that's a big plus.'

'Tell him he's in my prayers,' Kathleen said, preparing the

first dose of bryonia. 'And everyone back home. Make sure to tell him now.'

'I will,' Rory agreed, touched. 'Thank you.'

'OK now,' she said, showing him the medicine. 'We'll go and shoot this into Boyo's mouth, all right? We have to give him a dose every four hours. Without fail.'

'We as in?' Rory enquired, scratching the side of his head and wishing that he could stop feeling like a schoolboy every time he talked to this lovely girl.

'Every four hours, mind,' Kathleen repeated, looking sideways at him. 'From this little syringe, see?'

Rory followed her out across the yard, thinking that now she was back in his life the last thing he wanted was for her to disappear again. But he really didn't know how he could persuade her to stay. There was no money to pay for another pair of hands, and even though she had arrived uninvited he could hardly expect her to stay and work for nothing, particularly since his powers of eloquent persuasion seemed to have deserted him.

'What is it?' she asked out of the blue, after she had given the horse his medicine. 'You've gone all silent again.'

'No. It's nothing. Nothing, Kathleen. No, I was just thinking.'

'No harm in that, I suppose.'

'No, actually I was wondering . . . it doesn't matter.'

'For heaven's sake don't go doing that.' Kathleen sighed. 'Don't go starting something and then not bother to finish. That really is – it drives me mad.'

'You were really passing through, as you called it, were you?' Rory asked, picking up a bit of baling twine from the ground and starting to make it into a cat's cradle. 'You know – when you said – when you arrived that is, this time. You said you were passing through, but that isn't or rather wasn't what you were doing at all. Was it?'

'Does it matter, Mr Rawlins?' Kathleen asked, looking him right in the eyes. 'It's neither here nor there now, is it? What matters is getting Boyo here right, and if my being here helps, then let's just call it providential, OK?'

'Fine by me.' Rory offered her the cat's cradle. 'Know how to do this?'

'Know how to do it?' Kathleen laughed. 'I'm the Cronagh open champion.'

Expertly and deftly she took the cradle of string from him, turned it into the next complex and handed it back to Rory, who almost as quickly played on and handed it back to her. She smiled.

'Misspent youth, Mr Rawlins?'

'Too much time on my own,' he replied, getting stuck on the next move now that he had it back. 'No good. Can't do it.'

He held up the cradle as far as they had got it and raised his eyebrows at Kathleen, who shook her head at him, took the cradle and quickly polished it off.

'Told you I was the champion,' she said. 'It's a hard school, the Cronagh Cat's Cradlers. All-Ireland champions.'

Rory smiled shyly back at her, took the small ball of baling twine into which Kathleen had restored the cradle and pocketed it, finding himself vowing like a child never to part with it ever again, whatever happened.

Kathleen cleared her throat, tidied her hair with her hands and checked the bolts on Boyo's stable door.

'OK,' she said, a word that seemed to Rory to be her mantra. 'Better get back to what I was doing, then.'

Rory said nothing. He just watched her as she began to sweep and tidy the yard as automatically as if she was back home in Cork. He watched her check the water buckets and the bolts on all the stable doors when she was done sweeping, and he watched her as she put her broom away, dusted her hands together and stood with arms akimbo surveying the now immaculate yard.

'I can't offer you a j-j-job,' he said finally, picking up the smallest piece of straw imaginable and handing it to her with a straight face.

'Can't think how I missed that,' she returned, equally straight-faced.

'I w-wish I could.' Rory nodded. 'Offer you a j-job. But we can't afford it.'

'Did I axe for a job?' she said wide-eyed, thickening her brogue deliberately. 'I don't remember doing so.'

'You just came here to see the horse,' Rory offered, and then immediately regretted doing so when he saw the flash in Kathleen's green eyes.

'I did not come here looking for a job, as you call it, Mr Rawlins,' she all but snapped. 'I have a job at home, as you well know.'

'Sure.' Rory held his hands up in mock innocence. 'You were just passing through.'

Kathleen glared at him, but in truth she was more angry with herself than she was with him. She would have loved to tell him the truth, and not just the truth but the entire truth, because there was nothing Kathleen hated more than deceit, yet she knew she could not, for more reasons than just the one, so she had to bite her tongue and put up with what she saw as his facetiousness. She knew he knew that she had not just been passing through, as she had so lamely tried to convince him, but she knew that even if she told him a bit of the truth, that she had dreamed this terrible thing about her horse, that she had seen him sick and dying and that the dream had been as vivid and as potent as reality, she knew he would just think what she thought they all thought about the Irish, that they were full of nothing but whimsy and away with the fairies. So she put up and shut up, deciding to live in hope that what she wanted so much to happen might indeed happen, and she could somehow manage to stay here at Fulford Farm and look after a horse that although no longer hers would always belong to her in her heart as long as they both should live.

'Of course,' Rory began, twisting the ball of twine round his fingers out of sight in his pocket. 'Of course if you wanted to stay on for a while – see how your horse does – there'd certainly be no objections.'

Kathleen frowned but didn't say anything immediately. She looked past Rory into the distance and tried to work out how best to accept this invitation without making it seem that it was precisely what she had come for.

'OK,' she decided. 'But there's a proviso. If I was to do that – for a while, to see how Boyo does and all – if I were to do that I would have to work for my keep – and for nothing.'

'Yes – well, as I just s-said,' Rory replied, trying to keep the glee out of his voice, 'there wouldn't be any question of m-m-my paying you because there's nothing in that particular ker-ker-ker – *kitty*. You'd be looked after all right. I mean it might look a bit frayed at the edges, this place, but it's very comfortable. And warm. And of course you'd be able to keep an eye right on your horse.'

'Your horse, Mr Rawlins.'

'Fine. *The* horse, then. You'd be able to keep an eye on *the* horse.'

She turned her attention back to him, looking him once more directly in the eyes. Rory met the look and held her eyes with his. Even so, in spite of his determination, he found he dropped his first.

'Done deal,' Kathleen said. She pretended to spit on her hand and offered it to Rory, who took it and held it for as long as he dared.

'OK,' she repeated. 'But when Boyo gets better—'

'Yes.' Rory stopped her. 'If and when, which of course he will.'

'God willing,' Kathleen added. 'So when he does—'

'Let's cross that one when we come to it, shall we? That particular whatever,' Rory cut in. 'So now we've a deal, I'd better show you around and get you s-s-s-settled in.'

As they walked away together, behind her back Kathleen gave Boyo, who she knew was watching, the thumbs-up.

As soon as Rory had finished the full guided tour, including the rooms in a warm and comfortable little groom's cottage at the end of the yard, Kathleen set about her work. First, she saw to her horse, standing him in another box while she took his stable apart, disinfecting every inch of it, changing his bedding over to wood shavings – a supply of which Rory managed to scrounge from a friendly neighbouring trainer until he could get a full delivery – and washing out his mangers with boiling water. Then she disinfected his hay net and all the woodwork including the outside of the doors and windows, before finally giving the horse a thorough wash-down followed by a top-to-tail grooming. When that was done she went to find Rory, who was in his office checking the entries for his horses.

'If you don't mind my asking, Mr Rawlins,' she said, 'how often do you turn him out? Boyo, that is.'

'Well, I don't at the moment,' Rory replied, looking up from his paperwork in some surprise. 'If it's fine on Sundays some of them get run in the paddocks, but being short-handed and nearly in winter now we don't have the time or the m-man-power to clean off mud-covered horses.'

'But he needs to run out every day,' she told him. 'He always has. It's something he's been used to.'

'While he was growing, perhaps.'

'We run ours out even when they're in work.'

'As I just said, Miss Flanagan—'

'Kathleen.'

'As I just said, I don't have the – the – the—'

He knew perfectly well what he wanted to say, but the more he found himself looking at Kathleen the harder he found it to speak.

'I'm sure you could make an exception in his case,' she chipped in. 'It's what he needs. Look, I'll rug him up and I'll clean him off when he comes in. He really won't do good standing in all day like this.'

'We'll try it,' Rory agreed. 'But if anything happens—'

'Nothing will happen,' Kathleen replied, and finding himself rewarded with a smile Rory at once felt it had been not only the right but the only decision to take. 'Are you expecting someone?' Kathleen went on, having seen something through the office window. 'It seems you have a visitor.'

Rory got up to take a look for himself and saw a battered old yellow VW Beetle with blackened windows and a sawn-off exhaust pulling noisily up in a cloud of smoke and dust at the edge of the parking area. Barely had it stopped before the driver's window was wound down and the end of a cigarette flicked away by the still unseen driver. For a moment no one got out, then all at once the door was kicked open and one hand appeared to be hooked backwards over the edge of the car's roof where it remained while the fingers drummed out a brief tattoo. Finally someone emerged from the interior, a lean, athletic young man in oddly old-fashioned riding breeches, well-worn tan half-boots, an off-yellow anorak over a thin black polo-neck sweater, and aviator-style dark glasses.

The young man stretched, yawned, stretched again, and raising his dark glasses briefly, looked round the yard to see if there was any sign of life. Not yet having spotted Rory watching him from the office he kicked the door of his car closed with a backward shove of one foot then sauntered casually round the yard, peering into the boxes with his hands clasped behind him like a cleric.

Unable to contain his curiosity any longer, Rory stole out of the office and crept up on his visitor until he was right behind him.

'Can I help you?' he said suddenly, hoping at the very least to startle the young man. But far from being disconcerted, the stranger turned slowly round to face Rory, nodded, smiled and held out a hand.

'Mr Rawlins,' he said, in a lilting Irish brogue, as a statement of fact rather than as an enquiry. 'Blaze Molloy. How you doing?'

'Blaze Molloy?' Rory returned, shaking the black-gloved hand. 'Yes? So what can I do for you?'

'They said you might be looking for a rider,' Blaze said, walking on uninvited ahead of Rory to resume his inspection of the horses. 'And since I have meself just moved in near to this very locality—'

'Who said I might be needing a rider?'

'The grapevine, Mr Rawlins,' the young man replied, putting both hands up as if in surrender but continuing his stroll.

'What sort of rider did you have in mind?' Rory called after him.

'Work rider, race rider, stable jockey – anything that's going.'

'I can't afford to take any more work riders, sorry,' Rory said. 'I'm afraid you're wasting your time.'

Blaze went on walking, apparently unperturbed. 'Word has it you bought a nice horse from Padraig Flanagan,' he called back. 'Might I see him?'

'No, not really,' Rory said, catching up with him. 'He's not receiving visitors.'

'Not well, is he?'

'Had a dirty nose. Nothing serious.'

'Is that him? In the box down there?' Blaze pointed towards the horse's isolation stable and headed there before Rory could stop him.

'How did you know I'd bought a horse from Padraig Flanagan?' he asked when he caught the young man up.

'There's always talk when a horse crosses the water, Mr Rawlins, so there is,' Blaze replied. 'Particularly when it's to a betting yard.'

'This is not a betting yard. At least not when I'm in charge.'

'Rumour always was that your father liked a touch.'

'My father is in hospital at the moment.'

'I'm sorry to hear that.' Blaze turned to him, fixing him with a look of genuine sympathy. 'I hope it's not anything serious.'

'He had a heart attack,' Rory replied. 'And now he has a secondary infection.'

'Then may God help him,' Blaze said sincerely. 'He'll be in my prayers so. Now let's have a look at this horse of yours.'

'I'd rather you didn't disturb him, Mr Molloy,' Rory said.

'Blaze, please,' the young man insisted. 'And disturb him is the last thing I'll do.'

Rory sighed and stood by the half-open stable door while his uninvited visitor cast his eye over the horse.

'Not a lot of him,' Blaze observed. 'But he's got a good backside – and I hear he has a bit of a leap in him. Good legs too. And not far off racing I'd say, either. Long as he's well in himself.'

'I don't need a work rider, Mr Molloy, thanks all the same,' Rory said, closing the stable up behind the jockey.

'I'll ride work for nothing, sir. Not even the petrol.'

'Why would you want to do that?'

'Because I would, because of what I've heard about him,' Blaze replied, now dropping his laconic manner and becoming serious. 'Look, Mr Rawlins – I'll ride all the work you want in return for the ride. The first ride, mind. Just the first ride. I'm not asking for all of them. Let me ride his first race for you, that's all I'm asking.'

'I'm sorry,' Rory replied. 'I don't know anything about you. I don't even know if you can ride.'

'I can ride, Mr Rawlins, and if you let me ride the horse I'll win on him, for sure I will,' Blaze informed him, taking off his sunglasses and regarding Rory with large bright eyes the colour of cornflowers. 'And when I do, you'll want me to go on riding him, I promise you.'

'Do I look like a lemon? I don't know a thing about you, Mr Molloy,' Rory repeated. 'You could be the worst rider in Ireland for all I know.'

'No, he's certainly not that,' Kathleen's voice said behind Rory. 'He's not that at all, Mr Rawlins. They say this is a lad who's really going places.'

Rory turned round to stare at Kathleen and found her staring at Blaze.

'You two know each other?' he enquired.

'I don't know Mr Molloy,' Kathleen said. 'Not personally. But I know of him.'

'Then how do you know his name?' Rory frowned at her.

'I was – I was eavesdropping, I'm afraid,' Kathleen confessed. 'I'm afraid I was born nosy.'

'And you are?' Blaze asked, staring back at Kathleen.

'Kathleen Flanagan. Padraig Flanagan's daughter.'

'So you are,' Blaze said quietly. 'Is that right now? So you are, so you are.'

'I think this is utter – what do you call it? Blarney. Utter blarney. This is complete and utter blarney,' Rory protested. 'So you are – is that right now – yes you are. So you are, so you are.'

'Mr Molloy rides point to point, Mr Rawlins. And hunter chases.'

'Ah, but I have a proper licence this season, Miss Flanagan,' Blaze said. 'I can ride conditional.'

'I can vouch for his riding, Mr Rawlins,' Kathleen said. 'I saw him ride a grand double at Tramore in the spring.'

'But only point to point,' Rory said, becoming slowly aware of how the two were still regarding each other. 'Mr Molloy here is proposing himself to ride under Rules – and n-n-not only that – he's proposing he rides your horse here.'

'No, your horse, Mr Rawlins,' Kathleen corrected him. 'And you could do a lot worse,' she said.

'You won't do better, sir,' Blaze said with a sudden broad smile, taking off his cap and shaking out a head of curling blond hair. 'You wait and see.'

'If anyone else tells me to do that today,' Rory sighed, 'I shall give all this up and take up market ger-ger – *gardening*. Dammit, look – all right. Look, I'll put you up on something tomorrow – but only to see if you're as good as you seem to be saying you are – and when I've seen how you ride work, maybe I'll let you know my decision then.'

'God, now, that's fair enough,' Blaze said. 'God, thanks. God, that'll do me nicely.'

'I should think it is fair enough,' Rory muttered before turning his back. 'And you can leave G-God out of it.'

'So now tell me about yourself,' he heard Blaze saying to Kathleen as they walked away together. 'And how come and God knows why we've never met before.'

'Dunkum?' Rory called to his dog. 'Get in the car, boy – I don't know about you but I need a good long walk.'

By the time Rory had returned from a three mile point on Salisbury Plain, he was happy to see that Blaze Molloy had gone from the yard, just as he was happy to see that the yard was looking altogether smarter and tidier now that he had not only an extra pair of hands at work but hands that belonged to the skilled, devoted and beautiful Kathleen Flanagan. The clocks had long gone back so twilight was already setting in, the yard illuminated now only by the lights from the feed and tack rooms and those on the outside walls of the stables. Rory stopped and looked round him and thought what an oddly pleasing and happy sight it was, a racing yard at the time of evening stables, the horses all exercised and fed and most of them standing dozing happily at the doors of their boxes, or quietly munching a mouthful of fresh hay, while the stable cats stood stretching their backs and yawning in the anticipation of a good evening's mouse-hunting. Tonight all was quiet with not a horse kicking a door, the silence broken only by an occasional snort of equine satisfaction or the sound of one of them shaking itself after a good roll in its bedding. He had always enjoyed evening stables, ever since he was a boy, but now he was actually in charge he found he was deriving an even deeper sense of contentment from walking round the boxes, checking all the occupants and seeing them settled for the evening.

'Strange,' he said to himself as he made his way to the most important box on his round. 'I could be in Florence painting, doing the thing I do best, the thing I always wanted to do – and yet here I am, and really not minding at all. Which is really very odd altogether.'

He looked over The Enchanted's door and to his relief

saw that the little horse was at his manger, which he was busy licking clean. The horse cocked an eye at him then returned to his pot-scouring, his tail swishing occasionally as he searched vainly for one last mouthful. Having checked the rest of the yard Rory wandered over to the tack room and found Kathleen there in company of Teddy, cleaning saddles and bridles that now looked like new.

'Want a mug of tea, boss?' Teddy asked him. 'Kettle's just boiled.'

Rory accepted the offer and sat down opposite the two of them, picking up a racing saddle and beginning to clean it.

'This mysterious visitor of ours, Miss Flanagan – Kathleen,' he said, quickly correcting himself as he dipped a piece of sponge into a tin of saddle soap. 'What more do you know about him?'

'No more than I said, really,' Kathleen replied, glancing up at him from her work. 'He's made a bit of a name for himself riding point to point in the south-west – in Cork – and of course he rode in the Foxhunters at Cheltenham this year.'

'Did he finish? How did he do?'

'He was fifth, on one of Red Turvey's runners. I didn't see the race, but they say it was a good enough effort. He led for most of the race and he caught the eye enough to get a mention in the press.'

'And he wants to ride over here now professionally,' Rory said, wondering why. 'Rather than over there.'

'So it would seem, Mr Rawlins,' Kathleen replied, polishing the saddle on her knee. 'But then don't most Irish jocks come over sooner rather than later? There's a lot of opportunity and the pay's better, too.'

'Yes. Yes, that's true – but if you don't have much of a track record getting started isn't easy. Not even getting bad rides.'

'Which is why he's come here then, I'd say,' Kathleen

replied. 'Not for the bad rides—' She glanced up again at him, this time with a smile in her eyes. 'I meant to try to get a start.'

'Nothing to do with anything else, then?' Rory asked her, concentrating on cleaning the saddle he had on his knees. 'Or anyone?'

'I said I never met him,' Kathleen said, the smile now gone. 'And I have not so.'

'Fine.' Rory dipped his sponge in the soap again. 'But he thinks I'll just take him on just like that – sight more or less unseen.'

'You said you'd give him a trial. You couldn't have been fairer than you were.'

'I doubt he's much of a jockey yet, though.'

'Why would that be, Mr Rawlins?'

Rory shrugged and smiled at her. 'He still has all his teeth.'

'He has,' Kathleen replied, giving as good as she had just got. 'Which gives him the best of smiles.'

Favouring Rory with a deliberately overpolite smile of her own, Kathleen stood up, hung the clean saddle on the rack and took down another, leaving Rory with nothing except a deep desire to go and kick some furniture.

Chapter Fourteen

The Remedy

There was no doubt about it. Boyo was feeling better. Before, he had been feeling bad. His throat had hurt him and he'd felt as if he was full of dust, as if everything he'd eaten was dust. But now he felt good again, he felt right, so to tell her he went and kicked his stable door many times. Finally he threw back his head and bellowed because he knew this often got them running.

Sure enough, here they came – here *she* came, the one who had found her way here to be with him again. He'd been happy to see her and this time she was here for longer so he made a noise at her, blew at her through his lips, then pushed her with his muzzle because he knew this always made her laugh.

'So who's feeling better then?' she asked him, pushing him back, then running her hands up under his neck and tickling the bottom of his chin. 'Are you feeling all better then, Boyo? Because you look as bright as a May morning. Come on, let's take you out. Let's put a collar on you and walk you out.'

She unbolted his door and led him out. He stopped when

he was in the yard and pricked his ears, hearing something from a distant field, before giving himself a good shake.

'Mr Rawlins?' she was calling. 'He's eaten all his breakfast and the glands in his neck are right as rain!'

The man came over to him now and felt his neck and looked into his eye.

'Can I run him out? Let him have a bit of a blow?' she asked. 'He's been standing in a while so he could do with a blow.'

'His nose is clean,' the man said. 'And you're right about the glands. Just check his temperature, and if it's still normal—'

'Which it will be.'

'Which it undoubtedly will be, turn him out for an hour, and we'll see how he is then.'

Kathleen did as told and checked his temperature, which was, as she had predicted, still absolutely normal; then she rugged him up and took him to the home paddock where she let him go.

He stood until he knew she was safe then turned right round and bolted down the field as fast as he could, leaping in the air twice as he did so. He found the muddiest and the smelliest part of the paddock, bent his front legs at the knees, lowered himself carefully down then fell happily to one side, his shoulder splashing in the thick heavy mud. Once down he lay still for a moment then rolled on to his back, all four legs waving in the air as he tried his best to bury himself in the ground. He fell on to his other side and rolled there as well, then once he was sure he had well and truly covered himself in mud he got carefully to his feet, front legs first then a good push with the hind, shook himself thoroughly, jumped in the air, reared, turned round twice, then walked slowly away to begin grazing, safe in the knowledge that whoever lay in wait in the trees above him would no longer recognise his smell and so would no longer wish to eat him.

Kathleen watched him for some time, seeming to sense the horse's mood and condition, so that when she saw him running, rolling, shaking and jumping for joy in the air she knew he was better. Leaving him to his grazing, she hurried off to continue with her work.

Chapter Fifteen

A Piece of Work

'There's nothing wrong with his foot,' Kathleen insisted as she walked the horse up for Rory the next morning. 'Nothing at all.'

'No, he really was going short last night,' Rory insisted. 'If you'd just trot him up?'

'I put arnica on it!' Kathleen called over her shoulder, having turned the horse away first before trotting him back up to the waiting trainer. 'He must have stood on a stone in the paddocks.'

Rory felt like replying that it had been her bright idea to turn the horse out but thought it a cheap shot so decided against it.

'Fine, but we've been through all that, Kathleen,' he replied instead. 'What we have to make sure now is that he's nice and level. That it's not still bothering him.'

'Well?' Kathleen asked after she had trotted the horse up twice.

'Seems fine,' Rory said. 'As far as I can see he's totally sound.'

'Arnica is great for the bruises.'

'We learn a little every day,' Rory said, lightly, he hoped, but obviously not, he concluded, when he saw one of those quick but dark clouds scud across Kathleen's beautiful face.

'We do, don't we?' she replied. 'If we look and listen.'

'You can put the horse away now, thank you, Kathleen.'

'Think of the saving in vet's bills,' Kathleen called back to him as she put her charge in his box. 'How much is it for a call out now?'

'Enough,' Rory told her, following her into the stable. 'Thank you.'

'So are we on?' another Irish voice asked him from the door of the box. 'Is himself sound or what?'

'How did you know— Yes, wait a minute,' Rory said, turning to regard Blaze. 'You knew the horse— I don't understand.'

'Kathleen here rang me,' Blaze replied. 'She was worried she'd done something wrong.'

Rory gave them both a look before returning to Boyo and picking up and inspecting the hoof that had been damaged.

'If he stays sound, which let's just hope he will . . .' Rory said, cueing a glance between Kathleen and Blaze that he just happened to catch.

'God willing indeed,' Blaze added. 'God willing, yes indeed. That he stays sound, sir.'

'. . . I thought of giving him a piece of work tomorrow.'

'Tomorrow would be favourite, Mr Rawlins. Then we shall see what we shall see.'

'Most pro-pro-profound, Mr Molloy. I c-couldn't have put it better myself.'

'The horse looks grand, doesn't he? He looks well in himself to be sure,' Blaze observed.

'He's still got too much of a belly on him,' Rory muttered. 'But a couple of bits of f-fast work should do the trick. I'll put you up on him tomorrow. See how you get on.'

'Mr Martin along the way has just seen me ride – and he says I can ride for him.'

'So g-go – g-go and ride for him then,' Rory said, ushering Kathleen out of the stable and closing the door behind them.

'Wouldn't I rather ride for you?'

'Mr Martin along the way has over forty horses in training,' Rory informed him. 'You'd stand a far better chance of riding your winners there.'

'Riding winners is not what I'm after, Mr Rawlins,' Blaze said slowly, fixing Rory with his bright blue eyes. 'Riding good horses is what I'm about.'

'We pull out at nine,' Rory said, standing up. 'On the dot.'

'I shall be here be eight, sir,' Blaze said, touching his cap and just before taking his leave smiling just a little bit too long at Kathleen for Rory's peace of mind.

Duly summoned by Rory and alerted by Grenville, the new racing partnership were told to be in the yard at Fulford Farm at 8.45 a.m. sharp, well wrapped up for the gallops. Alice and Millie were the first to arrive, by which time five of the six horses that were to work that morning were already rugged up and walking round the edge of the square of grass in the middle of the yard, the work riders busy adjusting leathers and girths as their charges warmed up under them. As Alice and Millie sat watching from inside their car, Grenville's Jaguar pulled into the yard with the other three partners aboard.

'Morning, all,' Grenville called with a doff of his hat as he emerged from behind the wheel. 'Cold enough for the famous monkeys, I think, don't you?'

'I don't have the foggiest idea what he means,' Alice said *sotto* as she and Millie went over to greet Constance and Lynne, the latter looking like someone going on a *Vogue* fashion shoot in her fur-lined knee-high boots and new suede coat, also lined with sheepskin.

'I know.' Millie smiled. 'But I like Grenville. There's something almost quaint about him.'

'I could do with a hot toddy,' Constance complained. 'And what on earth am I doing here and not in Antigua?'

The women then fell to silence as Kathleen led their horse out of his stable. It was not the sight of The Enchanted that transfixed them, however, but the slim and elegant young man who now appeared from the tack room, ready to mount up.

'Top of the morning to you!' Blaze called, touching his crash hat. 'Let's hope we are going to see something special this morning, ladies!'

'I already have, thank you,' Lynne muttered. '*Who* is that bit of eye candy, please?'

'This is our mystery man, Lynne,' Rory said, coming to greet his owners. 'Blaze Molloy, if you would, freshly in from the land of Eternal Charm.'

'I often thought of going to live in Ireland,' Millie remarked. 'Now I well think I might. Talk about the world being bright and gay.'

'I take it that's a reference to his Irish eyes and not his private preferences, Millie,' Alice remarked, also unable to take her eyes off the slim figure in his tight riding breeches and shiny red windcheater.

'You betcha.' Millie laughed. 'But something tells me he bats for our team, Alice.'

'Did one hear right?' Constance wondered, looking in a vaguely accusatory way at Grenville. 'Did someone say his name was Blazer? What will parents think of next?'

'Blaze, madam,' their jockey corrected her as he prepared to be given a leg up by Rory. 'Blaze Molloy, at your service.'

'Most original,' Constance said with a nod. 'But not as good as my great-uncle, who was called Daisy.'

'Daisy, Lady Frimley?' Lynne frowned. 'You didn't actually have a great-uncle called Daisy?'

Constance sniffed. 'I most certainly did,'

'How on earth did he get to be called Daisy, Constance?' Alice enquired.

'Possibly because his preference was to dress as a woman.'

By now Blaze had swung easily into his saddle and gathered his reins, feeling the little horse feeling good and strong under him, both of them glad to be alive on this crisp, sharp winter morning. 'Let's hope your lovely horse goes as well as he looks, girls,' he said, before moving off to join the back of the string.

'I like "girls",' Constance murmured. 'I wonder if he has a father?'

'How do you think your horse looks?' Rory asked. 'I know he's still got a bit of a belly on him but that's only because he's short of a piece of work.'

'Nothing wrong, I trust?' Grenville enquired in line with his role as the partnership's racing manager. 'Nothing we should know about?'

'No – no, a couple of days in the sick bay with a dirty nose, but he's all better now, Grenville. If you'd like a quick cup of tea or coffee? Let's all have something. It takes them a good twenty minutes to get to the bottom of the hill.'

The party followed their trainer into the house, where they were all greeted joyfully by Dunkum. The lurcher took a particular shine to Lynne's new fur-lined coat, which had to be hung up well out of his range.

'He has a very bright eye, don't you think?' Alice remarked as Rory prepared the coffee.

'The jockey or the horse, Alice?' Lynne said.

'Our horse, Lynne. He looks – well. He looks rather full of purpose, I thought.'

'Let's hope you're right. You want a horse to be a bit of a street fighter,' Rory said, handing round the tea and coffee. 'And from what we've seen so far, Boyo doesn't like being taken on.'

'Not another candidate for the shades?' Millie wondered.

'Heavens no – no, the last thing he'll need will be blinkers, Millie,' Rory replied. 'Listen – soon as someone gets to his quarters he seems to find another gear. All right, OK, so he hasn't done a really serious gallop yet. This is only what I've seen so far, but we'll certainly learn a bit more this morning.'

'They're going to take each other on, then?' Grenville said. 'And in case you're wondering, ladies, what we mean by that is that some gallops are just precisely that. Horses coming up in line and not really racing each other. A serious piece of work should have the horses pitched against each other.'

'Not everyone would go for that though, Grenville,' Rory said. 'There's a theory that if you do that you can leave your race on the gallops.'

'Pass,' Alice said, with a shake of her head.

'Meaning you can cook your horse in before he gets to the races,' Rory explained. 'But don't worry. I'll try – I'll do my best not to let that happen.'

But Rory was a long way from as confident as he was trying to sound. As far as he was concerned this was where push very much came to shove, since in all his time as assistant to his father and during the weeks his father had been ill he had never really had to face the question of how far and how fast to work a piece of machinery as complex as a thoroughbred racehorse. He had seen how his father did it and there were many things about his father's methods that he criticised, but he had never so far had to put any of his own theories into practice. He knew that one piece of wrong work could quite easily spoil the newcomer and ruin his immediate chances, which would mean either a deeply disappointing first run or not running him at all for another month while they struggled to get the animal right again. So, smile as he might, as Rory drove his new owners up to the gallops his heart was well and truly in his mouth.

As indeed was Kathleen's. She too was riding work, having volunteered her services when one of Rory's occasional work riders called in to say he had the flu. She was riding Trojan Jack, with instructions to hit the front two furlongs from the end of the gallop and see if The Enchanted could get anywhere near the canny old handicapper. She knew from Teddy what a rogue Jack could be, but also that when he put his mind to it he could murder the rest of the Fulford string. So if he decided to put his best foot forward this morning Kathleen knew that her little horse would have his work cut out for him.

'Don't go soft on him now, Kathleen!' Teddy called as they reached the foot of the gallops and prepared to go. 'The boss wants to see what the new boy's made of, so you kick that old bugger on, right? I'm going to take him on as well!'

Teddy was riding Alone At Last, a relative newcomer to the stable who having taken time to grow into his frame was yet to race, but was now beginning to show the signs of some ability in his fast work. Now that he had strengthened, instead of looking like a giraffe the big horse looked purposeful and strong, as well as standing a good hand and a half over The Enchanted, who with the tall figure of Blaze in the saddle looked even smaller than he really was. Kathleen took a good look at the little horse, thinking the very same thing, yet noting that under his coat, which now had the beginnings of a real gleam to it, the muscles looked tight and hard.

'OK!' Teddy called. 'Kick on!'

A second later they were off and running.

When she felt what she had in her hands as well as under her saddle, Kathleen suddenly realised she had never ridden anything quite as fit, fast and strong as Jack, who had obviously decided today was going to be one of his good days. They had barely gone half a furlong before he had pulled himself clear into a two-length lead and was seriously motoring, really enjoying having the good turf under his hooves and a flyweight on his back. She heard Teddy yelling at her to take a pull as he got left behind, so she shifted her weight back a little and shortened up, but Jack had hold of the bit and was taking no notice. She tried to take a quick look round but the horse was pulling so much she was afraid of losing her balance and coming off, so she kept her head down, looking between his ears and doing her best to keep him balanced.

She had half expected and certainly hoped that halfway up the hill she might catch a glimpse of Boyo hacking up beside her, but there was neither sight nor sound of him, just the wind howling in her ears and the thunder of hooves on old turf.

'Dear God in heaven,' she prayed. 'Don't let me go beating my own horse now.'

'Here they come!' Rory told everyone, pointing to where the horses were just beginning to come into view – or rather one horse was, a horse that with only two furlongs left to run was well clear of the rest.

'Who is that?' Grenville called, peering at the distant animal through his race glasses. 'God, it's only Jack!' he cried. 'Going like a train, too!'

'It can't be,' Rory muttered. 'If it is, there's a glue factory waiting.'

He'd wanted The Enchanted to lie up so he wouldn't have a lot of work to do if he were to try to catch any horse leading him, but from what he could see it was Trojan Jack first, the rest nowhere, all of them stuck in a bunch some four or five lengths down. Then, as they got closer, with about a furlong and a half to run, he saw The Enchanted in the middle of the group. Blaze had him settled and the horse was moving easily but well within himself, his rider sitting as still as a statue and waiting for the moment, waiting for the time he would press the button and say go – at least so Rory hoped, although in view of how much Blaze seemed still to have under him, hope was growing fainter and certainty fast taking its place.

Jack was still galloping flat out, with no one else apparently making the slightest impression on him. Then, in a second, it was over. Blaze let out an inch of rein, his horse picked up and that was that. The little horse didn't look so little any more as he cut down the leader, ranged alongside and then left him, thundering past his trainer and his owners a good two lengths to the good and still hard held.

The others followed on in a cacophony of hooves on grass, leather slapping, riders shouting and whips cracking, but all to no avail. The Enchanted had murdered them, so comprehensively in fact that the moment he flew past Trojan Jack the beaten horse dropped his bit and slumped from first to last. Alone At Last came out of the pack to finish second, but looked and sounded cooked when Rory got over to where the horses were pulling up.

'Did you see that then?' Blaze grinned down at him from the saddle. 'But if I were you now, I'd keep it under your hat.'

'I just hope no one else is up here this morning,' Rory said with a shake of his head. 'Was that as easy as it looked?'

'That was just third gear, sir,' Blaze assured him. 'It doesn't matter how good or bad the rest of them are, this fella wasn't even in top, let alone overdrive.'

'He's blowing a bit,' Rory observed.

'Sure he is, but then isn't this his first bit of real work? It's a question of how long he blows *for*.'

Kathleen trotted Jack up to join them.

'Jeeze,' she said. 'One moment I saw his head and the next his backside. And this horse is nowhere near race fit.'

'Fine! Thank you!' Rory said, instructing his riders. 'Keep your horses moving, please! Don't let them stand still – particularly in this wind. Soon as they have their breath back, go back to the yard. Thank you!'

'Blaze said he never let the horse down, Mr Rawlins,' Kathleen whispered to him, bending down to him from the saddle, so close Rory could feel her warm breath on his cheek. 'He said he could have picked Jack off from ten lengths.'

'That's good, but it's early days yet, Kathleen, early days,' Rory replied. 'Now keep your h-horse moving, if you would.'

'The little horse really is something other, I tell you,' Kathleen said, before swinging Jack round to catch up with the others. 'Quite something else!'

'Ladies,' Grenville said when the partners and Millie were back in Rory's kitchen where Maureen was in the middle of making them all a fried breakfast. 'Ladies, I am here to tell you I think we have a horse.'

'He certainly looked jolly impressive,' Millie agreed. 'That was some gallop.'

'Was it?' Alice said. 'I say.'

'Absolutely,' Grenville continued. 'I think what we saw this morning was most promising, and I really do think we may have a rather good little horse here. He might well pick up a nice little race somewhere.'

'Less of the little, Grenville,' Lynne warned him. 'This little horse – our little horse – is going to win a lot of races and not little ones either. Any more of that little nonsense and Connie won't be the only one calling you Glanville.'

'OK,' Rory said, coming into the room, having finished his debriefing. 'Now then – look, I don't want anyone to get over-excited—'

'Oh, I don't mind,' Constance interrupted. 'I'd quite welcome it.'

'As you've probably gathered that was a very good piece of work we all just saw,' Rory said carefully, still not quite able to believe what he himself had seen. 'And I'm not going to make any great pronouncements – just this. There are such things as morning glories – horses that beat the birds on the gallops, but then when you get them to the course it's an entirely different matter. I'm not saying this is the case here, I'm really not. No, all I'm saying is we won't know how good or bad this horse is till we get him to the track, and with that in mind and with your say-so I think we should run him in the two-mile novice chase next week – at Wincanton again. It might be a country track but the going's invariably good, the racing's always competitive there so it's not a question of an easy option, and given that the horse looks as though he might have a bit of toe—'

'A bit of a toe?' Alice enquired.

'A bit of toe, duck,' Millie corrected her. 'Toe as in speed. Being a sharp track Wincanton might just suit him.'

'A sharp track?'

'Sharp as in fast, sweetie. A flat galloping track.'

'I thought we were going jump racing.'

'Flat as in level,' Millie sighed. 'There'll be jumps all right, don't you worry.'

'I'm getting there, slowly,' Alice replied.

'We'll give him another bit of fast work before then,' Rory told her, 'as well as lots of long slow stuff, but as he's small and appears to be quite naturally athletic, I don't think he needs a lot of hard work. So if it's all right with the owners – Wincanton it is.'

'What about a school?' Grenville asked.

'They want to send him to school now?' Alice enquired, deliberately wide-eyed.

'School as in jumping,' Rory explained. 'School him over fences. Yes, of course we shall give him a school – I was planning to do that tomorrow provided all is well. Although one thing I do know,' Rory added, remembering a famous rainy afternoon in Cronagh. 'I do know this horse can jump.'

The following day Blaze schooled the horse over the yard's four practice fences, jumping them twice. The first time they let him jump on his own, and he didn't put a foot wrong. The second time they jumped him in the company of two of Rory's neighbour's hunter chasers who were both schoolmasters when it came to jumping birch, and The Enchanted jumped all four fences alongside, straight and true, and most important of all, as Rory noted, landing and getting away from the jumps much more quickly and nimbly than the experienced duo schooling with him.

'You have to fancy his chances, Guv,' Teddy said when they were back in the yard. 'I know these two-mile novice chases take a bit of winning, but this horse doesn't seem to be a novice.'

'It'll be a hot race. Tony Pope's bound to run a couple,' Rory said. 'And I know Captain Timms intends to run a rather smart novice of his, so it's not going to be exactly a gentle introduction. Pope's will go off as if they've been scalded, and the captain's will be able to jump.'

'Nothing ventured,' Teddy said, taking the saddle from Rory, and starting to head for the tack room. 'This fella looks as if he was born doing it.'

'One thing's certain,' Rory said. 'He won't start favourite.'

Chapter Sixteen

Off and Running

The four of them sat round Rory's kitchen table studying the declarations in almost complete silence, as if the list of horses running was some rediscovered masterpiece. Occasionally Rory would click his tongue, or Blaze would inhale and exhale with apparent deep significance. Kathleen sat absolutely still, her lips pursed together so tightly that all the colour seemed drained from them, while Teddy chain-smoked his way through several cigarettes.

'There's no doubt about it,' Teddy said, finally breaking the hush. 'The captain's horse is the one to beat, given the way he trotted up at Ludlow.'

'My father says there's always one to beat, Teddy,' Rory said, waving away a cloud of smoke from Teddy's cigarette. 'If there wasn't we might as well keep all our horses in their stables.'

'But look at the way it's bred, boss,' Teddy replied, tapping his paper. 'This is a class horse.'

'Mr Pope's two have got form as well,' Blaze remarked. 'Both Taunton winners.'

'There's a decent-looking horse from Lambourn, too,'

Teddy added. 'One of David Chambers's. The yard's in form and the horse cost a packet at Doncaster sales.'

'Can we discount this unraced fella from Eddie Rampton's yard?' Blaze wondered. 'Isn't your man fond of using the racecourse as a schooling ground?'

'You want to watch what you're saying if Mr Rampton is anywhere in the vicinity,' Rory advised. 'Eddie Rampton's renowned for his short fuse. He's had several head to heads with reporters for hinting that he hadn't run some of his horses on merit recently.'

'He certainly has,' Teddy agreed. 'Eddie Rampton is not someone to cross. Before he took up training he was the stable lads' unbeaten lightweight champion for four years running.'

'His training methods aren't all that tasty either,' Rory added. 'Prone to hitching his horses to his Land Rover with a lead rope and making them gallop flat out behind him.'

'Imagine working for a guy like that,' Teddy muttered, returning to his study of the form. 'Anyway, all things considered, it looks as if it's going to be a hot one.'

'They're quoting our fella at anything from sixteen to twenty to one,' Blaze said. 'I'd say he's going to make some people very happy.'

'And I'd say that just about represents his chance,' Rory said, getting up from the table.

'Well, I'm going to have a touch,' Teddy decided, stubbing out his cigarette. 'In fact I'm going to have a wallop. Jack left a rather nasty hole in the savings.'

'You're very quiet, K-Kathleen,' Rory said, looking at Kathleen, who was still sitting stock still and had hardly said a word since they had all gathered round the table.

'I know,' she said quietly, swallowing hard. 'I think I have to say I've got what we call at home an attack of the reals. In fact I think I need a breath of fresh air.'

'Good idea,' Blaze said, getting up with her. 'After sitting next to Teddy here, I need fumigating.'

Rory watched the two of them cross the yard and walk over to The Enchanted's box. When he next looked, Blaze had his arm round Kathleen's shoulders and seemed to be talking to her most confidentially. The next time he looked, which he found he had to do, Kathleen had her hand in Blaze's and was walking away with him towards the paddocks.

'Don't they make a pretty couple?' Maureen remarked, handing him some letters to sign. 'They're both of them very good-looking.'

'Who's that?' Rory wondered, feigning ignorance. 'Sorry?'

'Kathleen and your new rider fellow.'

'Do they? I wouldn't know,' Rory said, glancing over the papers he'd just been given. 'I was looking at the skies. Seeing what the weather's doing.'

'Don't forget your appointment with your bank manager,' Maureen said, rolling her eyes up to the ceiling. 'You've less than an hour.'

It's a race, Rory kept reminding himself as he drove into Salisbury. *Or rather more specifically, it's only a horse race. And anything can happen in a horse race, and usually does.*

But however much he tried to convince himself that he must treat the outcome of tomorrow's race the same way he had seen his father react to racing's ups and downs – treating both impostors just the same, in the words of Anthony's favourite poem – he could not escape the feeling that he might just have a horse that was capable of winning what looked like a decent novice chase. There wasn't really another animal on the yard about which he could say the same; they were all either exposed handicappers that were capable of running a good sort of race off the right weight in moderate company, or horses that had been weeded out from some smart yard or other as being simply not up to their elevated standards, or promising moderately bred novices such as Alone At Last. There was nothing that excited him the way The Enchanted had done the morning he had got his first glimpse of what this youngster might be able to do. The times he could remember being excited racing were those rare and memorable occasions when along with other racegoers he had witnessed a horse with that special magic – the ability to find another gear and leave its fellow competitors stone cold. Most times, like everyone else, he enjoyed watching good honest horses racing courageously over stiff fences on a fair course. That was the nature of the sport as it was the nature of everything in life. What stopped people in their tracks, what made the hair stand up on their necks, what made them gasp, tingle or become speechless, was witnessing something not just out of the ordinary but quite extraordinary, and however much Rory tried to dismiss the notion, he found he was unable to stop believing that the result of tomorrow's race might actually prove to be a turning point in the fortunes of the yard.

More than anything he wanted this to be so, not for himself but for his father.

If it happens, he told himself as he walked towards the bank. *If and only if it happens, this might just be the tonic you need, Pop.*

'I quite understand your position, Mr Rawlins,' the bank manager told him. 'And please don't think I am not sympathetic to it.'

'Yes, well, you might be, Mr Hawkins,' Rory replied, 'but

certainly not the letter from the bank. The bank's letter to my father was most certainly not, not at all. I mean, the bank must know that he's lying in hospital not just seriously ill but he's there fighting for his life, and instead of that – that is, instead of giving everyone a little more time here, the bank is saying it feels it must call in the loan.'

'This is simply bank policy, Mr Rawlins. It is nothing to do with me personally. I have always done my best to find ways of helping your father and his racing business.'

'And in return you've had some more than good information, at least so my father told me, Mr Hawkins.'

'That is neither here nor there, Mr Rawlins,' the bank manager replied after quietly clearing his throat. 'All I am trying to point out is that these orders come from head office, not from me personally.'

'Yes, fine – but can't you put in a plea for special consideration?'

'I have done that, believe me. But while my superiors are naturally sympathetic it must be remembered that this is a bank, not some form of charitable institution.'

'So exactly how long do we have before you come and take the fixtures and fittings, then?'

'It certainly won't come to that, rest assured, Mr Rawlins.'

'You mean you'll accept an IOU.'

'I think we already have that in some form or another, Mr Rawlins. But to answer your question properly, as to how long we can extend the current overdraft facility on the yard itself, I would say we shall be looking at a time scale of four weeks.'

'If you wouldn't mind, because I've forgotten . . . How much exactly does the overdraft stand at?'

The manager turned the sheet of paper in front of him round so that Rory might be able to read it and pushed it towards him.

When he saw the figures, Rory froze inside. Whatever happened tomorrow or indeed in the next month or even the next six months, there was no way he was going to be able to find the funds to repay the debt his father had run up on the business.

'What about the farm?' Rory asked, when he had got his inner breath back. 'Leaving the racing business aside, if we can – or may— I mean, the farm itself must have a considerable value. More than considerable.'

'Indeed so, Mr Rawlins. And while the bank would have been quite content to take that as collateral—'

'Would have been happy?' Rory interrupted, frowning. 'Would have been?'

'Your father resolutely refused to let us have a charge on the farm in return for what is owed on the racing business. He has consistently maintained that he would rather go to prison than put the farm at risk and thus his family, meaning you in particular.'

Stopped in his tracks momentarily, since he had never realised this had been his father's priority, Rory attempted to marshal his thoughts.

'There must be some way we can use the farm now, isn't there?' he said. 'After all, look, if I am to inherit it—'

'Which I understand is exactly the case, Mr Rawlins.'

'Can't we somehow use it as security? I mean, if the worst comes to the worst—'

'I'm very much afraid that's exactly what would have to happen,' the manager replied, averting his gaze. 'If sadly your father were to—'

'No,' Rory said quickly and firmly. 'Come on now – there just has to be some other way.'

'The only other way would be for you to get your father to allow the bank to take a charge on the farm now. That way the loan would be permitted to stand, for a while anyway. But given your father's condition—'

'I couldn't possibly ask him to do that, not now!' Rory said. 'If he's been that determined to avoid putting the farm up, then to try to persuade him to change his mind now – I mean, can you imagine? For crying out loud, in his condition? No, I really couldn't do that. Really.'

'I understand.'

'Oh, no – sorry, but I don't think you do,' Rory said, beginning to get angry. 'What you want is either to take possession of the stables and everything to do with it, or else – or else you want my father to die, isn't that right? You would rather he died so that I can sign the other part of his life's work over to you – in order to wipe out a debt that compared with what the banks are losing left right and centre with their totally ill-advised investments—'

'I think that's enough, Mr Rawlins, don't you?'

'No I do not, Mr Hawkins. Enough? No, this is far from enough, Mr Hawkins. The money the banks are losing and lending quite indiscriminatingly overseas? That money is their customers' money, right? But in order to plug the holes in your boat—'

'I really do feel this interview has come to a close, thank you.'

'In order to try to balance your books,' Rory continued, 'what do you do? You start calling in every measly little overdraft you can find! And by doing so – by so doing—'

'Thank you, Mr Rawlins,' the manager said, rising from his chair.

'And by doing so, ruining good little businesses everywhere through your blasted impatience!'

'Thank you, Mr Rawlins,' the manager repeated as a security man appeared at the door in answer to a private summons made moments before. 'I think in future it would be better for both sides to conduct this business formally by letter. Good day.'

Before he left the building, Rory asked to see the balance on his personal account. He knew he was in the black not the red, but was surprised to see the amount he actually was in credit.

Where on earth did that come from? he wondered as he began the drive home. *I don't have anything like that sort of dosh.*

The mystery was cleared up when Rory examined his bank statements in detail when he returned home. The day before they had left for Ireland, it seemed his father had given in-structions to transfer the sum of two thousand pounds from the farm account to his son's account without saying a word about it. Rory stared at the details on the statement and, knowing his father, became convinced at that moment that he must have known that – as Anthony would put it himself – something was up.

Then he remembered the conversation they'd had over a dinner of delicious freshly caught mackerel and floury potatoes their first night in Ireland.

'You enjoying yourself, old chap?' his father had asked.

'Bit early to say, Pa,' Rory had replied. 'We've only just got back on terra firma. But the omens are good.'

'I meant in general. As in life in general, old thing.'

'Well, yes, Dad. Yes, I suppose so.'

'You suppose so? You *suppose* so?' His father had laughed, but not unkindly. His father wasn't given to unkind laughter. 'You can't be enjoying your life if you only suppose you are. The thing is – what you have to do,' his father had continued, pouring them both some wine, 'you must find and do something you love. Now I know what you want to do and if that's the case you simply have to go do it. You have to do what the man said – find out what you want and do it. I have to tell you that, leaving personal stuff aside' – Rory knew this meant the loss of his mother and the grief that had caused, something his father much preferred not to talk about – 'leaving that aside, I have to tell you that as far as my wonky old life has gone, I have enjoyed practically every minute of it. I've been very fortunate in doing what I do. I've met some wonderful folk, trained and worked with some cracking horses and above everything I've had *fun*. So now when it comes to it—'

'When it comes to what, Pop?' Rory had interrupted, wondering if there was something his father wasn't telling him. 'What do you mean? When it comes to it?'

'Oh, nothing.' His father had dismissed the question with an airy wave of his hand. 'Just a manner of speaking. What I meant was at this point of my life I can put my hand on my heart and say I really have enjoyed what I've done. That's all. Because I want you to be able to say the same when you reach my age – that you've done what you wanted to do and you have enjoyed your life. That's all.'

'I like working at the yard. Being your assistant.'

'Sure you do, old boy – but that's not what you *want* to do. You know what you really want to do. *I* know what you really want to do – so remember, it's never too late. It's never too late to down tools, say blow it – and bugger off and do the thing that really consumes you. That's all.'

So perhaps his father had known that he was ill, Rory thought, and in order to shore up the defences he'd deposited a sum of money in Rory's account to say to him, in this particular term of trial, *If all fails, old chap, you can always take off now and do your thing.*

That would be his father all over – and because this was what Rory knew and believed, it simply made him all the more determined to make the yard come good, one way or the other, because the yard was his father's life.

The only other thing he was left to wonder about was the fact that he hadn't stammered once during the interview at the bank.

'Are you frit, as they say oop north?' Millie asked Alice as they drove to the course. 'You definitely look a lighter shade of pale.'

'Of course I'm nervous, Millie, what do you think?' Alice replied. 'Don't tell me you don't get nervous when Jack runs?'

'I can hardly bear to look, if it were known, duck. I don't know why we do this to ourselves.'

'If I'd known I'd feel like this I think I'd definitely have had second thoughts,' Alice agreed. 'And this is only his first run.'

'Even so, it's exciting as well, right?' Millie enquired. 'Having a runner.'

'A runner's precisely what I feel like doing.' Alice sighed. 'I must be totally and completely bonkers.'

'Let's take a rain check on that, shall we? At least until after your chap's raced. In a couple of hours' time you might be feeling very different indeed.'

Lynne, Grenville and Constance were already warmly ensconced in the bar by the time Millie and Alice arrived. It was a cold but dry day, and with the promise of a good card the racegoers were arriving in force.

'Splendid,' Grenville said as Millie and Alice joined the rest of the partnership. 'Splendid – we are all met.'

'Isn't this something?' Lynne exclaimed. 'I am so excited I can hardly think straight.'

'I gave up thinking straight years ago,' Constance said. 'For all the good it was doing me.'

'Well now look,' Grenville said, tapping his hat against his leg. 'Since you ladies are all warm and cosy here, I am just going to pop out to the rails and see if there's an early betting show.'

'He's twenty to one in most papers,' Lynne said. 'And I am most definitely going to have a few quid each way at that price.'

'My money is staying in my purse, since I agree with whoever it was who said it,' Constance remarked, lighting a cheroot. 'Horse sense is the wisdom that keeps horses from betting on people.'

'*Very* good,' Grenville said, nodding and smiling. 'E'en so, and if you will excuse me, ladies, I to the bookmakers.'

On his way to the rails, Grenville bumped into Rory.

'How is the little horse, Mr Trainer?'

'He looks well,' Rory said, hoping to sound nonchalant. 'Travelled fine.'

'I'm off to see if I can get me better than twenties,' Grenville said with a smile.

'Teddy's got him at twenty-five.'

'Then I shall try to match him. See you in the paddock, old man.'

Rory watched the dapper Grenville head for the rails where the account bookmakers had their pitches, wishing that he too had an account. For a moment he thought of asking Grenville to lay his bet, but as soon as he realised he would have to disclose the precise size of his wager he thought better of it. His first intention had been to find a regular bookie with whom to bet, but being a less than novice gambler he was uncertain of the protocol. He had seen on several bookmakers' boards the slogan *No Limit*, but he also knew from past experience – his father's, not his – that some bookies had a habit of welshing on successful large bets, running away from the course before the winning punter could claim his cash, and given his intention

Rory could all too easily imagine himself being caught like that. So he knew the best, safest and only way was to bet with the Tote.

But he also knew enough about how the Tote worked to know that too large a bet placed too early could well attract the floating punters, the ones who watched the odds on the Tote shortening or lengthening to see where the money was or wasn't going. The way the Tote worked, the more money invested, the smaller the winning payout, so if he was going to use the Totalisator he was going to have to do so at the very last moment, just before the off. That is, if he placed a bet at all. The way Rory's mind was now working, the closer they got to post time the more absurd the thought of any gamble became, let alone the one he was contemplating.

The Enchanted's race was the second contest on the card and the runners for it were already being led up to the pre-parade ring, so since Rory had supervised all that he needed to supervise at this stage, he took himself off for what he hoped would be a calming walk round the enclosure, preferring to stay out of the bar and away from his owners lest their nervousness rub off on him. On his second circuit he bumped into Alice, who he discovered was also a refugee.

'I didn't realise I could get so nervous over a horse race,' she admitted to Rory as they walked into the Silver Ring to soak up a bit more atmosphere. 'Is he going to be all right, Rory? Please tell me he's going to be all right.'

'Of course the horse will be all right, Alice.' Rory did his best to comfort his ashen-faced owner. 'He's a tough sort and he can jump, so bar accidents of course he's going to be all right,' he added fatuously.

'That's what I mean,' Alice said. 'Accidents. It wouldn't be nearly so bad, I suppose, if there weren't any jumps, but I've just had a close look at those fences.'

'And you shouldn't have done,' Rory assured her. 'You're looking at them from the ground.'

'They're enormous.'

'Because you're looking at them from the ground, Alice. The horse is much bigger than you, and the jockey's on his back. To them – well, they're like athletes jumping hurdles. This is probably even easier.'

'They still fall, Rory.'

'He won't fall, Alice. No, let's put it more accurately than that – he shouldn't fall because he's a very good jumper. A lot of the horses in the race – remember, it's a novice chase, and believe me, most novice chases are exactly that – for novices, for horses with L plates on – a lot of the horses won't really know how to jump until they've run round here, and even then some will never learn. But our chap can jump, and since we're going to tell Blaze to keep up at the front and well out of trouble, I reckon he will be just fine.'

'I should never have said yes to this, Rory,' Alice said, as dismal as ever. 'It's really making me feel quite ill.'

'Come on, Alice.' Rory laughed. 'I think I'm going to have to force a brandy down you.'

'Best I could get was sixteens,' a puzzled Grenville informed his co-owners as they made their way out to watch the first race, a novice hurdle. 'Something's afoot.'

'News of the famous gallop has leaked, perhaps,' Millie said. 'There's absolutely no reason for him to be fancied.'

'Particularly since he's still only in the pre-parade ring,' Grenville added.

'What difference does that make, please?' Constance enquired, holding on to the top of her hat.

'Means he's still rugged up,' Grenville explained. 'Nobody can tell much when the horses are still rugged up, do you see. No, I think Millie here is right. I think some little bird has sung about his gallop.'

'I can't really watch this,' Alice said. 'My mind's not on it. I think I'll go and see how our horse is.'

'I'll come with you,' Lynne said, taking her arm. 'I must admit I'm feeling a bit Uncle Dick as well.'

While the first race was run, Lynne and Alice watched as Kathleen led The Enchanted from the pre-parade ring into the parade ring proper, where he joined only two other horses, some of the others already being tacked up in their saddling boxes, while the rest remained behind in the lower ring.

'How is he, Kathleen?' Alice asked as the girl led the horse past them for the second time. 'Is he all right?'

'He's fine, Mrs Dixon,' Kathleen replied, as Alice followed her round on the other side of the rails. 'He's actually switched himself off, which is pretty good.'

'How do you mean, switched himself off?'

'He's very relaxed. He's not wasting any unnecessary energy.'

'I just hope he's going to be all right,' Alice said yet again as she rejoined Lynne. 'Have you seen some of the other horses? They're enormous.'

'Size doesn't matter, Alice,' Lynne replied with a grin. 'Least so they tell me.'

'I remember Alex talking about boxing, and he said a good big 'un always beat a good small 'un, or something like that,' Alice muttered, taking some mints from her bag and offering Lynne one. 'I don't know about you, but I've got a terribly dry mouth.'

'Me, too,' Lynne agreed, accepting a sweet. 'What's wrong with us, anyway? This is meant to be fun.'

'I'd rather be having root canal treatment,' Alice said. 'Really I would.'

The roar from the stands told them that the hurdle race was reaching its climax, and within moments the crowds had streamed away from the course on their way either to collect winnings from the Tote or to stand round the winners' enclosure as the successful horses were led in. All except the four racing partners, who now gathered at the entrance to the paddock to cast their eye over the competition in a field of fourteen runners.

'One of Pope's horses has been withdrawn,' Grenville told them. 'Found him cast in his box this morning, apparently.'

'Cast?' Alice wondered. 'I thought that's what sculptors did.'

'It means basically he got stuck lying down,' Millie explained. 'They can jam themselves up against the wall and hurt themselves trying to get up.'

'Anyway, that's one less,' Grenville continued. 'The Chambers horse from Lambourn is also rumoured not to be quite right, but they haven't taken him out. There must be something up because he's certainly gone for a walk in the market.'

'Will that do him any good?' Alice enquired. 'I can't see going for a walk anywhere at this late hour's going to do much good, let alone in some market or other.'

'No, no, Alice,' Grenville said patiently. 'Going for a walk in the market equals the betting market. Look – you can see how his price has gone out.'

Grenville pointed to the Tote approximate odds board where it could be seen that a horse called Put Upon had drifted significantly from three to one out to five to one.

'While our horse is now only twelve to one,' Grenville said quietly. 'I wonder where the money's coming from?'

'Certainly not from me,' Constance assured him. 'My father always used to say a racehorse is the only animal that can take hundreds of people for a ride at the same time.'

Rory was standing in the centre of the paddock talking to another trainer. When he saw his group of owners he beckoned them to come in.

'I'm going to tell Blaze to either make the running or keep up with the pace,' he said. 'The seven pound allowance he gets as a conditional will certainly help, as long as he's up to the job.'

'I remember that bit.' Alice smiled. 'He gets a weight allowance because he's really only an apprentice.'

'Which is what these boys always used to be called,' Rory agreed. 'Until someone invented *conditional*.'

'Hope your belief in him is founded, Mr Trainer,' Grenville said as a line of jockeys now snaked its way into the paddock.

'He knows the horse, Grenville, and he hasn't put a foot wrong in his work so far.'

'He just hasn't ridden in a proper race, that's all.'

'This'll be a picnic after an Irish point to point, believe me,' Rory replied. 'And seven pounds is a lot of weight off this horse's back.'

As Blaze joined them, with a touch on the front of his cap, all eyes including his turned to the horse who was now having his rug removed by Kathleen. The moment she had it off his back, he gave a small buck born from good health and kicked his heels.

'Looks well, boss,' Blaze observed. 'Looks even better than when we boxed him up. Nice and bonny.'

'I like your colours,' Millie said to Alice, admiring the blue and claret shirt and cap. 'Very smart. Are they yours?'

'Apparently,' Alice replied. 'I chose them with the team, and Rory.'

'I think I might redo my bedroom curtains in that blue,' Constance said. 'It's not too bright.'

'You're not to go using that,' Kathleen said to Blaze, pointing to his whip.

'You giving the instructions?' Blaze replied, waiting to be legged up.

'Mr Rawlins?' Kathleen asked, as Rory legged their jockey up.

'He has to carry a whip, Kathleen,' Rory muttered. 'We've been through all this.'

'But he's not to use it,' Kathleen insisted. 'If he does I'll use it on him.'

'Just keep him handy,' Rory said to Blaze, as Kathleen prepared to lead them out on to the course. 'Get him into a nice rhythm and let him enjoy himself. But stay right in touch. If you can't make it, keep up with the pace. They go a fair old clip here.'

'Got you, boss,' Blaze said, making some final adjustments to his tack. 'I'll see yous all in the winner's enclosure!' he called over his shoulder.

'Don't you dare hit him, Blaze,' Kathleen warned him again as she walked the horse on to the exit from the paddock. 'I'm telling you.'

As the runners made their way to post, Rory excused himself and told his owners he'd see them up in the east end of the members' stand. As they hurried off to get a good vantage point to watch The Enchanted on his way down, Rory hurried off to the Tote.

'Little horse is going down well,' Grenville observed through his glasses as the line of horses made their way across the centre of the racecourse and past a fine old stone barn on their way to the two-mile start. 'As if he's been doing it all his life.'

'I feel sick,' Lynne said. 'I think I'm going to have to go and sit in the bar.'

'I'll join you,' Alice said. 'In fact why don't we just go and get legless, Lynne?'

'You'll be fine, both of you,' Grenville assured them. 'This is the worst part, believe me. Now, Captain Timms's horse is favourite,' he continued, training his race glasses on the bookies' boards in the next enclosure. 'Roaring Cavalier at five to four, so they *really* fancy that one – Pope's horse as well – Go Fast Carb two to one, while poor old Put Upon is still going walkies at five to one now and six to one in places.'

'And The Enchanted?' Millie enquired.

'Pretty solid at twelve to one,' Grenville replied. 'Making my sixteens look better by the minute. But who's backing him – and why, I do wonder? And where's our trainer gone?'

The horses were all down at the start now, the last arrivals having their girths checked by the starter's assistant while the starter himself climbed up on to his rostrum ready to call them into line.

'Where on *earth* is Rory?' Grenville wondered again. 'He's going to miss the start.'

Rory was standing alone at one of the Tote windows, the rest of the punters having all placed their bets, as the race was about to start. Rory had the money in his hand, but found himself still unable to do the deed. He was trying to convince himself that because it wasn't his money there really should be no problem, particularly since it had obviously been deposited in his account as his do-as-you-like fund. But then if it was his father's and he lost it all, it would matter. At least, according to the way Rory's mind was working it would – because if he lost it all on one ridiculously chancy gamble there would be no getting out for anyone.

'The starter's calling them into line . . .' he heard a voice announce on the tannoy. 'They're under starter's orders . . .'

'Fifteen hundred pounds to win horse number nine,' he heard a voice saying. He saw a hand pushing the money across the counter and under the glass and the operative's hand taking it. It wasn't until he had the ticket in his hand that Rory realised the voice, the hand and the money were all his. The bet was on – and the horses were off.

'And on the run to the first it's Go Fast Carb already in a clear lead,' he heard the course commentator calling as he ran back to the members' stand and up the steps to join his group.

'And they're all over the first,' the commentator continued. 'Go Fast Carb landing well clear of Roaring Cavalier in second, third Put Upon who jumped it particularly well, and then a gap to So I Gather, Lilac Daisy, Wender, Please Sir and The Enchanted.'

'So much for riding to orders,' Rory observed, now he had his glasses up. 'He must be ten lengths off the leader.'

'They are going a hell of a crack, Rory,' Grenville replied. 'But the little horse is certainly not being run off his feet.'

'I really can't look,' said Alice's muffled voice from behind Rory's back. 'Will someone please tell me when it's over?'

Out on the course itself Blaze thought he was sitting quite pretty, with his horse settled into a nice regular rhythm, jumping the second and third easily enough and lying nicely in about sixth place on the rails, some eight lengths off the leader, who really seemed to have bolted. He knew what his instructions had been, but once the Pope horse shot off like a bolting hare there was no way he was going to kick his horse on after it and waste all that precious energy. He wanted to keep The Enchanted sweet, wanted him to swing along nicely on the bridle, wanted him to have plenty of time to see his fences and plenty of time to take them in his stride. Already the tactics of the jockey up on Go Fast Carb were apparently rattling several of the novices, two of them crashing out at the first open ditch and another falling heavily at the cross fence. By the time they were turning into the home straight for the first time Go Fast Carb had failed to increase his lead although his jockey was shaking his reins and had given him a couple of hard slaps in his attempt to poach the race, while both Put Upon and Roaring Cavalier were still on the bridle and jumping like seasoned horses rather than novices.

Up the rise into the straight they rode, into the first of three big black fences and past the grandstands, Go Fast Carb's lead now no more than three lengths over the next two horses, with The Enchanted still biding his time in sixth. But Blaze could see that the two horses immediately in front of him were already labouring, finding the pace too hot and the fences too stiff. At the last fence in the straight they lost So I Gather who nose-dived on landing, his spread-eagling fall then bringing down the already beaten Wender whose rider stepped off in mid-air and managed to land on his feet and running, earning a round of applause from the spectators. Blaze saw the first horse fall and swung The Enchanted to the left, not snatching him up but just easing him to the outside of the fence in order to avoid what he suspected might be carnage on the landing side.

'Did you see that, Rory?' Grenville asked. 'The boy rode that fence like a real pro.'

But Rory was not really looking. He could hardly bear to do so. As far as he could see The Enchanted was still just cantering, but given the pace of the contest he knew it simply could not be so and that he must be kidding himself, indulging in more than a little wishful thinking. So, trying not to let anyone in his group notice, he dropped his race glasses, closed his eyes and began to sing a particularly difficult song to himself in his head.

All the field bar one had now safely negotiated the water jump positioned somewhat recklessly just before the turn into the back straight, the faller being Please Sir who dropped his legs in the water and slithered to his belly, giving his jockey no chance of staying in the plate. As they swung round the sharp right-hand bend the horse immediately to the left of The Enchanted failed to negotiate the turn and grabbing its bit swerved out across the track towards the slope that led down to the boundary of the course, consequently running out at the next fence.

'Six gone, six still standing,' Millie remarked. 'They're sure not taking any prisoners out there.'

A weak and watery sun had now come out, shining directly in the eyes of the riders and the horses and making it difficult for them to get a clear view of the fences. Blaze could see fine, but it was bothering two of the leaders who stepped into the bottom of the second fence down the back but somehow managed to get away with it. As for The Enchanted, Blaze didn't need to look for a stride because the horse under him was foot perfect, finding his own distance from the fences as if he'd been jumping all his life and getting quickly away from them on the other side without losing his rhythm. By the time they had flown the open ditch and picked up two lengths in doing so Blaze knew the little horse was going far and away the best of all of those still racing.

Again at the cross fence they lost another horse. Blaze had no idea who it was – all he heard was the crash of something heavy hitting the birch and a yelled expletive as the jockey was catapulted over his mount's head. The Enchanted, on the other hand, had met the tricky fence perfectly, again picking up a good length in the air and landing with ears pricked and still on the bridle. Into the straight now for the last time Go Fast Carb was beginning to tread water and was being reeled in by Put Upon and Roaring Cavalier, who had both now engaged top gear. The Enchanted was lying fourth.

'Time to make a move, I'd say,' Grenville informed his party. 'If we're going to get in the frame.'

'How many more times do they have to go round?' Constance wanted to know, turning her pocket race glasses on some of the more attractive older gentlemen in the grandstand. 'I've quite lost count.'

'This is it, Connie!' Lynne called to her over the increasing din. 'I think these are the last three jumps!'

'I still can't watch,' Alice cried, her head buried in Rory's back, unaware that their trainer also was standing with his head bowed and his eyes still fast closed.

'Hello?' Millie cried. 'He's got a double handful, chaps! He's cantering all over them!'

'I cannot watch!' Alice yelled. 'I cannot *bear* it!'

'You are going to have to watch, duck!' Millie shouted back. 'Your little horse is going like a winner!'

'What?' Rory said, now forcing himself to look. 'Bloody hellfire!' he exclaimed when he saw what was happening. 'Crikey almighty!'

Unlike her guv'nor, Kathleen had seen every stride of the race from her perch on the little hill at the end of the grandstand from which the lads always watched their charges, and she had known the outcome of the race as her horse had galloped past her the first time.

Bar a fall, Boyo, she'd whispered. *It's all yours, Boyo – bar a fall.*

As they ran to the third from home the race was now on in earnest, at least as far as the first three horses were concerned. The three leading jockeys all thought the race lay between

them, unaware of the outsider who was lying about four
lengths behind them, swinging along as if out for an exercise
canter, his rider sitting motionless while the three up front
were all kicking, changing their hands, throwing their reins
at their horses' heads, beating their horses regularly – in fact
doing everything in their power to win the race. All three rose
and cleared the third last together, followed by The Enchanted
still four lengths off, but as they landed Put Upon suddenly
slowed almost to a halt, his jockey's silks splashed with blood
from the burst vessel the horse had just suffered. The sight of
the distressed animal momentarily caught Blaze's eye as he
passed it, causing him temporarily to lose his bearing so that
when he turned his attention back to the business of the race
he found he was all but running up Roaring Cavalier's back
end as they ran to jump the second last.

'If that horse falls,' Rory muttered, more to himself than
to anybody else, 'God, we are history. He'll bring us down for
sure.'

'Get away from him, Molloy!' Grenville yelled fruitlessly.
'For God's sake get away!'

Blaze had seen what was happening in time and if ever his
lack of racing experience was to show, this was the moment.
Were a jockey to take a pull at this stage and at this pace he
could easily unbalance and unsettle his horse, with the result
that it might either put down at the fence and so take it by its
roots and fall, or simply just panic, balloon the fence and fall
on landing. Yet if the rider remained just where he was and
the horse right in front of him fell there would be no way of
avoiding crashing into it. And the time in hand to make a
decision was possibly less than one second.

In the end Blaze didn't do a thing, at least nothing physical.
All he did was call out something to his horse, something in
a language not known to his rivals, and as soon as he heard

the call The Enchanted did the rest. Seeing nothing but horse slap bang in front of him and nothing but hedge beyond that, the horse jumped the moment after his adversary did, but instead of rising in a dead straight line he swung himself to the left in mid-air, not enough to throw himself off balance but enough to land clear of Roaring Cavalier, who as it happened didn't fall but landed well and still running. But The Enchanted landed even better, not crooked and not in the slightest unbalanced, although his evasive action had cost him what normally might well prove to be an all-important length, because as they began their run to the last the little horse was still three or perhaps four off the leading pair, Go Fast Carb and Roaring Cavalier, who were now running neck and neck.

'What's happening!' Alice cried. 'Someone please tell me what's happening!'

'Oh, for goodness' sake, Allie!' Millie shouted back. 'Take your fingers out of your ears and take a look for yourself!'

'And as they come to the last it's still Go Fast Carb in the lead but only just!' the commentator called. 'Roaring Cavalier is right there with him with The Enchanted now beginning to make significant progress!'

The din that had swelled to a roar as both the favourites seemed to have the race between them now died considerably as one of the outsiders laid down what in other circumstances would appear to be a hopeless challenge, with the two leaders still four lengths clear at the last and neither of them showing signs of weakening. But the roars were lessening because of the notable ease with which the unknown and unfancied little horse was racing. He was running so easily that, as every seasoned racegoer in the crowd knew, provided he jumped the last as well as he had jumped all the previous fences, this horse was going to win doing cartwheels.

Blaze knew it, too. As they thundered towards the last he could see the jockey on Go Fast Carb hard at work, giving his mount two sharp ones behind the saddle before he left the ground, while the rider on Roaring Cavalier, who had chosen to come up the rails, was shouting and yelling blue murder for room as Go Fast Carb suddenly swerved across in front of him. The fence was wide open for The Enchanted who stood so far off Blaze thought he was gone and buried and all but closed his eyes. It was the longest and greatest jump he had ever sat on any horse, The Enchanted practically taking off outside the wings and yet landing lengths clear the other side.

A roar went up from the stands when the racegoers saw it, their indifference now turned to genuine admiration and respect as they realised they might be witnessing the debut of a really special animal. A few more strides were all that were needed to silence anyone still doubting, The Enchanted coming away from the last three lengths down on the leaders who were both still racing flat out, catching them both hand over fist, and in a matter of a few lengthening strides, in the time it took for Rory to put his race glasses back up, in that brief moment the battle was won. Blaze didn't even have to shake the reins at his mount. He didn't have to shout at him the way the other two jockeys were berating their brave horses. He didn't have to touch him. He didn't have to do anything more than let out the same amount of rein as he had up on the gallops and the race was over. The Enchanted went into top gear and flew.

'It's The Enchanted now!' the commentator called. 'The Enchanted is simply flying! He's right alongside Go Fast Carb – and he's past him! He's flown past Go Fast Carb and Roaring Cavalier! And to add insult to injury he's putting daylight between himself and the second two! It's The Enchanted by two, by three, by four lengths now, and Blaze Molloy still hasn't moved on him! And on the run to the post it's The Enchanted going away from them still – and it's The Enchanted – The Enchanted wins by six lengths!'

The grandstands were buzzing as everyone began discussing what they had just witnessed, while the little group of those who owned him stood in stupefied silence as they tried to come to terms with what they too had just seen.

'What happened?' a small voice said from somewhere behind Rory.

'He won, that's what happened, Alice!' Rory laughed, turning and swinging her round to face him. 'He's only gone and won! Didn't you see any of the race?'

'Not one bit,' Alice said. 'I didn't hear anything, either.'

'Because she had her ears blocked,' Millie groaned. She turned to her friend. 'I bet you were singing loudly, too, the way you always did at school when you didn't want to hear anything.'

'He really did win?' Alice said, wide-eyed. 'I mean really? This isn't all a dream?'

'He not only won, my dear Alice,' Grenville said, whacking his leg with his hat, 'he blooming murdered them!'

'Come on,' Rory said. 'You lot have got to go down and lead your horse in. Yes, and there's a cup to be collected too. Wow – yes, this is a very big day, everyone – and oh my heavens above—'

Rory stopped as if pole-axed as he remembered, as he felt the winning Tote ticket between his fingers in his coat pocket, realising how well and truly this would now see the wretched bank and its equally wretched manager off.

'Oh my goodness gracious me,' he said again. 'Right. Yes. Yes – this is really quite a very big day.'

They made their way down the stands, Alice with her eyes

full of tears, arm in arm with Millie who was laughing her head off, Grenville still beating himself up with his trilby, and Constance now singing at the top of her voice.

'We've got a horse right here!' she sang. 'And he's a little dear!'

'Of course it's only a novice chase so it could mean anything,' a rather mean-faced military-looking man was saying behind them. 'The horse was carrying seven pound less than any of the others, and for God's sake, have you seen the way it's bred? Or rather isn't? No, I don't think we have to go getting carried away here, do you know?'

'Pooh,' Constance said, turning round to him. 'You're talking twaddle. And you look quite as silly as you sound.'

'Here are the Tote returns on the last race to a pound stake,' an announcement rang out over the tannoy. 'Horse number nine – win nineteen pounds seventy, place three pounds fifty . . .'

The rest of the prices were lost to the group who with the exception of Constance had all backed the horse, Grenville on the rails and Alice, Millie and Lynne on the Tote – and of course Rory as well.

'Eighteen and a half to one, old chap,' Grenville said to Rory. 'And the best I could do was sixteens. So two and a half points better on the Tote – except— poor chap.' Grenville suddenly stopped and pulled a sympathetic face at Rory. 'Of course. Poor Rory. You didn't have a bet, did you?'

'No – no I didn't,' Rory answered with perfect candour. 'I didn't have a bet personally. But my father did.'

There was a terrific buzz around the winners' enclosure as the crowd waited for The Enchanted to be led in. To the side of the pen where the victorious horse would stand was a small dais on which stood a table bearing a large silver cup, while photographers and press hurried back from the course and down from the press room ready to fire questions at the winning trainer and take pictures of the winner.

'I think Constance should accept the cup on our behalf,' Alice suggested. 'If that's all right with everyone else?'

'Absolutely,' Grenville agreed, although he had been just about to propose that Lynne accept the cup, hoping thus to give an added boost to his chances there. 'I couldn't think of anyone better.'

'Will I have to speak?' Constance wondered, looking round at the gathering crowd. 'I would really rather not, don't you know.'

'You absolutely do not have to speak, Constance,' Rory assured her, still unable to believe what had just happened and afraid to pinch himself just in case. 'Just smile and accept the cup, that's all. Just be your lovely gracious self.'

'I do know rather a good poem,' Constance said as they continued on their way towards the enclosure. 'A very smart lady named Suki, said she liked to mix business with nookie – before every race she'd go home to her place, and curl up with a very good bookie.'

'Oh, I think you must say that,' Millie said. 'You'll bring the place down.'

'Should I really?' Constance asked, wide-eyed.

'Most certainly not, my lady,' Grenville laughed. 'You'll be up before the stewards.'

'I think I'd quite enjoy that,' Constance sighed. 'Oh well.'

They were just in time to see a radiant Kathleen leading in their horse. A great round of applause began and lasted until Teddy had thrown a rug over the winner's quarters and Rory had gone to the horse's head to pat his neck and congratulate him. As is so often the case with horses after they have won, The Enchanted now looked quite a different animal; not only did he seem to stand taller but the look in his eyes suggested that he sensed what he had just done. As he looked imperiously around him he looked altogether stronger and even more purposeful, ears pricked, eyes bright and so full of himself that it took all Kathleen's skill to keep him contained in the small enclosure.

Grenville escorted his three co-owners into the pen, hat off and smiling broadly. Alice and Lynne went shyly to join Rory, who was calling them over to the horse's head so that they could all have their picture taken with their hero and their jockey, who was smiling broadly and hugging the horse's neck.

'And Constance?' Rory looked round. 'Where's Constance gone?'

'She's up on the podium already,' Grenville said, spotting her. 'Waving to her subjects.'

After they had all been photographed, Grenville took Alice and Lynne with him to the podium while Rory was besieged by the racing press. A cheerful woman in a large felt hat and horn-rimmed glasses announced her pleasure in presenting the trophy to the winning owners, the cup being accepted on their behalf by a mercifully silent Constance. The presentation was followed by yet another photograph session.

'The last time I saw as many cameras as this,' Constance remarked loudly, 'I was not wearing anything like as much clothing.'

The party were then finally led away by two of the course's directors, to enjoy a celebratory bottle of champagne in a small back room heavily decorated with photographs of famous horses winning famous races at the track.

'Good race, Blaze,' Rory told his jockey in the weighing room after Blaze had weighed in. 'Well done.'

'Nothing to do with me, boss,' Blaze replied. 'That horse is magic.'

'Got a bit of toe, hasn't he?' Rory said. 'Jumps, too.'

'Did you see the way he took the last?' Blaze asked, his smile replaced now by a serious expression. 'It was as if he had wings on him. Listen now, I could have picked the leaders up any time I wanted to, boss. I never got a feel like it. I never asked him a thing, not once. I never asked him to pick up, I never asked him to see a stride, I didn't even have to ask him to jump round that other horse at the second last. He did it all himself. And when I let out that much rein . . .' Blaze opened his index finger one inch away from his thumb. 'That's all. When I let out that much rein – whoosh. He quickened so fast I hardly even remember the final furlong.'

'He hardly blew after it, as well,' Rory remembered. 'While you have to say the second and third were out on their feet.'

'Congratulations, young man.' A tall, distinguished-looking man with a racing saddle slung over one arm stopped to offer his good wishes. 'That was some performance.'

'Thank you, Captain,' Rory replied. 'Thanks a lot.'

'I never mind losing to a good horse,' the captain replied. 'And that is most certainly a very good horse.'

'Captain Timms,' Rory said. 'You probably don't know my jockey, Blaze Molloy.'

'Well ridden, young man,' Captain Timms said. 'Well ridden indeed. I shall keep my eye on you. And by the way, Rory, did you get the time? A new course record for two miles. Well done indeed.'

'A new course record?' Rory repeated when Captain Timms had left them. 'A course *record*? I thought it was a fast pace, but a course record? It can't be. It looked as though you were easing up at the finish.'

'I was, Mr Rawlins,' Blaze replied. 'Or rather the horse was.'

Kathleen had almost finished washing her horse down when Rory found her.

'I said this was a special horse, Mr Rawlins,' she said, throwing the last of the bucket of water under the horse's stomach to cool him. 'Didn't I say just that?'

'He was certainly d-d-dreadfully impressive,' Rory agreed. 'I don't mean dreadfully. I meant he was certainly – he was certainly – he was – ter-ter-*terrifically* impressive. Wasn't he?'

'Didn't I just say so? This is a very gifted horse, so this is,' Kathleen said, straightening up and looking into her horse's eye before kissing him on one cheek. Rory watched, wishing for the first time in his life that he was a horse, here and now.

'OK,' he said, bringing himself back to earth. 'What have I got to do? Yes – yes, I have to go off and join my owners, but look, what about later? I mean, what about when we get h-h-home this evening . . .'

Kathleen glanced at him then carried on fussing her horse.

'Thanks, but we're all going down the Chequers,' she said over her shoulder. 'Blaze asked me just now. Teddy, Pauline, Blaze and I. After we've done stables.'

'Oh. Right. Fine.' Rory nodded. 'Yes of course, that's fine. Yes. I just – I just wanted to make sure you all had something organised.'

'You're more than welcome to join us, Mr Rawlins.'

'Am I? You mean . . . ? Right. Right, thanks, but no, we're all going out as well. The owners and I. I think I said I'd take them all out to dinner. Something like that. After all,' he added, 'this isn't exactly the sort of thing that happens every day.'

'It most certainly is not,' Kathleen agreed, now turning to look at Rory, to stare right into his eyes. 'But then this is not exactly an everyday sort of horse.'

Before going out to dinner, Rory called in to see his father.

'Any improvement, Dan?' he asked the doctor, catching him just before he went off duty.

'I was going to ring you, as it happens, Rory,' the cardiologist replied. 'I think we might have turned a corner.'

'When?' Rory asked as the two of them walked down the highly polished corridor that led to Intensive Care. 'What, you mean there's been a general improvement in the last couple of days?'

'I would say today, actually, Rory. This afternoon to be exact.'

'This afternoon?' Rory said, feeling his blood change. 'Right. Tell me, yes – why this afternoon exactly?'

'I looked in on your father this morning and he was much the same. Sleeping, as he mostly does, although quite comfortable. But his temperature was still raised – we can't really seem to get it to come down and stay down, not safely, that is. And while as we all know a temperature means the body is fighting the infection, in infections such as the one your father is suffering from, and particularly following several heart attacks, obviously it's not only worrying, it's very debilitating for the patient. Anyway. Anyway, all said, until the nurse called me at – what was it? About quarter past two.'

'Round about the time we were weighing in,' Rory muttered.

'Sorry? What was that?'

'Nothing. No, I was just – it doesn't matter. Go on with what you were saying.'

'The nurse said your father's temperature had dropped down to normal. So of course I went across to see him at once . . .'

'And?'

'And not only was it normal, but the patient was awake,' Dan said. 'His temperature has stayed down ever since.'

Dan pushed open the door to the side ward. Rory's father was sitting propped up on his pillows, looking while not exactly the picture of health considerably improved since the last time Rory had seen him, when he had thought he might lose him at any minute.

'Hi, Pop,' he said, going in.

'Hello, old boy,' Anthony whispered. 'Haven't got much of a Hobson's, I'm afraid. So if you want to hear me, best pull up a chair.'

'I'm sorry to say I've come empty-handed, I fear,' Rory said, sitting by the bed by his father's head. 'I didn't know you were back with us. By that I mean awake and everything.'

Anthony cleared his throat and then put one long-fingered, elegant hand on his son's.

'I had the very devil of a dream today,' he said, barely audibly. 'There was this horse. And it had wings. I was on it, do you see, this flying horse. It had somehow rescued me from the sea, I knew that. It was a very rough sea, and very cold. Then I was on this horse's back and it flew me to safety. The devil it did. It plucked me out of the sea and flew me to safety.'

Chapter Seventeen

Headlines

'Hey, Gerry?'

'I'm in the bathroom!'

'Wait till you see this!'

Maddy stared again at the news stories in Gerry's copy of the *Sporting Life* and the racing pages of the *Telegraph* and the *Mail*. The Enchanted's victory was a major sports story in both dailies.

'You just wait till you see this,' Maddy said, pushing the *Sporting Life* Gerry's way as he came into the kitchen in a white towelling dressing gown, still drying his hair.

'So where's the fire, then?' he asked. 'What's all this about?'

'Get reading and you'll find out, lover.'

Maddy poured herself another cup of black coffee and sat watching Gerry read, coffee cup held two-handed, both her elbows on the table.

'I wish you wouldn't do that,' Gerry said, having glanced up and noticed what she was doing. 'It's dead common.'

'I am dead common,' Maddy replied, remaining exactly as she was. 'Anyway, dead common according to who?'

'You know who,' Gerry replied, sitting down with the paper. 'Bloody hell.'

'Yeah,' Maddy agreed. 'How about that?'

'How long has she had a horse? I mean, it can't be long. We haven't been divorced that long.'

'Well, she's got one now, Gerry. And not only a horse, a winning horse and all.'

Gerry read on, shaking his head.

'"The Enchanted,"' he read out from the *Life*. '"A breeding mystery."'

'Yeah, I know, I read it,' Maddy said, still watching him.

'"The easy winner of yesterday's Markham Novice Chase at Wincanton as far as the stud book goes is a completely unknown quantity."'

'Her mug is staring out at me everywhere,' Maddy complained. 'Look!'

She turned her copy of the *Daily Mail* to Gerry, simultaneously tapping the picture on the front of the *Sporting Life* with a long, manicured, bright red fingernail.

'I mean, look, Gerry!'

'I'm looking, Maddy. I'm looking.'

'"Lynne Faraday, one of the four owners of the debuttant horse . . ."' Maddy read out to him, taking her paper back.

'Debootant,' Gerry corrected her. 'That should be debootant horse, Maddy.'

'Yeah, yeah.' Maddy sniffed. '"Lynne Faraday blah blah blah expressed herself *delighted* with the horse's performance and said as a first time owner she never for a moment imagined herself as being a winning owner. Certainly her part-owned young and unconsidered horse won a fast-run race with considerable authority and without making the semblance of a mistake. The Enchanted has to be one for the notebook and certainly goes on my list as one to follow, as indeed does his lovely co-owner." I mean, that just isn't *fair*, Gerry!'

'What particular part just isn't fair, Maddy?'

'She's got her picture in every blooming newspaper, that's what! It just isn't fair!'

'So what am I meant to do about it, my love?'

'I dunno, Gerry! But I do know something.'

'You do? I'm dying to hear. What do you know?'

'That you are going to have to *do* something!'

'Mum? Is this true?' Georgina was asking Alice on the phone. 'I mean, I am looking at this picture of you in the *Daily Mail* and it says—'

'It's all perfectly true, Georgina,' Alice replied, picking up Sammy's water bowl to freshen it.

'So what are you groaning for, Mum?'

'I'm groaning—'

'I'm the one who should be groaning, Mum.'

'I was groaning because I was bending down, dear. To pick up Sammy's water bowl.'

'Just tell me this isn't true, right? Seriously? That you've bought a *racehorse*?'

'Part of a racehorse, Georgina dear. A share in a race-horse.'

'Are you completely out of your head, Mum? Have you totally lost it?'

'Not at all.'

'First of all you suddenly decide to move *miles* away from your family, without so much as discussing it with us, then the next thing we know is you've bought a *racehorse*.'

'A share in a racehorse, Georgina. Do get your facts right. A share in a *winning* racehorse.'

Alice smiled to herself and sat down on the old sofa she'd

put under the kitchen window in the cottage, patting her knee for Sammy to jump up. It was a cloudless winter day, and the wonderful views she now enjoyed were lit by a gentle early November sun.

'I honestly don't know what to say.' Georgina sighed down the phone.

'You could try "Well done. Congratulations",' Alice suggested.

'Mum?' her daughter replied in her particularly irritating sing-song way. 'Mum, do get real.'

'Actually, Georgina,' Alice said, 'I think that's precisely what I am doing. Bye-bye.'

Instead of being cross, which she felt she should be, Alice found herself first smiling and then laughing out loud. Now that the little horse had won she was even more determined to stand firm and be free. She was no longer invisible. And she had ended another telephone call by putting the phone down first.

Chapter Eighteen

Back Across the Wather

'There is only one certain remedy for a sore head,' Michael Doherty announced to his fellow sufferers in the snug of Finnegan's Exclusive American Cocktail Lounge in Cronagh, 'and that is to avoid excess in the first place.'

'And if they was to mind you, Michael,' Donal replied, polishing a pint glass with a tea towel decorated with the head of Arkle, 'what would I be doing for a living?'

'And where would we be doing our drinking?' Tim O'Cloughlan asked from further down the bar. 'Perish the thought altogether and have another. That's generally considered to be the best cure-all for this sort of malarkey. Donal? Fill all the glasses again, man, for God's sake now.'

'Let's hope for the sake of all our sanities this is not going to be a regular occurrence,' Padraig muttered, leaning on the bar and holding his head. 'I have a large motorway gang at work in here.'

'This business about a statue,' Eammon pronounced Yamon said from his usual standing position in one corner of the snug. 'Was this a serious thing or was this just a jest?'

'Who said anything about any statue?' Padraig groaned. 'A statue of whom, for heaven's sake?'

'Not of yourself, Padraig,' Donal told him, wiping the bar with Arkle. 'Of that you can be sure.'

'I'm not following you one whit, Donal.' Michael frowned at the landlord. 'If there's any statue to be posted, then I think most certainly Padraig here should be in the running.'

'Whoever heard of posting any statue?' Tim wanted to know. 'Meself I never heard the like.'

A red-faced man with a large powdered nose burst into the snug, shaking his head violently.

'May I never live through such a time again, so help me God,' he announced, collapsing against the bar and resting his head on it. 'May I never bear witness again to the like.'

Donal filled a tumbler with a double measure of John Jameson and put the glass on the bar for the new arrival.

'Will the bank not recover then, Mr Coulihan?' he enquired politely with a wink at the others, throwing Arkle over his shoulder.

'The bank?' Coulihan wondered, standing upright now and regarding his peers wild-eyed. 'The bank indeed? I doubt if the entire Irish economy will ever get back on its feet. I have never seen such a run on our money.'

'Your money?' Padraig muttered. 'And there was I going round thinking now the money belonged to the depositors.'

'Never mind that,' Michael said. 'What about poor old Tobias Tandy? Surely he's the one facing the ruin? All you did is what you always do – give us some of our money back that you've been making yourself even fatter on.'

'The problem with you people is that you do not have a proper grasp of banking in any way whatsoever,' Coulihan retorted. 'There is a lot more to banking than just counting out money, you know.'

'That's the bit you enjoy, Mr Coulihan,' Donal said, with a nod. 'The rustle of all them new green ones sent down from Dublin. I've seen the expression on your face.'

'Tobias is never ruined now, surely?' Padraig said, concerned. 'I'd never forgive meself if Tobias was done out of it.'

'He's a bookmaker, Padraig!' Michael said fiercely. 'He's there to be done out of it!'

'He was in and out of the bank like a hen on fire,' Coulihan told them. 'For him to meet his obligations to his customers, sure the bank had to take a charge on his shop.'

'What he means is Tobias had to cancel the charge he has on the bank,' Michael said with a broad grin. 'Isn't that so, Coulihan? Wasn't it yourself that had the very worst of times this last Cheltenham?'

'Mr, if you don't mind, Michael Doherty. That is if you want me to go on cashing those rubber cheques of yours.'

'And did you have a bet, Mr Coulihan?' Yamon bellowed from the back of the snug. 'They say you took the twenties!'

'I'd have been no sort of financier not to have done so, Yamon,' Coulihan replied. 'I could hardly call meself any sort of banker if I'd eschewed such an investment opportunity.'

'Padraig here is suggesting we put up some sort of a statue to your man,' Donal told Coulihan. 'Your man with The Horse, this is.'

'I couldn't but agree.' Coulihan nodded. 'There's astute trainers, there's very astute trainers, and there are the inspired ones, and your man over the water falls well and truly into the latter catechism.'

'Hadn't we all been sitting here watching and waiting for The Horse?' Michael asked rhetorically. 'Waiting to see him properly declared and entered, for then we knew he'd be off.'

'We all knew he was off,' Padraig said with a nod. 'Helped be word of the daughter who kept us regularly posted about his work.'

'She said his first piece of fast work scorched the turf,' Michael said, dropping his voice to a whisper. 'She said she'd never seen the like. Said he buried the rest of the string and wouldn't have blown a candle out after it.'

'What was the worst anyone took, I wonder,' Coulihan said, holding his now empty glass out for a refill.

'The twenties you had, Mr Coulihan,' Michael said. 'Sure we all had the thirty-threes.'

'All except himself here,' Tim said with a nod to Padraig.

'And what price did you get him at, Padraig?' Michael enquired. 'Did you do better than our thirty-threes now?'

'Maybe I did and maybe I did not,' Padraig said with a careful nod of his throbbing head. 'Let's just say I had him backed at extremely good odds to win the very first race he ran in.'

'So they'd be longer than ours, so.'

'They'd be considerably longer,' Donal said, handing the bank manager his fresh drink. 'So if the Irish economy needs boosting, you'll know whose bed to be looking under.'

Chapter Nineteen

The Morning After the Day Before

Grenville went to collect the morning papers, which he gathered were left in a large box inside the main front door of Brook House. Since there seemed to be no one else about he thought it perfectly safe to do so in the large white towelling dressing gown that he had found hanging behind the bathroom door. Padding barefoot down the polished wooden stairs he found himself singing to himself with happiness, something he very rarely did – something in fact he couldn't remember doing for far too long a time.

'I've got the world on a string, sitting on a rainbow,' he crooned. 'Got the whatsit round my doodah – what a world, what a life – I'm in—'

'Fielding?' a voice from behind interrupted him. 'Grenville *Fielding?*'

Grenville stopped dead in his tracks, his moment of unbridled joy spoilt. He knew the owner of the voice without even having to turn round to identify him.

'Barrington,' he intoned. 'Montague Barrington, I do declare.'

'I say,' said his investment client, 'I say, Grenville, what on earth are you doing in this neck of the woods, eh?'

Grenville slowly turned about, putting a polite smile on his face. 'Just visiting actually,' he replied lightly. 'And you, old chap?'

'Got an apartment here. Had quite enough of SW3, thanking you kindly. Thought I would take me to the country instead. I like the casual look, Grenville. Very *soigné*.'

'Just getting the daily rag,' Grenville replied, pulling his borrowed dressing gown more tightly round his midriff. 'If you'll excuse.'

'I'll come along with you, dear boy,' the portly Montague told him, falling into step alongside Grenville as they crossed the large marble-floored hall. 'L. F.,' he commented, noticing the monogram on the dressing gown's top pocket. 'Undercover, are we? Jolly good. Or are those the initials of some hotel you nicked the robe from? Eh? Right?'

'Belongs to a friend,' Grenville explained.

'Oh I say.' Montague smirked. 'Oh I say, I say, I say.'

'So you just said,' Grenville remarked. 'Look – tell you what, if you're around later, perhaps we might have a drink, yes? But at the moment—'

'At the moment I should think so too,' Montague cut in, giving Grenville an over-suggestive wink. 'What? I should say.'

'Which is your apartment, Monty? I'll come and take a drink off you lunchtime, if you're around.'

'Good thought, Gren, but I'm off shooting all day. But should you be around this weekend, I'm in apartment six. *Ciao*, Casanova!'

Relieved to see him go, Grenville found himself puzzled by why he should have felt so embarrassed, as if he'd been caught doing something he shouldn't instead of something of which he should be proud. He could only put it down to his mother's prevailing influence on his life. Fond as he was of his mother, he resented her still constant interference in and regular criticism of his private life and affairs. But because his parents had divorced after his father had been found *in flagrante* with his secretary, Grenville felt sorry for his mother and so had remained loyal to her, even though she had never met his kindness and understanding with any real kindness or understanding of her own. Worst of all she was a purely dreadful snob, an affectation that had been directly responsible for the ruination of several of the young Grenville's love affairs, most particularly the termination of his engagement to the charming, sweet and pretty Jane Denton, whose only failing was her family's modest beginnings.

As Grenville padded back upstairs with the newspaper tucked under his arm, he wondered what his mother would make of the young woman with whom he was now – as he liked to think of it – *associated*, and when he thought of it he literally stopped to think about it, halfway back up the polished wooden staircase. And to his joy he realised he didn't care what she thought.

Better than that, he told himself, *I won't even ask her what she thinks because I won't even introduce her to Lynne. Or rather I might not*, he decided, re-forming his thoughts as he continued on his way. *And even if I do decide to take Lynne home to meet her, it will not matter a single jot if she tries to make any of the usual sort of trouble. Not a jot.*

'Grenville?' a sleepy voice called from the bedroom as he let himself into the apartment. 'That you?'

'It's only me,' Grenville called back to reassure her. 'Like some coffee? I thought I'd make some coffee.'

'OK,' Lynne called back. 'I'll be up in a jiffy.'

Grenville put the newspaper on the table, and went to tidy up his makeshift bed on the sofa, taking the quilt Lynne had given him and stacking it neatly with the pillow on top of the pile of his immaculately folded clothes on a nearby chair. After straightening the creases out of the sofa he plumped up the cushions, squared the bright-coloured Scandinavian rug in front of it, and finally pulled the curtains back at the sitting-room windows, flooding the room with pale winter sunlight. Before going to the kitchen to make the coffee, he stood for a moment admiring the apartment, once again finding himself surprised by his reaction, since never for a moment had he thought he would end up approving of such a Spartan style of interior décor. As far as furnishing and design went, he was a dyed-in-the-wool traditionalist, preferring brown furniture to white, chintz to single bright colours, and portraits of ancestors to geometric abstracts. Yet Lynne had chosen to decorate and furnish her new apartment in the sort of style he would have thought would be anathema to him, and he found himself admiring it.

The decoration and furnishing were only in the initial stages, with the walls freshly painted in what Grenville thought would probably be described as a subdued white. The sofa and armchair were large, modern and upholstered in single-coloured tweeds, the chair in an Etruscan red and the sofa in dull ochre. Two of the walls were hung with large, bright and beautifully executed landscapes, one of mustard fields, the other of pale mountains shrouded in a light mist. The bathroom was furnished with a large modern tub fitted with oversize chromed taps and its window fitted with handmade American-style shutters, and the large modern kitchen dazzled with clean lines and an abundance of worktops.

'All so very uncluttered,' Grenville observed to himself as he made his way to the kitchen. 'Rather like the way one hopes one's life is now going to be.'

'I'm sorry about last night,' Lynne said to him as they

sat drinking their coffee in the sitting room, Lynne in her pyjamas with a cashmere sweater pulled over the top and thick white ski socks on her feet, Grenville still in her dressing gown. 'Really I am. Sorry.'

'There is nothing to be sorry about, Lynne,' Grenville assured her. 'Absolutely. And do stop apologising for everything.'

'Sorry,' Lynne said, pulling a face.

'Lynne?'

'No, I am sorry about last night,' she insisted. 'I had far too much champagne and everything—'

'You were celebrating. We all were.'

'I know, but I did – I had far too much.'

'You mean nobody else did? I didn't?'

'Yeah – but then you sleeping on the sofa and everything. Did you get any sleep?'

'I slept like a top, thank you, Lynne. Like a top.'

'You got a hangover?'

'I could have a coffee or ten, certainly.'

'Me too.' Lynne sighed. 'That was some party. I didn't make a fool of myself, did I?'

'Depends how you define that,' Grenville replied, pouring some more coffee. 'If you think being totally delightful—'

'Me?'

'Totally delightful,' Grenville assured her. 'Funny, interesting, wonderful dancer—'

'Course, we danced, didn't we?' Lynne groaned in recollection, head in hand. 'Back at Rory's.'

'And sang.' Grenville laughed. 'Though not me, you'll be happy to hear. A foghorn in distress is infinitely more musical than yours truly. You sang, Rory sang—'

'He was at the piano, wasn't he?'

'Pretty fair too, on the old ivories. Constance was the star of the show, however.'

'I remember that all right. She was marvellous.'

'Yes,' Grenville said thoughtfully. 'Yes, she was, wasn't she? Mysterious old thing, isn't she?'

'I'm really fond of Connie,' Lynne said. 'I think she's had a really tough life.'

'I don't really know anything about her life. She seems to have married quite a lot.'

'So she says. I think she's probably rather lonely. Which is why this is good.'

'And she was obviously once a bit of a looker,' Grenville remarked. 'Wouldn't you say?'

'I'd say she still is, Grenville. Just because she's older doesn't stop her being beautiful.'

'No,' Grenville agreed, such a thought never having occurred to him before. 'No, I don't suppose it does.'

Lynne put down her coffee cup and leaned across to touch Grenville's hand.

'Sorry you only had a sofa to sleep on,' she said. 'As you can see, I've hardly really started furnishing this place.'

'It's very nice, you know,' Grenville replied, pretending to look round him at the apartment to take his mind off the warm hand that was resting on his. 'I really like this plain, uncluttered look.'

'Why *did* you sleep on the sofa, as a matter of interest?' Lynne asked him, frowning. 'No, I didn't mean to ask that. Sorry.'

'You really must stop apologising for yourself all the time,' Grenville told her, patting her hand with his. 'You have nothing to apologise for.'

'I don't apologise for myself all the time, do I? Really?'

'I'm afraid you do a bit, yes.'

'Do I really? Oh. Sorry.'

'You really have nothing to apologise for. You're a wonderful girl. You're bright, you're funny, and you're – you're really very pretty.'

Overcome, Lynne stared at Grenville for a moment, then dropped her eyes.

'And you dance quite beautifully,' Grenville added.

'And you're a . . .' Lynne began, 'you're a real gentleman.'

'Why, Lynne,' Grenville said, his whole face brightening. 'Why, Lynne, what a very nice thing to say.'

'Well you are, Grenville,' Lynne assured him. 'I can't tell you how nice it is to be with someone who treats you – well, who treats you with respect. I can't tell you what it's like. It's so – I don't know. It's so different. It makes you *feel* so different.'

'Thank you.'

'I mean, a lot of men might have taken or tried to take a bit of advantage last night or something,' Lynne went on. 'You know, your horse wins, you have a lot of champagne, you party and dance and everything. A lot of people would have tried to take advantage.'

'Lynne—'

'No. No, you really don't have to explain, Grenville. All I want to say to you is thanks. Really. You're such a nice man.'

She smiled so sweetly at him that Grenville could no longer help himself. The next moment they were kissing and only a short time after that Grenville found to his delight he would no longer be sleeping on the sofa.

Alice was also nursing a sore head, the first one she could remember having since Alex and she had drunk too much champagne on the night of their silver wedding anniversary. In the belief that a hangover shared was a hangover slightly spared she had telephoned Millie, who she thought might also be suffering since they had all insisted she come to the party as well, reasoning that if it hadn't been for Millie Alice would never have met Rory and they would never have formed the partnership.

Millie had thought it an excellent idea to share the hangover and had the iced and spiced Bloody Marys all ready and waiting in a large glass jug when Alice turned up with Sammy and a box of home-made spaghetti carbonara from her deep freeze. After a couple of drinks and a restorative lunch the two of them sat in front of a roaring log fire while the November winds lamented round the grey and cold landscape outside, with Sammy and all of Millie's dogs, two pugs, a bearded collie, a rescued mongrel and an oddly self-assured whippet, sleeping peacefully at their feet.

A ringing telephone woke them from the sleep into which they had both fallen.

'It's Rory,' Millie told Alice, handing her the receiver. 'He rang earlier because he couldn't find you – you'd obviously left already – so I said you were coming over here and he said he'd ring back. I forgot to tell you. He wants a word with you.'

'Not bad news, I hope?' Alice asked when she got on the phone. 'The little horse is all right?'

'He's fine, Alice,' Rory replied. 'Didn't Millie tell you? He's come out of his race really well.'

'No, Millie didn't tell me,' Alice replied, giving her friend the mock evil eye.

'I didn't tell you because I thought you'd like to hear it for yourself,' Millie excused herself quickly.

'I'll talk about plans for the future in a minute,' Rory said. 'But first I have to tell you what's happened.'

'Something has happened.' Alice all but groaned. 'I thought you said the horse was all right?'

'The horse is *fine*, Alice.' Rory laughed. 'He's eaten up, had a run out in the field, and at the moment is having a total body massage from the lovely Kathleen. No, what I have to tell you, although it concerns the horse, is nothing about his health or fitness. And I'm obliged to tell you about it although I hope I know what your answer will be.'

'Yes? So?'

'I had a call. Someone wants to buy the horse.'

'What?' Alice said, astounded. 'But he's not up for sale.'

'Who's not up for sale?' Millie mouthed. Alice turned her back to her, flapping one hand at her friend to try to stem further interruptions.

'Why should anyone think they can buy the horse?' Alice wanted to know.

'This is the sort of thing that happens in horse racing,' Rory replied. 'People see a winning horse, particularly a young winning horse, and out come the chequebooks.'

'Well, he's not for sale,' Alice said. 'At least my leg most certainly isn't.'

'I'm relieved to hear that.' Rory laughed. 'After the agony you went through during the race I thought you might be glad to get rid of him.'

'Nonsense,' Alice reproved him. 'I've never enjoyed not enjoying myself more. How much did they offer?'

'Do you really want to know?'

'Just for the record.'

'Fifty thousand.'

'Fifty thousand guineas?'

'Fifty thousand guineas.'

'That's more than four times what we paid for him.'

'That's what people will pay for a winning horse. A special horse.'

'What has everyone else said?'

'Grenville said no, Lynne of course said no, and Constance said something I can't repeat.'

'Suppose one of us wanted to sell?'

'By the terms of your contract, if you couldn't come to an agreement then the horse would have to be sent to the sales,' Rory told her. 'But since none of you want to sell . . .'

There was silence from Alice.

'Alice?' Rory pressed her. 'Are you having second thoughts?'

'Of course not. I was just wondering who on earth had the cheek.'

'No sale, my love,' Gerry reported to Maddy later in the day. 'Went as high as I dared, but no takers.'

'So what are you going to do, Gerry?' Maddy demanded, pouring herself another glass of champagne. 'You're not just going to sit down on this, are you? Because if you are—'

'Yes, my love? If I am, what?'

'Never you mind. Just don't expect *me* to be around while you do.'

'While I do what, lover?'

'Sit down on it, that's what, Gerry!' Maddy yelled at him. "Cos if you are, I am not!'

'All this just because Lynne got herself a bit of a horse?'

'This is not all because of that at all, Gerry! Look – I'm a model, right? Not far off the top, neither, and I do not want some nothing and nobody knocking me out of the papers, right? Got it? I mean, who does she think she is anyway? Poncing around all over the place mouthing off as if she's just won the bloody Derby or something!'

'All right, all right,' Gerry said, holding up both hands. 'All right, all right!'

'No it is not bloody well all right all right, Gerry!' Maddy all but screamed back at him. 'You told me when we got together I could have everything she had and more, right! So go get it, Rover! I want everything she's got and more!'

Gerry shook his head and went out to stare at his new BMW

coupé, wondering why women couldn't be more like cars, beautiful yes, sexy certainly, but under your control, with your foot on the accelerator and your foot on the brake. It was at times like this, and in Gerry's view recently there had been a few too many times like this, but it was at times like this that he began to miss Lynne. Lynne might have been a bit boring and a little too compliant and even dutiful as far as Gerry was concerned, but at least she wasn't given to these sorts of you-just-wait rages, the terrible spoilt tantrums that Maddy was beginning to throw all too frequently. But it was too late now, he thought to himself as he walked round his gleaming red car, idly kicking its wheels. There was no going back now. Lynne and he were divorced, a settlement had been made and Maddy had well and truly moved in, in more ways than one.

Maybe the fact that he hadn't married her yet was what was making her so mouthy, Gerry supposed. Or maybe it was all to do with this hormone thing he was always hearing about; maybe it was just her hormones playing her up at her time of the month or whatever. What did he know and how was he to know? He was just a bloke and, like so many of his mates, he admitted that women were more than a bit of a mystery to him. When they behaved the way Maddy was behaving they became totally inexplicable. Worst of all, he realised as he walked slowly back into the house, the reason didn't make the slightest bit of difference, because life would in no way return to normal till Maddy got what she wanted. And if she didn't get what she wanted, Gerry was beginning seriously to dread what might indeed happen to him. After all, not only wasn't he getting any younger, what was worse, he wasn't growing any new hair.

Chapter Twenty

Kicking On

The horse was due to run next at Huntingdon. Rory was astonished at how well his charge had come out of his first race, which even though he had won it with ease had been run at a track-record-breaking pace. Yet the horse had come home, eaten up every oat that evening, slept like a baby and run out in the paddock next day with the sort of energy that made Rory think he could have raced again that very afternoon.

'I see they're running Fly The Flags,' Grenville observed on the morning of the race, when he called the trainer before leaving for Cambridgeshire. 'Quite a useful novice, I gather. He's won his first two races by healthy margins, beating some other half-decent novices into the bargain.'

'Yes. I asked Dad about him, now he's sitting up and reading the racing papers—'

'He's that much better, is he?' Grenville interrupted. 'I'm so glad to hear that.'

'Thanks, Grenville. Anyway, what the old man said – I think I should stop calling him that, actually – what my father said is that his connections have always seen him as a Cheltenham horse and so far nothing he has done has made them think of reconsidering.'

'So the little horse will have his work cut out. Fly The Flag's owned by some Yank or other, correct?'

'The some Yank or other, for your information, isn't just any Yank or other. He has six horses with Geordie Mainstone,' Rory informed him. 'He also owns the runner-up in last year's Grand National and—'

'Of course he does,' Grenville ad-libbed. 'I've been a bit out of touch since Papa bolted. We used to race all the time.'

'Eddie Rampton's running one of his hot hopes as well, and he doesn't send them this far if he hasn't had a good touch.'

'And you don't think the increase in distance is going to bother the little horse?'

'Don't think so. According to our pilot, our fellow hasn't just got toe but stamina as well.'

'Yes, right, Rory – but untested stamina.'

'No – no, that's why we decided to try him out over two and a half miles, Grenville. Huntingdon's a flat track like Wincanton – another fast galloping track – so it's not going to ask too big a question of him.'

'Fine,' Grenville replied. 'Right. Jolly good – see you at the track, then.'

As he hung up the phone, Rory could almost see Grenville tipping his hat on the other end of the line.

In spite of having bought herself a nice low-mileage second-hand Renault 5, Alice did not feel sufficiently roadwise to drive herself all the way to Cambridgeshire from Dorset and so had persuaded Millie to drive her there – not that her friend needed very much persuasion.

'It's very flat, Cambridgeshire, isn't it?' Alice observed after they had motored a dozen or so miles into the county. 'Alex always said it was murderers' country.'

'The Fens are worse,' Millie replied, 'Lincolnshire particularly. I don't think I could stand living in a flat county. How are you feeling, duck? Getting the wobbles yet?'

'Nowhere near as badly as last time. Although I must admit to feeling slightly nauseous.'

'The horse must have a good chance.'

'Perhaps we should have called him that,' Alice continued. 'Slightly Nauseous. On the other hand, I don't think so.'

'I don't think you can change a horse's name once it's registered,' Millie told her. 'At least, if you do – if indeed you can – I do know it's considered the most frightful bad luck.'

'Even if we could and we wanted to, I couldn't possibly change his name. I've always felt sure the horse was called The Enchanted because that's exactly what he is.'

'An enchanted horse, indeed,' Millie mused. 'Certainly looked like it at Wincanton. And today perhaps he'll look even more so.'

'Rory says it's quite a hot race.'

'If he's a good horse he has to beat good horses,' Millie said. 'And here we are – we've arrived.'

It was a mid-week meeting, but due to the quality of the racing there was a good crowd, despite the rain that had now begun to fall, accompanied by a biting east wind. After Alice had picked up her complimentary owner's tickets, she and Millie walked out on to the course with the first race only five minutes from the off. Alice's increasing nervousness was allayed by the good-humoured atmosphere, the vibrant colours of the jockeys' silks and the elegant beauty of the thoroughbreds parading in the paddocks. As arranged, they met up with Lynne, Constance and Grenville just outside the weighing room, then went and had a drink to refresh themselves after their long journeys.

'Right,' Lynne said, opening her racecard, after they had all sat down at a table. 'Let's see which ones are going to make us rich today then.'

'A man I knew once, can't remember his name,' Constance said, 'he was a reformed gambler who always maintained that the only people who made money from following the horses were the ones with a brush and a shovel.'

'You're full of those things, aren't you, Connie?' Lynne remarked. 'Full of equine bon bons.'

'Bons *mots*,' Grenville said, helping her out.

'Thank you, sweetheart,' Lynne replied, putting a hand on his, and cueing an exchange of looks between Alice, Millie and Constance.

'Trouble was, that's about all he ever did say,' Constance concluded. 'He was the most frightful old bore. And totally bald, which made it even worse.'

'Rory tells me the word is out for Fandangle, another west country horse, in our race,' Grenville said. 'Won easily a couple of weeks back at Devon and Exeter from a big field of novices, including two Lambourn hotshots.'

'You've seen Rory already, have you?' Alice asked.

'We have indeed,' Grenville replied. 'He said the little horse is very well and travelled up fine. But I'm afraid he *will* be favourite.'

'He's favourite in about eighty per cent of the papers,' Millie said, having consulted the tipster's table in the *Sporting Life*. 'I must say I always hated it when Jack was favourite. Seems you're there to be shot at, instead of just another runner.'

'That's racing.' Grenville sighed. 'Time to go and look at our runner, I'd say.'

*   *   *

The Enchanted started at an even shorter price than forecast, finally going to post at six to four on, four pounds on to win six, in spite of the fact that this was only his second race in Britain and he came from a small and what was largely regarded as an unsuccessful west country yard, was trained by a novice assistant trainer and was ridden by a conditional jockey who was having only his second ride in England. Yet throughout the race there was never really a moment's doubt in anyone's mind that the horse was going to win. This time, with no front-running Pope horses entered, Blaze jumped his mount off in front and let him lead the rest of the field the merriest of dances. Three fences out he was an easy twelve lengths clear of the chasing bunch, who were all quite obviously beaten horses, and the race was his bar a fall.

'I've warned Blaze about the last two fences here,' Rory said, as he watched his horse cantering into the straight, with Alice once more hiding herself behind his back. 'They've just rebuilt them and they're very stiff. Dad had a horse here at the opening meeting who took one heck of a fall at the last.'

'Thanks for sharing that with us now,' Grenville said, his large race glasses trained firmly on The Enchanted. 'He's coming to the last now.'

They all held their breath, particularly as having nothing to race against the horse was seemingly beginning to idle, but closer inspection revealed Blaze sitting as still as a fox watching chickens, his eyes only on the last fence, his hands still full of horse. The nearer they got to the fence the more he felt his mount regain his rhythm, putting down foot perfect and still on the bridle with ears pricked, not touching a twig of the formidable black wall of birch, and landing still full of running. This time, having taken a quick look after clearing the last at the distance between them and the rest of the field,

Blaze eased his horse back and they passed the post at almost a walk.

'He's only done it again,' an incredulous Grenville said, as the cheering that greeted the little horse's victory began to abate. 'And if anything, even more easily.'

'Blooming heck,' Lynne said, grasping Constance by the arm. 'Two in a blooming row.'

'What else can you expect?' Constance replied. 'With such distinguished owners?'

'He didn't really win again, did he?' A white-faced Alice had finally emerged from behind her human shield. 'This is getting ridiculous.'

'This is getting unreal,' a none the less delighted Rory said. 'Seriously. Come on – let's get down and lead him in.'

'Thanks, boss,' Blaze said, when he'd been congratulated by his trainer, full of smiles and positioning himself for the team photograph. 'And didn't I say he'd stay? He could have gone round again. And again.'

'Very well done, if I may say so,' a tall and distinguished-looking American said to all the partnership met to greet their returning hero. 'If I may intrude on your celebrations, I just wanted to say I thought your horse ran a simply marvellous race. If you ever feel like selling him . . .'

He had a smile on his face which was reflected in his large blue eyes as he teased them, standing hatless with his hands clasped behind his back and his silver hair blown by the stiffening wind.

'How very kind,' Constance replied at her grandest. 'But I doubt that you could afford him.'

'I doubt that too, ma'am,' the American replied. 'Though I sure would like to own him.'

'The only way you'd be able to do that,' Constance told him, 'would be to marry one of the owners. Or perhaps all three of us.' She turned to her fellow partners and opened her eyes very wide.

'Mr Lovell,' Rory said, entering the conversation rather hastily, having dispatched Blaze to weigh in. 'If I may – can I introduce you to everyone? Everyone, this is Mr Lovell who owns Fly The Flag.'

'I thought your horse ran a very decent sort of race,' Grenville said, after they had all been introduced. 'Ran on to be second, I believe.'

'He certainly did, Mr Fielding,' Harrington Lovell replied. 'He ran a very good race and he came home sound, which is what I always pray for. But he couldn't hold a candle to your fellow. Not a lot of him, I dare say, but what there is is all heart and class. So my congratulations – and who knows? We may cross swords again some time. I very much hope so. Ladies.'

And with a small half-bow and another smile he took his leave.

'What a very nice man,' Constance observed. 'I think I shall go and marry him.'

'Not a chance, Connie,' Lynne said. 'You're far too young for him.'

'Lovely old world manners,' Alice remarked, looking after the departing American. 'I do like that.'

'My turn to buy the champagne, I say,' Rory said, handing Grenville some money. 'Even if it isn't I'm buying – I'll meet you in the bar after I've made sure Kathleen hasn't forgotten about his dope test.'

'Kathleen said it took him twenty minutes to do a wee at Wincanton,' Lynne informed the rest of the party as they made their way to the bar.

'I trust you're talking about our horse and not our trainer,' Constance remarked.

Harrington Lovell was at the bar when Grenville went to buy the champagne. 'Why don't you let me do that, Mr Fielding?' he suggested. 'I had a good wager on your horse so I feel the need to celebrate as well.'

'I have an even better idea, Mr Lovell,' Grenville replied. 'Why don't you come and join us? I gather from the young lady at the bar here that the winner's champagne is on the house, which might make the offer even more attractive.'

'That's very kind of you, Mr Fielding. I would certainly appreciate the company.'

'I gather you make it a habit to come over here to see your horses run,' Grenville said as they sat down at their table.

'Whenever it's possible I do,' Harrington agreed. 'As a matter of fact I would live in this country if I could, I love it so much.'

'And your family?' Grenville wondered. 'Are they Anglophiles as well?'

'Sadly my wife died some six years ago and my family have all long flown the nest. Only thing keeps me home are my dogs.'

'You like dogs?' Alice chimed in. 'How many dogs do you have?'

'Far too many, ma'am.'

'Alice, please.'

'Far too many, Alice. Two Lhasa apsos, that were my wife's originally, a French bulldog, a Standard poodle and two mongrels, both rescue jobs and consequently my friends for life.'

'Perhaps you're a little like me then, Mr Lovell,' Constance said, lighting a cheroot. 'The more I see of dogs the more I wish I was one.'

'You want to be careful there, Connie,' Lynne whispered.

'That sort of remark could be whatever. You know. Mis-what-ever.'

'Misconstrued?' Millie said helpfully.

'If you say so,' Lynne agreed cheerfully. 'I doubt I could even spell it.'

'And I agree with you, Constance,' Millie added. 'When I see how spoilt my dogs are, I think you're exactly right.'

'Your very good health, everyone,' Lovell said, raising his glass of champagne. 'And health to your quite magic little horse, too.'

Blaze found Kathleen coming out of the dope box with her horse. They said nothing to each other about the race, because they did not have to. All they did was exchange smiles, smiles perhaps a little longer than those they would normally give each other, and share a big, long, strong hug, which Rory happened to see on his way to find his horse. Unaware of him, Blaze then wandered off to watch the next race, and Kathleen went to prepare her charge for his return journey while Rory hung back, then turned and wandered back to the bar.

'What is it they say?' Grenville mused, offering Rory a refill from a fresh bottle of champagne.

'Not for me, Grenville,' Rory said, putting a hand over his glass. 'I have to drive.'

'Jolly good,' Grenville replied, topping up the glasses of all those in the rest of the party who weren't going to get behind a wheel. 'Now what is it they say? Keep yourself in the best company and your horses in the worst, yes? Or is it the other way round? No – no, I think that's the right way round, and if so, and *à propos* of the fact that I don't know your exact think-ing—'

'I don't know my exact thinking either – in fact I'm usually the last person to know what I'm thinking,' Rory agreed. 'But it might help if I had the slightest idea what you were on about, Grenville.'

'Plans,' Grenville replied, taking off his spectacles and carefully cleaning them on a spotless white handkerchief. 'Plans for the little horse.'

'I think they say, what is it? Keep horses in the worst company and yourself in the best, isn't it? Not that I think he should run against the rubbish because that's not going to get us anywhere.'

'But if you're thinking what I'm thinking, Rory—'

'Sorry – one thing at a time, Grenville. What I was going to say was it might be a bright idea to keep away from the grade-one tracks and the more – how shall I put it? – the more spotlit races. Keep a low profile, in other words.'

'Then you are thinking what I'm thinking.'

'Just keep a low profile,' Rory repeated. 'Until we know exactly what sort of horse we actually have.'

'Gotcha.'

'And I think we should certainly run him over three miles next time. Blaze said he wasn't in any way cooked, and finished full of running.'

'Can anyone else join in this?' Alice wondered. 'Or is it boys only?'

'Of course, Alice.' Rory moved his chair slightly away from Grenville's and turned to Alice. 'All we're doing – we were only discussing the next race.'

'Yes.' Alice nodded. 'Well, I know we're not exactly *au fait* with all that stuff, the distaff side as it were,' she added, indicating Lynne, Constance and herself. 'But we do have something to say, and the point is that if you two are hatching some sort of plot to enter our horse in the Grand National you can forget it—'

'Alice—'

'Seriously, Rory.' Alice overrode him. 'Because that's what we've been discussing, the three of us, and Millie, while you two have been talking. And the Grand National is over our dead bodies.'

'Mine too. I couldn't agree more,' Rory assured her. 'Not that it would be on even if we thought it was a good idea, because the horse is still a novice, and the National is no place for novices. Even so—'

'Even when he's not a novice,' Alice insisted. 'None of us want him ever to run in the National.'

'I couldn't agree more,' Grenville said. 'Too many good horses get injured in the National, and usually through no fault of their own. So you mustn't worry, Alice, because that was not what we were discussing at all, I do assure you. We have our eyes on something quite different.'

'Grenville here has his eyes on something quite different,' Rory said with a frown. 'I prefer to look not quite so far ahead. I'll send you all a list of suggested entries in a day or two, but now if you'll excuse me I have to hit the road. My father's coming home from hospital tomorrow, and I have to make sure everything's in place.'

'That's wonderful news, Rory,' Millie said. 'When did he turn the corner?'

'After Wincanton, would you believe?' Rory said. 'After the horse's first race.'

Since they had come such a distance to see the race, now their horse had won again none of the owners was in any great rush to get home, so they all decided to stay and enjoy the rest of the excellent racecard. The feature race was a three-mile handicap chase, the betting for which was dominated by Insider Trading, a big grey horse from Eddie Rampton's yard ridden by Sandy Bridger, his retained jockey, a man with a reputation as formidable as the trainer's.

'Think I should have a flutter?' Lynne asked Grenville as they stood at the paddock rails watching the sharp-faced jockey receiving his instructions from the pug-nosed, broad-shouldered Eddie Rampton. 'It's not much of a price.'

'I think that's because it's considered one of those nailed-on certainties, my dear,' Grenville replied. 'If I were you I'd go for something a little longer priced, some little each way chance.'

'Who's that dreadful-looking villainous type in the Al Capone hat?' Constance wondered, pointing at Rampton who was now turning round to face their group. 'He looks as though he should be carrying a gat.'

'Careful,' Grenville warned her, dropping his own voice as he thought he caught a glare from the trainer while quickly lowering Constance's accusing finger. 'And I'm sure Nanny told you how rude it is to point.'

Having both decided to back Whistlestop, one of the rank outsiders, Lynne and Alice hurried off to the Tote with Millie while Constance and Grenville made their way to their appointed spot in the grandstand. By the time the others finally found them, the race had started.

'Did you get my bet on, Millie dear?' Constance enquired.

'Certainly did, Constance,' Millie said, handing Constance a Tote ticket. 'Two pounds each way number seven.'

'You've had a bet, Constance?' Grenville asked in surprise. 'You the great anti-gambler? You who said no one ever put enough on a winning horse?'

'Just a smokescreen, young man,' Constance replied, putting her ticket in her bag. 'I have a whole multitude of hidden vices.'

'Number seven,' Grenville said, looking at his racecard. 'Piper Aboard. No chance.'

*   *   *

With two miles of the three completed, Insider Trading was lying second and going easily, his jockey already looking around for any sign of danger.

'The way he's going, five to four looks generous,' Grenville remarked, as the favourite ranged up alongside the now struggling leading horse.

'Thanks for that,' Lynne said. 'I could still have made a packet. And where's blooming Whistletop, girls? I thought we were going to get rich.'

'In your case rich*er*, dear,' Constance said. Then, startling them all, she suddenly called at the top of her voice, 'That's the one. Come on, Piper Aboard! Stuff that great big grey carthorse!'

Most people in the immediate vicinity smiled or laughed, all except naturally the horse's bullnecked trainer, who was standing right in front of Constance, who having heard Constance's exhortation turned round to stare at her with a considerable degree of menace.

'Pipe down, you silly old woman,' he commanded.

'I most certainly will do no such thing,' Constance replied. 'Not even if you say please.'

For a moment those witnessing this brief but pointed exchange believed that Eddie Rampton was about to add to his notoriety by hitting a woman in public, so dark had become his countenance, but the call of the racecourse commentator drew his attention back to the race, much to the relief of those in Constance's party.

'And coming to the second last it's now Piper Aboard who's laying down the challenge to Insider Trading, on whom Sandy Bridger is now hard at work . . .' the commentator called.

'He's hitting that poor horse far too much,' Alice remarked,

319

an observation which earned another look of consummate fury from the animal's trainer. 'That is just awful.'

'And Piper Aboard and the favourite Insider Trading rise at the fence together! And land together – neck and neck!' the commentator continued. 'And if anything Piper Aboard has got away from the fence the better!'

'Come on my horse!' Constance yelled. 'Come on my lovely little horse!'

'Somebody should shoot that jockey!' Alice insisted. 'Surely he's not allowed to hit his horse like that?'

'He'll be up before the stewards don't you worry,' Grenville whispered to Alice, not wanting to incur another fit of rage from the man in front of them.

'My horse has done it! He's only gone and done it!' Constance cried whacking Grenville on his hat with her rolled-up racecard. 'The carthorse is estuffadoed!'

Everybody nearby held their breath waiting for the inevitable eruption. But it seemed that the notoriously short-fused trainer was far too taken aback both by the performance of his hot favourite and the behaviour of some mad punter behind him to do anything other than give Constance yet another drop-dead look.

'And as they approach the last it seems Piper Aboard has got the favourite's measure!' the commentator called. 'He's drawn a length clear now and at the run to the fence he definitely has the measure of Insider Trading, who in fact might even be beaten into third place by Whistlestop!'

'Whistletop!' Lynne shrieked. 'Come on, my son! Come on Whistletop you beauty!'

'And as they land over the last it's Piper Aboard clear by three lengths from the fast tiring Insider Trading – with Whistlestop closing on the favourite now – and passing him easily – it's Piper Aboard increasing his lead to four to five lengths now, with Whistlestop running on in second, two lengths ahead of Insider Trading who's in danger of being caught on the post by Catzoff – and Catzoff just catches the favourite on the line to snatch third place!'

'We won – we won!' Constance carolled, waving two triumphant arms in the air. 'My little horse won!'

'Will you shut up about your wretched little horse woman!' Eddie Rampton finally warned her, turning to face her. 'Some of us do this for our living!'

'I do *hate* bad losers,' Constance groaned. 'It's only a race, chum – it's only a silly old horse race.'

'Get me out of here,' Eddie Rampton rumbled. 'Before a terrible tragedy occurs.'

'Oh pooh!' Constance sighed after the thickset retreating figure. 'What a dreadfully rotten sport.'

'Yes indeed Constance,' Grenville agreed, taking her arm to lead her off in the opposite direction. 'But he is absolutely not someone to cross swords with.'

After the three women had collected their winnings from the Tote they walked past the unsaddling enclosure where to judge from the sound of raised voices it seemed that Eddie Rampton had not yet regained his composure. Grenville tried to chivvy his party through and past the confrontation but Constance was having none of it.

'Don't be such a spoilsport Grenville,' she said, detaching herself from his arm, 'I want to hear what Al Capone is sounding off about now.'

Rampton was addressing the small company of racing journalists who had gathered around him to learn his thoughts on the race.

'It is a perfectly disgraceful situation,' he announced loudly. 'Certain trainers run their horses in handicaps not on their merits. We all know this for a fact – that they do it to get the weights down when their horses are fly weighted then what a surprise! They trot up in handicaps such as this. And no one says a bloody thing. No one.'

'Except for you, Eddie,' one of the braver scribes suggested.

'The horse that won today hasn't even been placed for eighteen months, he's getting a stone and a half from my horse and you saw the result!'

'Isn't that what handicaps are for, Mr Rampton?' another journalist wondered. 'To give horses such as Piper Aboard a chance to compete favourably with higher-rated horses?'

'When horses are run on their merit it's a level playing field.' Rampton replied in no uncertain tones. 'When they are not, it's a bloody travesty.'

A heavyweight man with what looked like visibly high blood pressure pushed his way through the throng.

'I hope you are not suggesting I've not been running my horses on merit!' he asked in a west country accent. 'One of the reasons my horse hasn't won for eighteen months is because he was swallowing his tongue.'

'Too right he was, Peters,' Rampton growled. 'More's the pity you don't follow suit.'

'We tied his tongue down today, you oaf,' the other trainer replied. 'Hence the improvement.'

'And you never thought of doing that before? Don't take it, pal. You're not doing yourself any favours here. Now bugger off before I make your nose bleed.'

With that Rampton pushed his blackcurrant-complexioned rival out of the way and stormed out of the enclosure, passing right by Constance and her group. 'And as for you,' he said, stopping briefly to eye Constance. 'Don't you *ever* be fool enough to stand anywhere near me on a racecourse ever again!'

'Not unless you have full police protection,' Millie murmured as they made their way back to the bar. 'What a sweetie.'

On their way to the bar, they passed a short, thin-faced man with sleek oiled-down hair and darting eyes, dressed in a double-breasted pinstripe suit, standing gossiping with a small crowd from the county set just past the unsaddling enclosure. Suddenly noticing Constance, he stopped and stared at her, then looked sharply at her again.

'Sylvia?' he said, breaking away from his associates and pursuing her.

Constance, who had been idling along at the back of her group with Grenville, grabbed Grenville by one arm and began to hurry him forward.

'Quickly, Grenville,' she urged. 'You're being the most awful Mr Slowcoach.'

'Sylvia Topsham?' her pursuer repeated, now almost alongside Constance. 'It is you, isn't it?'

'It most certainly is not,' Constance replied haughtily, hurrying on even more quickly. 'Now go away at once. I have no idea who you are.'

'You mightn't know me, Sylvia,' the man insisted, following on, 'but I think I know you all right. You're Sylvia Topsham, aren't you?'

'Grenville,' Constance muttered, dropping Grenville's arm and preparing to flee forward. 'Get rid of him. Lose him. See him off. I mean it.'

'Look here,' Grenville said, placing himself between the rapidly departing Constance and her pursuer, 'I'll be most obliged if you will stop pestering my mother.'

'Your mother?' the man said with a frown, stopping in his tracks.

'My mother, precisely,' Grenville assured him. 'My mother,

Lady Frimley, who for some reason you mistakenly believe is someone else, apparently.'

'Lady Frimley, did you say?' the man repeated, raising his eyebrows. 'Your mother. Apologies. OK – sorry, but I could have sworn—' He stopped, looking in the direction in which Constance had now disappeared from view. 'Excuse me,' he said, and left.

Grenville waited and watched to make sure he did not double back in pursuit of the obviously distressed Constance before going after her himself to make sure she was all right, but although he looked everywhere he could find no trace of her. None of the others appeared to know where she had gone to either, although Millie thought she had seen her hurrying away, hand on hat, towards the owners' car park. Grenville went there at once, happily to find Constance all but hidden behind his car.

'Constance?' he called in bewilderment. 'Constance . . .'

Instead of replying or greeting him, Constance simply put a finger to her lips and remained where she was, stooped low beside the passenger door of Grenville's Jaguar.

'What on earth is the matter?' Grenville enquired, begging the question.

'Please open the car,' Constance hissed at him. 'And then please take me home? Please?'

Too much a gentleman to refuse, Grenville opened up his car, went to find Lynne, explained the situation to her, and returned with her to the car park.

'Right,' Grenville said, starting the car. 'London first, everyone.'

'I don't care where you take me,' Constance muttered from the back, sitting down in her seat with her face turned well away from the window.

'I thought you wanted to go home?'

'And I said I don't care where you take me,' Constance repeated. 'As long as it's away from here.'

Grenville frowned at Lynne beside him as he backed out of his parking space. 'Sorry,' he murmured. 'You'll be awfully late home.'

'It doesn't matter,' Lynne said quietly. 'I can stay in London tonight and take the train home tomorrow. Long as that's all right with you.'

'Yes, yes of course,' Grenville said quickly. 'I should have suggested it. Sorry.'

'You really must stop apologising for yourself all the time, Grenville,' Lynne teased him, putting a hand discreetly on his knee. 'You really have nothing to apologise for. Nothing at all.'

On the road now and headed south, Grenville glanced in his driving mirror to see Constance slumped down even further in her seat, a handkerchief held to face.

'There's something the matter,' Grenville said *sotto* to Lynne. 'Perhaps if we stopped and put you in the back . . . ?'

As soon as he could safely do so, Grenville pulled the car off the road and Lynne slipped into the rear seat.

'It's OK, Connie.' Lynne took one of her hands, leaving Constance to dab at the tears on her face with the other. 'Listen, if you want to talk, I'm here.' Constance just shook her head. 'Look – something's upset you, and that's terrible. I mean, on a day like this. Of all the days to be upset . . .' Still Constance tried to tough it out, shaking her head again and clasping her handkerchief even more tightly to her mouth. 'Did someone say something to upset you, darling? Or what? Why don't you tell us? It'll be much better if you talk about it. Honestly.'

'It was something that happened long ago,' Constance whispered, glancing red-eyed at Lynne over her hankie. 'And if I told you, you'd only hate me.'

'I couldn't hate you, Connie,' Lynne assured her. 'Don't be daft. I love you.'

'You wouldn't. Not if you knew. Not if I told you.'

'Was it anything to do with that man at the racecourse, Constance?' Grenville asked from the driving seat. 'The chap who thought he recognised you? As a matter of fact I thought I recognised him from somewhere.'

Connie nodded and carefully wiped her eyes with her handkerchief.

'He's that gossip columnist johnny,' she said. 'And he did recognise me.'

'Sylvia – what was it?' Grenville frowned at her image in his driving mirror. 'Sylvia . . .'

'Topsham,' Constance replied. 'My married name. I was born Sylvia Barton, which was my professional name as well.'

'Professional?' Lynne asked. 'Professional as in what, love?'

'I was an actress,' Constance replied. 'Before you were born, dear, so don't worry.'

'Sylvia Barton,' Grenville said to himself. 'You were more than just an actress, Connie. You were a bit of a film star.'

'A bit is about right, Grenville, dear.' Constance sniffed. 'Rank School of Charm.'

'What's that when it's at home?' Lynne asked.

'The J. Arthur Rank studios, just after the war, dear. Made all those British films, and put a lot of us girls and boys under contracts. Trained us up the way he wanted us to go. I was what was called a Rank starlet. Which is not quite what everybody called us – as you can imagine.'

'You were in some rather good films, Connie,' Grenville said.

'Didn't have much to do with making them any good, dear. I was there purely as decoration.'

'Yes, but even so, Connie,' Lynne continued, with a reassuring smile, 'I don't see what's so dreadful about being a starlet. I mean that's hardly going to make us hate you, is it?'

'You are so sweet, Lynne,' Constance said, squeezing her hand. 'I've really grown terribly fond of you.'

'I told you, I love you too.'

'Very American,' Constance returned, trying to smile.

'Doesn't matter. I happen to mean it.'

'It's got nothing to do with my being an actress, you're quite right,' Constance continued, beginning to recover her composure. 'It was my marriage. Or more particularly one of the men I married. You're too young to remember, sweetie – you probably both are. It might just ring bells with Grenville. One of my husbands happened to be a somewhat notorious fellow called Andrew Topsham.' She waited for the expected reaction but all she got was silence from both Grenville and Lynne.

'See?' Lynne exclaimed after a moment. 'Nothing to us. Not a thing.'

'Andrew Topsham,' Grenville said slowly. 'It does ring a bell somewhere or other. Yes.'

'Let me save you the trouble, dear,' Constance said. 'He was a spy. Cold War jobby. He spied for the Russkies.'

'Red Andrew, of *course*,' Grenville exclaimed. 'Defected, didn't he? Sometime in the early sixties, if my memory serves me.'

'I met him just after the war. He'd had a rather good war, so I was told, if there can be any such thing, which I very much doubt. He was frightfully well connected, knew all the right people, terribly dashing, but – well, a little peculiar I thought, but we won't go into all that. Anyway, the point was he worked for Intelligence, or *in* Intelligence or whatever they call it, but all the time he was stealing stuff for his Red friends. He got out, defected, and left me behind, high, dry and stranded. The so and so had implicated me as a sort of red herring—'

'I remember now,' Grenville said. 'It's all coming back to me.'

'I thought it had gone away,' Constance sighed, turning to stare out of the window at the rain-lashed winter landscape flashing by. 'I was finally given the all-clear, but of course you know what they say about mud. It does stick, you know. By George it does. So they advised me to go on holiday, a long holiday, which I did. I went to a friend's in South Africa, a chum from the Rank school of little charmers who had married really rather well and lived out there until a few years ago. Met someone there, as it happened, and got involved. An absolute beast of a fellow who went in for a lot of beating up. Wouldn't think it to look at him. Looked like an angel, sweetest little baby face and lots of curly blond hair, and drank himself to death.'

'Lord Frimley, perchance?' Grenville wondered, giving her a smile via the driving mirror.

'Sir Peter Frimley, as it happened,' Constance replied. 'Don't laugh, dear, that really was his handle, though don't ask me. So I took his title since I thought that was the least he owed me and back I came, thinking the dust must have settled by now, because I was frightfully homesick, don't you know. Pretended we'd been wed. It worked because no one remembered me, not as Lady Frimley. They hadn't a clue. All washed up and long forgotten.'

'You obviously haven't lost your looks, Connie,' Lynne said.

'Obviously not,' Grenville agreed. 'Hence the tripe hound's recognising you.'

'For the life of me I don't know how,' Constance said. 'As a girl I was raven-haired and now I'm grey as a ghost; a little shrunken, invisible old woman.'

'Oh yes?' Lynne laughed. 'I've seen the heads still turning.'

'Pooh,' Constance said, but with a half-smile.

'Anyway,' Grenville said. 'So what if he thought he recognised you? It's all over. Dead, gone, buried.'

'You know the papers, dear.' Constance sighed. 'They'll dish it all up again. Red Andrew's scarlet woman and all that nonsense. I really don't want it all dragged out of the cupboard yet again.'

'We'll take care of you,' Lynne assured her, linking her arm in Constance's. 'We won't let the illegitimates get you.'

'I do hope you won't,' Constance said quietly. 'I think it would finish me. Just when everything was at its very best, too. Do you know something? I think this is the first time I've ever had any fun, first time I've been really happy, since I was a gel, as we used to say in those days. This is the very first time in such a long time I've felt really happy.'

Before they began their own journey home, Alice and Millie treated themselves to some tea and cake. While they were enjoying their refreshment, Alice noticed Harrington Lovell looking at her occasionally from his own party across the room, but thought little of it until, after Millie had disappeared to the ladies preparatory to leaving the course, she found Harrington standing at her table, hands clasped behind his back and inclining himself forward as if he wished to speak confidentially.

'Alice,' he began. 'Forgive the intrusion, and I'm not quite sure how to put this without seeming too forward . . .'

'You're not intruding at all,' Alice assured him. 'Would you like some tea?'

'No thank you.' Harrington gave a cautious smile. 'No, what I really wanted was to know – well. How can I best put this? I wondered when you might be racing your horse again.'

'Why's that, Mr Lovell?'

'Harrington, please. Or better still Harry. That's what all my friends call me.'

'Sorry. Of course,' Alice said. 'Why do you want to know when the horse is running again? Do you want another bet?'

Harrington laughed. 'No. No, the reason I wanted to know is because I'd like to know when I might see you – you all – again.'

Alice looked up at him quickly, and found to her interest and surprise that her heart was suddenly beating a little bit faster.

'To be truthful, I don't know,' she said. 'Rory's sending us a list of entries later in the week.'

'I see.' Harrington nodded, not knowing quite how much further to go, before deciding to cut his losses and leave. 'In that case, best thing I can do is to keep an eye on the racing papers,' he said, straightening up. 'Or have my trainer let me know.'

'Of course,' Alice agreed. 'Except now I'm curious,' she added. 'I don't mean to be rude—'

'I doubt very much whether you could be, Alice.'

'But since you have horses of your own, I was just wondering why you were so keen to see ours running.'

'It isn't your horse I want to see, Alice.' Harrington leaned forward again. 'Actually it's you.'

'Oh,' said Alice, finding herself unexpectedly on the back foot. 'Oh. Oh, I see. Or rather I don't. I don't see.'

'I'd like to say because me Tarzan, you Jane,' Harrington replied. 'Except I think I'm a bit too old now for that to sound convincing. So let's just say it's a man–woman thing, Alice. I've enjoyed meeting you, and now I find I would like to see you again. That is, provided it's all right with you.'

'It's perfectly all right with me, Harry. I've enjoyed meeting you as well. Very much.'

'So,' Harrington concluded, straightening himself to his full and still impressive height as he saw Millie making her way back to the table. 'To the next time. To our next time.'

Then he was gone.

'So what do I spy here?' Millie said, collecting her things off the table. 'Got yourself a heavy date, sister?'

'Never you mind that,' Alice replied, getting up to leave. 'That was just horse talk.'

Even so, as she left the bar, Alice couldn't resist one last glance over her shoulder, and, when she looked, she saw that apparently Harrington couldn't resist one either.

Chapter Twenty-one

Best Laid Plans

Rory was sitting studying the Racing Calendar with his mind on entries when Kathleen walked into his office. He had been doing his very best to keep his mind off the subject of Miss Kathleen Flanagan ever since it had become obvious to him that she and Blaze Molloy were an item. Up till now, he had been managing the task better than he thought he might, using what little free time he had in trying to make his convalescent father as comfortable and happy as possible. He was surprised but pleased to see that Anthony seemed more than happy to watch the activity of the yard from the warmth and comfort of an armchair in the drawing room, and to catch up on all the news at drinks time over a weak whisky and water, rather than try to take back hold of the reins.

There was concern, however, over the exact condition of Anthony's health, Dan having told Rory privately before sending his patient home that in an ideal world he would have the sort of heart surgery that currently was only being practised in America, and at a price. As it was, they had done everything they could and would continue to do so in order to keep their patient up and about, as Dan put it, which Rory took to mean they would do everything possible to keep his father alive and well enough to enjoy life for as long as they could. That was all that was said, because on their side of the Atlantic that was all that could be done.

But now Kathleen was standing on the other side of Rory's desk, looking even more beautiful than ever, Rory thought, if such a thing were possible. Being at Fulford Farm obviously suited her for since she had come to work in the yard everything about Kathleen seemed to have become more exceptional; her skin gleamed, her eyes shone, her hair looked more lustrous, her figure even shapelier, and her personality was ever more vibrant. It was as if she was in training herself and blooming under her new regime.

Despite all this, Rory wanted her to disappear from his life, while with all his heart he wanted her to stay, because he knew from the bottom of that same heart that he could have no chance with her, not since the arrival of the handsome, laid-back and highly talented young jockey Blaze Molloy. It seemed every time he looked up or turned round there they were, deep in conversation, Blaze with an arm draped round her shoulders, or Kathleen just smiling across the yard at him as she went about her work, or the two of them in deep and private debate on the course, or celebrating their horse's win with their peers, while the only time he himself spoke to Kathleen in any depth was when they needed to discuss matters concerning Boyo. Every time Rory thought he might try to dig a little deeper, either someone or something interrupted them, or Kathleen excused herself on the pretext of having to do something to or with her precious charge. So Rory had resigned himself to an existence that now included a seriously unrequited love.

'We have a problem, Mr Rawlins,' she was saying, her cap off, gently tossing back her head of long dark hair. 'He's off his food.'

'Since when?' Rory asked, getting up immediately. 'He's been eating up everything. So when did this start?'

'He started picking at it yesterday, and now today he won't go near his pot.'

'Right. Fine. I'll come and have a look,' Rory said, thinking that although going to stare into the horse's manger was hardly going to work the oracle, at least it would afford him some time with the object of his affection.

'What I was wondering was why you'd changed the supplier,' Kathleen remarked as they crossed the yard. 'I'm sure you had good reason.'

'Changed the supplier?' Rory stopped and looked at her. 'I don't understand what you mean.'

'It wasn't the usual corn merchant who delivered the last lot of fodder,' Kathleen told him. 'The man said someone had rung him and transferred all the stable orders to his firm.'

'I don't understand,' Rory said again, his brow furrowing. 'We had a new supplier and no one thought of mentioning it?'

'You weren't here, Mr Rawlins,' Kathleen replied, looking as though she were mortally affronted. 'It was the day you were collecting your father from hospital. And since it was exactly the same food we'd been having before, no one thought anything of it. Anyway, Pauline said it was all in order, that there'd been some problem or other with the last people, and so we never thought another thing about it.'

'Pauline? But it isn't really Pauline's – look, we'd better f-f-find Pauline, because I don't like this at all. I certainly never authorised any such change – not m-me.'

'But Pauline's not in. Didn't you know? She's been off for a couple of days, and she called this morning to say she was still unwell.'

'Why am I always the last to know any – it doesn't matter.

334

Forget it,' Rory muttered, hurrying now towards the feed room. 'How many feeds has B-Boyo had? From this famous new delivery?'

'You don't think—'

'I th-think a lot of things, but first things f-first.'

'He's only had supper last night and breakfast today from the new stuff, because I don't like waste and I thought we should finish the last consignment first. It's just the way I was brought up.'

'Ker-ker-ker – *quite* right too, Kathleen,' Rory said, inspecting the new consignment of fodder. 'You might just have saved the day.'

Noel took the foodstuff away for analysis, having thoroughly examined the horse and found nothing apparently amiss with him, although as a precautionary measure he also took away a blood sample and a specimen of the horse's droppings for analysis. After Noel had departed, Kathleen insisted on giving her charge a purge as well, assuring Rory that the mixture she intended to use was purely herbal and would leave no unwanted medicinal traces.

'Obviously you think it was doped with something,' his father observed at drinks time. 'Although if someone's keen on stopping the horse, wouldn't they wait till nearer the time of his next race?'

'Well, yes, I suppose so, but this could be – couldn't it? – one of those slow-term drugs you were on about,' Rory replied. 'Something they might simply want to get into the horse's system, that works insidiously; some sort of dope that – you know, something that might slow him up a bit on the gallops, but not sufficiently so for us to get worried.'

'But then when you get him to the races—'

'There was that horse you swore was stopped end of last

season? One of Dick Anderson's up at Haydock? And then it went and dropped dead in the paddock after the race.'

'Lovely thing to do to an animal,' Anthony observed. 'Nice people.'

'And that chap you know – the security guy from the Jockey Club,' Rory continued. 'Didn't he tell you there was this new stuff coming in from Scandinavia that left absolutely no trace? That it was worrying them all sleepless?'

'How long before you get the result?'

'Twenty-four hours, tops. Noel's giving it priority. And can you believe they got at Pauline, of all people? You just can't tell with people.' Rory shook his head in dismay and poured himself another beer.

'And she's done a runner, you say,' Anthony said.

'Well, of course. Could be anywhere by now. Who'd want to do this anyway? We're not exactly a big betting yard or anything. Bastards.'

'We don't know what they've done yet, old chap – if anything,' Anthony remarked, holding up his own glass for refreshment. 'But it wasn't very subtle, was it? Somebody's going to remark on the change in the food merchant sooner or later, sooner more likely than later. And the moment they do, end of story.'

'They probably thought that with me in charge nobody would bother to remark on it. Not the sort of thing anyone would get past you.'

'Don't be hard on yourself, Rory. You're doing well, so don't beat yourself up – there's no need.'

'I forget to book the dentist, I left the horses on contaminated straw when we'd discussed putting them on shavings, I let Kathleen turn the horse out in the paddock – we were lucky to get away with that one – and now someone's sending us unauthorised fodder.'

'Rory?' his father interrupted. 'You've had a lot on your mind, and I wasn't here.'

'I can't have been paying that much attention when you were here, can I?'

'You've also trained a horse to win two races.'

'I've also got a horse who's won two races.'

'What is this about anyway?' Anthony asked. 'This isn't like you at all. So what is it about?'

'It's about me thinking I could just take over just like that and manage, Dad, that's what this is about,' Rory replied. 'Instead of thinking what I was doing. Instead of asking for advice. I should have asked for advice instead of just going ahead thinking training horses and running a yard was . . . was – I don't know. Child's play.'

'That isn't what this is all about at all, old chap. You've got something on your mind.'

'I've got a stable full of horses on my mind, Dad, that's what. And if Kathleen hadn't brought the subject up, this latest thing – the change in supplier – it might have gone unnoticed for days. Maybe the others thought with the way things have been – with the way they still are, actually – maybe they thought there'd been some problem or other over the bills, let's say, and if so they might have been too tactful to mention it.'

'What did our regular suppliers say? Mortons? I take it we're back with them?'

'Mortons told me someone had rung a few days ago cancelling the order but without any explanation.'

'A woman?'

'A man, oddly enough. Pauline's contact, presumably. And yes – I put our order back in place.'

'Makes your hair stand on end,' Anthony said, draining his glass. 'The lengths people will go to stop a horse.'

'People as in bookmakers?'

'The poor old bookmakers,' Anthony said wryly. 'They get to carry the can for everything. This sort of thing can be down to anyone, you know. A rival. A soured ex-owner. An embittered bloodstock agent – the racing world is full of people carrying grudges, real and imagined. Let's wait on the tests. Maybe they'll give us some sort of indication.'

'Maybe they will,' Rory agreed. 'Now if you don't mind, I think I'll take Dunkum out for a bit of a walk.

He took the lurcher for a long walk round the farm, trying without success to sort out his head and his heart. He hated both making a fool of himself and being made a fool of, so he resolved at least to put a stop to both of those, determining to ask for advice when in doubt and not to say yes to anything equine when he either meant no or just don't know. Horses were an unknown quantity even to the most experienced of trainers, so to Rory, who considered himself well and truly still an apprentice in the craft, it seemed absolutely vital that every decision regarding the yard must be thoroughly discussed and not arrived at on the wings of some whim or other. He would make lists, he would have charts, people would have specific tasks delegated to them, and nobody would do anything without the properly considered consent of both him and his father.

As for his affairs of the heart, he would really have to stop mooning about like some lovesick schoolboy and simply realise that Miss Kathleen Flanagan was spoken for, and that even if she was not he could think of not one good reason why he should ever be of the slightest interest to her. Besides, even if her heart did not fully belong to Mr Blaze Molloy, it was certainly given long ago to the little horse who was now the star of the yard, and not for one second did Rory imagine that even were Kathleen free she would find either time or reason to take the very slightest of interests in someone as incompetent and as diffident as he.

'All we want to know is what we're meant to do about Christmas, Mum,' Georgina was saying on the telephone. 'It's not a lot to ask.'

Alice felt like reminding her daughter what they and everyone else were meant to do at Christmas, but resisted the temptation.

'I'm not sure what I shall be doing yet, Georgie,' she replied instead. 'Our horse is meant to be running somewhere on Boxing Day, so I'm not making any hard and fast plans till we know where.'

'It's not exactly as if we're seeing a lot of you at the moment,' Georgina continued inexorably.

'I know, love, but what with moving and everything . . . Once spring comes, and summer, then you must all come down.'

'But what about Christmas, Mum?'

'You're more than welcome to come down here, I told you that.'

'All of us? Plus Christian *and* his new girlfriend?'

'He's got a new girlfriend?'

'Not in touch, then?' Georgina sighed. 'Yes, he's got a new girlfriend who if anything is even more frightful than the last one – and they are an item. Yes? So all of us coming down would be a little out of the question? In your cottage, Mum? Do get a little bit real. No, much the best if you come up here to Richmond.'

'When I know where the horse is running, and if he is—'

'I hear he won again,' Georgina cut in. 'Thanks for telling us.'

'I didn't know he was going to win!' Alice laughed. 'And can you imagine if he hadn't won? And I'd told you to back him? Can you imagine?'

'As it happened Joe backed him, but at pretty miserable odds.'

'He *was* favourite, darling. Anyway. Let's discuss this as soon as I know my plans this end.'

'Mum?'

'Georgina?'

'Nothing.'

But Alice was getting stronger. She still managed to hang up before her daughter.

Rory and Maureen had just finished entering The Enchanted up for several good-looking races on the great feast of National Hunt racing otherwise known as Boxing Day, when the telephone rang.

'Noel,' Maureen said, holding the receiver out to Rory.

'Noel? I thought he was meant to call yesterday,' Rory said with a frown, taking the phone. 'Noel?'

'Yes, I'm sorry for the delay, Rory,' his vet said on the other end of the line. 'We all wanted to be absolutely sure before we made any pronouncement, but the feed was definitely tampered with, no doubt at all.'

'Right. Really? With what, Noel?'

'Steroids,' his vet told him. 'There are definite traces of steroids in the food, and if anyone had gone on using this food – and why the hell shouldn't they? – there'd have been enough there to show up in any dope test.'

'Which of course means . . .' Rory said, trying to remember the exact rules.

'Automatic disqualification, Rory, and not just from any new race,' Noel reminded him, 'but from any races recently won.'

'Nice,' Rory said. 'End of the horse and nice for the yard. We can't get any winners, so we give them steroids.'

'It's a bit of an amateur plan,' Noel said. 'Yet one that just might have worked. There are a lot of yards where this sort of thing could well go unnoticed until too late.'

'One month's supply of fodder. And by the time the change in corn merchant is noticed, it could well be too late. The race could have been run.'

'That's possibly a very good horse you have there, Rory. So be vigilant.'

'As of now I am riding shotgun, Noel.'

From then on security became of paramount importance. Kathleen, Teddy and Rory took it in turns to sit on watch during the nights, and no one was allowed into the yard without advance permission. All gates were kept locked and Dunkum roamed freely in the role of watchdog.

'He might be as kind as a saint,' Rory told Kathleen, 'but the bark is quite off-putting.'

'What else can go wrong, Mr Rawlins? Whoever it is, they're up to right mischief, I'd say.'

'We've hardly caned the bookies,' Rory replied. 'His first race he was any price. If you ask me, the money that shortened his odds all came from your homeland.'

'Tell me something that would surprise me.'

'And all right – he was favourite for his second race, but it was hardly a hot betting race. No, this is about something else altogether.'

Oddly enough, Rory might have put two and two together and made a decent stab at four had he read the racing papers more carefully that morning instead of getting some of the more important news second-hand from Maureen when he returned to his office.

'There's still plenty of it about,' Maureen commented,

looking up from the *Sporting Life* she was reading at her desk. 'The favourite for the King George, My Pal Joey? He's been sold for what they call an undisclosed sum.'

Rory stopped and looked at his secretary, who was back to reading the paper again, sticky bun in hand and a mug of coffee beside her.

'Who'd want to sell a horse like that?'

'One of those offers you can't refuse, maybe?'

'He's also ante-post favourite for the Gold Cup,' Rory said. 'Who'd sell a horse like that? Mind you – yes. Yes, there were rumours that the present owner wasn't at all well. So maybe . . . no, I don't know.' He shook his head. 'I still don't get it. Think I'll go and see what the old man makes of it.'

'"The deal was brokered by bloodstock agent Roddy Downes,"' Maureen read, '"on behalf of Mr G. Fortune." As in G for good, I imagine.'

But when she looked up Rory had already gone.

There was more bad news on Christmas Eve. When Rory came down to the yard at first light he found an agitated Kathleen waiting for him.

'Not the horse?' he asked quickly, seeing the expression on her face. 'Please tell me there's nothing wrong with the horse.'

'There's nothing wrong with the horse, it's all right, Mr Rawlins,' Kathleen assured him. 'But there's plenty wrong with his jockey.'

Blaze had been set upon. It was as simple as that and yet just as baffling. Kathleen, Teddy, Teddy's girlfriend Julie and Blaze had gone as usual for a drink at the local after evening stables, a safe and friendly pub that was even more so than usual because of the time of year. Everyone had been full of peace and goodwill towards their fellow men right up until the moment the three from Fulford Farm and Julie wished everyone a Merry Christmas and walked out into a starlit night, whereupon three men in balaclavas and anoraks had set about Blaze, and only Blaze. Teddy, who was brave but only a lightweight, was soon dealt with, felled by a single punch, leaving Kathleen and Julie to scream blue murder as the hoodlums went to work on Blaze, but because everyone was singing 'Hark The Herald Angels Sing' at full volume in the bar, no one heard their shouts for help.

Blaze could look after himself but only up to a point, and by the time Kathleen had run back into the bar and brought half a dozen of their racing friends rushing out to help, Blaze was on the ground and being given a serious kicking. The cavalry soon saw the thugs off and then the soberest among them drove Blaze to Salisbury General Hospital, where they found he had a split lip, a broken nose, and severe bruising to the ribs and back where he had been kicked. When Kathleen had left to come back to the farm Blaze was still waiting to be X-rayed.

'There'd been no sign of bother inside the pub?' Rory asked.

'Not a bit of it, Mr Rawlins,' Kathleen told him. 'It had been the very best of nights. They were lying in wait outside, pure and simple. Waiting to do him over. But why? Everyone loves Blaze. You couldn't meet a sweeter man.'

'Yes,' Rory said, preferring to avoid the subject of Blaze's exemplary character and concentrate on the aftermath of the affray. 'He's not going to be fit to ride Boxing Day, then.'

'Now we don't know that yet, Mr Rawlins,' Kathleen said quickly, with obvious concern. 'He's as tough as old boots, Blaze, and if he can ride, sure he will, he will.'

'There are other jockeys, Kathleen.'

'You said yourself – I heard you, Mr Rawlins, talking to Maureen – what a lottery getting a jockey was on Boxing Day. How many meetings are there?'

'Far too many,' Rory retorted, knowing that all the decent jockeys would have long been booked for the best rides over the holiday.

'You don't want to go trusting some untried lad on Boyo, I know you don't,' Kathleen persisted. 'I'm sure Blaze will be fine, Mr Rawlins. He has a whole day to recover.'

'I won't put him up if there's any doubt about his fitness, Kathleen,' Rory said. 'I'd rather not run the horse.'

'But you have to!' Kathleen insisted, before immediately recovering herself. 'I mean, the poor owners, Mr Rawlins. They'd be mortally disappointed, so they would.'

'That's not why you said I have to run him.'

'That's all I meant.'

'Hmm.' Rory looked at her, then shook his head. 'We'll wait and see how the lad is,' he decided. 'Your precious Blaze.'

As soon as he said it he knew he shouldn't have, since it sounded churlish and childish even to his own ears. Kathleen said nothing. Nor did she smile; nor did she frown.

'Thank you, Mr Rawlins,' was all she said, at last, before hurrying off to do her duties.

When Blaze appeared in the yard the next day, he looked as though he'd been acting as a punchbag for a heavyweight contender. Besides a thick lip he had two black eyes, and his nose, although apparently mercifully not broken after all, was heavily strapped across the bridge. In spite of his battering, however, he was his usual jaunty self, although he must have been feeling a long way from good.

'You're not expecting to ride tomorrow, are you?' Rory said the moment he saw him. 'Surely not.'

'I am indeed, guv'nor,' Blaze replied. 'This is not as bad as it looks. Believe me.'

'But how does it feel? That's the important thing,' Rory said. 'If you've any cracked ribs—'

'Devil the one. I'm a bit black and blue, but sure I'm all in one piece.'

'I think I'd rather put someone else up, even so. Just in case.'

'Tell you what, boss,' Blaze said, following him across the yard. 'See how I do riding work this morning. Put me up on old Jack since he's not running over the holiday, and I'll give him a blast. The both of us will know after that, particularly if you put Kathleen up beside me. She'll tell you right enough.'

'Isn't she a little biased?' Rory said sarcastically, then immediately kicked himself.

'In favour of the horse, Mr Rawlins,' Blaze said with the best smile he could manage through his swollen lips. 'She won't let me near him if she thinks I'm not up to him.'

So to the gallops they all went and Blaze passed the test with flying colours, giving Jack such a good ride he won the gallop. Afterwards Rory insisted on Blaze's schooling one of the younger horses over the practice fences to make sure he was as confident jumping at racing pace as he was just galloping, and again there seemed to be no visible chink in his physical armour. Finally, since by chance Dan had dropped in to have a Christmas Day drink with Anthony and to check up on his well-being, Rory got their doctor friend to give Blaze a quick physical to make sure he really was fit enough mentally as well as physically to ride.

'He might not be a very pretty sight at the moment, Rory,' Dan told him when he had finished his examination. 'But there's absolutely nothing to make you think he can't ride the horse. He's a very strong and very fit young man, which is probably how he walked away relatively unscathed.'

'OK, buster,' Rory told Blaze in the yard. 'You're on. Now go away and have a quiet – and I mean quiet – Christmas Day. And a happy one.'

'Happy Christmas to you as well, boss,' a delighted Blaze returned. 'And God bless you.'

Rory watched as Blaze hurried off to find Kathleen to tell her the news. She was just finishing grooming Boyo, and after she had put her box of brushes and combs away in the tack room Rory saw her making for Blaze's car. He'd thought of asking her to have Christmas lunch with himself and Anthony, but had not, because Kathleen had volunteered the information that Blaze and she had been invited to spend Christmas Day with Teddy and Julie at Teddy's parents', so once he was sure all the horses were fed and watered he took himself back into the house to have his Christmas lunch with his father.

In the end, Alice had gone up to London to spend Christmas Eve and Christmas Day with Georgina, Joe, Christian and the new girlfriend, Sofia, at Georgina and Joe's house in Richmond. Her daughter and she cooked lunch on Christmas Day and the whole event passed off happily and peacefully, with no anxieties being aired, and no quarrels being picked between brother and sister as they usually were when all the family were gathered. The only bone of contention arose when Alice was helping Georgina clear up the debris of lunch and tea, while the men were doing their best to dispose of the endless amount of decorative wrapping paper and cardboard boxes that now littered the sitting room.

Somehow, right out of the blue and without prompting, Georgina had managed to turn the conversation to her greatest ongoing preoccupation, the matter of her children's school fees. There was no direct request for help, just a long conversation full of hints and bewilderment.

'I just don't know what we're going to do, Mum,' she kept saying. 'Joe ran up the latest projections on the cost of privately educating two children the other day and *it was horrific*. I just don't know what we're going to do.'

'You could send them to state schools, Georgie,' Alice said, carefully drying the set of cut-glass Waterford wine glasses she and Alex had given their daughter as one of her wedding presents. 'You were saying the other day that there are some good state schools in this area.'

'There were, Mum,' Georgina sighed. 'You should see them now. They are *huge*, and it's pretty obvious children like ours are not particularly welcome. Anyway, the feeling's quite mutual really, after what I've been hearing about what goes on in these places. Last week one of the teachers was so terrified by her class that she barricaded herself in her office and wouldn't come out.'

'Then in that case you're going to have to find schools you can afford,' Alice said, with perfectly good common sense. 'Other people manage, so I suppose you and Joe are going to have to do the same.'

'Great,' Georgina replied. 'While you go and blow all the money Dad earned doing a job that finally killed him on some stupid racehorse.'

'That's enough, Georgina dear,' Alice said, folding up her tea towel now she had finished drying up. 'I don't think this is the sort of conversation we should be having, particularly today of all days.'

'When else are we going to have it?' Georgina demanded. 'We don't see anything of you nowadays.'

'Georgina.'

'Do stop calling me Georgina.'

'I don't see why. It's the name we christened you.'

'You only call me that when you're cross.'

'So you're forever telling me,' Alice replied. 'But let's just get one thing straight, shall we? I have only just moved to the country. I'm hardly even settled in. When I am, then from the spring onwards we can see as much – or as little – as we like of each other. And as for blowing all the money you say your father earned, for your information your father and I always saw the money he earned as being our money – not his, ours. That was your father's idea. As it was that when . . . when he was gone, any money he left me should be mine to do with as I pleased. We used to joke about it. He was always telling me to shock everyone by going on a round-the-world cruise, or buying a fast car, or a wardrobe of brand-new clothes – *Anything you like, Alice*, he used to say. *But for God's sake, Alice, make sure you enjoy the rest of your life, because you've earned it. All you've done all your life, he'd say, is work, work, work – for me, and for the kids, so you just promise me you'll do what you like, and have a good time.*'

'Yes,' Georgina said, her mouth tightening. 'But that – that was just Dad. The last thing Dad would really have wanted was to see you squandering all his hard-earned on a racehorse.'

'You know that for a fact, do you?' Alice queried. 'I see. Then all I can say is that obviously you knew your father a lot better than I did.'

She went to her room and quietly packed her things. She had intended to stay over until the morning, leave early to avoid the traffic and drive straight to the races. But all of a sudden she was filled with an enormous longing to return to her cosy little home in the west, to light a fire, open a good bottle of wine, and dream of what might or might not happen on Boxing Day. She waited till all was quiet downstairs, with the adults sleeping off the effects of their lunch and tea, and her grandchildren sitting mesmerised by some traditional Christmas Day movie, before stealing outside to put Sammy and her belongings in the car. Then she wished everyone a fond but quick goodbye, resisted all protests against her leaving already, and drove off into the peaceful Christmas night.

Grenville took Lynne home for Christmas to meet his mother. This was something on which he had not been overly keen, but owing to his feelings for Lynne and the feelings she had for him it was something that he knew he would have to do sooner rather than later. He warned Lynne what his mother was like, and although Lynne said little in return it worried her and Grenville saw that it did so.

'It doesn't matter, Linnet.' Grenville smiled, feeling strangely proud of the pet name he had given his beautiful girlfriend. 'It really does not matter one jot, tittle, whit or scrap. It's simply a formality.'

'I know, Grenville, you're sweet and I'm sure it's all fine,' Lynne replied. 'It's just I'd much rather have Christmas with just you. *Chez* me.'

'Me too, dearest girl. But one has always felt one should have Christmas at home, especially since the old man went AWOL.'

So he drove them to Esher, to his mother's house, which was situated at the end of a lane well away from the town and the main road, a small but very pretty redbrick Queen Anne house Grenville's grandfather had lived in before bequeathing it to his only child, Grenville's father. Since Grenville's father's disgrace, as it was known in the family, his mother had been granted custody of the house in which she resided and over which she presided like a Victorian matriarch. As small as her son was tall, Catherine Fielding was famous for the sharpness

of her tongue as well as her arrant snobbery, and as a conse-
quence had an exceedingly select circle of friends, a company
of like-minded people who saw modern life as a shocking
disgrace, particularly the change in social and moral values,
which they all considered – and not particularly privately – to
be the beginning of the end of civilisation as they had known
it, and a terrible waste of all the lives that had been sacrificed
trying to preserve it.

Her only weakness was her son, Grenville, whom she had
always considered to be something extraordinary, in spite of
an extremely average career at school and the attaining of a
less than distinguished university degree. To her Grenville was
simply a late developer, like so many brilliant people in life,
and once he achieved a certain seniority he would come into
his own. For the early part of Grenville's life such an indulgent
maternal attitude was nothing but harmful, spoiling the child
by giving him an inflated sense of his own ability and worth.

Fortunately his father was an altogether stronger character,
and besides taking the wise decision not to send Grenville to
Eton, which he himself had hated, while he remained married
to Grenville's mother he did at least manage to teach his son
some of what he considered the more masculine virtues and
interest him in some manly pursuits. Terrified that his son
might turn into a mother's boy, he made sure Grenville went
to boarding school from the age of seven, and when he was
a teenager encouraged him to take a healthy interest in the
opposite sex, something of which Catherine Fielding most
certainly did not approve.

'So why exactly are you taking me to meet her, Grenville?'
Lynne asked him on their way there. 'If what she thinks
doesn't matter a dot, whittle, scrip or scrap, then why are we
doing it instead of getting legless at home and watching *The
Wizard of Oz*?'

'It's just a formality really, Linnet,' Grenville assured her. 'Don't worry your pretty head. We'll just put in an appearance, have lunch and then take off back to yours.'

The one thing of which Grenville was sure was how pretty Lynne looked that Christmas Day, dressed in a black and white silk and wool dress worn under a beautifully cut crimson velvet jacket, her hair piled expertly on top of her head, and her long elegant legs clad in a pair of black silk stockings, one of the gifts he had bestowed on her. He was happy to see her looking so elegant, because he knew that yet another thing his mother was picky about nowadays was appearance, taking every chance she could to pronounce that people simply did not know how to dress any more.

'Ah, Mummy,' Grenville said on finding his mother sitting waiting for them in the drawing room, ostensibly working on a sampler on her knee.

'Grenville, dearest boy,' Mrs Fielding replied, remaining seated while Grenville came over and kissed her on the cheek. 'I was beginning to worry.'

'Quarter to one, you said, Mummy,' Grenville said, tapping his watch. 'Quarter to one on the dot.' He hated still calling her Mummy but knew that if he tried anything else all he would get in return was a severe dressing-down.

'I am sure I said quarter past twelve, dear,' Mrs Fielding replied with a small shake of her head, before turning to regard Lynne with a pale smile. 'Good. And you must be Anne,' she said, offering a hand vaguely.

'Lynne, Mummy. This is Lynne.'

'It's my great age, Grenville, darling boy.' Mrs Fielding sighed. 'Things just go. Names particularly. I lie awake at night going through my address book in my head. I'm on the Gs at the moment, and not, I have to say, doing all that brilliantly. Do forgive me, *Lynne*.'

'It's fine, really, Mrs Fielding,' Lynne replied with a quick reassuring look to Grenville. 'You can call me whatever you like.'

'I do so like your jacket, *Lynne*, and such a – such a nice *bright* colour,' Mrs Fielding continued smoothly. 'Have you been to cocktails somewhere on the way?'

'No, no.' This time it was Grenville who gave Lynne a reassuring look. 'No, of course not, Mummy. No, we came *straight* here.'

'I find everything so confusing nowadays, don't you, *Lynne*? People do such different things. In such different ways. Shall we have some sherry, Grenville? Traditional, isn't it, sherry at Christmas? Ever since you were a boy. The first time you drank it you must have been . . . eight, yes?'

'Eleven actually.'

'And you got terribly squiffy. Then you were sick after lunch. There's only the three of us, I'm afraid, Lindy.'

'Lynne,' Grenville corrected her.

Lynne smiled. 'I don't mind Lindy. Lindy's fine.'

'Most of one's friends are dead. Or losing their minds. Alas. The perils of great age. It will come to you, my dear, just as it will surely come to me.'

'Let's talk of something more cheerful – Christmas and all that,' Grenville said, pulling a small face.

'What was that you said, Grenville? I missed it.'

'Nothing, Mummy – nothing at all,' Grenville said hastily. 'Do you need any help in the kitchen? Sprouts need doing or something? Can we do anything?'

'Mabel is here.' Mrs Fielding gave a little laugh then rose from her chair to accept the sherry Grenville had poured for her. 'Mabel is here and everything is in hand.'

'Mabel?' Grenville frowned. 'I thought you'd – I thought you'd dispatched Mabel.'

'Did you?' His mother stared and then smiled slightly at him. 'Mabel is undispatchable, Grenville dear. You know that as well as I.'

Grenville tried to put on a brave face, and failed. The thought of Mabel's dreadful cooking filled him with gloom. She had been his mother's housekeeper since time immemorial. Food inedible, Mabel unsackable, it all contributed to the general atmosphere of immutability in this house where nothing that needed changing was ever changed, and no discussion wanted or allowed either.

'Perhaps Lynne and I could go and give Mabel a hand?' he suggested, hoping it might still not be too late to salvage something of the lunch that was being prepared.

'Oh, no, really, Grenville, darling. I hardly think that's necessary. Of course if Lynne here would like to go and help . . . ?'

'No, I think we should both go,' Grenville suggested, finding himself defying his mother for the first time in as long as he could remember. 'Take Mabel a glass of sherry and wish her the compliments of the season, yes? And since it's Christmas, in the spirit of Christmas we could also see if she needs a hand.'

'I see.' His mother regarded him without even the semblance of a smile. 'Very well. But please do not be long. I shall stay here by the fire. By myself.'

Grenville rolled his eyes privately to Lynne as they left the room, and Lynne grabbed his hand as soon as the door was closed behind them, kissing him quickly.

'Stop looking so tragic,' she whispered. 'You said yourself it didn't matter and it doesn't. So come on, let's go and get old Mabel tiddly.'

*   *   *

353

Mabel needed no help. Grenville and Lynne found her in the kitchen singing an incomprehensible carol with a nearly empty bottle of Fine Old Tawny open on the table. Happily they were just in time to do a rescue operation on lunch, Grenville pouncing on the sprouts before they turned to water, taking out the potatoes and sausages before they went quite black, and managing also to salvage the turkey before it was reduced to the size of a quail, removing it from the oven and wrapping it in tinfoil while Lynne concocted what smelt as if it was going to be a most delicious rich gravy. Leaving the Christmas pudding to steam gently and Mabel likewise, they repaired to the dining room where Grenville carved and Lynne served what was, while not the best Christmas lunch they had ever eaten, most certainly a more than serviceable one.

'Do you see now, Grenville?' Mrs Fielding asked her son after sampling her food. 'You do see what I mean about Mabel?'

'We saw exactly,' Grenville replied urbanely. 'All to the good that you dispatched us to the kitchen.'

'So,' Mrs Fielding continued. 'And what are you young doing for the rest of the holiday, might I ask?'

'We're off racing tomorrow,' Grenville replied. 'Lynne and I have shares in a horse that's running—'

'Perhaps you would like to come with us?' Lynne put in, to Grenville's surprise.

'Not on Boxing Day, I don't think so. The crowds are simply frightful. In more ways than one. They most certainly do not consist of what I would call true racing people.'

'It would still be fun. This horse we have, he's really rather promising.'

'Perhaps some other time, Grenville dear. I was thinking we might go to Royal Ascot this year, for Ladies' Day. Have you ever been to Ascot, Lynne?' Mrs Fielding enquired, slowly turning to gaze at her.

'Not really,' Lynne replied. 'I mean not Royal Ascot. I've been to Ascot, but only to ordinary Ascot. Not Royal Ascot.'

'I think I understand what you mean, thank you.'

'I don't know whether I could now, anyway,' Lynne continued, after taking a sip of her claret. 'Don't they still have some rule or other about divorcees?'

Grenville took a deep breath and stared up at the ceiling.

'And that might concern you perhaps?' Mrs Fielding asked. 'Are you saying that you, personally are divorced?'

'I don't know whether it's actually possible to be divorced *im*personally, Mummy,' Grenville chipped in, hoping to create a diversion.

'I was divorced only a few months ago, actually,' Lynne admitted.

'I see,' Mrs Fielding said. 'I see.'

She took a sip from her wine glass and looked away from Lynne, as if it would be improper to go on addressing her directly.

'A lot of people get divorced nowadays, Mrs Fielding,' Lynne said. 'And a good thing too, if you ask me.'

'Really?' Mrs Fielding sniffed. 'I wonder why you should nurse that particular sentiment? I personally have always believed in the sanctity of marriage and, please God, I always shall.'

'Yes, I'm sure,' Lynne replied. 'But all that left the men free to do just what they wanted, right? Which is not always such a good thing.'

Mrs Fielding tapped the mahogany table in front of her and shook her head. 'People of my generation never believed hurting the children helped anything. And as for airing one's marital difficulties in the divorce court, just try to imagine the effect on one's family.'

'I can understand that,' Lynne agreed. 'Luckily, in my case there are, or rather were, no children.'

Mrs Fielding looked at her. 'And had there been?'

'Maybe it would have all been different, who knows? The last thing I would ever want to do would be to hurt my kids.'

Mrs Fielding dabbed her lips with her linen napkin. 'I see.'

'Lynne was the totally innocent party,' Grenville said carefully, mindful of the dangerous ground they were still on. 'Her husband was flagrantly unfaithful.'

'Grenville,' Mrs Fielding warned him. 'I have just said I do not wish to hear about it. As I have always believed in the sanctity of marriage—'

'Even though Papa was serially unfaithful and left you to run off with another woman?'

'Grenville?' Lynne pleaded quietly.

'Whatever your father might or might not have done, Grenville—'

'There's no might or might not about it, Mother,' Grenville insisted, brave enough now to dare a change of address.

'Grenville? I can look after myself, sweetheart,' Lynne said to him. 'It's OK.'

'Whatever your father *might* have done, Grenville,' Mrs Fielding persisted, 'it remains something between your father and me. It was certainly something he and I would never have wished to have resolved in the divorce court.'

'Mother—' Grenville started, now determined to see his mother off for the first time. But seeing the look in his eyes Lynne hastily put a hand over one of his and came in quickly.

'Your mother is absolutely right, Grenville,' she said. 'Marital difficulties should if possible be sorted out between the partners, not by a lot of greedy lawyers – particularly when there are children involved.'

Grenville was about to disagree but, seeing the look of kindness in Lynne's eyes as well as the small warning frown on her forehead, he pulled back from the brink.

'Of course, Lynne,' he said quietly. 'Sorry, Mother – that really was uncalled for.'

'That's perfectly all right, Grenville dear,' Mrs Fielding replied, now sensing the understanding as well as the love that Grenville and Lynne shared. 'I was probably speaking somewhat out of turn myself.'

'So now it's my turn,' Lynne said, taking a deep breath. 'To speak out of turn, as it were. The point is, Mrs Fielding, although I'd far rather you and I got on, Grenville is my real concern, and I don't want anything to spoil what we feel for each other. You see I love your son, Mrs Fielding. He's just about the kindest, sweetest and gentlest man I have ever met and I really do love him very much, OK? Just in case you've got it wrong – which I'm sure you haven't, but just in case. And you see, I don't care what anyone is or was or whatever because what matters now is what's in the future because that's the only thing we can really affect. We can't change the past but we can care for the future. OK? That's all.' She smiled. 'Sermon over.'

'Thank you.' Grenville took her hand. 'I feel the same – exactly the same – about you and about everything, now that you have put it so well, which I most certainly could not have done.'

'It's all that matters,' Lynne said quietly. 'You said so yourself on the way here – you said it didn't matter what anyone might think and all that, and I really go along with that. We just have to follow our star and feel what we really feel. Life's too blooming short.'

During the silence that ensued Grenville looked first at Lynne, then at his mother, then back to the woman he loved.

'Happy Christmas,' he said, raising his glass. 'Happy Christmas to us all. I have a feeling this is going to be one of the best Christmases ever. If not the very best.'

'Good,' Mrs Fielding said after a moment spent carefully wiping her mouth on her napkin. 'Now I do hope you two are not dashing off somewhere – at least not until after the Queen's speech. Then of course there's the Tree. Mabel and I went to a lot of trouble decorating the Tree, or rather, truth to tell, I spent a great deal of time redecorating the Tree after Mabel had finished ruining it.'

Grenville and Lynne laughed quite genuinely at her observation, a reaction that pleased Mrs Fielding no end.

'And then,' she continued, 'after that, perhaps we might play a game. Monopoly – or Cluedo, maybe. We always so used to enjoy playing Cluedo.'

'Me too,' Lynne agreed. 'Colonel Mustard in the conservatory with the candlestick. I think it's my all-time favourite board game.'

'I rather agree,' Mrs Fielding said. 'I never really tire of it.'

'Whereas with Monopoly,' Lynne observed, 'someone's always got a hand in the bank.'

'Then Cluedo it shall be, Lynne,' Mrs Fielding decided. 'And now if you'd like to pour us all some more of this excellent claret you brought, Grenville, I'd quite like to finish my equally excellent lunch.'

Chapter Twenty-two

Lost in the Furze

Rather than reveal that their pilot had been the victim of an unprovoked physical assault, Rory had already excused his appearance before Blaze came into the racecourse paddock. The jockey, he explained, had suffered a riding accident.

'Taken a bit of a bashing off someone else's horse, but he's all right now, passed fit to ride.'

And in fact, thanks in part to Kathleen's powdering down the black and blue bits, other than the thin strip of plaster across his nose, as he stood taking instructions from Rory, Blaze did indeed look nearly, if not quite, himself.

'It's a good field, but not the strongest,' Rory told the owners and their connections, as they gathered together just before the race. 'That's what my father says is the good thing about racing on Boxing Day. Too many meetings and not enough horses to go round.' He stopped before going on. 'Where's Connie?'

'She couldn't come,' Lynne said quickly. 'We'll explain afterwards.'

'Rory?' Grenville said, bringing a well-dressed woman to the fore. 'I don't think you've met my mother.'

'Mrs Fielding,' Rory said, taking off his hat and shaking her hand. 'How do you do?'

'How do you do, and good luck with your horse, Mr Rawlins. I have heard great things of him.'

'Fingers crossed.' Rory smiled before turning to Lynne. 'Is Connie all right, Lynne?'

'Not really,' Lynne told him. 'I mean – sorry – she's not ill or anything. At least she's not sick. She's just not quite herself. We'll tell you later.'

Once an oddly quiet Blaze had been legged up by Rory they took their places in the stands to watch the race.

'They're difficult fences in the home straight, so be warned, everyone,' Rory said, taking his race glasses out of their leather holster. 'You come uphill off the bend and the camber's tricky. Tips towards the rails. The fences are pretty stiff, too, and claim quite a few fallers, particularly when the horses are tiring.'

'Thanks for that, Rory,' Alice said. 'I wish I'd stayed in bed now.'

'They're off and running,' Rory muttered. 'Good luck, everyone.'

Blaze had intended to try to make it all as instructed, but two of the fancied runners, the favourite and joint second favourite, stole a march on him, their jockeys forcing him off his preferred berth on the rails as they waited for the starter to set them off. Blaze had barely finished the turn he had been instructed to take on his horse when they were off. In no time, The Enchanted was a good ten lengths down on the leaders, but seeing the scorching pace they were setting, and remembering what Rory had told him about the two hills he would face on the course and the fact that the going had been declared as good to soft, he decided not to waste any petrol by taking off in pursuit. There was plenty of time. The important thing was to get his horse jumping in a good rhythm, which he had done by the time they had jumped the third fence.

The two leaders were still ten lengths or so in front, but the rest of the field were well bunched, and judging from the conversation between the jockeys round him no one was particularly worried about the situation, confident that as the race developed they would be able to close the gap at will. Blaze felt the same, remembering that when he had walked the course that morning he had been surprised at how long the run without fences was when the field left the back straight to descend downhill towards the home stretch and the final four jumps. It seemed there was plenty of time to make up ground, and since it was all downhill he kept The Enchanted cantering along with the rest of the field, heading them by about a length, perfectly happy at the way his horse was going and jumping.

It was only when they reached the top of the hill to turn into the back straight that Blaze's best-laid plans began to go astray. Coming to the last fence along the back, an island fence with a drop on landing, and with the leaders now only half a dozen lengths at most in front, in an effort to pass him in the air the horse alongside The Enchanted suddenly jumped sharply to the left, going through the top of the birch and cannoning into his horse.

For a moment it seemed they would be knocked out of the race as his horse lost all momentum, knocked sideways by the impact of his rival, but somehow – and Blaze would never know how – The Enchanted managed to get his front legs un-tangled although he landed almost on his nose. Instinctively Blaze slackened his reins and sat back, giving the horse every chance of recovery, but as the horse pitched on landing his head came up and back, and hit the jockey in the face.

Blaze could see nothing except a wall of red. His head felt

as if it had been chopped in half by a meat cleaver and his mouth filled with blood. At that moment he wanted nothing more than to fall off the horse and roll to the ground, but that option was out of the question. Not only had he a race still to ride, he had a race to win. So he shortened his reins, took a lot of deep gasping breaths, closed and reopened his eyes several times in an effort to clear the fog and got himself balanced again in the plate, aware only of what was now the distant noise of the race and the vague shouting of the jockeys round about him.

It all seemed a hundred miles away from where he was, but then as the intensity of the pain faded a terrible giddiness set in. He could see now all right, but what he saw was blurred and very far away. What he could see was a field of small blurred horses galloping in the distance while the ground seemed to be falling fast away in front of him. He was running downhill.

I'm going down the hill and there's something I have to remember, he told himself, shaking his head and taking one hand off the reins to wipe the blood from his nose. *But I have plenty of time to get Boyo back in the race because we have to go round again. And if we have to go all the way round again, then we have the time, Boyo. I have time to get my head back, I have time to settle my horse, and I have time to make up the ground – next time round. Good. Good. I make up the ground next time round.*

He settled his horse back at the head of the chasing group as they turned into the home straight. Still thinking he had all the time in the world, he didn't ask his horse, instead letting him bowl along in the same rhythm and at the same pace, as they approached the first fence in the home straight.

'What the hell does he think he's doing?' Rory suddenly asked himself and his group as they stood up in the stands watching. 'They're going for home now and Blaze is just sitting there.'

But even in what he realised afterwards must have been a semi-conscious state Blaze could not help being aware of the activity around him as they ran uphill to the first fence in the straight.

'Where's the fire?' he shouted to a jockey busy beginning to go to work on his horse. 'Haven't we to go round again?'

'Do as you please, Paddy!' the jockey shouted back. 'But this is where we get off!'

It was then that he finally got the picture. Now he understood what all the shouting and the beating and the kicking was about – this was it. This was the finish. No going round again, not for him, not for anybody. He had the last line of fences to ride and after that was the lollipop. Way ahead of him they were already gone for home. As he landed over the fourth from home he could see vaguely the leaders heading for the next fence, half a dozen or more lengths clear of him, and racing hard. But The Enchanted had landed perfectly yet again, passing two of those racing alongside, horses who were visibly tiring, so he knew he had them beat, but not the ones in front, not yet. He let out more rein than he had ever let out before and sat and pushed – and pushed, shaking the reins at his horse's head but never touching him with the whip. All he did was shake the reins, call to the horse and sit. He'd change his hands if he must, but he'd not hit him – don't hit him – he remembered that – don't hit, just sit, and ride him, ride him, ride him! Before he even had to change his leading hand he felt the horse responding to his urgings. He felt the horse coming alight. He felt him flying.

He could also hear a sudden and almost overwhelming wall of sound, a roar from the grandstands as the racegoers saw what was happening.

'He's left it too late!' Rory shouted, watching as the horse flew the second last fence, passing the horse lying in third who was still a good eight lengths behind the two leaders, who were locked in battle on the run to the last fence, both of them still racing although both of their jockeys were hard at work. 'He's left it far too late, for crying out loud!'

'Please tell me he hasn't!' Alice yelled from her hiding place behind his back. 'Please tell me, please!'

'He hasn't!' Lynne shouted back over the cheering, watching transfixed as their horse continued inexorably to close the gap, coming to the last fence with Blaze still just pushing at him with his hands and his heels. 'He's catching them hand over whatsit! Look, Alice! You've got to look!'

'I can't!' Alice cried. 'I'd have a heart attack!'

'Come on, Enchanted!' an astounded Grenville heard his mother shouting, and turned to see her waving her rolled-up racecard in the air. 'Come on Grenville's horse!'

Out on the track Blaze thought he saw a stride before the last fence and was just about to ask the horse to put in a big one when the horse beat him to it, jumping once again, just as he had done in his last race, from practically outside the wings as he soared into the air and over the top of the black birch without disturbing a twig. There was a huge gasp from the stands, followed by a roar as the racegoers realised that what they were witnessing was a singular performance by what was definitely a singular horse.

After landing over the last The Enchanted ate up the ground and the six lengths' difference between himself and the two leading horses. All at once they were no longer alone, but being passed.

'He's done it!' Lynne yelled, jumping up and down in her excitement before throwing her arms round Grenville and knocking his hat to the ground. 'He's done it, everyone! He's only done it!'

It was an unforgettable sight.

And that would have been exactly how it finished had not something else happened, something that would stamp this race even more indelibly on its witnesses' memories. No more than fifty yards from the post and now easily five lengths clear of the beaten horses, Blaze eased both himself and his horse back and in that moment his heroic effort abruptly ended as suddenly a wall of darkness fell about him and he passed cleanly and entirely out.

Everyone watched aghast from the stands as just yards from the post the winning horse lost his pilot, the comatose Blaze falling sideways from the saddle to the ground, his feet mercifully coming free from the irons, leaving his triumphant horse to gallop joyfully past the winning post with an empty saddle.

They carried the bloodstained jockey on a stretcher to an ambulance that had been rushed up to the winning line. 'His poor old face was just covered in blood,' Kathleen told Teddy as he held the horse's head while Kathleen washed him down. 'It was awash with it. He must have taken some sort of bang out there in the country somewhere.'

'If only he could have hung on till he'd passed the damned post,' Teddy growled. 'If only he'd just hung on somehow.'

'If he got a crack in the face out in the country, Teddy,' Rory pointed out, having joined them for a few seconds to see the little horse, 'Blaze did wonders to stay up that long, let alone ride the race he did. Now I have to go and explain to our loyal owners what happened – then I'm off to see our pilot.'

A few minutes later, looking at the concerned faces surrounding him, Rory realised he was one very spoilt trainer. These owners, this bunch of anxious people, only wanted to hear about Blaze and the little horse; there wasn't a mention of their disappointment.

'Our little chap won it anyway,' Alice said, after a small pause, because she knew from everyone's faces that she was speaking for them all. 'I think that's pretty obvious. So it really doesn't make any difference.'

'Other than the fact that we're out of the money. Come on, I'll buy you all a nice strong consoling drink before I chase after the ambulance.'

'What do you think actually happened, Rory?' Alice asked when they had all repaired to the owners' bar.

Rory shrugged his shoulders, handing round the drinks.

'Bad luck, that's what happened – jockey injured, stayed on brilliantly, lost consciousness as he came up to the post. Fell off. Bad luck. That's racing.'

'Which is something I must speak to you about, if I may,' Grenville murmured.

'Can it wait till I've got back from the hospital?' Rory asked, already making for the door.

'Of course, yes. I mean no – if you could wait just a second.' Grenville dropped his voice. 'It's just that I got an unofficial timing from a chum of mine who's one of the stewards here, and it appears they're all talking about it. It seems that was the second fastest time ever posted here.'

'I know what you're thinking, Grenville: the same as you were thinking the other day when you phoned me. So you know what I'm thinking too. Same as I told you the other day. Big dreams and small horses don't mix.'

'I know, I know, Rory. But this hadn't happened then. I mean, by any standards that was a remarkable performance, regardless of the fact that the jockey finally fell off.'

'The horse is only a novice, Grenville,' Rory replied, putting his race glasses back in their holster. 'He was also only carrying around eleven stone today, with Blaze's allowance taking another seven pounds off his back—'

'I know, Rory, I know.'

'In the race you have in mind he'd be carrying twelve stone with no allowances. If Blaze rides him in a Grade One the horse carries the same weight as the others. But the real point is, they're both still novices, Grenville, The Enchanted and the boy. Speaking of which, I have to dash off to the hospital – so if you'll all excuse me?'

With a doff of his cap, Rory was gone.

'He's not going to, is he?' Lynne asked, joining Grenville after Rory had left. 'He won't, will he?'

'All it is is an entry, that's all.' Grenville sighed as they headed back out on to the course. 'Just an entry, Linnet. We don't have to do more than just enter the little horse.'

'Yes, but you could tell by the look on Rory's face that he doesn't think it's a good idea, honey.' Lynne slipped her arm through Grenville's and smiled up at him.

'We're the owners. We pay the bills.'

'Rory and his dad – they know all about these things.'

'And we're learning.'

'You more than anyone, Grenville. You're becoming a little bit of a turf expert,' Lynne teased him affectionately. 'My own little walking, talking *Sporting Life*.'

Grenville shrugged. 'It's only an entry. At this stage of the proceedings there are going to be all sorts, shapes and sizes entered. So what does it matter? There's no risk to putting a horse in for a race, is there?'

'Yes, but be honest, Grenville. You don't think he should be just an entry, do you? You think he should run.'

Grenville looked down at Lynne, and smiled.

'Chances like this do not come round twice, Lynne,' he said. 'Believe me, they don't.'

* * *

As he headed for the car park, Rory reconsidered the conversation he'd just had and shook his head. He knew perfectly well what Grenville was thinking, but it made no difference. He had no intention of going down that path.

'Mr Rawlins?' he heard a familiar voice call from behind him. 'Would it be all right if I came to the hospital with you? I've done Boyo and Teddy's going to box him up. So would it be all right if I came along with you?'

Looking at Kathleen it was perfectly clear to Rory that he could think of nothing he would like more.

'You're not suggesting Teddy drives the box back alone, Kathleen, surely?'

'He's got Julie with him,' Kathleen replied. 'They'll be perfectly all right, because if anything happened Julie knows the ropes. She drives George Clement's horsebox, after all.'

'In that case, hop in. I'll be glad of the company.'

'As long as you don't mind,' Kathleen said, suddenly sounding a little shy and looking up at Rory from underneath her fringe. 'I won't jaw on, or anything. Leave you to your thoughts, and all that kind of thing.'

'You can jaw on as much as you please, Kathleen,' Rory replied, unlocking the car. 'As I said, I'd be delighted.'

He opened the passenger door. Kathleen was about to step in when she saw the inside spilling out towards her, a forest of old racing papers and racecards, sweet and chocolate bar wrappers and empty plastic water bottles.

'Right,' she said as Rory got in beside her. 'Since I forgot to give you a Christmas present, to make up I shall spring-clean your car for you.'

'It really isn't necessary—'

'It really is, Mr Rawlins,' Kathleen assured him. 'This is not a car anyone civilised would drive. It must be a health hazard, and we're not even at the hospital yet.'

When they arrived they learned that although Blaze had regained consciousness he was still not making much sense. The doctor in charge told them there should be nothing to worry about, since this was a fairly common symptom of concussion, but even though there appeared to be no fractures they were keeping him in for observation.

'Can we see him?' Rory enquired. 'Just to say hello?'

'Of course – but no excitement, please,' the doctor added after glancing appreciatively at Kathleen.

When they approached the bed the figure in it looked pathetically small, as if Blaze had been shrunk by the ambulance service.

'Blaze,' Rory said, raising his voice, as the eyes barely opened. 'We just thought we'd look in and see how you were.'

'Hi there, Blaze,' Kathleen said, bending over the figure in the bed and kissing him gently on the forehead, which apart from his eyes was about the only non-bandaged part of Blaze's handsome face. 'Haven't I told you before, this sort of thing just isn't funny?'

Blaze stared at them, trying to focus his eyes.

'How's my horse of Mananan come through the race?' he enquired. 'And didn't I tell you he could fly?'

'He's come through the race just fine,' Kathleen said, with a quick glance up at Rory, who was standing on the other side of the bed. She took one of the jockey's bruised hands in hers. 'They said no excitement now.'

'The horses of Mananan . . .' Blaze murmured.

'You certainly took a terrible smack in the face, you poor lad, did you not?' Kathleen said quickly. 'They're keeping you in until you're fit for a pretty girl to look at without screaming.'

'He doesn't know about the horses, though,' Blaze said, looking at Rory with eyes that Rory could swear had changed colour from the last time he saw them, although being a man he was never too certain of the colour of people's eyes. 'You don't, do you, Stranger?'

'This isn't a stranger, Blaze,' Kathleen said. 'This is Mr Rawlins now. Mr Rawlins trains the horse you were riding, doesn't he?'

'There was a kingdom below the sea, once,' Blaze muttered. 'A long time ago there was a kingdom . . .'

Kathleen nodded down at the bed, worried. 'He really shouldn't be talking, Mr Rawlins,' she murmured. 'So tiring for him. I think we should leave him, so.'

'Of course we must, Kathleen,' Rory agreed. 'And just as I was enjoying the story too.'

'The horses belonged to Cuchulain, the god of the sea,' the voice from the bed continued. 'It was said they were once the waves on the sea which was why they could go over anything . . .'

'We'll come in and see you tomorrow, Blaze.' Kathleen nodded briefly at Rory, indicating that she thought they should be heading for the door.

'The horses had endless power and they would weep tears of blood if one of the warriors was killed. Cuchulain's horses were immortal and possessed a divine knowledge of Fate,' the voice from beneath the bandages continued.

'As Kathleen just said,' Rory told Blaze, following her to the door, 'one of us will look in tomorrow. You just get better quickly. And completely.'

'Some of them – some of them were sent from the kingdom,' Blaze went on, speaking in snatches. 'Some of them – some of them left Mananan to be sent out from the sea, and when they reached the shore . . .'

"Bye, Blaze,' Kate said, easing Rory out of the door before her.

'Once they were ashore they took the earthly form and went into the world to perform all manner of wonders.'

'See you tomorrow.' Kathleen shut the door on Blaze and his ramblings.

'They went forth into the world,' Blaze went on, now quite alone, 'to do wondrous things, to do the magic that would make the people understand, love and worship horses. Those were the wondrous horses that were from Mananan, the horses that have come down to us to this very day.'

'What was all that stuff about horses of Manahan or wherever?' Rory wondered as the two of them walked out of the hospital.

'Mananan,' Kathleen corrected him, looking away across the car park. 'He's obviously still concussed.'

'Horses that could weep tears of blood and had – what was it? Had a divine knowledge of Fate,' Rory mused. 'I just loved that. A divine knowledge of Fate.'

'I hope he's going to be all right, Mr Rawlins,' Kathleen said, changing the subject, zipping up the front of her anorak and tossing back her head of long black hair. 'I really do hope with all my heart he's going to be OK. He took a right old knock, so he did. I don't know how he stayed on as long as he did. Yes, well, I do actually. He stayed on because Blaze Molloy is something special. Something very special. At least I think he is.'

'You do? You think so?' Rory said, with a quick glance at her across the roof of his car as he unlocked the door.

'Of course,' Kathleen replied. 'Don't you?'

'Yes, but it's different for me. By that I mean, yes, I think he's . . . he's special, but perhaps in a d-different way.'

'You're a man,' Kathleen said, waiting to be let into the car. 'You're bound to see it differently.'

Rory frowned, got into the car and opened the passenger door.

'What I meant was I think he well might be an exceptionally talented young jockey,' he continued, settling into his seat. 'While what you th-think of him—'

'What I think of Blaze was firmed up the moment I saw him, Mr Rawlins.'

'Really?'

'I think he's already very special. Yes.'

'Yes, I see. As far as riding g-goes? Or – or . . .'

'Or what, Mr Rawlins?' Kathleen asked, looking round at him with what seemed like genuine bewilderment on her beautiful young face.

'Well,' Rory muttered, firing the ignition. 'You and Blaze – n-n-not that it's any of my business—'

'If you say so, so then it isn't.'

'I don't understand what you mean by that. I was being p-p-polite.'

'Of course you were,' Kathleen agreed. 'And I was being polite as well.'

'L-look,' Rory grunted as he drove out of the hospital car park. 'How this all started – I was simply wondering—'

'Then don't, if you'll excuse me. Wondering usually leads to the wrong conclusions.'

Rory took a deep breath. 'You like Blaze.'

'Of course I like Blaze. Don't you?'

'Of course I like B-B-B-Blaze!' Rory returned, banging two clenched fists on the steering wheel.

'Be careful now,' Kathleen warned him. 'I don't think you saw that bus.'

'I saw the b-b-b-bus. *I saw the bus*, thank you.'

'Not that it's easy driving in this rain – and in this light.'

'I was simply trying to establish . . .' Rory tried yet again. 'All I was wondering was in what *way* you – you know . . .'

'Sorry?' Kathleen frowned and looked round at him again. Rory glanced back at her, taking his eyes off the road, and a car hooted angrily at him.

'Careful—'

'It's all right. It's all right, I s-saw him,' Rory replied, eyes back firmly to the front.

'All you were wondering was . . . ?' Kathleen prompted him.

'It doesn't matter,' Rory replied with a shrug, feeling that he had tied himself completely in knots. 'It really d-d-doesn't matter.'

'OK,' Kathleen said brightly. 'Then if it really doesn't matter, we won't bother going on with it, so.'

'Kathleen . . .' Rory groaned.

'It's OK,' Kathleen replied, looking quickly away out of her window. 'No worries.'

'Kathleen.'

'Really, Mr Rawlins. No worries at all.'

'I do wish you wouldn't call me M-Mr Rawlins.'

'I work for you, Mr Rawlins,' Kathleen replied, still looking out of her window. 'I couldn't possibly call you anything other. It wouldn't be fair on everyone else.'

'One day, maybe,' Rory muttered.

'Of course,' Kathleen agreed politely. 'What will be.'

Unable to think either of how to reanimate their conversation or of anything fresh to say, Rory lapsed into silence, as did Kathleen, both of them wondering at their failure to connect, Rory ascribing it to Kathleen's obvious interest in Blaze and Kathleen to Rory's equally obvious lack of interest in her. Finally, unable to contain himself any longer yet still unable to think of quite what to say, Rory shook his head and turned briefly to her, to find her sitting staring down at her hands, which were clasped in her lap.

'OK,' he said. 'So. Penny for them.' Kathleen looked up at him, a worried expression now clouding her beauty. 'Penny for your thoughts.'

'I was just thinking I really shouldn't have done this,' she replied. 'Gone to the hospital. I really should have gone back in the box with Boyo.'

Sensing they were now on ground where the very angels might fear to tread, since once again his companion had turned herself away to look out of her window on the dark landscape flashing by, Rory sighed quietly to himself and put a music cassette in the car radio, drowning himself and his private consternation in the sound of Arthur Rubinstein playing the Chopin ballades. Finally, as they had all but reached Fulford Farm and the tape had finished playing through the first side, Rory ejected the cassette and tried one last and different approach.

'This is really à propos of nothing in particular, Kathleen,' he began. 'J-j-just a completely general enquiry – but when you came here, when you agreed to work in the yard, did you put a t-time limit on it?'

'Why do you ask that?' Kathleen asked quickly, thinking that she must somehow have displeased her employer and he was now wondering whether to ask her to go. 'Have I done something wrong?'

'No.' Rory laughed, although his mood was a far from happy one. 'No, of course not. You do everything right. Just right. No, no – I was just wondering what your plans were.'

'In truth I'd hoped I'd be able to stay as long as I was needed, Mr Rawlins. But if you'd rather I went – that is, if you feel that I'm *not* needed any more—'

'No, I didn't say that, K-K-K-Kathleen—'

'Sure I've done what I came to do, Mr Rawlins, so you'd only be right,' she said as the car turned in at the top of the long drive down to the yard. 'We have the horse fit and well, he's winning his races, you've staff enough now – and anyway, my father's at me to go home all the time so really it would be best all round if I were to go back as soon as is convenient.'

'This is entirely your call, not mine,' Rory replied, now parking the car at the yard gates. 'What do you really want to do?'

'What do you really want to do, Mr Rawlins?' Kathleen asked in return, turning a pair of now dark and troubled eyes on him. '*Really.*'

'That's neither here nor there, K-Kathleen – what I really want to do. We're talking about y-you here.'

'Is this what you want?'

'Is *what* what I want?' Rory shook his head, finding himself unable to cope with the way the conversation was going hither and thither, sensing a subtext but unable to quite make sense of it. 'I really c-c-can't follow this.'

'I don't think this is what you want at all,' Kathleen said quietly. 'Not one bit of it.'

'Are we talking in general terms here? Or are we being specific? What I was asking—'

'And what I was meaning, if you'll forgive the interruption, was that I've always sensed you're only marking time. But then that's me being previous and that I mustn't be, so forgive me.' She smiled at him, almost formally, then opened her car door. 'I'll be gone as soon as is convenient – and thank you, Mr Rawlins. It has been great, but as they say, all good things . . . Thanks, anyhow.'

Then she was gone. He watched her walking into the yard then breaking into a run as soon as she was through the gate, hurrying to Boyo's box to make sure her horse was safe and sound and had travelled home all right. She shut him up for the night and walked quickly off to her quarters, with Rory still sitting in his car watching her. He hoped she might stop and turn round, the way they often did in films, to take a look back, and if she did he would be out of the car, running into the yard and taking her up in his arms – but that was not the way it happened. Life was not like the movies, Rory told himself. Life was far more prosaic, harder, less forgiving. In real life people did what Kathleen was doing now – continued to walk to their destinations without a stop, a pause or a backward glance.

Anyway, as far as Kathleen Flanagan was concerned, Rory decided that he was hopeless – or rather perhaps that *it* was hopeless. Kathleen Flanagan quite obviously loved another, so as far as his own aspirations went he might as well try to catch a moonbeam, or light a penny candle from a star.

'Yes, well!' Anthony Rawlins shook his head and laughed when the two of them had finished watching the video tape Rory had brought back from the course of The Enchanted's race that afternoon. 'Good heavens, it's hard to believe it's the same little horse we bought that day when we were both tight!'

'I was the one who was footless, Dad, not you.'

Anthony smiled. 'Forget about beware the Greeks when they bring you gifts. More to the point would be to beware the Irish measure, my son.'

Rory took the tape out of the video player. 'Well, you've seen the videos of his other two races, so what do you think?'

'I have to say – with a certain amount of caution, naturally – that I can actually see what the excitement is about, Rory.'

'When you think that this is only his first season and that was his third race. His third *proper* race . . .'

'It's a race often won by younger horses, old man, there's that in his favour,' Anthony said, holding up an empty glass to be refilled. 'The point is, you don't want to run him at Cheltenham, but your little quorum do. It's the usual dilemma with trainers and owners. A race like the Gold Cup can ruin a young horse, as we both know.'

'There'll be plenty of other chances, Dad, God willing.'

'I always used to think that, you know,' Anthony replied, sipping his whisky and water. 'Until I was persuaded to run Starlight Fleet in the Schweppes at Newbury. He was ten pounds out of the handicap. Didn't think he had a hope. I told the owner the selfsame thing. The horse was young, he hadn't many miles on the clock, and there'd be plenty of other chances, I said. But the owner stuck to his guns and you know the rest of the story.'

'He sluiced home by a distance.' Rory looked rueful as he remembered.

'Which is exactly why we trainers don't like running our horses out of the handicap. It makes it look as though you haven't been running them on their merit.'

'The Gold Cup isn't a handicap, as you well know, Dad.'

'Same point. For weight, read class.'

'What you're saying is if owners insist on running their horses—'

'Then you must run them,' his father replied. 'Or make it look as though you will. You do at least have to make the entry. What you can do then is try to advise them against it. Talk them down slowly, use reason and gentle persuasion, and ninety-nine per cent of the time the owners will come round to your way of thinking, because at the back of their minds they know or they think you know best.'

'But if they don't come round?'

'Then you have to run. The owners own their horses. The

owners pay the bills. So the owners have the right to say where their horses run. Remember dear old Eileen Nesbitt? When she had her horses here, she insisted they only ran in televised races, when in fact they were barely out of egg and spoon class. But since her health prevented her from racing and she wanted to see them run, the only way to do that was to run them in televised races. It was agony for me, old man – can you imagine? Time after time they'd trail in last, if they finished at all, so that was *very* good for one's reputation, I don't think. For a while I was a complete laughing stock. But there you are. They were her horses, and she paid the bills.'

'Point taken. Now come on, time to eat. We have a mass of turkey to finish up.'

'Rory?' his father said as he followed Rory out. 'I do appreciate what you're doing, you know.'

'Oh, nonsense. I'm not doing anything.'

'Yes, but sooner or later, and preferably sooner,' Anthony insisted, putting a hand on his son's shoulder for support, 'we're going to have to make some other sort of arrangement.'

'Everything in due course,' Rory said, holding the kitchen door open. 'That's what you always say – everything in due course. Now come on – we've got some rather good burgundy to finish off.'

The following morning it began to snow. At first it snowed only in light flurries, but by mid-afternoon when Rory was sitting in the office with Maureen preparing the entries and catching up with his paperwork, the fall had become a blizzard.

'I do hope we're not in for a freeze-up,' he said. 'My father always says this is the curse of racing at this time of year. You get your horses right just at the time winter decides to kick in.'

'Luckily it's a level playing field, Rory,' Maureen reminded him. 'At least it is this time round because apparently, according to the news, the whole country's blanketed.'

'Sure,' Rory sighed. 'But some of the rich boys in Lambourn have got covered canters so they can at least keep their horses moving, keep them in work. You know what our gallops get like here when it snows. Talk about north to Alaska. And who on earth's that?'

Rory rubbed some of the condensation off the window and stared at a small figure battling its way through the blizzard, one arm held up face high in protection against the snow. He got up quickly from his desk and hurried outside.

'Hello?' he called. 'Who is that?'

'No, please!' a small female voice answered him. 'Please don't worry! It's only me!'

As soon as he was outside and got a better look at their unexpected visitor Rory thought he knew who it was, yet he could hardly believe his eyes when finally he helped Constance out of the storm and into the warmth of his office.

'What on earth . . . ?' He came in behind her, closing the door. 'Connie, what are you *doing* here?'

'Don't even ask,' Constance replied. 'This is not a day to remember.'

On her way down to stay with Lynne, Constance had missed her stop. Lynne had invited her because, having read the rehashed stories in the newspapers concerning Red Andrew and his once equally suspect wife, anticipating her friend's imminent distress, she had telephoned Constance at once and offered her refuge, an invitation that Constance had gratefully accepted, only to miss her stop at Andover. It had begun to snow heavily in London long before the weather hit the west, so by the time Constance was able to get off the train at Salisbury, the next stop down the line, the services had been so disrupted by the snowstorms that all trains in and out of the capital had been cancelled.

Unable to get back to Andover by rail, Constance had tried to get a taxi to take her, but to no avail, all drivers flatly refusing to take the risk of driving anywhere other than within the city itself. Panic stricken, and after a moment of not knowing what to do, she remembered that Rory lived close to Salisbury. She decided to try to get herself transported to Fulford Farm, which she imagined to be only a short hop from the city. Again every driver she asked to take her there refused, advising her to book into a hotel until the weather cleared. Constance was about to throw in the towel and find a room when a local lad in a large truck, overhearing her dilemma, offered her a lift since Fulford Farm was on his own way home.

'I couldn't telephone you to warn you, because the queues at the public telephones were right round the block,' Constance explained as Rory took her soaking wet overcoat to hang it over the Aga in the kitchen, and then filled the kettle for tea. 'And the lad who brought me here was quite understandably anxious not to delay any longer than was necessary.'

'He didn't bring you all the way down here, surely?' Rory asked. 'Even with four wheel drive I doubt if he'd have got back up again.'

'I walked from the top of the drive,' Constance said, in a forlorn voice, standing with her back to the Aga. 'I got utterly lost twice.'

'You poor thing,' Rory said, putting a cup of tea in front of her. 'Well, I'm afraid you're not going to get to Lynne's today and I doubt very much if you'll make it tomorrow either. In fact, according to the forecast, we could be snowed up here for a good few days. So I hope you've brought your toothbrush.'

*   *   *

'I've just been reading all about you in the papers,' Anthony told Constance when Rory took her through to the drawing room, once she had defrosted.

'Oh, please, don't,' Constance groaned, putting her hands to her face and sinking into an armchair by the fire. 'The very reason for my flight.'

'Nonsense.' Anthony laughed. 'Water under the bridge. Besides, you don't want to take any notice of these gossip columnists. No way to earn a living, I always say. Not what I'd call a proper job, more an improper job.'

'Can I know what you're both talking about?' Rory asked, throwing some more logs on the fire and earning himself a hard stare from the dormant Dunkum in return. 'What exactly was in the papers?'

'Here,' Anthony said, fishing out from under himself a well-squashed tabloid. 'In the diary.'

'You really don't have to,' Constance muttered. 'I would much rather you didn't.'

'Nice picture of you, though,' Anthony said in admiration. 'You know, I think I probably saw all your films.'

'They were hardly my films, Mr Rawlins,' Constance replied. 'You mean the films I passed through.'

'Far too modest, Lady Frimley.'

'Do call me Constance.'

'You're far too modest. *The Lady Returns*, for instance. You had a very decent part in that and gave a very decent perform-ance, too. Saw it again only the other day.'

'Did I?' Constance frowned. 'I don't remember.'

'I was madly in love with you, I have to tell you.'

'Do you know, I watched some old film or other I was in on the television recently, and do you know, I don't even remember making it. That's how memorable most of my films were.'

'*All At Sea*? I bet you remember making that one. You had a smashing love scene with that rather dishy dark-haired bloke.'

'Who would have been a great deal happier kissing the actor who played my fiancé, I can assure you.'

'Yes, I have to say we were all in love with you, my friends and I.' Anthony sighed. 'Before I was married, of course.'

'I don't think you need get upset about this, Connie,' Rory said, having finished reading the item in the paper.

'And then when I married it turned out that my darling wife said she'd modelled herself on you.'

'I shall certainly look forward to meeting your wife, then.'

'Alas not,' Anthony said with a sad shake of his head, turning to look at his late wife's photograph in her Court presentation dress. 'I lost her some years ago now.'

'I'm very sorry to hear that.'

'Thank you, Constance. She was a wonderful woman.'

'Then that makes it all the sadder.'

'No, this is all water under the bridge, Connie.' Rory threw the paper into the log basket, and shrugged. 'I don't see the point in bringing it all up again.' He sat down on the sofa beside Constance. 'Although I agree with my father – smashing photo.'

'Once upon a long time ago.' It was Constance's turn to shrug her shoulders. 'Yes, indeed a long, long time ago. But this.' She pointed at the crumpled newspaper. 'This is ridiculous, this piece. Hardly one word of truth in it. For a start I most certainly did not have an affair with that awful blackshirt Bolton. I hardly even knew the fellow. And I did not flee abroad. I said at the time I was determined to stay here and prove my innocence—'

'Which you did?'

'Yes, and when I did go abroad it was only on the advice of

the Home Office. The way that horrid little gossip merchant, that peddler of the misery of others has written it up, it makes it sound as though I vanished at the same time as my wretch of a husband, when in fact it was a long time after. Ages after, in fact.'

'They shouldn't publish such an inaccurate piece.' Anthony frowned. 'Like me to do something about it?'

'I would love it, of course,' Constance said. 'But what can you do?'

'The chap who's the editor,' Anthony told her, reaching for his telephone book. 'When he was something else – features editor, I think – he had a horse with me. He'd had it with someone else who shall be nameless, but he got fed up and sent it to me – and he won a couple of races while he was here. Three, in fact. He's always said if there was anything he could do in return, so now seems to be a very good time to call in the favour.'

Anthony excused himself and took himself off to his study to telephone his journalistic contact.

'This is very good of your father, Rory,' Constance said. 'He doesn't have to do this, you know.'

'That's my father. A friend of his told him the reason he'd had a heart attack was that his heart was too big.'

'How is he now? He looks very well.'

'He's much better; be even more so if we could find some way of getting him to America. According to his specialist, they have a procedure there which would be just the job. But it's very expensive and Dad thinks he isn't worth it.'

'While you obviously think he is.'

'Of course. But try telling him that. Besides, we're a bit short of beans at the moment.'

'I know it's really none of my business,' Constance said after a moment, 'but what if he doesn't have the operation?'

Rory pulled a wry face. 'Your guess is as good as mine.'

'All done and dusted,' Anthony told them on his return. 'Apology in tomorrow, and he's promised it won't be hidden down the bottom of page two either. They wanted to ring you for a quote but I said I didn't know where you were.'

'I very much appreciate that, Anthony. Thank you.'

'It's nothing. Glad to be able to help. So . . .' He looked at the snowscape outside the drawing-room window, and then at Constance. 'It looks as though we shall be having the pleasure of your company for a day or so.'

'Afraid so,' Constance said, fishing in her bag for her cheroots. 'Sorry about that.'

'I dare say we'll manage,' Anthony replied. 'Long as we don't run out of Scotch.'

It turned out they were snowed in for six days. The weather was so bad they were unable to do anything with the horses other than walk them round a track they had cleared and kept having to clear round the yard. After the initial two days of heavy snow the blizzard stopped, but then it froze, which made any horse exercise impossible. So the string were confined to their boxes and their diet changed from a full training and heating one to half-rations supplemented by plenty of fresh, damp hay.

'If this goes on, Pop,' Rory said to his father, 'if we have another week of this, it'll be the equivalent of losing a month's work. And you know what that means better than I. If the owners are even vaguely thinking of Cheltenham we've got to get another run into the horse, but to get him fit enough for that would take at least three weeks' full work. So suppose the weather doesn't relent until late January? We wouldn't be able to run him till near the end of February, which would only leave us about a fortnight to the race itself. And I don't think that would be enough.'

'You're talking in ifs and ands here, old chap,' his father replied. 'It all depends when the thaw comes and how hard it thaws when it does come.'

Having talked to his owners and made sure they had all seen a recording of the big Kempton race so they knew exactly the sort of opposition they might face at Cheltenham, Rory had done as requested and at least made an initial entry for The Enchanted in the big race, feeling a little happier to do so since the handicapper had raised the little horse's rating another five points. Rory knew a lot could happen between early January and the second week of March, so while not particularly happy about entering the horse he knew that so far there was no commitment other than the financial one the owners had been prepared to shoulder when they requested the entry in the first place. When the list of first entries was duly published, as far as non-combatants went there were no surprises. All the top cup horses had been entered, as had the top half a dozen or so handicappers, while there were only two novices in the list, a little heard of Irish horse and The Enchanted. But as the weather showed no signs of breaking, Rory began to feel that time might be on his side, since the longer it froze the less time he would have to prepare such a young and inexperienced horse, which would give him every reason to opt the horse out and save both his own and his father's faces, convinced as he was that the whole professional racing world would be laughing at him.

The only other good thing to come out of the freeze was Kathleen's continued presence at the yard. When she was unable to make the journey back to Ireland on the day she had planned to do so, Rory had been only too happy to agree to her staying on.

'Not that I ever wanted you to go in the first place,' he'd told her.

'You did not?' Kathleen had replied with a frown. 'You said there was nothing left for me to do here.'

'No. No, *you* said that, Kathleen. I didn't say anything.'

'Comes to the same thing though, does it not?' she had asked in return, turning a pair of large green eyes on him. 'Your saying nothing told me there was no point in staying.'

'Don't let's start all that business up again, shall we?'

'I'm not starting anything up, Mr Rawlins,' Kathleen had replied, walking away from him, before calling back over her shoulder, 'You were the one who said nothing!'

Afraid to go up that particular dark alley again, Rory had given her best, just happy that she wasn't leaving.

Then the thaw came, and when it did, it did so as dramatically as it had snowed. Just six nights after the first blizzard, they all went to bed in sub-zero temperatures and woke in the morning to find water everywhere. Thawed snow was pouring in wide rivulets off the stables roofs into gutters quite unable to cope with the torrent. The yard was ankle deep in slush, and the paddocks themselves were beginning to resemble small lakes.

'At least the gallops will be rideable,' Rory observed as he lent a hand sweeping water into the yard drains. 'Although judging from the amount of slush we're facing we'll probably have to swim up there.'

But in another two days the last of the snow and slush had completely disappeared, the yard was back in business, and Constance was on a train to London, her newly formed friendship with Anthony foremost in her mind.

First thing every morning for three days the horses were walked for five miles on the roads before breakfast and then another five miles in the early afternoon, before anyone was allowed near the gallops, and when they were finally allowed up the hill it was only for a couple of long steady canters. After such a long lay-off the last thing anyone wanted was to have a horse pulling a muscle or doing a leg, so caution was the byword.

'Slow and steady!' Rory would remind his work riders as they left the yard. 'I don't want anyone going on. I just want to see you all swing up and by. OK?'

Blaze, who had returned from hospital and was now completely recovered from his fall, thanks largely to Kathleen's tender care, was given the leg up on Boyo and rode him exactly to orders. As far as anyone could tell the horse was as fit as he had been before the snow arrived. Every morning he would appear at the crest of the gallops cantering over his stablemates, only to thunder past Rory with his head in his chest and his big ears pricked, full of premature joys of spring, a season which to judge from the bitter winds on the downland was still a long way off.

'I'm entering him at Devon and Exeter, Ludlow and Towcester, all three-mile races, and since all the races have good prize money and everyone with a decent horse is looking for at least one more run before March, we can expect good fields everywhere – which is what we want if we're all being serious about this.'

Rory had called a meeting of the owners to discuss their strategy, and now it was Alice who spoke up. 'I don't understand why we shouldn't be being serious about it,' she said. 'We all think – no, sorry. We all *know* Boyo is special and we all of us believe he deserves to run in one of the special races, if not the most special race.'

'I know, Alice. And I'm not trying to talk any of you out of it.'

'Oh, but you are, Rory. Of course you are. Millie said you would, because trainers are infinitely more sensible than owners, she said.'

'I'm not sure I want to be remembered for being sensible.'

'Very well, more knowledgeable then. More pragmatic, if you like.'

'I don't think I want to be remembered for being either of those either.'

'It's your job to be realistic,' Alice persisted. 'Not ours. Our job is to dream, and we all dream the same, the four of us. We all dream of The Enchanted winning at Cheltenham.'

'You wouldn't prefer to put it on hold for say another year? Just to see how right or how wrong we all are? Another year on the horse could make a whole lot of difference.'

'Another year on the horse could see him injured or worse,' Grenville said. 'There's nothing to say he'll be any better next year than he is now. He's six. Six-year-olds often win these sorts of races.'

'But he's not very big, Grenville. He's not really built for this.'

'He's not going to get any bigger in a year, Rory. Who knows? He might be at his very best now, and if he is, there's nothing to stop us running him.'

'As long as he's qualified.'

'He's practically qualified already, and anyway—'

'Grenville—'

'No, seriously, old man, do hear me out on this,' Grenville insisted. 'A chum of mine who was at school with the handi-capper had a private word on our behalf. It's all right, it won't go any further. The handicapper's also married to my chum's sister, if you get my drift. Anyway, he had a word in the old ear, and *el handicapper* said that even if the little horse's rating stayed the same – which it will not – but even if it does, and we want to run him, he would let us do so, which he can if he thinks the horse jumps and races well enough.'

'As long as you all know what it means.' Rory sighed, finally getting the feeling that he was being strong-armed into doing what they all wanted. 'We could be a laughing stock, you know that?'

'You mustn't mind what people might say,' Lynne said. 'Grenville says you're worried because people are already saying novices have no place in Gold Cups.'

'It could well be so, Lynne. It's not really a race designed for novices.'

'Not novice novices, it isn't,' Lynne agreed. 'Sorry – I mean, that is according to Grenville. I'm only quoting Grenville here. But since we all of us think that The Enchanted isn't a novice novice, that answers that, really.'

'And I've just had a long talk with your father,' Constance chimed in. 'Because frankly I wouldn't know one race from another. As far as I'm concerned they go hoppity-hoppity-hoppity for a few miles while Alice and I close our eyes—'

'You don't close your eyes, Connie. You watched every inch of the race at Huntingdon, when we all thought Eddie Rampton was going to murder you.'

'That wasn't Boyo's race, clever dick. That was another race, the race I had a bet on. Ever since he won his first race at wherever it was I haven't been able to watch a thing. Anyway, beside the point, I fear – all I want to say is that I listened to what your dear father had to say.'

'And?'

'And I didn't understand a word of it. But I do so love talking to your father. He's a very good listener, and he has such a lovely voice.'

Rory smiled and left it at that. As far as he was concerned the little horse was entered up but no decisions were to be made until it was seen how he ran in his next contest. As for other matters at Fulford Farm, another decision seemed already to have been made concerning Constance, for it now appeared that although the brief freeze was over and the brouhaha in the newspapers concerning her had quickly and completely died down, at the express invitation of Anthony, Constance was back at Fulford Farm not just for a meeting, but to take up residence in one of the farm cottages, where she said she would be out of everyone's way, everyone, that was, other than Anthony, who judging from the increasing amount of time he spent with Constance in the cottage seemed also to be changing his place of residence.

But of course, as Rory well knew, there was a downside to the change in the weather. Now that the freeze was over and road and rail were all but back to normal, there really was nothing to keep Kathleen at the yard any more – nothing, that was, except the horse.

Chapter Twenty-three

Re-enter My Pal Joey

The horse hadn't run as planned in the big race on Boxing Day, the King George VI Gold Cup, even though he had been the firm co-favourite in all the ante-post betting lists and in spite of Eddie Rampton and his connections maintaining he would. Instead he was withdrawn on the morning of the race, the veterinary certificate stating that a foreign body had been found under a shoe, the result being an infection. Naturally the punters who had taken the price on offer ante-post were not best pleased, although the majority of them, as they tore up their vouchers, might have been heard to mutter a more colourful version of *that's racing*.

The truth of the matter was that the trainer liked to play the waiting game to unsettle the opposition. He was also a gambler who liked to take the odds ante-post, and he also particularly enjoyed winning valuable races for his owners, most of whom also enjoyed a tilt at the ring. But what really rocked Eddie Rampton's boat was beating those trainers whom he perceived as belonging to the Smart Set, the loud-talking, party-going, arrogant young men most of whom had inherited the family stables and whom, Rampton had long ago decided, looked down their noses at the likes of him, and him in particular. So he derived a peculiar pleasure from rattling their cages. And, it had to be faced, having the favourite for the Gold Cup offered him ample opportunity to indulge his chip. He knew most of his rivals preferred to avoid taking on any of his good horses before the big Cheltenham meeting in March so he took great delight in spreading as much misinformation about intended and non-intended runners as possible, after which he would sit back to watch his rivals getting into flat spins as they tried to decide whether or not to run their own charges.

This was by far his favourite time of year – the run-up to Cheltenham, and yet another chance to win the most coveted racing trophy of them all, the Gold Cup. So far Eddie Rampton had been twice denied a triumph he thought was his as two of his horses, on separate occasions, had galloped up the famous hill after the last fence looking certain to win, only to tire and be caught at the post by horses trained by two of his most despised rivals. But this year was different: this year he knew he had a worthy favourite in My Pal Joey, who had won his two preparatory races this year with the sort of consummate ease that is the hallmark of an exceptional horse.

My Pal Joey was a large horse, standing at a full seventeen hands, and for his size he was blessed with stamina, an exceptional cruising speed, and a prodigious jumping ability. Such was his presence that he normally had his rivals beaten a long way out simply by dominating the race with his sheer physical presence. Given a trouble-free run-up to March, Rampton considered he had his best chance yet to triumph in the Gold Cup. His only regret was that the horse's terminally ill owner had known that he himself wasn't going to make it to Cheltenham and so had sold his horse in order that someone else could enjoy the thrill of having not only a runner in the Gold Cup but possibly the favourite and perhaps even the winner. But even though he had lost an owner of long standing, Rampton very soon realised that My Pal Joey's new owner was a man after his own heart. A real go-getter, someone determined to win at all costs. There was no coming second in this man's book – it was win, and win whatever the cost.

So as soon as the entries were published in January the favourite's new owner and his trainer put their heads together to hatch various stratagems, shortly after which Eddie Rampton initiated his campaign of disseminating misinformation, a process that began with the last-minute withdrawal of My Pal Joey from the big race on Boxing Day.

On the other hand, Rory and his four owners put all their cards on the table as far as their horse was concerned. Not that there was a lot of undue interest in his possible participation in March even when his name appeared among the initial entries. To the racing and betting public he was a largely unknown and hard to rate quantity, certainly a promising novice steeplechaser but one whom the cognoscenti were ready to dismiss because of his size, his lack of breeding, his relatively inexperienced trainer and the fact that the horse had only run on what they liked to call the gaffe tracks, the smaller and less fashionable country racecourses. So when the bookmakers made their first ante-post lists it was no surprise that the price quoted against The Enchanted to win the Grade One Cheltenham Gold Cup on 13 March, to be run over three miles two and a half furlongs for five-year-olds and upwards, was a hundred and fifty to one.

When Alice noted the apparent generosity of the odds, she began to fashion a plan of her own, and once she had considered it carefully she made two telephone calls, one to her bank for information on the state of her current account and the other to her friend Millie for advice on a certain bit of protocol.

As far as the owners of The Enchanted went, no one had yet realised who the new owner of the star of Eddie Rampton's yard was. Rory's secretary Maureen so far had been the only person to spell out the name, but since she had no idea that Lynne had once been Mrs Fortune, and not so very long ago at that, the name of the new owner did not mean anything to her. The Enchanted's owners were not always glued to racing on the television or reading every item of gossip in the racing papers, and by the time they turned their attentions to any other horse that might be taking on their own in March the story about My Pal Joey's changing hands had long gone cold. So it was not until Grenville and Lynne happened to be sitting in front of the television in Lynne's now fully furnished apartment one wet Saturday afternoon that the penny finally dropped.

The racing was from Ascot where one of the contests, according to Grenville, was looked upon as being a good trial for any Gold Cup candidates who wanted to pit themselves against stiff well-made fences on what was reckoned to be a seriously testing course. Before the race was run, to kill time as the horses were cantering down to the start, one of the presenters informed the viewers that he was about to interview the owner of a horse which had been one of the favourites for the Gold Cup until recently, when it had suffered an injury that had, according to the interviewer, indeed prevented the animal from running in this prestigious Ascot race this very afternoon.

Whereupon the new owner was introduced to the public.

'Bloody hell – will you look at who it is?' Lynne exclaimed. 'By all that's Satanic and evil, it's only my bloody ex!'

And sure enough, there was Gerry, wearing a fashionably overlong black overcoat with matching fedora, Maddy by his side, dressed in a red leather overcoat and a Dr Zhivago-style fur hat.

'What do they look like?'

'I'm too much of a gentleman to say,' Grenville murmured. 'An updated Bonnie and Clyde, perhaps?'

'But he doesn't know any more than I do about racing! All he knows about is blooming dodgy motor cars!'

'I've always been mad about racing and horses,' Gerry was saying, smiling urbanely into the camera. 'Ever since I was a nipper.'

'Baloney,' said Lynne. 'First time he ever went racing was with me.'

'My dad always had horses,' Gerry went on.

'And they pulled carts,' Lynne retorted.

'So, you know, horses have always been part of my life.'

'Mine as well,' Maddy simpered, tightening her grip on Gerry's arm. 'I had my first pony when I was seven. He was a little skewbald called Paintbox.'

'And it lived in a toy cupboard,' Lynne hissed.

'Now, now, Linnet,' Grenville remonstrated. 'One mustn't speak ill of the brain dead.'

'Course I'm sad that the guy who owned the horse previously won't be here to see him run,' Gerry continued. 'But I think he'll be watching anyway. From his cloud up there.'

'He'll be taking Holy Orders next,' Lynne said.

'Or holding up banks,' Grenville remarked. 'Particularly in that coat.'

'So what's the news on your horse, Gerry?' the interviewer was asking. 'Is he over the setback that prevented him from running in the King George?'

'He's certainly back in work,' Gerry replied, returning to

the script Eddie Rampton had prepared for him. 'It's a bit early to say whether he's fully over it. It was a real nasty infection.'

'Got right in between his poor toes,' Maddy added helpfully.

'Right in his hoof,' Gerry corrected her as quickly as he could. 'Right in the – you know. The outside bit.'

'Inside the outside bit.' Maddy again.

'The bit right under the shoe,' Gerry said with a nod. 'Very painful. Anyway, as I said, he's back in work now but we're taking it day by day.'

'And if he does make it to Cheltenham,' the interviewer said, 'which of course we are all hoping he does, which horses do you most fear?'

'You would have to say County Gent,' Gerry replied, looking at his most knowledgeable. 'County Gent, certainly.'

'Yeah,' Maddy agreed. 'You would have to say County Gent.'

'And the Irish horse,' Gerry added. 'Spun Silk.'

'Right.' Maddy nodded. 'And the Irish horse, Spun Silk. Course.'

'I think most of all you'd have to say County Gent,' Gerry said, summarising. 'And the Irish horse Spun Silk.'

'Good. Thank you both very much,' the interviewer concluded. 'Hope to see you both again in March.'

'You bet!' Maddy said, leaning to camera and holding up her free hand clenched in a fist. 'Cheltenham here we come!'

'They really should give them a show of their own,' Grenville said, lying back on the sofa with a deep sigh. 'One of those in-depth chat shows.'

'Must be because of us,' Lynne said, sitting back on the sofa. 'Only reason Gerry muscles in on something is when he thinks his precious nose is out of joint.'

'Really?' Grenville pulled a face. 'Rather an expensive get-you, isn't it?'

'You don't know Gerry, Grenville,' Lynne said, still staring at the screen. 'And you certainly don't know Maddy. Hold on – isn't that that American's horse? Fly The Flag? You know, that nice bloke we met at Huntingdon.'

Grenville checked the runners in the paper just as the odds were being flashed up on the screen.

'Right, it is,' he said. 'Should be favourite.'

'It is favourite,' Lynne replied. 'Two to one.'

They watched the race, a three-mile handicap with Fly The Flag carrying top weight of 11st 9lb, a burden that certainly didn't stop him winning as he liked, sauntering home in the soft going by an easy four lengths.

'Another one for the notebook,' Grenville observed. 'He also holds an entry for the Gold Cup.'

'But we're not sure we'll go to Cheltenham,' Harrington Lovell said when he was interviewed in the unsaddling enclosure. 'If the ground dries up, which it usually does, he might be found out in the speed department. There are some fast horses entered, and really our fella's bred to stay, so we might be looking at Aintree instead. It's always been on the wish list, the Grand National, and you know, from the way he ran today, he could go close.'

'Yes,' Grenville agreed from his armchair. 'But we did beat him somewhat easily at Huntingdon, so although he has to come into the reckoning he's not my major worry.'

'Who is, sweetheart?' Lynne wondered, getting up to go and make them both some tea.

'Your ex's horse, I suppose,' Grenville replied. 'A little bird told me they'd laid him out to win.'

*   *   *

Kathleen turned the television off in her cottage and sat back in her chair. In front of her on the floor stood her bags, already packed ready for the journey she intended to make that evening, a journey she had been intending to undertake in fact for the past three days, but having warned Rory of her intention she had found herself finding plenty of reasons for delaying her departure, all of them concerning Boyo, who she kept discovering needed just a little bit more care and supervision with every day that passed.

She had hoped that Rory would notice her increased diligence and invite her to stay on just in case Boyo needed her, even though they both knew there was nothing about the horse to cause even the slightest concern. But he had said nothing at all, not one word. In fact, if she didn't know Rory for the kind-heart that he was, she would have said he was doing his best to ignore her altogether. So finally, now that Saturday had arrived, the day, she had told Rory, on which she simply had to leave because of pressing matters at home, Kathleen realised that she was going to have to be as good as her word and take her leave of the place where she knew she had found true happiness.

Of course, what she had just seen televised from Ascot racecourse was only making her job harder. Most of the talk had been about the Gold Cup, and although no mention was made of The Enchanted in the entire broadcast the fact that the chances and merits of all the favoured horses were being so readily discussed and compared only served to make her departure more of a terrible wrench. For a moment she had even seriously contemplated going to find Rory to ask him directly if perhaps she could stay, pleading her special relationship with Boyo as her reason, only to remember it was too late, since Rory was at Ascot and Blaze was coming to pick her up in half an hour to take her to the station.

'You sure you know what you're doing, Kate?' Blaze asked her yet again as he drove her off to Salisbury.

'Just leave it alone, will you?' Kathleen replied, turning away from him. 'And leave me alone as well.'

'You're mad,' Blaze said. 'You've completely lost it.'

'That's my business,' Kathleen insisted. 'The whole thing is a lot of baloney anyway. Boyo'll be fine, and so too will everyone else involved.'

'Sure,' Blaze said. 'Everyone, that is, except you.'

All the way back from the race meeting, which he left early, Rory found he could do nothing but think of Kathleen. The main reason he had gone to Ascot was not to see the competition but to be away from the yard when Kathleen left it, thinking that if he remained he would only do what he had resolved not to do, namely beg her to stay. Now, as he was driving back in more than a slight panic, he knew that was exactly what he should have done and never minded the consequences. Life at the yard was not going to be the same without the beautiful Kathleen and he had let her go. Worse, he had let her go without having made any really serious attempt even to interest her, let alone win her heart, and when he realised this he felt ashamed of himself for making such a feeble fist of it.

Leaving before the second last race, he reckoned, gave him an outside chance of getting home before she left, but thanks to an accident on the motorway slip road his journey took him half an hour longer than usual and so he missed her.

'You haven't missed her by that much, Guv,' Teddy told him when he asked. 'She can't have left more than twenty minutes ago.'

Without stopping to think, Rory got back into his car at once and headed fast for the station. He didn't know what he was going to say to her, but since Salisbury was a good fifty minutes' drive away he reckoned he'd have time enough to come up with a good reason for asking her to change her mind – that is, if he managed to get there before her train left. Motoring faster than he had ever driven, he made it – by the time he had hurled himself out of the car and run into the station – with a minute to spare.

He saw her just about to get into the train and started to run along the platform waving frantically at her, hoping to catch her eye before it was too late, but she wasn't looking his way. She had turned away to embrace the man who had come to see her off, to throw her arms round his neck and lay her head on his shoulder. Rory recognised the man immediately and stopped dead in his tracks, about to turn tail and leave when she looked up and saw him. Rory froze, unable to move or think. They stared at each other and then after a moment Kathleen put up one hand and slowly waved to him over Blaze's shoulder. Absurdly enough, Rory found himself waving back.

As they watched each other without moving, people arriving to catch the train at the last minute hurried down the platform, pushing their way through the throng and into the nearest available carriage, while Rory and Kathleen remained exactly where they were, until Blaze finally turned round and saw the man who was also his employer staring at the girl in his arms.

Finally, as the guard blew his whistle and the train prepared to leave the station, Rory began to walk towards Blaze and Kathleen, pointing at the train, which was now starting to move.

'You'll miss it!' he called, beginning to run. 'You'll miss your train!'

By the time he reached her the train was moving too fast for her to get on it – not that Kathleen showed the slightest intention of trying to do so. Instead she waited calmly for Rory to reach her.

'Your train,' he gasped. 'You've missed it.'

'So I have,' Kathleen said, looking round at the departing transport. 'I have so.'

'Well, now you'll m-miss everything!' Rory shouted over the increasing noise. 'You'll n-never catch your ferry now!'

'Ah no, she won't do that either,' Blaze agreed with a smile.

'I don't know what you're both looking so pleased about,' Rory yelled. 'I thought the whole intention was for K-K-Kathleen here to return h-h-home.'

'That was her intention, guv'nor, not mine,' Blaze assured him.

'No. No, it wouldn't be, would it?'

'No, it would not indeed. No, sir.'

'But even so,' Rory stuttered, turning his attention to Kathleen, who was still staring at him. 'I don't understand why y-you didn't get on the train.'

'Because I saw you, Mr Rawlins,' Kathleen said, as if it were obvious. 'When I saw you running on to the platform, sure I thought there must be something wrong back at the yard which would explain why you were here. What else was I to think now?'

'There's nothing wr-wrong,' Rory assured her through gritted teeth, realising that the whole thing had now gone seriously pear-shaped. 'At least not at the yard, there isn't.'

'So what is it, then?' Kathleen enquired earnestly, as Blaze picked up her bag and began to saunter back down the platform. 'Something must have happened to bring you here.'

'It's nothing,' Rory said in haste, turning his attention to Blaze. 'And where does he think he's going with your bags?'

'There's precious little point in staying here, boss!' Blaze called over his shoulder. 'The horse has long bolted.'

'So what was it, Mr Rawlins?' Kathleen enquired once more, catching up with Rory. 'What exactly's the matter?'

'There's nothing the m-matter, Kathleen,' Rory said slowly, trying to mind what he said, knowing Kathleen's propensity for taking things wrong. 'It's just—' He stopped to scratch his head. 'It's just – it's j-just – it's jer – *just* – it's just that I don't w-wan— I don't think you should go, that's all.'

'Why?' Kathleen wondered, shaking her head so that a thick lock of dark hair fell across her eyes. 'Why ever not?' she asked again, brushing the hair slowly aside and looking right at him. 'Is it something in particular? Or just nothing really at all? Just a whim?'

'It is *not* a wh-whim,' Rory said, almost crossly. 'I just don't happen to think you should go, that's all. That's all there is to it. All right?'

'Because?' Kathleen wondered, widening her eyes at him.

'Because – because of the horse, that's what!' Rory retorted. 'Because of the Gold Cup! You know he's running in the Gold Cup—'

'I didn't know for definite, Mr Rawlins.'

'Well he is. It's definite – and I'm s-sorry for shouting. It's just that I got a bit – I was a bit thrown when I realised you'd gone and that they want to run him definitely in the Gold Cup and so I thought if anyone should be there – that is, if anyone shouldn't be here – no, I mean if anyone *should* – if anyone should be here then that someone would be yer-yer-yer—' Rory came to a standstill, word-bound, staring back into the pair of green eyes that were staring so solemnly at him.

'Me?'

'Yes,' Rory said. 'You l-looked.' He smiled at her while frowning at the same time.

'OK,' Kathleen said, clasping her hands behind her and

nodding. 'That seems only sensible. In that case, 'tis just as well I missed the train.'

'Yes,' Rory agreed, his frown deepening. ''Tis just as well you did.'

Shortly after teatime on the same day, Alice's telephone rang.

'Harry?' she said in wonder. 'This is a surprise.'

'I got your number from Rory,' Harry replied. 'I hope that was all right?'

'Well, of course,' Alice replied. 'And congratulations. I just watched your horse winning. Well done. He won jolly easily.'

'Thank you. I'd sort of hoped you might be there – except when I saw the runners, I thought no chance.'

'I think we're headed for Devon and Exeter next. And that'll probably be his last race.'

'I'm sorry?' Harry sounded startled. 'You don't mean for the season, surely?'

'Oh, no.' Alice laughed. 'No, of course not. I meant before Cheltenham.'

'You're really intending to run there, then?'

'It rather depends on how we do at Devon, I think. Why? Don't you think we should? You sounded doubtful.'

'My, Alice,' Harry replied, 'that really wouldn't be my place, and anyway it's absolutely not what I'm thinking. I think if you want to go run, so you should. Your horse has earned a place in the line-up, whatever they say.'

'You've heard, have you?' Alice asked. 'Even the other side of the pond, as you call it? A lot of the wiseacres are saying the race is no place for novices.'

'Don't listen to them. Listen to your trainer and to yourselves. He's your horse, and you run him where you like. It's a sport, not a religion.'

'Thank you, Harry. I shall treasure that advice. And what about you? Cheltenham or Aintree?'

'Tell you what,' Harry replied, 'why don't we discuss that over lunch? Or even dinner? I'm coming down to London tonight to stay for a couple of days. I would love it if you came out for a meal.'

'You would?' Alice was unable to stop the catch in her breath.

'I really would. But if it's too much of a slog, you know – for you to get up to town – I don't mind a day out in the country.'

'No, Harry.'

'Please don't say no, Alice.'

'No, Harry,' Alice assured him. 'I wasn't going to say no. At least not to you. I was about to say no don't worry about coming down here. I'd actually like a day in London. I have some things to do.'

'Lunch or dinner?'

'I think dinner.'

'Better by the minute. I'm staying at Claridges. Let's meet in the bar at around eight tomorrow, OK?'

'Of course. I shall be there.'

Before she left to go to London to meet Harry, Alice wrote two brief but affectionate notes to both her children, enclosed the two vouchers that she had received that morning in the post and then drove into the village to send the letters recorded delivery. After that she drove to the station, parked her car and caught the train to Waterloo.

From Waterloo she took a taxi to Sloane Square, spent an hour shopping at Peter Jones, had her hair done, checked into a small hotel off Lower Sloane Street that offered special rates for country visitors, changed into her new clothes, then took a taxi to Mayfair, arriving at one minute to eight o'clock.

Harry was waiting for her in the bar, dressed in an immaculate dark suit, handmade white shirt and dark red silk tie. He stood, took her hand as if to shake it, and then decided to kiss it instead.

'My. You look beautiful.'

'And you look very handsome.'

'A mutual admiration society it is, then.'

Offering her a chair, he asked her if champagne would be all right, and after Alice had accepted the offer he sat down opposite her, started to speak and promptly fell to silence. As they waited for their champagne to arrive, neither of them spoke. They just looked at each other and after a moment smiled. Finally Harry breathed in deeply, and shook his head slowly, while Alice smiled once more and putting her hands together leaned forward slightly to speak to him.

'Don't let's waste time at our age, Harry,' she said. 'I think I feel exactly the way you do.'

'You do?' Harry's eyes widened. 'You really think so?'

'Absolutely,' Alice replied with a nod of her head. 'And if I'm right, if that's the case, we don't have to say another thing. All we have to do is enjoy ourselves.'

Which is exactly what they both did, and after a fine dinner and long and wonderful conversation, rather than take a taxi Alice and Harry decided to take a walk on what was a fine, albeit frosty, winter night, the two of them strolling arm in arm out into Park Lane, down round Hyde Park Corner and into the Brompton Road, stopping now and then to look into the brightly lit shop windows in Knightsbridge, before cutting down the side of Harrods to Alice's small hotel, where Harry wished her a very good night, kissed her once, but only briefly, and then with a wave of his hand walked all the way back to his own hotel.

*   *   *

When they all arrived at Devon and Exeter racecourse, set high on Haldon Hill, the rumours were of abandonment, so heavy was the mist that enveloped the track.

'It's always like this,' Rory said, taking them all to the bar. 'Nearly always. This course is famous for its mists and fogs, as well as for being the longest oval track in the country.'

'I don't understand, Rory,' Alice said. 'How can one track be longer than the others when the races are the same length – no, I see what you mean.' She laughed. 'You mean longest all the way round.'

'With most other tracks – well, all other tracks really –' Rory replied, 'for a three-mile chase you have to go round at least twice, sometimes near enough three times. But here – if you look at your racecard, the three-mile chase starts here . . .' Rory pointed out the spot on a map on the card. 'The circuit being two miles, you just go round one and a half times, and although it looks flat there's quite a steep pull up the back straight, which at the moment you can't see at all, so it calls for not only speed but stamina.'

Half an hour later a breeze got up and began to shift the fret that had all but obliterated the course, and after a further short delay it was announced that racing would go ahead.

By the time they got to the three-mile chase in which The Enchanted was running, the mist had thickened again, making it once more impossible to make out what was happening on the far side of the course. Even so, the runners went to post, with The Enchanted second favourite at five to two, the market leader being another of the season's most promising novices, an athletic-looking grey called Mossman, from the same yard as County Gent. Once off, and past the stands for the first time, the field of ten runners disappeared into the mist, the commentary petered out, and nothing more was heard or seen of the action until the horses reappeared coming off the bend on the home turn to head for the two fences in the straight.

There were three horses in a line, well clear of the rest of the field, which remained invisible, but at first the race reader was unable to call them with any certainty, finally naming them as Mossman, Pondarosa and Penny Off.

'Where's Boyo?' Lynne cried, turning to Grenville. 'Where's our horse gone?'

'What do you mean?' Alice cried from behind Rory's back, where, as usual, she was hiding. 'What do you mean, where is he?'

'Something must have happened out in the country,' Grenville said, adjusting his race glasses in an attempt to get a better and more focused view. 'Except – wait a minute . . .'

'And as they land after the second last it's still Mossman in the lead, but only just, and now with Pondarosa beaten and dropping back it's Penny Off who's laying down the challenge – except . . .'

'Except that isn't Penny Off,' Grenville cried.

'Except it isn't Penny Off!' the commentator agreed. 'My mistake – it's The Enchanted!'

'It's Boyo!' Lynne cried joyfully. 'Come on, Boyo! Come on, our little horse!'

'Yes, it's not Penny Off, it's The Enchanted who's now laying down a serious challenge to the favourite – and on the run to the last there's nothing in it between Mossman and The Enchanted – whose rider Blaze Molloy appears still to have a double handful—'

'Come on, Boyo!' Alice yelled from behind Rory.

'Come on, The Enchanted!' Grenville shouted. 'Come on, Boyo! Go for it!'

'And as they jump the last it's the two market leaders neck and neck,' the commentator called. 'But as they land Mossman pecks, but it's too late anyway because The Enchanted has landed flying – and as they run from the fence The Enchanted has already opened up a two-length lead . . .'

'Come on, Boyo!' his owners shouted, Lynne jumping up and down as always, and Alice now daring to peep out from her hiding place. 'Come on, the little horse!'

'It's OK,' Rory managed to say, the first words he had spoken since the horses had disappeared into the fog. 'He's home and hosed.'

'And it's The Enchanted who is first past the post,' the commentator announced, 'by what looks like a good five or maybe six lengths, with a very tired Mossman just hanging on to second from what looks like an equally exhausted Penny Off.'

'First number five, The Enchanted,' came the official announcement. 'Second number three, Mossman, and third number four, Penny Off.'

'If you want to know, guv'nor,' Blaze said after he had hopped off the horse in the winners' enclosure, 'don't ask me, because you weren't the only ones who couldn't see a thing.' Blaze looked round him in case the journalists had arrived yet, but seeing they were still alone except for the owners the jockey dropped his voice and continued, 'We'd have won by a street if we hadn't been all but knocked out of it – four from home, I reckon it was. Don't ask me which horse it was either, because I hardly saw it, but Jeeze – it barged right into us and oh so nearly carried us out. I had to take a huge hook, but this little horse is something else. We were into the bottom of the fence but he still managed to pick up and jump it – no, fly it. But whichever horse it was took two others out, and one of them had the unholiest of falls. I hope to God he's all right.'

With a tip to his cap Blaze was gone to weigh in, the thanks of the owners ringing in his ears.

'Wonder which horse it was? I didn't see the Rampton horse come in. But then we're never going to be any the wiser, since nobody could possibly have seen anything that happened in the back straight any-old-how.'

'There's a horse coming back now,' Grenville pointed out. 'Someone caught him over there. By the last fence.'

They all watched through their binoculars as the loose horse was brought in, minus its saddle but otherwise seemingly unharmed, unlike, they soon discovered, its trainer, none other than Eddie Rampton, who had all but broken a blood vessel himself in his rage.

'You!' he yelled, stomping across the paddock with a thick finger pointed at Rory. 'You. Rawlins or whatever your name is!'

'Sorry? Are you talking to me, Mr Rampton?' Rory wondered, pulling a help-me face.

'What the hell do you think you're playing at?' Rampton continued, pushing Grenville, who had stepped in front of Rory, out of his way. 'Or rather what does that idiot of a boy you allow to ride your horses think he's playing at? Eh?'

'Matter of fact your guess is as good as mine, Mr Rampton,' Rory replied, retreating from the thick finger that was attempting to stab him in the chest. 'Or rather it's probably a lot more creative.'

'Don't you get fancy with me, Rawlins,' Rampton warned him. 'Your boy apprentice rode my horse off out there! I've just heard it all from my jock!'

'Ah yes, Kevin Billings, right?' Rory asked, consulting his card with a studied frown. 'Yes, I gather he always has a tale to tell.'

'I said don't get fancy with me, d'you hear?' Rampton

roared, attracting the attention of several racegoers. 'Your blasted learner jockey – for want of a better word – rode my horse off! Cut right across him five from home and ran my horse out! And I'll tell you something else, shall I? We were cantering all over your stupid little horse! And furthermore it wouldn't surprise me in the least if he and his idiot pilot missed out a couple in the back straight!'

'Careful what you say, Mr Rampton,' Grenville said, in his gravest voice. 'I happen to be a lawyer.'

Eddie Rampton spun round and stared at him, his mouth opening and closing like an oversize carp's at feeding time.

'We'll soon see about that.'

'Yes, we no doubt will,' Grenville replied. 'Whatever that may mean.'

'I'm off to see the stewards,' Rampton shouted. 'I am off to lodge a formal complaint! You just wait, Rawlins! You haven't heard the last of this yet!'

'I have a feeling we might have,' Rory turned to his startled owners. 'The patrol cameras out there won't have been able to pick up much, you see, but if they have, I bet they'll find we're completely in the clear. And if they haven't been able to pick anything up then old Eddie won't have a leg to stand on.'

'Thank heavens he didn't shout like that at me,' Constance sighed from under her large hat. 'I might have been forced to teach him a lesson.'

In the event, the stewards threw out Eddie Rampton's complaint without even calling in any jockeys, since the far-seeing senior steward had positioned several of his staff at all the fences in the back straight to keep an eye on things in view of the lack of visibility and two of them had already reported an incident at the fifth fence from home where it appeared the horse trained by Eddie Rampton and ridden by Kevin Billings had been seen to dive and cut across the horse on its outside, the horse believed to be The Enchanted. The only thing the witnesses had to add to their official report was a commendation to the young jockey riding The Enchanted for managing his horse so well at the fence in question that an accident had unquestionably been avoided.

'Don't think you've heard the last of this, Rawlins,' a furious Eddie Rampton warned Rory later in the car park when he passed him.

'On the contrary, Mr Rampton,' Grenville replied, stepping in front of Rory. 'If you do not desist, you can expect a formal letter of complaint from my client. I hope that is understood. Good afternoon to you.'

'Don't you just love that? "Good afternoon, to you!"' Lynne laughed, catching at Grenville's arm. 'Talk about old-fashioned cool.'

The call Alice had been expecting came that evening when she got back from the races.

'Mum?' Georgina said down the telephone. 'Mum – please – *what* is this?'

'What is what, dear?' Alice enquired. 'I can't see down the telephone.'

'This – this *thing* that's arrived in the post. From some book-maker or other. I don't want to open a bookmaker's account, thank you.'

'It isn't a bookmaker's account, Georgie. If you look properly—'

'Mum?' Georgina interrupted. 'There is this thing that says quite clearly on the top the name of a well-known bookmaker. OK?'

'Yes. And what else does it say?'

'I really don't know. I have only just got in from a seriously exhausting day – I've got Will in bed with a sore throat and I think Finty is now sickening for it, Joe has got problems at work, and I come home and find this. This bookmaker's thing.'

'Your tone seems to have changed, Georgie.' Alice smiled to herself. 'Have you noticed something?'

'I don't understand, Mum,' Georgina returned, her tone indeed changed. 'It seems to be some sort of betting slip. For rather a lot of money.'

'That's exactly what it is, darling.'

'Why? What's this about? Do you want us to hang on to this for you for safe keeping or something?'

'Why don't you just read the note I wrote? In fact if you'd read the note first instead of just grabbing the telephone . . .'

'Mum?' All at once her daughter sounded just how she used to sound, before she had decided life was turning against her. 'Mum, I really don't understand. This is for a thousand pounds.'

'No, it's not, not really,' Alice explained. 'It's not worth a thing, unless the horse wins, which probably won't happen. It's what's called an ante-post voucher.'

'For a thousand pounds?'

'Yes,' was all Alice could think of to say. She had been about to go into a long explanation of the whys and wherefores, but had quickly thought better of it. The deed had been done and now everyone concerned just had to go along with it.

'I still don't understand, Mum.' The edge was beginning to creep back into Georgina's voice, and, hearing it, Alice took a long, steady and deep breath. 'No, OK, I think I do. You have bet a thousand pounds on your horse? A *thousand pounds*?'

'Georgina darling, it is my money. And yes, I have bet a thousand pounds on our horse.'

'And you want me to have the voucher – for safe keeping.'

'No, you silly daft girl!' Alice found herself suddenly laugh-ing at the ludicrousness of the situation. Here she was having given her daughter the chance – albeit an outside one – of making a lot of money without raising a finger, and here was her daughter criticising her for it. 'No, I want you to have the voucher! It's for you – for what you're always so worried about. School fees. But look, if you don't want it—'

'No, hang on.' Georgina stopped her. 'It says here – it says one thousand pounds bet at odds of one hundred and fifty to one.'

'Sounds about right.'

'So if the horse won—'

'If,' Alice interrupted. 'And you must understand it's a very big *if* we're talking about here. That's why the odds are so very long, apparently. Anyway, the point is I haven't got enough money to give you anywhere near the amount you say you need to educate your children – my grandchildren – but this at least gives you an outside chance. And before you say anything else I've done exactly the same for your brother. For Christian. Not for school fees, obviously, but to help him out. But you're not to tell anybody. Not a soul. It's bad luck, right? And chances of its happening are not only extremely slim but probably non-existent. Anyway.'

'Mum?'

'Yes?' Alice asked carefully, wondering what the objection might be this time.

'Mum, I really don't know what to say,' Georgina said, her voice dropping almost to a whisper. 'Except – except sorry.'

'Sorry? What on earth for, Georgie darling?'

'For being such an A1 prat.'

'You have been nothing of the sort. Nonsense. Now all we have to do is hope he runs. And if he does run, I understand he won't start at anything like that price. I'll keep you posted.'

'You'd jolly well better, Mum. And Mum?'

'Georgie?'

'Love you.'

'I know, darling. The feeling is entirely reciprocated. 'Bye, darling.'

Dear old Mum, Georgina thought to herself as she put down the telephone. *Still can't say it. Oh well . . .*

While as she was putting down the phone her end Alice was thinking *And now all we can do is get out the prayer mats, light the votive candles, keep everything crossed and not walk under any ladders. In other words, just hope and pray the little horse stays in one piece and gets to the races.*

Different hopes and desires entirely were entertained by a certain other person who, as Alice was busy praying and hoping, was equally busy scheming and plotting, trying to imagine every single possible way she could thwart the aspirations of all her rivals, real and imagined.

Chapter Twenty-four

Creeping Murmur and the Poring Dark

It was Kathleen who saved the day.

With the big race now only a week away and the owners in full agreement about running The Enchanted and the horse going from strength to strength in his work, the security blanket round Fulford Farm was pulled even tighter than before, particularly after a couple of alarms and excursions when both Teddy and Kathleen had sworn they had heard the sound of would-be intruders late at night when they were on watch. Dunkum gave chase on both occasions, only for the prowlers to escape over the perimeter fencing. Kathleen then came up with a plan with which Rory immediately agreed and put in motion at once.

The horse was due to have only one more piece of fast work before the big day so what was proposed was eminently feasible, relying only on the discretion of the staff at Fulford Farm and the assistance of Rory's friend Henry Carmichael, a keen horseman who trained his point to pointers and hunter chasers from a yard on a farm less than five miles away. Oddly enough, despite its risks, the very simplicity of the plan was its strength.

'I thought we were going to have to hire some muscle, p-p-perhaps,' Rory told Kathleen the first night the plan was put into effect, when he came down at midnight to take over her watch. 'Yet here we are, quiet and safe as can be, and it's all really th-thanks to you.'

'Not a bit of it,' Kathleen replied, getting up from her seat at Rory's desk from where she had been keeping an eagle eye on the yard and on the all-important stable directly in front of her. 'Anyway – your shift.'

'My shift,' Rory agreed. 'Ab-ab-absolutely.'

'Might I ask you something now?' Kathleen enquired. 'Without upsetting you, that is.'

'From what I know of life, when a w-woman asks you that sort of question – you know – ther-ther-the would-you-mind-if-I sort of question – they're going to anyhow. So yes – f-f-fire ahead.'

'It's just I was wondering,' Kathleen said, hesitating by the door. 'I was just wondering if I – do I make you nervous?'

'N-n-nervous?' Rory returned, doing his best to laugh lightly. 'Y-you? M-make me nervous? Why on earth – wh-what on earth would make you ther-ther-ther-*think* ther-that? H-heavens above.'

'It's just that I couldn't help noticing you only seem to have trouble when I'm around,' Kathleen persisted. 'You know – you don't seem to stammer so much with other people. If at all. Not as much as you do when I'm around.'

'I don't know what you m-mean,' Rory lied, pinching the fleshy part of one of his thumbs between thumb and index fingernails to try to control his speech. 'I don't know what you're talking about, actually.'

'That's all right then,' Kathleen said with a polite smile. 'I best be getting along now.'

'Did you see the l-latest ratings?' Rory said, calling her back with a wave of a sheet of print. 'They arrived this morning.' Unable to resist getting an update, Kathleen came back and stood just behind Rory's shoulder while he pored over the figures. 'Better than you might think,' Rory continued, glad of her return. 'They put County Gent top obviously, with a rating of 156, but our horse has gone right up and n-now they rate him 132. With a plus mark, d-denoting his improvement.'

'If racing were all done be ratings, Mr Rawlins—'

'Yes I know, Kathleen,' Rory interrupted her, turning round and finding her face considerably closer to his than he had been expecting, a sight that stopped him midstream. He swallowed hard and frowned at her.

'Yes? Something the matter?'

'Yes – no. No,' Rory corrected himself again. 'Form also notices his jumping, is what I was about to say. They make special – you know. They remark on his j-jumping.'

'And so they should, too,' Kathleen replied, now standing away from Rory. 'He's more than earned the right to be in the line-up. None of the others jump like him.'

'You're not alone in th-thinking that,' Rory added. 'There's been money for him.'

'That wouldn't surprise me a bit, Mr Rawlins.'

'The first shows had him at a hundred and fifty to one, if you remember. He's now a sixty-six to one chance, which one would h-have to say – ther-ther-that's quite a reduction.'

'He won't start at that on the day either, you can be sure of that,' Kathleen said, with a stretch and a yawn. 'I'd say you won't be able to get better than twenties on him for a starting price.'

'Who am I to argue with the Oracle of Cronagh?' Rory replied. 'Anyway – th-thanks. I'll take over now.'

'Have you had a stammer all your life?' Kathleen asked out of the air. 'If you don't mind my asking, that is.'

'I thought the Irish axed rather than asked,' Rory replied, trying to work around the question.

'Have you?'

Rory drummed his fingers lightly on the desk as he tried to prepare his answer. No one had ever asked him directly about his stammer, no one except his therapist, the woman who had taught him the coping mechanisms that had gradually fallen out of use as his control had increased, to the point where he had thought he was completely cured – until Kathleen came into his life.

She put a hand on his shoulder, making him start. 'That was very tactless of me. I'm sorry.'

'It wasn't at all tactless, as it happens, Kathleen,' Rory said, sitting back in his chair and closing his eyes while Kathleen's hand remained still on his shoulder. It took all his emotional strength not to reach up and hold it in return. 'Actually I wish more people had asked rather than pretend it wasn't happening. Might have helped me cope with it better. I haven't stammered for years, not really. Not since I played Henry the Fifth – at school, of course. Of all things – I mean, I was still stammering fit to bust then – but I had this great English teacher who'd sussed that I hardly stuttered at all when I was reading and took this huge risk of getting me to play Henry Five.'

'End of stammer, was it? Being onstage? I'd have thought that would have made it worse.'

'Yes,' Rory agreed. 'Me too. But it didn't, believe it or not. Soon as I started being someone else, that was it.'

'And after the play was over?'

'Yes – well, it came a bit, but not nearly so badly. Course, when my therapist heard – and saw – when she realised this could be a key she changed her treatment and besides giving me key words and finger clicks and all that, she suggested that when I hit a bad patch I pretended to be someone else. Sounds a bit facile, but it worked.'

'So why do you think you—' Kathleen began, then stopped.

'Go on,' Rory said.

'It's none of my business.'

'I think it is actually, Kathleen.'

'Not a bit of it,' Kathleen said crisply. 'Now I must to bed – leave you in peace.'

'Kathleen—'

'If I'm to be of any use in the morning, which it is now, I have to get some sleep,' she insisted. 'Now if you're OK? I rather enjoy this, don't you? Sitting up on watch.'

'Yes, I do actually,' Rory agreed. 'As it happens it always makes me think of the play – of *Henry the Fifth*. It's a bit like the night before Agincourt. *Now entertain conjecture of a time when creeping murmur and the poring dark fills the wide vessel of the universe. From camp to camp, through the foul womb of night, the hum of either army stilly sounds, that the fix'd sentinels almost receive the secret whispers of each other's watch.*'

'What was that?' Kathleen suddenly asked, looking out of the window in front of them. 'Didn't I hear something just then? I could swear I did.'

Rory was on his feet and at the office door. Whistling for Dunkum, he picked up the heavy knobkerrie he kept in his office as a precaution and went out into the yard. With one hand on his dog's collar and his stick in the other, and Kathleen carrying a searchlight torch, the two of them made a tour of inspection, but found nothing amiss. All the horses were either fast asleep or idly munching at their hay, while all the gates and doors were shut and locked. Happy there had been no intrusion, Kathleen finally took herself off to her bed, leaving Rory to settle down in his office to his own spell of duty.

Rather than read, Rory sat and drew, something that allowed him to keep an ear out and also helped him keep his eyes open. The first night watch he had ended up reading, only finally to fall fast asleep, so he decided he would use the time instead to do some sketching. He had started a series of horse studies and the concentration needed to work on these kept the adrenalin flowing enough for him to stay on full alert. Two hours later, when it was time for Teddy to come and take over, Rory had no idea of where the time had gone.

Each night up to the eve of the race the procedure was the same, and each night – nothing. Two nights before the big day, however, when Rory came down to take over from Kathleen he found her closely studying the sketchbooks he had left on his desk.

'I take it these are yours?' she asked, apparently unashamed to have been caught in the act. 'They're wonderful. Really. I hope you don't mind – I'm a dreadful snooper.'

'It'd be a bit late if I did,' Rory replied. 'Mind, that is. Of course I don't. Mind that is.'

'They are wonderful,' Kathleen said once more. 'They are really beautiful.'

'They're only sketches,' Rory insisted, suddenly feeling shy. 'It's only work in progress, as they say. Which is a terrible ex-pression. Sounds as if you're digging a road up.'

'You have an amazing talent,' Kathleen said, taking no notice of his protestations. 'And surely isn't this something you should be doing seriously?'

'You mean rather than falling about laughing?'

'I mean seriously,' Kathleen chided him. 'You know what I mean. People who can draw like this—'

'It's nothing,' Rory said, wanting to dismiss the subject, and trying to close the sketchbook. 'It's just something I do.'

'This isn't something anyone just does. This is a gift.'

Kathleen looked round at him with something in her eyes Rory didn't think he'd ever seen before. Then she returned her attention to the next and largest sketchbook, opening it carefully at the page on which Rory had last been working.

'Look at this now,' she said. 'This one of Boyo. It catches everything about him, including—' She stopped, and frowned.

'Including? What? Yes? Including what?'

'The special thing he has,' Kathleen said slowly and quietly. 'His magic.'

'Do you really like it?'

'Like it? This is just brilliant.'

'OK,' Rory decided. 'Then it's yours.'

He took a small penknife from the desk and carefully cut the drawing out of the sketchbook.

'No,' Kathleen protested. 'No, please. Please. What are you doing?'

'I want you to have it.'

'I couldn't. I couldn't take it – I simply couldn't.'

'If you don't . . .' Rory said, holding the drawing up. 'If you don't . . .' He moved as if to tear it in two.

'Are you crazy?' Kathleen said, grabbing hold of his hands to stop him. As she held them in hers, they both fell silent and looked at each other. This time Kathleen was the first to drop her eyes.

'Good,' Rory said finally, setting the drawing down and covering it with a sheet of tissue paper. 'It isn't fixed. I'll do that in the morning.'

'Fixed?'

'Stuff you spray on to stop smudging. A fixative.'

'I don't think you should give this to me at all,' Kathleen muttered behind his back as he finished covering the drawing. 'I really don't.'

'Why not?' Rory shook his head in bewilderment. 'I want you to have it. Because of the horse. Because of everything you've done here with him. Because I just – look, I just want you to have it. Knowing that you have it, that you love it – well.' Rory stopped and swallowed. 'That's great.'

'Rory?' Kathleen said after a moment.

'Rory?' Rory repeated, genuinely astonished. 'I can't have heard right.'

'The thing is, Rory,' Kathleen began, lowering her eyes. 'I really don't feel right – not you giving me this, but me taking it. I really don't.'

'Because?'

'I'd rather not say.'

'Oh, and why would that be?' Rory wondered with an exaggerated sigh. 'Let me guess. Could this be something to do with Blaze Molloy, I wonder?'

'Well – yes. Yes and no. Both really. Yes and no.'

'What a surprise,' Rory said, giving his head a quick scratch. 'Well, it doesn't matter. I'm not taking the drawing back. I still want you to have it – in spite of Mr Blaze Molloy.'

'In spite of—'

'Yes. In spite of. In spite of Mr Blazes Molloy.'

'Oh, I see. Of course.' Kathleen sighed all of a sudden. 'What an idiot. *What* a total idiot.'

'Who – me?'

'No, you fool – me!' Kathleen returned, her eyes flashing. 'Why didn't I see? Of course there was you thinking—'

'What am I meant to think?' Rory demanded. 'Every time I look he has his arm round you, or you're holding hands – or you're in his arms at the railway station, or you're . . . oh, I don't know – so I really don't see what else I'm meant to think.'

'But it isn't like that, Rory,' Kathleen assured him. 'I know that's what it must look like—'

'That's exactly what it looks like.'

'OK,' Kathleen said, changing her tone. 'So suppose it did. So what? I mean, so why should it matter? Why should it matter to you?'

Rory said nothing. He just stood looking at her, scratching the side of his head.

'Rory?'

'Did I say it mattered?' he asked all but inaudibly.

'You started pulling it-matters faces as soon as you mentioned Blaze. *Oh, I suppose this is all to do with Mr Blaze Molloy.* Remember?'

'So?' Rory shrugged, feeling the rug being pulled slowly but surely from under his feet.

'And you know something else?' Kathleen started to smile. 'You haven't stammered or stuttered for a while. Not since you got all hot under the collar about you-know-who.'

'Of course I have,' Rory protested. 'Don't be silly. Of course I – I must have done.'

'Well, you haven't so.'

'Look – Kathleen,' Rory began again, wondering how best to regain the lost ground. 'What you feel about Blaze really – it's really no skin off my nose.'

'I've never known what that meant exactly.'

'Does it matter? Anyway, it isn't – whatever it may mean. Whatever you and Blaze are – whatever you feel about each other—'

'Blaze is my half-brother,' Kathleen interrupted quietly, putting a hand on his. 'I know. I should have told you—'

'Your half-brother?'

'Yes, my half-brother – and yes, I told him to come over. I lied to you, and God forgive me for it, but I only did it for the best.'

'The best being? Not that I mind,' Rory added hastily. 'I

don't mind if you lied. Not that sort of lie. I really don't. Your half-brother? Can I ask how come?'

'After my mother died, and not that long after – because my dad went completely to pieces and people do the strangest things when they're like that, you know – when they're deep in their grief. Anyway, the long and short of it is, he and this woman . . . Da had a child be her, and of course he couldn't – not that he would have anyway – he couldn't marry her because of the way he is and the way my mother and he were . . . and the result was Blaze. Blaze grew up in a village not far away with this woman and her brother, and everyone thought they were man and wife, but that was only because they pretended to be, for Blaze. Then one day Da told me. He said you have another brother, or should we say half-brother, and it was Blaze. And young Blaze be then was making a bit of a name for himself – even though he was still a nipper – pony racing. On the strands. He went on doing just that for a while, then he started riding points – then he came over here.'

'At your instigation.'

'I admit that quite readily. Yes.'

'So why didn't you say? Why the need for subterfuge?'

'Now we didn't know how you'd take it,' Kathleen argued. 'How could we? I'd been as bold as brass anyway, the way I came here, the way I just elbowed me way in. So can you imagine? Imagine if I said *Oh and by the way, here's a relative of mine. I want him riding for you as well*. No, I don't think so, Rory. I don't think that would have been the best way at all.'

'So you pretended he was your boyfriend instead.'

'I never did! Didn't I say we'd never met before?'

'And weren't you off with him the very next minute? Do you think I never smelt the tiniest bit of rat there?'

'I'm devoted to Blaze,' Kathleen said quietly. 'He's a very special boy.'

'He's certainly a very talented one.'

'Anyway. Enough of that,' Kathleen decided. 'As I said earlier, what's the fuss? Why should it matter?'

'Oh, because it does,' Rory groaned. 'Because it does matter. What do you think? Why do you think it matters? Of course it matters.'

'I can't imagine why it should.'

'Are you fishing? Because of course that's something else the Irish are dab hands at.'

'Fishing for what, pray?'

'Fishing to find out why it matters!' Rory mock-glared at her, then groaned again. 'Why do you think it matters? One person being – well. One person minding that another person seems to be – seems to be – well. Attached to another person.'

'You were . . . jealous?' Kathleen finally asked, visibly amazed. 'You?'

'Yes,' Rory insisted. 'Yes, all right. Yes I was jealous. Does that surprise you?'

'Yes.'

'Yes?'

'Yes.'

'Why should it surprise you? You're surprised that I – that I was jealous about you and Blaze?'

'Yes.'

'Why?'

Dumbfounded, for once Kathleen found herself all but speechless.

'Kathleen?' Rory prompted her.

'Because never for one moment did I imagine that some-one like you could possibly be in the slightest bit interested in someone like me, that's why,' she finally replied in a near whisper. 'That's why.'

'Someone like me?'

'Yes! And do stop repeating everything I say! Yes, someone like you!'

Rory stared at her. 'I don't know what someone like me seems like. Not to someone like you.'

'Different. Rich. Sophisticated. Successful. And now, as we gather, a brilliant artist.'

'While you, of course – and by the way you can forget the rich bit – in fact you can forget all the other bits too because it's complete nonsense, your assessment of me – particularly when compared to you.'

'Me as?'

'Well,' Rory said, shrugging hopelessly. 'You as in by far and away the most beautiful girl I have ever seen—'

'Me?'

'Don't start that. You're doing it again. Yes, you. You are . . . you are beautiful. In fact I would go so far as to say ravishingly – no, that's a terrible word. What's wrong with just beautiful? You are the most beautiful girl I have ever seen, as well as the liveliest, the most warm-hearted and just about the sweetest and funniest—'

'Funny? I'm not at all funny.'

'Ah, but you agree with the rest of it, right?' Rory teased her.

'I most certainly do not. It's a load of cod.'

'No, it is not. You're all of those things and more – and you're a brilliant horsewoman as well as everything else.'

Kathleen just looked at him, at an utter loss for words.

'And do you want to know something else, Kathleen Flanagan?'

'If it's worth hearing,' Kathleen replied, tongue in cheek, 'then certainly.'

'I'm very glad you didn't get on that train,' Rory said. 'I really am.'

'And do you want to hear something as well, Rory Rawlins?' she asked in return.

'If it's worth hearing, then certainly.'

'I'm very glad I didn't get on that train as well,' Kathleen said. 'Sure as eggs.'

But all the time they were beginning to declare their true feelings for each other, and explore their hopes for the future, in the yard outside – so very close to where they were standing – there were others who knew exactly what they hoped for the future and were in the process of making sure it happened.

It wasn't until the next morning that everyone found out how close they had been to disaster. No one knew when it had happened exactly, nor at first did anyone know how. Teddy was the first to blame himself, but it was no fault of his. He was just finishing his watch, dawn was breaking, and even though it had been yet another quiet night he thought he would check all the boxes once more before the stable woke up and clicked into its normal routine.

As always Teddy went straight to Boyo's box. This morning he found the horse standing on three legs. Initially he thought the animal was still half asleep and only resting a leg, until he picked up the limb in question, looked at the hoof and found a rusty two-inch nail driven into the sole of the horse's foot.

'Mother of God,' Kathleen sighed when she arrived and saw the damage. 'He never stepped on that, so he didn't. As sure as anything that nail was driven in.'

'And no one heard anything,' Rory repeated, just in case any of his team had overlooked or forgotten anything. 'No one dropped off, or went to spend a penny or anything? So they could have missed something?'

But no one had, and Teddy insisted on blaming himself because according to both Rory and Kathleen, when they had checked the horses at the end of their respective watches, all were apparently sound and healthy.

'But whoever it was would have had to get through the stable door, which is right slap bang in front of the office window,' Rory said. 'Yet nobody saw or heard anything.'

'Boss?' Teddy called from the back of the stable. 'Look.' He pointed up to the roof above him. 'That's how they got in. They lifted the sheeting on the back of the roof. They must have climbed across the other stable roofs and dropped down into this one.'

'OK,' Rory said, having eased the nail out of the horse's hoof as carefully as he could. 'I'm going to call the vet, and Kathleen's going to poultice this hoof, and we're all going to thank our stars and Kathleen here that it wasn't Boyo's hoof they nailed, but dear old Flibberty Gibbet's.'

He shook his head and went off to telephone for the vet.

It had been as easy as that.

After the first suspicion that they were going to attract the wrong kind of attention from intruders, Kathleen had suggested stabling Boyo somewhere anonymous, which was where Rory's friend and neighbour Henry Carmichael had come in. Henry rented Fulford Farm gallops, so the morning after their first nocturnal alarm, once Boyo had finished his piece of work, Rory and Kathleen boxed him up in Henry's horsebox and Henry took him down to his own modest yard, along with the couple of hunter chasers he had been exercising.

Since it was a matter of only a few miles away, Kathleen could easily commute between the two yards to feed, look after and ride the horse in his road work which, aside from one last long easy canter before the race, was all that was planned.

And no one suspected a thing.

The only ongoing argument that still remained unsolved

was who was to ride the horse in the race, the diehards insisting that the best and most experienced jockey should be put
up, while the owners lobbied insistently for their own so far
faultless rider. Rory, who was still keen to listen to both sides,
once again consulted his father.

'Look, Rory, this is a case for common sense. If you could
utilise the boy's weight claim then I could see why you would
still be considering it, but since that doesn't come into the
equation, what's the point in risking using someone who after
all is nothing more than an apprentice? He's ridden once
round Cheltenham in a hunter chase, which to my mind is not
enough. Nor is it the same thing as the hottest Group One race
in the calendar, and you know as well as I do that Cheltenham
takes all the riding there is, and then some more. You have
the breakneck pace of the race to contend with, you have to
be able to deal with the tactics of the best and the toughest
jockeys in the land, you have to be able to handle that terrible
downhill run, keeping your horse balanced at all times so he
doesn't take those two fences by their roots, and then you have
to know how to ride a finish up that heartbreaking final hill.
Now if you think young Molloy is up to that, fine, but if I were
you – and the boy will understand it, sooner or later – you'll
offer one of the top lads the mount. I see there are quite a few
without rides still, and if I really was you, old boy—'

'Which at this very moment you are.'

'—I'd offer the ride to Richard Durden. His intended has
just been withdrawn with a leg.'

'I already did, Dad.'

'And what did he say?'

'He said he wanted to sit on him first.'

Since Rory had given the horse his last piece of fast work at
the weekend, before this final argument had really come to

a head, all he could offer Richard Durden was the chance to ride the horse in an exercise canter. However since Boyo was the type of horse who told you as soon as you sat on him exactly what you had in your hands and under you, Rory was confident that a horseman as skilled and as experienced as Durden would be happy enough just to work the horse at half-speed. Boyo had other ideas.

As soon as he was saddled up and brought out of his box it seemed he knew something was afoot, and laying his ears flat he began to swish his tail ominously. Having walked round the horse a couple of times to get his measure, Richard Durden then asked for a leg up from Rory, and as soon as he was in the saddle he was out of it again, decanted summarily.

Kathleen got a firm hold of the horse's bridle and they tried again. They tried twice more, but Boyo was having none of it.

'Bad-tempered bugger, isn't he?' Durden said, dusting himself down grimly. 'Well, we'll have to show him who's boss then.'

And he promptly vaulted up unaided on to the horse and raised his whip, but it got no further than shoulder height before Boyo bucked him off again, this time so hard that the jockey was flung far further, into the muck heap.

'This horse got a cold back or something? Or is he just some sort of nutcase?'

'There's really nothing the matter with the horse, Mr Durden,' Kathleen informed him.

'Then let's see you sit him,' the jockey said, handing Kathleen the reins.

'Sure thing,' Kathleen said, and vaulted up herself. As soon as he saw who was about to mount him, Boyo had pricked his ears and stopped swishing his tail.

'Fine,' Durden said, staring. 'Obviously a cold back.'

Next time Rory tried to leg Durden into the plate, the horse simply stepped smartly away and swung himself round, leaving his would-be rider with nowhere to go but the ground.

'Thank you,' Durden said, picking himself up for the last time. 'I hope you all enjoyed that. I'd say this horse is unfit for anything except a tin.'

'You got a fan there all right, Guv,' Kathleen laughed as they watched the stained and furious figure disappearing into his car and driving off. 'He'll ride for you any time.'

'I think that certainly answers the question as to who's going to be riding. By the time this gets round the weighing room there won't be a fee big enough to tempt anyone. Anyone good, that is.'

The decision reached, Blaze was informed he had the ride. There was a long silence at the other end of the telephone, broken finally by a quiet voice in Rory's ear.

'You'll not regret it, boss,' he said. 'God bless you.'

Everything was set fair until the next morning, when they all woke up and found everything outside once more frozen hard.

Chapter Twenty-five

Come the Hour

The freeze continued into the weekend, giving the racing Jeremiahs endless pleasure as they all prophesied the cancellation of the great National Hunt meeting scheduled to open on the Tuesday, and when by Monday morning the course was still frozen there was every indication that at the very best they would have to forfeit the opening day and hope to fit in and run all the cancelled races on the next two days, weather permitting.

But then, shortly after seven thirty that very morning, it being the fickle and changeable month of March, the temperature suddenly rose and the heavens opened, deluging the whole of the south of England in thunderous showers followed by an afternoon of strong wind and spasmodic March sunshine. By eight o'clock that evening, Edwin Armstrong, the diligent and urbane clerk of the course, announced that subject to a 6.30 a.m. inspection the following morning the meeting would go ahead, and with Tuesday dawning dry, bright and blustery every road to Cheltenham was choked with traffic and every train headed west was packed with punters.

With no other runners at the meeting, Rory and his

staff stayed at Fulford Farm for both the Tuesday and the Wednesday, not taking their eye off the ball for a moment. The little horse was still at Henry Carmichael's, eating and looking as well as ever, and yet in spite of a total shut-down on any information coming from the stables, a rumour – among many rumours that week – began to circulate that The Enchanted had met with a setback. His price began to drift, the ante-post market showing twenty-five to one across the board by midday.

'If you ask me,' an ex-jockey who was one of the experts on one of the preview programmes opined, 'horses such as The Enchanted have no real place in a Gold Cup line-up. Rumour has it that Dick Durden went down to have a look-see after he'd lost the ride on Sportsmaster, and that he said not only is the horse a pony, but he's got several screws loose.'

'Oh dear,' Grenville had remarked when he had watched the programme with Lynne before setting off for the course. 'Another little soul off the Christmas card list.'

Having never been to Cheltenham before, when she got her first proper view of the wonderful Cotswolds racecourse set in the bowl of Prestbury Park, Alice was impressed. In spite of the vagaries of the weather the track looked in superb condition. It was as if the grass had just been planted and grown for this one occasion. The sun was shining with the particular March light that brings hope and spiritual refreshment to the long wintered soul, the sky was blue, the clouds were high, and the place was packed.

'It's all right,' Grenville assured them as he led Alice, Constance and Lynne along a concourse thronged with racegoers and past packed bars. 'Rory's got a box for us all – belongs to a friend of his old man. The box's owner can't be here today which is tough on him, but lovely for some, namely us.'

Once they were safely ensconced in their private box, which directly overlooked the home straight and from which they could see the whole of the racecourse, the party began to try to relax a little, but the atmosphere was far from the seemingly light-hearted ones that had accompanied their horse's previous appearances. Although naturally nervous on those occasions, they had had nothing to lose. Boyo was unknown, nobody was risking real money on him, the pundits had little or no interest in him and their ambitions had consisted of little more than seeing the horse get round and come home safely. The fact that he had won his first race and then his second was nothing short of miraculous, and at that point they might perhaps all quite happily have drawn a line under it and called it a day. Only their wildest dreams had brought them this far, to have their horse running in the most prestigious National Hunt race not just in the country but in the world.

'If anyone's nursing any second thoughts,' Grenville said as he handed out the racecards, 'I'm afraid it's way too late now. Here are the runners for the Gold Cup,' he explained, open-ing the card, 'and here is our horse.'

'Isn't this odd?' Alice stared at the details of their horse and the colours he would be carrying. 'What is it – a bit less than six months ago? About six months ago we didn't even know each other, and yet here we all are.'

'And what a thing, too,' Millie remarked, her invitation earned by the fact that if it hadn't been for Millie in the first place none of this would have happened.

'But it is extraordinary, really, when you think about it,' Alice continued. 'And never mind what happens or doesn't happen, because rather like Humphrey Bogart in *Casablanca*, we shall always have this. Always.'

'I'll certainly drink to that,' Grenville said, handing round the champagne. 'Mind you, today I shall drink to most things, but first to what Alice has just said. To The Enchanted Partnership.'

They all raised their glasses to make the toast. 'The Enchanted Partnership.'

'And may the best horse win,' Grenville added.

'And let that one be ours,' Constance said firmly. 'I need the money.'

'Don't say you still haven't paid for your share, Constance,' Grenville teased her.

'Cheque's in the post, Glanville,' Constance replied, with a wink to Alice. 'First-class stamp, too.'

'Only pity is Anthony couldn't be here today,' Alice said. 'But, of course, too much excitement would not be good news.'

'There's going to be too much excitement anyway,' Constance told her. 'Anthony said he's had what he calls a bit of a tilt. Says if the horse wins it'll pay for his op and a recuperative cruise. For two,' she added with another wink. 'I told him I'd stay home and try to keep his lid on, but he insisted I didn't miss the race – and anyway, what chance would I have with someone who escaped from Colditz twice? We locked him up in his bedroom without even a telephone, in case he rang one of those racing line things. We also gave him an old klaxon horn Rory found in the garage which he can sound in case of an emergency, because Maureen's on watch. And she's been told to keep an eye on him and to tell him the result. So now. What are the chances of us all becoming squillionaires, please?'

'The prize money's excellent,' Grenville told her, pointing to the figures on the card. 'A hundred and twenty thousand pounds to the winner, but since anything has to be divided by four less Rory's percentage, even if we did win I don't think we'd be sailing the Mediterranean in our private yachts, right?'

'Don't be so vulgar, Grenville,' Constance reprimanded him. 'I'm not talking money money. I'm talking about just supposing we won. Winning something like this makes you a squillionaire, which is nothing to do with money. Winning a race like this must be something money can't possibly buy. This sort of thing can stand life on its head. So here's *hoping*,' Constance concluded, raising her glass, 'and here's *toping*.'

Rory put his head round the door of the box just before the second race.

'Horse is fine, everyone,' he said, trying not to sound breathless. 'Travelled fine, looks fine. Anyone know where I can be sick?'

'You do look a little pale.'

'I feel a little pale, Alice.' Rory breathed slowly in and out. 'No, I'm fine really. And everything's fine. The horse is fine, so there we are, and here we are. Everything will be fine. Don't worry. See you all down in the paddock.'

Down in the pre-parade ring, with less than forty minutes now to go to the off, Kathleen kept her charge walking round in an easy swinging rhythm, talking quietly to him all the time and sometimes singing to him. Then, shortly before she was due to take Boyo into the main parade ring, she happened to look up and away from her horse for the first time for a long time and saw her father and brother leaning on the rails smiling at her.

'Looks a picture, Kathleen,' Padraig said with a whistle and a tilt of his head. 'You've done him proud, my girl, you have so.'

'Everyone's over,' Liam told her the next time she came past them. 'Practically the whole of Cronagh.'

'The church is clean out of candles!' Padraig called after her, on her last lap. 'Good luck, now, girl!'

'Good luck, Katie!' Liam shouted. 'And to the little horse, God bless him!'

The parade ring was packed to the very top with everyone anxious to get a closer look at the contenders for the Gold Cup. Kathleen could hardly believe that she was here and this was really happening. The atmosphere was electric, the buzz around the ring making her flesh turn to goose bumps. She put a hand up to stroke Boyo's neck. But the gesture was more to calm herself than to soothe her horse, who wasn't turning a hair, even though the animal in front of him was beginning to boil over already, swishing its tail and kicking out now and then with a hind foot. She glanced up at the huge electronic price board that showed the approximate odds and saw to her astonishment that the price of twenty-five to one that had been on offer some ten to fifteen minutes ago for The Enchanted was now as little as fourteen to one.

Now the parade ring was filling up with trainers and connections – owners, officials, television commentators and reporters, and finally the jockeys, streaming out from the weighing room in their brilliant colours, some of them joking with their colleagues in order to allay the nerves they were feeling, others careless of showing their tension, tapping their boots with their whips as they made their way to touch caps to their owners and take their last instructions from their trainers. Then they were mounting, legged up by trainers, some of whom walked with their mounted horses round the last couple of circuits of the parade ring, calling up their last thoughts, while some of the horses began to prance and play up, others started to break into a slight sweat, and some were as calm as police horses facing a riot. Racegoers abandoned their positions by the ring to hurry to the Tote windows or the bookmakers, while others rushed back to the stands to get the best vantage point possible, as a now orderly line of horses made their way from the paddock to parade in front of the grandstands, lads and lasses at their heads, some assistants following out on to the course in case of any accident or mishap. Red-coated huntsmen on strapping horses waited to escort the parade, and cheers were already rising from the jam-packed stands as the line of horses and handlers walked and jogged in front of them.

'The runners are parading in racecard order,' the course commentator called. 'At the head is the favourite, County Gent, followed by number two, Duke's Biscuit, three, Jenrich, followed by number four, Jenuflecked, five the French challenger, Le Corbeau, six the second favourite, My Pal Joey, number seven one of the Irish, Na Shonaca, followed by Rumbledumble, number eight. Out of order at nine for some reason is number ten, Stopdat – then number nine, another Irish challenger, Spun Silk, number eleven is The Enchanted, followed by the raider from north of the border, Ticketpleez, number twelve, thirteen is Tyron, fourteen is Vulcan Flyer, fifteen is Welsh Harebit and last but not least the only mare in the field, Moosey.'

A great roar went up as, with the parade over, the horses, released by their lads, about-faced to the left and began to canter down to the start at the bottom left-hand corner of the track.

'My,' Alice sighed, standing at the front of the box and watching the spectacle. 'What excitement.'

'Don't tell me you're actually going to watch the race, Alice?' Grenville laughed.

'Of course not,' Alice replied, heading for the door. 'I shall be out here if anyone wants me.'

'Did he go down all right, Grenville?' Lynne asked, still

watching through her race glasses. 'I don't know the difference between going down well and going down badly.'

'He's nice and calm, if that's what you're worried about,' Millie told her. 'One or two of the others have got pretty hot, even though there's quite a cold wind.'

'I'd have thought horses would run better hot than cold,' Constance said, lighting a cheroot. 'I was always better for the sun on my back.'

'Hot as in sweating up, Connie,' Grenville said. 'Means they start taking it out of themselves.'

'Of course, horses can sweat, can't they?' Constance mused. 'It's only we ladies who glow.' She thought she felt and looked calm. It was only when she put her glasses to her eyes that she realised she was having difficulty keeping them steady, to say the least.

'They're under starter's orders!' the course commentator called, as the horses got into line by the starting tape, only for two of them to break the formation and so necessitate another call-in from the starter.

'He's squeezed right up on the rails,' Lynne observed. 'Hope he's OK.'

'Rory's told Blaze to try to get an inside berth first time round, and also to kick on if he can and make it,' Grenville put in.

'No – a horse has come right in front of him!' Lynne exclaimed. 'Practically pushed him through the rails!'

'They're in line . . .' called the commentator.

'It's number thirteen,' Millie observed. 'Eddie Rampton's other runner.'

'And they're off!' the commentator announced, his proclamation almost drowned by the almighty roar that rose from the grandstands and enclosures as the race began.

'They're away to a good level start – except for Vulcan Flyer who's wheeled round, and The Enchanted who must have lost a good six lengths as they set off.'

'Blast,' Grenville cried. 'That looked quite deliberate to me.'

Blaze knew it was deliberate. He'd had Kevin Billings's mount Tyron in his own horse's face ever since they filed out on to the racecourse proper, Billings shadowing Blaze's every move and leaning his horse on Boyo at every opportunity, so Blaze knew something was up. He kept trying to avoid Billings, and then just before the tape was released Blaze and Boyo were all but knocked sideways through the guard rail by Tyron. Seeing the field charge off without him, Blaze thought better than to panic his horse by kicking and flapping at him, so once he had got him straight he jumped him off just as if he hadn't missed the break at all. Boyo picked up at once, deciding for himself to cut down the distance between himself and the back markers, an objective that by the time they cleared the first fence to all intents and purposes he had achieved. In the run from the second fence to the next, Blaze and Boyo made up more ground, going from tenth place into seventh, only to have Billings on Tyron loom up on their outside.

'Going somewhere, Mick?' Billings yelled at him, over the thunder of hooves, the slapping of leather and the shouts of the other riders. 'Because if you are, I'm coming with you!'

'What's going on out there?' Grenville wondered, race glasses trained hard on the action. 'It's that horse again – Tyron. He's crowding Boyo!'

'What?' Lynne cried. 'God, he is too! Look – he's running into him!'

'And as they approach the third,' the commentator called, 'My Pal Joey continues to make the running a good two lengths clear of Le Corbeau, while behind there seem to be some traffic problems with Tyron, The Enchanted and Duke's Biscuit – and Duke's Biscuit has gone at that one! Tyron appeared to cannon into him and Duke's Biscuit has gone – leaving The Enchanted now third with Tyron ranging once more up alongside him as the rest of the field have all flown that fence – with Le Corbeau still in second, Tyron now third, The Enchanted fourth, followed by Spun Silk, County Gent, Jenuflecked, Na Shonaca, Rumbledumble and the mare Moosey.'

'He's trying to break his rhythm,' Grenville said over the commentator. 'Look! Every time Boyo goes to pass him, the other horse cuts in front of him and then slows down. What a dirty trick. What a simply filthy trick!'

'Is it allowed?' Constance wondered. 'Should they not perhaps stop the race?'

'They can hardly do that, Connie!' Grenville called back, glasses still trained on the action. 'Blaze is just going to have to find a way of dealing with it!'

At the first of the line of fences in the back straight, having forced Blaze to take a pull on The Enchanted to avoid being run into the wing of the fence, Billings straightened his horse and did his best to run into the back of the French horse that was still lying second. Disturbed by the proximity of the animal all but jumping up on him, Le Corbeau made a mistake, went through the top of the fence and down on to his nose on the landing side. His jockey made a fine recovery to get his horse racing again, but by then Billings had pushed Tyron past Le Corbeau so that he was lying in second place, some four lengths off My Pal Joey, exactly where it had been planned he should be. As soon as he slotted himself in behind the leader, Billings kept his mount in hand, all the time glancing over his shoulder at what was coming at him, then riding across any horse that tried to overtake him. At the last fence along the back straight Tyron ran Na Shonaca out, to the sound of a huge roar of disappointment from the enormous Irish contingent, many of whom, knowing a thing or two, had backed the horse in from twenty-five to one to sixteens.

Swinging out of the back straight and heading now downhill for the first time the field faced two of the most formidable fences on the course, both downhill, the second one being the harder since the ground on the landing side fell away while the running rail into the straight suddenly came into play, bowed as it was into the course so as to carry the horses out before they swung left-handed into the home straight.

Blaze knew what was going on. He had ridden in far too many bareback, rope-bridled pony races on the strands of Cork and Kerry not to know a dirty trick when he saw one, so the slow, slow, quick-quick slow tactic employed by the broken-nosed Billings came as nothing new to him. But what it did mean was that Blaze could not now allow Boyo to run his usual race, which was of course the whole point of the exercise. Rory, Blaze and Anthony had gone through every possible aspect of the event the previous evening, a discussion that had left nothing to chance and so had included possible spoiling tactics, the sort of so-called jockeymanship that had previously marred several of the more prestigious races, particularly those with a lively ante-post market.

'Which is why I always say we should have a Tote monopoly, like the French,' Anthony had pronounced. 'About the only thing I like about the French, though.'

'Besides their wine, their food, their women, their cities, their bread, and practically everything else,' Rory had replied.

And so now here it was happening to Blaze and Boyo as the race unfolded, a horse entered deliberately as a spoiler, a horse whose jockey was riding under strict instructions to do everything he could within a certain amount of reason to put off the opposition and allow the stable's favoured horse the best and most trouble-free run possible. So Blaze and Boyo's only hope of salvation lay in running a race that was the opposite of those they had run so far, a dangerous tactic which could easily backfire, since it meant dropping the horse out of the race – and often when a rider did that the horse switched off and the day was lost.

But there was nothing else Blaze could now do. Ahead of him he saw Billings perched up on his tall and burly horse's neck, taking good looks around him as they approached the first of the downhill fences. It was clear this was not going to be a short-lived diversion, so Blaze knew he had to start steadying his horse without for a moment allowing him to become unbalanced – and all of this at the most dangerous part of the course. Any loss of momentum coming downhill could easily result in the horse's not having enough power to take off safely as it ran towards the intimidating obstacle, and that would mean end of story. So Blaze chose to decelerate not going into these two downhill fences but after them, as he and Boyo turned into the home straight for the first time – if they got that far. This meant he now had to outsmart Billings, and once again his pony-racing skills came to the fore as he feinted to come up on the inside of Tyron, only at the last moment, as Tyron closed the gap, to switch to the outside, hoping and praying that in doing so he hadn't broken The Enchanted's fine rhythm.

He hadn't. Swinging right of Tyron at the first downhill fence Boyo jumped fast and immaculately, landing running, but not quite fast enough to get clear of Tyron, on whom Billings was now hard at work, beating the horse and turning the air blue with his curses against Blaze and Boyo. Dropping down faster and faster to the second downhill fence, again Blaze pre-guessed his adversary, reckoning that Billings, predictably enough, would think Blaze was about to do the same thing at this next fence – go round the outside – which indeed Blaze feinted to do. Billings immediately pulled Tyron wide to cut off all sight of the fence whereupon Blaze at once shortened his left rein to cut inside and safely up and over, using to the full the deftness and agility of the little horse.

'What is happening, please?' Alice asked, putting her head round the box door for the first time. 'Are we still in one piece?'

'Just about, Alice,' Grenville called back to her. 'You ought to come and see this. This promises to be the race of a life-time.'

Alice crept into the box and half hid herself against the wall at the edge of the open window, peering round through half-closed eyes as the race continued.

'But this I don't understand,' Grenville continued. 'Just as he appeared to have the measure of that horse, Blaze seems to be taking a pull.'

'Yes, he does,' Millie agreed. 'I hope everything's all right. I hope the horse hasn't gone wrong.'

What Blaze was hoping was that the horse wouldn't go wrong, that he wouldn't switch off and go to sleep. Knowing Boyo he somehow doubted it, but equally well did he know that horses have minds and moods of their own, and that the one thing a really good horse hates is being disappointed. So somehow – and he didn't know quite how – he had to keep the horse sweet. He had to keep him believing. So as he eased him ever so slightly back off the pace, Blaze began to sing to him. As he turned the horse into the home straight, in a fine lyric tenor voice Blaze sang 'The Minstrel Boy' to his horse, to the slack-jawed astonishment of other jockeys now ranging up alongside them.

He saw Billings looking round again, and guessed that

seeing Boyo dropping right back through the field, the mean-minded rider would turn his attention to more ready dangers, which indeed he did as the field jumped the two fences in the straight for the second time. Billings now proceeded to try to disrupt the rhythm and racing flow of what now appeared to be My Pal Joey's closest rivals, Jenrich, who had made a move up through the field, Spun Silk, who was going exceptionally well and the bay mare Moosey who as always was running her gallant heart out.

'So as they go out into the country for the last time,' the commentator called, 'and with Stopdat and The Enchanted going backwards through the field, both appearing to have run their races, it's still My Pal Joey taking them along at a really good gallop, My Pal Joey, Jenrich, Spun Silk, Moosey the four leading horses with Tyron still in close attention and now moving up to jump into third place at that one, almost carrying Moosey out through the wing there . . .'

With the hill in the straight climbed and now behind him, to everyone watching it might seem as though The Enchanted had indeed shot his bolt, and yet even as he began another verse of his song Blaze felt the horse come back on the bridle, which was what he had been praying for all the way up the stiff climb past the grandstands. Of all places to choose on the course, switching a horse off when it was going uphill was the most dangerous, as passing the winning post the horse could easily think his work for the day was over. So when Blaze asked the horse to pick up he half expected Boyo not to do so. Instead, to his delight, Boyo took a hold once more of the bit and swung back out into the country full of running and – Blaze suddenly felt – determination.

At the first open ditch in the back straight Rumbledumble fell, the horse simply failing to pick up and crashing through the fence, sending his jockey spinning over his head and also bringing down Welsh Harebit, who seemed to be going particularly well at the time. The falls happened in front of Boyo but by then Blaze had tracked to the inside and so had a good, clear and unimpeded run at the line of fences, a row of obstacles that finished before the turn downhill with another ditch where the horizon lay so far below as horse and jockey jumped that it appeared as if they were jumping off the edge of the world. Boyo flew it, landing full of himself and swinging left downhill with only the lightest of instruction from Blaze.

Ahead, with four fences to jump, they had only five horses now in their sights, Boyo having moved up easily but not overly quickly through a fast depleting field, past other horses beaten now but not fallen, more or less running on empty, two of them looking as though they might be pulled up at the top of the hill, so murderous had been the gallop. Blaze wasn't exactly sure which horses were ahead of him, although he could make out My Pal Joey's colours, and those of Spun Silk and the mare Moosey, who was still somehow hanging in there, in spite of the regular interference she was suffering from the horse in the hands of Billings. The leading quartet, or maybe quintet, Blaze thought, seemed to be coming back to him, or else Boyo was even more full running than he had thought, but whatever was happening he knew if he hugged the rail down the hill and into the home turn he could come off it at speed, pick up the best of the ground and give it his best shot.

It was then that he heard the sound of a horse behind him, the noise of its rhythmic breathing, the powerful thrumming of its great hooves, and up alongside him, on the very inside of him, up through a gap Blaze had carelessly left, moved the forgotten man of the race, County Gent. As he galloped past The Enchanted, his rider not moving, Blaze felt his blood change. He felt himself suddenly grow cold and he felt suddenly dense and very stupid. For the one thing he had not thought about since he had dropped his own horse back was the chance of some other horse picking him off, having done exactly the same thing.

He remembered seeing Dennis Maloney as he had eased his way back to the pack of chasing horses, sitting as still as a mouse on the big black horse from Lambourn, the easy winner of the King George VI chase. He should have known then to watch for the horse, to trail him if necessary, for the big horse had one weakness. He liked to come from behind and he did not like to be challenged once he had made his move.

Twice before when this had happened the horse had simply downed tools and lost races he was winning easily. Blaze should have remembered this and he knew he should have done so, because during his pre-race briefing the fact had been dunned into him. And now the big horse was through.

Over the first downhill fence they both flew, Boyo now a good length down on a horse that still seemed to be only in third gear. Knowing he couldn't take his rival here, Blaze did some quick thinking, and then on the run to the next fence he thought some more, but nothing occurred to him until they were flying the most dangerous fence on the course for the second time, the third from home, the last of the downhill fences, where just ahead of them Blaze saw Spun Silk make a mistake that cost him half a dozen lengths and meant Moosey's pilot had to check her and pull her round the still stumbling Irish horse.

Roars and cries and cheers rose from the stands as the field turned for home, a great wall of sound, a noise that had so intrigued the mighty Arkle long ago that he had turned to stare at where the noise was coming from and nearly fallen for doing so. But today the noise thrilled and inspired not only Blaze but the brave horse under him, who all at once quickened, well before Blaze had even thought of asking him to do so, hugging the rail on his left so tightly that he could have been running on tracks.

'And now as they turn for home it's still My Pal Joey!' the commentator called. 'My Pal Joey who has made every inch of the running then Jenrich, who will not be shaken off, Tyron, who at last seems to be weakening, Moosey whose task now seems impossible, with Spun Silk, who made that serious blunder at the last dropping back fast – but County Gent is starting his run! County Gent who has been making ground hand over fist downhill is now swinging wide into the straight – followed by The Enchanted! The Enchanted is tight on the rails – The Enchanted, who has also made up an enormous amount of ground to get back into the reckoning – there's only half a length between County Gent and The Enchanted – and now the two of them are only three or four lengths behind the leaders as they approach the second last!'

First of all Blaze wanted to see where Tyron was, in case the horse was still in the reckoning, and on the run to the second last he could see him only a length or so ahead of him, zigzagging across the course from sheer exhaustion, being severely beaten up by his jockey. Someone behind Blaze yelled at Billings to pull his horse up, but Billings took no notice, driving his semi-conscious horse on in the hope of carrying out yet another challenger. Again Blaze had only a split second to make up his mind about where to jump and how, yet it seemed Boyo made up his mind for him, jinking first to the right then changing legs and heading left of a horse too tired to be able to obey the wilful demands of his rider even if he had wanted to do so. Tyron staggered as Boyo ranged alongside him and in that moment Blaze saw his opportunity and asked Boyo for a big one. At once the horse came up in his hands and they were airborne, yards outside where the leading horses had left the ground, but as they flew Billings took one last chance, sticking his left leg out as Blaze and Boyo sailed by him and catching Blaze's right foot, knocking it clean out of its stirrup.

How the blow didn't knock Blaze completely from the saddle he would never know. Perhaps it was due to his legendary 'stick' or perhaps it was due to Boyo's beautiful balance. Whatever the reason, Blaze's right foot was out of the pedal and swinging loose and in a flash, he pulled his left foot free as well, all at once realising that if he landed acey-deucy, one foot in and one foot out, the odds were one hundred to one on that he would be catapulted out of the saddle and out of the Gold Cup.

So he landed with his horse on the far side of the fence sitting right back in his saddle with both legs stuck out in front of him and reins as long as curtain pulls. Yet he stayed there, he stuck on the horse, and even as Boyo began to power away from the fence the nimble Blaze, blessing his days as the champion pony racer in the west of Ireland, was already slotting his feet back into the irons and gathering his reins for one last fight.

'Dear God above us!' Grenville cried to the rest of the box. 'Did you ever see anything like that!'

'I didn't!' Alice shouted back over the tumult, her hands in front of her eyes. 'I didn't see a thing! What's happening, someone?'

Then she looked and what she saw was what everyone that day saw, one of the very best and most inspiring finishes to a horse race any of them had ever seen.

'There really is very little in it now!' the commentator was shouting over the tannoy and above the ever growing crescendo of sound. 'As the field runs to the last My Pal Joey has finally surrendered the lead to Jenrich! But County Gent is not finished with yet – nor is The Enchanted, in spite of the rider's losing his irons at the last fence! So on the run to the last there are four horses together – Jenrich, My Pal Joey – the still improving County Gent, who seems to have timed his run just right – and The Enchanted! The Enchanted, who seems to have caught his third if not his fourth wind! And at the last they all rise together – Jenrich landing first and My Pal Joey now making a mistake! The horse's first mistake and he's all but down on his knees – and now he's passed by County Gent who landed yards the other side of the fence – then The Enchanted! The Enchanted lands third, a length down, and still running on – but they both have to face the hill now! The famous Cheltenham hill now faces both these brave horses – and it's County Gent now! It's County Gent who is lengthening his stride and beginning to put daylight between him and The Enchanted, who doesn't seem to have anything left!'

'Damn, damn, damn,' Grenville said to himself through gritted teeth.

'Oh, Geoffrey Alcott Wilson!' Alice shouted, watching the finish unfolding. 'Hell and dam's ladders!'

'I'm afraid we're roasted,' Constance observed sadly, putting her binoculars down.

'Hang on, everyone,' Millie said. 'Hang on – hang on in there!'

Blaze knew he had to wait his moment. If he moved too soon there might not be enough gas left in the tank to complete his challenge, and if he moved too late the huge-striding County Gent would have swallowed the ground up and galloped past the post. He had to time it just right. He knew there was something left in his horse because he felt it still there in his hands, but he also knew he couldn't and wouldn't beat the effort out of him, so he waited. And waited. And waited.

And then he pounced.

He was only a length down but there were only a hundred and fifty yards to run and he waited for a sign and when he saw the sign he pounced. They both did.

There were in fact two signs. First County Gent's head went up – only marginally, but one thing young Blaze had learned on the sands of Kerry and of Cork is that the very second an animal's head goes up is the moment it is beat; and the other sign was from Dennis Maloney, from the champion jockey in person, who could not resist a quick look round. It was only a very quick look, but he looked over the wrong shoulder. Expecting the young thruster to be coming up on his inner, he took a split-second look over his left shoulder and when he saw it Blaze knew he had got him.

Down in the drive position he sat, down he went and hard he drove, throwing the reins at the back of Boyo's head, shouting battle cries of victory at him in Gaelic, thrusting and driving the horse up the final lung-bursting, heart-popping hundred yards, the two horses now neck and neck, Dennis Maloney throwing everything at his horse, producing all his great skills, riding one of his greatest finishes ever – but it just wasn't enough. It just wasn't enough to beat the horse racing at his side, sticking out his proud head, all but leaving the ground to fly home the winner, finally by no more than a head.

For a moment no one knew who had won. The crowds that had been roaring a sound that could be heard for miles fell all but silent as the two gallant horses slowed to a canter then to a trot and finally to a leg-weary walk as they too awaited the result.

'Did you get up, lad?' Dennis Maloney gasped, barely able to catch his breath. 'God, I don't even know who you are.'

'Blaze Molloy, Mr Maloney sir.' Blaze grinned at him, sticking out a muddy hand, which Dennis shook.

'There's a thing,' the other Irishman grinned. 'They'll all be saying – *look at those two fine sportsmen* – when little will they know all we're doing is introducing ourselves!'

'Here is the result!' the official announcement rang out. 'First number eleven – The Enchanted—'

Boyo's name was hardly heard, such was the roar from the stands.

'First number eleven – The Enchanted!' the official repeated. 'Second number one, County Gent—'

Drowned by another mighty cheer.

'And third number three, Jenrich! The fourth horse was number nine, Spun Silk.'

'Well done, Blaze,' Dennis said, this time putting an arm round the young tyro's shoulders. 'Say what you like about old Mother Erin, but she doesn't half turn us out.'

Blaze touched his cap to one of his great heroes, thanked him, then turned Boyo round to face the stands and the long walk back into the unsaddling enclosure. He had never even imagined this moment, not in his wildest dreams, so he had no idea of what it might be like. In spite of his bravura, the most Blaze had ever hoped and prayed for was that one day he would just ride in a race at Cheltenham, and now that it had happened he still didn't know how. Nor had it really sunk in that not only had he ridden in a race, he had ridden in the greatest steeplechase of them all. And not only that – it seemed he had won it.

Kathleen was waiting for him at the entrance to the track that leads past the stands and into the unsaddling enclosure. She had watched the entire race away from everyone she knew. Once she had turned Boyo away to the start she had taken up her selected position, and simply prayed. Now she was proudly leading in her horse, the horse she had helped deliver into the world, the horse she had reared herself. The people in the enclosures she and her horse passed by were still beside themselves with the power and magic of the great race, showering love, compliments and congratulations on horse and jockey alike. Television crews with cameras on their shoulders and microphones stuck on sticks ran backwards before them, twenty thousand flash bulbs burst around them, hands were clapped sore, throats were roared red. Yet nothing could match the noise and tumult that awaited them in the unsaddling enclosure.

Rory was there, waiting at the last turn in the path before it opened to reveal the packed enclosure. Kathleen put out her free arm and hugged Rory to her and he hugged her to him. He slapped Blaze on the thigh and Blaze took Rory's cap and threw it into the crowds. As soon as the people saw the horse and rider a roar went up that was loud enough to have announced victory in a great battle. Eyes filled with tears, hats were thrown in the air and the police had to link arms to cordon off what looked as if it might be a stampede to greet the victors in what would go down as one of the most enthralling Gold Cups ever run. And there in the paddock were waiting Boyo's faithful band of ecstatic owners: Constance, Alice, Lynne and Grenville, transformed by the horse, transformed by the moment.

As things began to calm down and the snappers came forward to take their pictures, a most beautiful Irish tenor voice was raised somewhere in the middle of the throng. And at the sound of it, everyone stopped to look and to listen.

'Bless this horse, O Lord we pray!' the singer sang, and when they heard the words the crowd roared once again, before the song was taken up by a whole choir of racegoers from Ireland.

'Bless this horse, O Lord we pray –
Make it win a race each day!
Bless the jockey, chimney thin –
Bless his mum for feedin' him gin!
Bless this horse that we may be
Richer for each victor – eee!'

'Three cheers now!' another Irish voice commanded. 'Three cheers for Blaze Molloy – and three more for a great racehorse!'

'Well,' Constance said when the cheers had died down. 'I think that's the last we'll ever hear of his being little, don't you?'

Then all at once, as the sound of the cheering died away, the odd and quite unexpected sound of the very opposite was heard coming from a crowd that had gathered round the unmistakable figures of Eddie Rampton and the owners of My Pal Joey.

'Well I'll be blowed,' Lynne said, having caught sight of the objects of the crowd's derision. 'If it isn't my ex and my ex.'

'Ex and ex what, precisely, Lynne dear?' Constance wondered, putting up her race glasses and directing them at what seemed now about to be a skirmish.

'Ex-old man and ex-best friend.' Lynne grinned. 'Seems they're getting the bird.'

'You're going to enjoy this, Rory,' a tall, languid man remarked, joining the group by the winners' enclosure. 'You should be there, rubbing your hands in glee. And by the way, one and all, well done with your horse. What a champion, eh? James Roderick from the *Sporting Life*.' He shook all their hands and gave The Enchanted a well-earned pat on his steaming neck.

'What's going on exactly, Jim?' Rory asked. 'It seems the people are taking against Eddie Rampton. Right?'

'Spot on, cocky.' James laughed. 'He can never shut it, can he? Starting mouthing off his owners, saying his jockeys' race tactics were all their idea. At which the owner, whatever his name is—'

'Gerry Fortune,' Lynne volunteered. 'He can never shut it either.'

'Too right, my lovely. Mr Fortune started slamming back at old Eddie, saying he'd cooked it all up and that he never knew a thing about it. Whereupon all hell broke loose, and . . .' He stopped to look round at the crowd surrounding the still wildly gesticulating figure of Eddie Rampton. 'And to judge from the sound of it,' he continued, 'is breaking even more loose. Not the sort of thing one wants to see here in the Holy of Holies.'

At that moment a tall, well-dressed figure with a pair of large race glasses slung over one shoulder appeared on the scene, followed by a retinue of assistants, reporters and policemen, all headed for the skirmish.

'Ah,' James said. 'The cavalry have arrived. I would say any moment now the connections will be called in to have a quiet word with the stewards – or, seeing it's old Eddie, not so quiet will be more the order of the day.'

'And what will happen to them, do you think, James?' Lynne asked, giving him her very best smile, much to the discomfort of Grenville, who began slapping the side of his leg with his racing hat. 'I do hope they'll all be clapped in irons and set adrift.'

'Very possibly, Miss . . . ?'

'Faraday,' Lynne replied. 'Lynne Faraday.'

'Soon to be Lynne Fielding,' Grenville said with a smile and a nod. 'Very soon to be Lynne Fielding.'

'Well, Miss Faraday soon to be Mrs Fielding,' James said with a grin, 'I would say there's every chance of that happening. Mr Rampton is forever getting himself into trouble, and having seen that race I doubt if this time he'll get off with just a warning, I don't think any of them will. One thing racing's powers-that-be most certainly do not like is anything that brings the sport into disrepute – and there's no doubt that the way they ran that second horse did exactly that.'

'Goody.' Lynne laughed. 'I shall stand outside wherever it is—'

'Portman Square,' Rory volunteered.

'I shall stand outside Portman Square and throw rotten eggs at all of them.'

'And I shall be there right by your side, my dear,' Constance assured her. 'What an awful lot of flotsam.'

'Oh, my,' Alice said as they all waited to be presented with the Gold Cup. 'I've just remembered the children.'

'I didn't know your kids were here, Alice,' Lynne said, as Edwin Armstrong beckoned them to come forward to receive the most coveted trophy in National Hunt racing.

'They're not.' Alice smiled. 'But I do hope they were watching.'

One of them had been. Although Joe and Georgina were unable to get to the course itself because of Joe's work and the children's schooling, Joe watched it in a betting shop round the corner from his office while Georgina managed to watch at home, having persuaded her friend and neighbour to do the return school run. By the time The Enchanted was making his effort up the hill Georgina was standing on the sofa screaming so loudly that two passers-by – thinking someone was being murdered – rang her doorbell to make sure everything was all right.

'Yes! Yes!' Georgina laughed. 'God, I'm sorry – it's just – it doesn't matter. Yes it does!' she suddenly shouted at the two utterly nonplussed strangers standing staring slack-jawed at her. 'Yes it does matter! My mum's horse has just won the Cheltenham Gold Cup!'

As she tried to persuade the bewildered but now beaming young couple to come in for a celebratory drink Georgina's phone rang.

'Hi!' she said happily as she answered it. 'Hi – Chris! Chris – were you watching? You were watching, weren't you?'

'Yeah, well, no actually,' Christian confessed with an embarrassed laugh. 'I mean I actually forgot.'

'You what? You forgot?' Georgina repeated in disbelief.

'Yeah, I know, sis. But honestly, at that price – like one hundred and fifty to one? I thought, *Come on – what sort of a no-hope is that*? So I forgot – yeah.'

'But he won, Chris! Mum's horse won!'

'I know, I know,' Chris laughed. 'Why I'm ringing. I was in Horrids – in the audio and television department looking at stuff and there was Mum all over the screen. Getting this little gold cup. I mean – what? But he wasn't anywhere near one hundred and fifty to one, sis.'

'No, you dibbock!' Georgina laughed. 'But you had him at a hundred and fifty to one! Like me! That's what an ante-post voucher is, apparently – that's the price we had him at. You realise how much money you have just won?'

'You are kidding me,' Christian said, his whole tone of voice changed. 'Seriously? You really are kidding me.'

'I am not kidding you, Chris,' Georgina assured him. 'You are a rich young man.'

'Fantastic.'

'You can say that again.'

'No – *fantastic*, sis. I mean wow.'

'You bet, bro. So too do I.'

'Hey!' Christian said, as if suddenly realising something. 'This is cool – because you know what this means, right? This is cool because it means I can pay Mum back what I owe her.'

'No, I don't think so, Chris,' Georgina replied. 'I don't think either of us is ever going to be able to do that.'

Epilogue

MAY

Turned Away

Summer came early. April was fine and warm, with little rain, but May simply burst into spring which in two weeks became summer. Kathleen and Rory roughed their newly crowned champion off as soon as the celebrations had died down and turned him out in his favourite paddock with plenty of company. At first, as if back home in Ireland, he had hardly strayed from the area around the gate, happy to graze on the fresh spring grass that was already full of goodness but seemingly loath to turn his back on human company. But a week or so later he was gone from the gate, and when Kathleen went to check his welfare morning, noon and night she would find him in what had fast become his favourite spot, a shady oasis afforded by two enormous horse chestnut trees under which lay a shallow spring-fed pond from which Boyo and his playmates could drink and in whose mud they could lazily roll and cool.

The oddest thing was that he no longer looked smaller than his companions. It was as if the race had made him grow

459

taller, and when Rory and Kathleen had put a measuring stick to him, something they had never done in fact, just in case he turned out to be as small as his critics would have him be, they found to their delight and astonishment that in his shoes he stood at fifteen hands three, no longer the size of a milk pony. His six months as a racehorse had certainly brought him on, although nothing did so to such purpose as his magnificent, heroic and famous run in the Gold Cup. When the four owners and their trainer had stood admiring him in the unsaddling enclosure they had all remarked on how much more of a horse he seemed to have become, which they say is often the way with winning horses. They look like winners. They look stronger for their race. They look altogether bigger for their victory – and Boyo was no exception. As he had stood there proudly in the enclosure with the steam of his efforts rising from his heaving flanks and the breath of his labours steaming from his flared nostrils, he had looked mighty. Not tall, not huge, not statuesque, but strong and mighty, as if his victory had already transformed him from a good athletic and burly sort of racehorse into the near mythic creature he was to become, the winner of twenty-eight races including two Cheltenham Gold Cups, three King George VI Steeplechases, one Whitbread Gold Cup and an Irish Grand National, the last two named races being the only two handicaps in which he ever ran, notable contests he won carrying top weight, the Whitbread by an easy four lengths and the Irish National by a jaw-dropping ten. But now as his first summer at Fulford Farm unfolded, and as if mindful of the battles that lay ahead of him, Boyo switched himself off and grew fat on the fine farm grasses, coming back into his stable to sleep the day away when the sun got too hot and being turned out in the fields at night when all was cool and the flies had gone.

As for his human friends, all was as well with them as it was with himself. Constance insisted on accompanying Anthony to America for his operation, flown there in Harrington Lovell's private jet and back again after the procedure had been successfully completed. Meanwhile, Harrington and Alice, his soon to be wife, found a fine but manageable house in a little-known part of Somerset where they would spend the rest of their days in peace, quiet and deep contentment. Grenville and Lynne married but went on living exactly as they had been, happy to keep Grenville's elegant Knightsbridge flat for their London life and Lynne's spacious country apartment for their rural days. Grenville ceased his dabbling in the world of investments, on Lynne's suggestion founding a racing club for people who could not afford to buy horses or even legs of horses but wanted the fun of ownership. In the first season the club had fifty subscribers, a membership that ten years later had swelled to over twenty thousand happy punters. The Fieldings had two children, neither of whom had the slightest interest in horses, their daughter becoming an opera singer and their son a chef.

As for the boys across the wather, there was never a race The Enchanted ran when the money wasn't down. Cronagh prospered, and the citizen who prospered most was Padraig Flanagan, thanks initially to the fact that Rory credited him with the breeding of his Gold Cup winner in his post-race press conferences, a credit that soon brought the dealers, bloodstock agents, pin-hookers and well-heeled owners to the door of his modest smallholding in south-west Cork, an establishment that thanks to the continued wondrous success of The Enchanted, ten years later had grown into one of the most successful small stud farms in Ireland. The fact that neither the so-called sire or dam of The Enchanted had lived to see their son's first success had no bearing on the events whatsoever, for all the horse people wanted was to be privy to the skills and the magic of a man already rumoured to be a singular breeder of outstanding national hunt horses. This was a reputation that Padraig very quickly and truly deserved, himself and Liam going on to breed the dual winner of an Irish Champion Hurdle and three fine and strong steeplechasers that all went on to win at the Cheltenham Festival, which perhaps only goes to show that as far as equine breeding goes, very often the stud book is as much use as a tuning fork is to the tone deaf.

When Anthony returned from America with his life expectancy greatly increased, decisions had to be made about the future of Fulford Farm.

'The first thing I would like to do and intend to do, as it happens, Dad, is to get married,' Rory told him.

'I would have to say that is one of your better ideas, Rory,' Anthony replied. 'And after that, what then?'

'That rather depends on what you're going to do.'

'Well, I'm going to enjoy myself,' Anthony told him. 'Connie and I have got one or two things we'd like to do and a couple of places we'd like to go and see, but before I can do that, I have to know what's to become of the yard.'

'I can go on running it, if it's all right with you. Or rather we can. Kathleen and I, that is,' Rory said, taking Kathleen by the hand.

'And that's all? That's it, is it?' Anthony sighed. 'You're just going to train horses for the rest of your days and do nothing else.'

'No, of course he's going to do something else, Mr Rawlins,' Kathleen reassured him. 'In fact, if I have anything to do with it, soon he'll not be training the horses at all.'

'Is that so, Katie?' Anthony laughed. 'Mind you, I rather thought it might be.'

'He's to spend the rest of the summer painting,' Kathleen said.

'Are you going to Florence after all, old man?'

'And no, he's not,' Kathleen chipped in. 'That has been decided against.'

'By herself here,' Rory said, indicating Kathleen with a nod of his head.

'Rory can paint horses like nobody's business,' Kathleen continued. 'Haven't I already got him half a dozen commissions, and in a couple of years won't Mr Rory Rawlins here only be one of the top equine artists in the country?'

'With no time to look after the yard,' Anthony commented.

'Go on.' Kathleen laughed. 'Now you know well enough who'll be doing that, Mr Rawlins. And if it's all right with you, I can't think of anything I would want to do more.'

'It's very all right by me,' Anthony said mock-seriously, 'as long as you stay as beautiful as you are and don't turn into another Eddie Rampton.'

'Fat chance,' said Rory.

So while Kathleen trained, Rory drew and painted, and in time they had three children, two daughters and a son, their son's most notable achievement being the riding to victory of one of his parents' horses at Aintree in the Foxhunter's Steeplechase, otherwise known as the Amateurs' Grand National.

And all this time Boyo continued to run his heart out and to enjoy doing so.

'When he stops enjoying it, that's the day we retire him on the spot,' Rory and Kathleen agreed, and indeed the day finally dawned when the great horse was retired to grass, though not because he was no longer enjoying his races, but because he developed arthritis. He spent the rest of his days being as mollycoddled as he would allow, which wasn't very much since even though his legs were stiffening and his back was aching the one thing Boyo could not abide was being shut in his stable doing nothing. So whenever the weather allowed, the horse was given the freedom of the field, well rugged up in winter and always brought in when the flies became bothersome. Never short of company, he ran with the youngsters Kathleen introduced to him and taught them his ways, and he tended to the older racehorses, making sure their well-earned holidays were spent with as few interruptions from the youngsters as possible. He was parent and nanny goat, guardian and grandfather, a perfectly tempered animal who looked after his pastoral kingdom with great care and compassion.

His favourite spot to lie was a fold in the home paddock just under the shade of the biggest of the chestnut trees, a haven to which he would take himself off to sleep when the aches in his bones became too much and finally when the sun could do his discomforts no more good. It was there that Kathleen and Rory found him late one summer evening, fast asleep for ever now, his life over, his great and indomitable spirit having been quietly taken away by a tall and beautiful young man with eyes the colour of coral, to be returned to the kingdom under the seas where his heart had always belonged.